Pe[illegible] Jordan

Born in Preston, Lancashire, **Penny Jordan** now lives with her husband in a beautiful fourteenth-century house in rural Cheshire. Penny has been writing for over ten years and now has over seventy novels to her name including the phenomenally successful *Power Play* and *Silver*. With over thirty million copies of her books in print and translations into seventeen languages, she has firmly established herself as a novelist of great scope.

Penny Jordan

GAME OF LOVE

and

TIME FOR TRUST

Harlequin Mills & Boon Limited,
Eton House, 18-24 Paradise Road, Richmond, Surrey, TW9 1SR

GAME OF LOVE and TIME FOR TRUST were first published in separate single volumes in 1990 by Mills & Boon Limited

ISBN 0 263 79314 1

Set in Times Roman 11 on 12 pt
05-9508-97668 C

Printed in Great Britain by
BPC Paperbacks Ltd

GAME OF LOVE

CHAPTER ONE

'TASHA, I think I'm going to need your help.'

'What, again?' Natasha Lacey queried humorously, looking up from her work to smile at her cousin. 'What is it this time? Another crisis over the bridesmaids' dresses? If you want my honest opinion, my love, you're never going to make your Richard's sister look anything other than the little dumpling she is. Poor girl. I can well remember what it feels like to be fourteen, chubby and detesting every female in the world who isn't.'

'When you add to that the fact that she virtually worships Richard, it's no wonder that she isn't exactly overjoyed about your marriage.'

'No, it isn't Sara . . . not this time,' Emma Lacey interrupted hastily. 'Nothing so simple. I only wish it were.'

Natasha's frown deepened. Three years her own junior, Emma had always been more like her sister than her cousin. They had lived in the same small cathedral city all their lives, their parents close friends as well as relatives, both of them glad to have a peer with whom to share the burdens of growing up.

Perhaps because she was the elder, she had always been the calmer, the more logical of the two of them, her emotions and moods controlled and predictable where Emma's were subject to wild variations and swings.

In the family it was tacitly acknowledged that the death of Emma's father when she was fifteen years old had to have been the cause of the sudden wild streak which had then developed in her behaviour—a wild streak which had led her into scrape after scrape, some of them so serious that they had led to a rift developing between the two cousins. Emma, bored and rebellious, had insisted on leaving school at sixteen, while Natasha had gone on to university, calmly and determinedly working her way towards the qualifications she needed while Emma had played her way around the world.

However, if Emma had been a little wild, that part of her life was behind her now, and no one could be more pleased than she was herself that she had fallen in love with Richard Templecombe.

It was true that the Templecombes were not perhaps as happy with the match as Emma's family. For one thing, the Laceys were not and never had been part of the ecclesiastical life of the city, and even though both families had lived there for several generations they inhabited two very different worlds. The Laceys represented commerce and worldliness, the business which the first Jasper Lacey had established on the outskirts of the city over seventy years before being, after the church, the largest employer in the area. The Templecombes, on the other hand, prided themselves on being above such materialistic things as commerce. Their connections with the cathedral and the church went back even further than the

Laceys' connection with the city. Richard's father was dean of the cathedral, he and Richard's mother acknowledged leaders of local ecclesiastical society, and it was generally accepted that, one day, hopefully Richard would follow in his father's footsteps.

A thought struck Natasha and her heart sank. The wedding was less than a week away now, but her sudden fear had to be expressed. 'You haven't . . . you're not having second thoughts, are you?' she asked.

Emma shook her head and gulped. 'No, I'm not . . . but Richard probably will, once Luke tells him what I've done.'

'Luke?' Natasha questioned her, snapping off a thread with expert care, and frowning over the repair she had just completed. It seemed ironic that, having spent all those years qualifying and then travelling the world as an embryo news reporter, she should suddenly discover when she was twenty-five years old that the place she really wanted to be was here in this quiet cathedral town, and the thing she really wanted to do was to work with the rich fabrics and embroideries of that world.

She was establishing quite a name for herself now. A couple of prestigious magazines mentioning the quality of her stock, and the sudden demand for fabrics more suitable for the refurbishment of the ancient piles now being acquired by the migrant tide escaping from London, had helped—as had the fact that she had been able to bully her father into expanding the range of ecclesiastical fabrics the company produced so that they had a more general appeal.

'Luke?' she repeated encouragingly. 'I don't think...'

'He's Richard's father's cousin. You won't know him, but he's a typical Templecombe,' Emma told her tearfully. 'Narrow-minded, bigoted, just waiting for me to do something wrong so that Richard will break our engagement.'

Being used to her cousin's emotional highs and lows, Natasha merely said calmly, 'Emma, Richard is twenty-seven years old, and quite plainly besotted with you. I can't imagine what this Luke——'

'You don't understand,' Emma interrupted, and then told her dramatically, 'Luke saw me leaving Jake Pendraggon's house.'

Now Natasha did begin to understand and her heart sank a little, although she didn't allow Emma to see it.

Jake Pendraggon had arrived in the city just over a year ago, as colourful a figure as his name suggested, Cornish by self-adoption rather than actual birth, or so Natasha suspected. Certainly he had cleverly, if not too subtly played up the effect of tanned skin, wildly curling black hair and eyes so blue that she thought he must wear contact lenses.

Certainly anyone knowing Emma as Natasha knew her must have realised immediately that Emma would be drawn to Jake Pendraggon like a lemming to a cliff. Certainly it came as no surprise to Natasha to learn that the acquaintanceship between the two of them had obviously developed into something far more intimate.

She herself had been travelling to Italy, Portugal and Spain for much of the time Jake Pendraggon had been living in Sutton Minster, looking for samples of the kind of cloth she wanted her father's factory to reproduce for her, suitably adapted for a non-ecclesiastical market. Her travels had produced some marvellous fabrics, so rich, so mouth-wateringly desirable that her eyes grew dreamy as she remembered the pleasure of discovering them, of——

'Tasha, you must help me. It was all a mistake—I'd only gone to see Jake to tell him that everything was over between us, that I loved Richard. But he was right in the middle of one of the most important parts of his novel. He begged me to stay and type up his notes for him and we worked all night on them. Nothing else happened. But of course Luke would have to be walking down the close just as I opened Jake's door to leave, and, of course, I would have to be wearing the evening dress I'd had on for our engagement party.' She pulled a face. 'I loved that dress... Richard's mother hated it, of course.'

Natasha brushed aside this incidental chatter and demanded fatalistically, 'You don't mean you went straight from your own engagement party to Jake Pendraggon's house, and were then seen leaving it first thing in the morning by Richard's cousin?'

'He's Richard's father's cousin, but in essence...yes.'

'And you never said a word to Richard...never explained.' Natasha frowned. 'But, Emma, if this Luke didn't say anything to Richard at the time, what on earth makes you think he's going to do so now?'

'I heard Richard's mother talking to him. I'd gone round there to see Sara, and the sitting-room door was open. Neither of them knew I was there. Richard's mother was saying how much she wished Richard were marrying someone more suitable.' Emma pulled a face. 'Well, I already knew she doesn't approve of me, and I'm not bothered about that, but then I heard him—Luke—saying in a sort of sinister way, "Well, you don't know—they aren't married yet. Maybe Richard will have a change of heart," and I knew instantly...'

She paused dramatically while Natasha wrinkled her forehead and asked patiently, 'You knew what?'

'That Luke had been waiting until the last possible minute to tell Richard what I'd done, and I know when he's going to do it—tonight at the pre-wedding party. The one your parents are giving for us.'

'Oh, I'm sure you're wrong,' Natasha tried to comfort her. 'I haven't met this Luke, but I'm sure if he had wanted to tell Richard he would have done so months ago—as you should have done yourself,' she added forthrightly. 'It's still not too late,' she continued more gently, knowing her cousin's stubbornness of old. 'Why don't you simply explain to Richard what happened? After all, if it was as innocent as you say——'

'What do you mean "if"?' Emma demanded belligerently. 'Don't you believe me?'

Natasha sighed faintly. 'Yes, I do,' she confirmed. 'But——'

'Exactly!' Emma pounced. 'And it's that "but" that stops me from telling Richard. Everyone knows that Jake and I went out together a few times that time when Richard and I broke up.' She ignored the ironic look Natasha gave her at her deceptive description of the ragingly public and passionate affair Emma had had with the writer while he was supposedly researching his latest blockbuster. 'But I explained to Richard that if he hadn't got cold feet about loving me I'd never have even looked at Jake.' She ignored the look Natasha gave her and added miserably, 'I know he'd *want* to believe me, but given my reputation and the fact that Luke saw me leaving Jake's house...'

'I *can* see the difficulties,' Natasha admitted. 'You know, you should have explained to Richard right away.'

'I should have but I didn't,' Emma said morosely, 'and now, because of that, Luke is going to tell Richard, and then Richard will break our engagement, and my life will be ruined, unless...you must help me, Tasha. Please...'

'I think the best person to help you is yourself, by confiding in Richard,' Natasha told her severely. 'He *is* an adult, Emma, and I'm sure this Luke whoever he is won't be able to stop Richard from loving and marrying you.'

'You don't know him,' Emma told her starkly. 'He's a typical Templecombe, only worse.'

'Worse?' Natasha questioned. 'How?'

'Well, for a start he's completely anti-women. Oh, not in that way,' she hastened to assure her cousin, when she saw Natasha's expression.

'According to Richard he's had women virtually coming out of his ears, since his early teens. And for all that he's even more strait-laced than Mrs T now. According to Richard there was a time when the family almost disowned him, he was so wild.'

'Well, then, he should sympathise with you,' Natasha murmured, picking up another piece of embroidery and examining it lovingly, wondering how it would look hanging on the wall in her own small house, perhaps over the fifteenth-century oak coffer she had been lucky enough to buy at a local auction.

'Not him,' Emma assured her bitterly. 'He's the original reformed rake. He's already advised Richard that we'd be far better waiting another year to marry, and he's told him that he's not sure that I'm the right wife for him, given his calling. Who says that a vicar's wife has to be like Mrs T?' Emma began indignantly.

'Who indeed?' Natasha agreed *sotto voce*, knowing that if she let her cousin run on for long enough she would eventually run out of steam.

'You will help me, won't you?' Emma pleaded, her face suddenly crumpling with real emotion as she said shakily, 'I couldn't bear to lose Richard now, Tasha. I really couldn't. Before... before we were engaged and we had that row, and I got involved with Jake... well, I thought I *could* live without him, that he was just another man, but it isn't like that. I really do love him. I know he loves me too, but——'

'But you don't think he'll believe you if you tell him what you were doing with Jake Pendraggon.'

'He'd want to, but he *is* only human, and if our situations were reversed... Well, I know how I'd feel if I heard that he'd been seen coming out of an ex-lover's house at that time in the morning.'

'What is it you want me to do?' Natasha asked her. 'Kidnap this Luke and keep him out of sight until after the wedding?' she suggested facetiously.

'Don't be silly,' Emma said severely, making Natasha reflect that her cousin *had* changed a little. Time was when she would very probably have suggested just such an outrageous solution to her present problem. 'No, all I want you to do is to pretend to be me—that is, I want you to pretend that it was *you* Luke saw leaving Jake's house. After all,' she continued, warming to her theme and ignoring the stunned look in Natasha's eyes, 'we *do* look alike. We're both blonde and we both have grey eyes; we're both around the same height——'

'We're cousins, not twins,' Natasha interrupted her drily, 'and we don't look anything like that similar. I'm taller than you for one thing, and——'

'Tasha, please listen. Luke doesn't know me all that well. He only saw me briefly.'

'He saw you wearing the same dress you had worn for your engagement party,' Natasha reminded her very firmly. 'Emma, love, much as I want to help——'

'No, you don't,' Emma interrupted her bitterly. 'You want to stay nice and safe in your own cosy little world. I bet you think just like Luke really, that I don't deserve someone like Richard. Everyone knows that, if Richard had to marry into our family, Mrs T would have much preferred to have you as a daughter-in-law. After all, before you went off to university you and Richard dated for a while.'

'I like Richard as a person, I'm delighted that the two of you are in love, and as for being like this Luke...' Natasha began, determined to nip any further emotionalism in the bud. 'What exactly does he do, by the way?'

'He's an artist,' Emma told her truculently, totally stunning her. 'He paints landscapes. He's quite well known, apparently.'

'Luke Templecombe? I don't think I've ever heard of him.'

'You won't have done, he uses another name—Luke Freres.'

'Luke Freres? *The* Luke Freres?'

'Tasha, please help me. My whole life's happiness could depend on it,' Emma added theatrically.

'What do you want me to do? Wear a placard tonight saying, "It was me you saw leaving Jake Pendraggon's house, and not Emma"?'

'That's not funny. I just want your permission, if Luke does say anything, to deny it by saying that it wasn't me and that it must have been you. After all, what does it matter to you?' Emma pleaded when she saw her cousin's face. 'It isn't as though there's anyone in your life at the moment.'

'And so *my* reputation doesn't matter, is that it?'

Emma looked cross. 'Oh, for goodness' sake, must you be so old-fashioned? Honestly, Tasha, you're archaic. You must be the only twenty-seven-year-old virgin left.'

'A situation which you want me to claim I tried to rectify via a night in Jake Pendraggon's arms,' Natasha derided, ignoring the jibe. 'Come on, Emma. There might be certain similarities between us, but Luke Freres is an artist. Do you honestly think for one moment he's going to believe he saw me when he saw you?'

'It doesn't matter what *he* believes, only what Richard believes,' Emma told her fiercely. 'But, of course, I should have known you would refuse to help. After all, you don't want to lose your reputation as Miss Pure-and-goody-goody, do you?' she added nastily. 'Oh, no, you'd rather Richard broke our engagement and my heart.'

'Stop being so dramatic. I don't think for one moment that Luke Freres will say anything to Richard. Not at this stage, but in the unlikely event that he does——'

'You'll do it! Oh, Tasha, thank you. Thank you!'

Natasha grimaced. She hadn't been about to volunteer to do any such thing, merely to advise her volatile cousin to put her trust in Richard and tell him the truth, but Emma was on her feet, dancing round the attic workroom of the four-storey building which housed Natasha's home, office and work-place, blowing extravagant kisses at her as she headed for the door.

'You don't know what this means to me. I knew you'd help me. I'm so relieved. Let Luke do his worst—he can't hurt me now. Oh, Tasha, I'm so relieved!'

'Emma, wait,' Natasha protested, but it was already too late.

Her cousin had opened the door and was hurrying downstairs, calling back, 'Can't, I'm afraid, I've got a final fitting for the dress and I'm already late. See you tonight at home.'

'Tasha, where on earth have you been? You know everyone's due at eight. It's half-past seven now.'

Natasha stopped on the threshold of the bedroom which had been hers all the time she was growing up and which she still used whenever she had occasion to stay at Lacey Court overnight.

Emma was standing in the middle of the room, dressed in a fetching confection of satin and lace, delectably designed to show off the prettily tanned curves of her breasts and the slenderness of her thighs in a way that was just barely respectable.

'If you're planning to wear that for dinner, then I think you're making a mistake,' Natasha told her thoughtfully, eyeing the camisole and its matching French knickers consideringly.

Emma grinned at her. 'Don't be silly—as though I would.'

'No? Am I or am I not talking to the girl who appeared at her own eighteenth birthday party wearing a basque and little more than a G-string?'

'That was for a dare,' Emma pouted, 'and, anyway, it was years ago.'

'A millennium,' Natasha agreed drily, adding, 'But, if you don't want Richard's parents to catch you wearing such a fetching but highly inappropriate outfit, I suggest you go back to your own room and finish getting dressed.'

'Not yet. I wanted to see you first, and besides, my dress is silk and will crease if I sit down in it. Listen, I've been thinking—tonight you'd better wear your hair like mine, and if you could wear this as well...'

She reached behind her back and lifted something off the bed, holding it up in front of her.

'That's the dress you wore for your engagement party,' Natasha recognised.

'Exactly. I thought if you wore it tonight it would help to convince Luke that it was you he saw and not me.'

'But, Emma, he must know that you were the one wearing it the night you and Richard got engaged. And, besides, it won't fit me. I'm at least five inches taller than you, and two inches wider round the bust.'

'Yes, it will—the top was very loose and skirts are being worn shorter this year.'

'Not that short, and certainly not by me.'

'But you promised,' Emma began, and, to Natasha's exasperation, large tears filled the soft grey eyes so like her own. Even knowing they were crocodile tears and a trick Emma had been able to pull off from her cradle didn't lessen the effect of them. The trouble was that she was *programmed* to respond to them, Natasha decided grimly. Well, this time she was not going to. She would look ridiculous in Emma's dress. Her cousin loved bright colours and modern fashions, but, for some reason, when she and Richard got engaged she had decided that a sober, sensible little dress in black was bound to appeal more to his parents than her usual choice of clothes. No doubt it would have done so if Emma had stuck to her original decision and not been swayed by the appeal of a dress which, while it was black, shared no other virtues in common with the outfit she had gone out to buy.

True, the dress did have long sleeves, but it also had a bodice which was slashed virtually to the waist front and back. True, it was not made of one of the glittering, eye-popping fabrics Emma normally chose. Instead it was made of jersey—not the thick, sensible jersey as worn by Richard's mother and aunts, but a jersey so fine, so delicate that it was virtually like silk. Worn over Emma's lissom young body, it had left no one in any doubt as to its wearer's lack of anything even approaching the respectability of proper underwear between her skin and the dress—a fact which had obviously been appreciated by the less strait-laced of the male guests at the party.

It was the kind of dress it took an Emma to carry off with aplomb and certainly not the kind of dress Natasha herself would ever dream of wearing. She was just about to tell Emma as much when her bedroom door opened and her mother walked in. Like Emma, she adored clothes, and they adored her, Natasha acknowledged as she studied her mother's appearance admiringly. Tall and still very slim, her mother was wearing pale grey silk, the simplest of styles and one which Natasha suspected had had a far from simple price-tag. Diamonds glinted discreetly in her ears, her hair and make-up were immaculate; she looked the epitome of the elegant and understated wife of a rich and indulgent man.

She frowned when she saw them, exclaiming, 'Emma, here you are! Darling, you ought to be ready. You'll want to make an entrance. I'll keep everyone in the hall when they arrive and then you'll come downstairs——' She broke off when she saw that Emma was crying. 'What is it?'

'It's Tasha. I wanted her to wear this dress, but she won't. She says she's going to come down to dinner in that awful beige thing she's had for years. You know how we planned everything so that we'd all be in white, grey and black so that the table would look just right with the Meissen dinner service, and now Tasha's going to spoil it all.'

'Really, Tasha,' her mother disapproved. 'You *are* being difficult. You can't possibly wear that dreadful beige.'

'Neither can I wear this,' Natasha told her mother through gritted teeth. Emma was an arch manipulator when she chose. She'd deal with her later, though. 'Remember it—the discreet little number Emma wore for her own engagement party, the dress that virtually gave the archdeacon apoplexy every time Emma leaned forward.'

'Oh, that dress——'

'Tasha's exaggerating,' Emma interrupted. 'It wasn't *that* bad. I only want her to wear it because I want her to look her best. She never makes the most of herself—you've said so yourself. With her hair done like mine instead of screwed up at the back of her head, and this dress . . . It's time people saw how attractive she really is. Do you know, I heard Mrs T actually telling Sara that she needn't worry about how she looked in her bridesmaid's dress because Tasha was bound to look worse, and, while Sara is still young enough to improve, Tasha is virtually on the shelf.'

Natasha closed her eyes and mentally cursed her cousin. If her mother had one fault, it was an almost obsessive antipathy towards Mrs Templecombe, coupled with a desire to upstage her on each and every opportunity—a discreet and very ladylike desire, of course, but nevertheless...

'Oh, did she?' she declared grimly now. 'Emma is right, darling. That dress would look wonderful on you. You're tall enough to carry it off.'

'Am I? And what do you propose I should do about this?' she demanded grittily, picking up the dress and holding it in front of her by the shoulders so that her mother could see the full effect of its plunging neckline.

'It's perfectly decent,' Emma interposed quickly. 'It only looks as though——'

'It's about to fall off,' Natasha finished acidly for her. 'I am *not* wearing this dress.'

'Oh, dear, I'm afraid you're going to have to,' Emma told her, managing to look both guilty and triumphant at the same time. 'You see, I went through your wardrobe when I arrived and...'

Natasha rushed past her and threw open her wardrobe doors, staring at the empty space where her clothes should have been. She always kept a few things here—her formal evening clothes, her gardening wear and one or two other outfits.

As she closed the door she was more angry with Emma than she had ever been in her life. 'I am not wearing that dress, Emma,' she told her icily. 'Even it if means staying up here all night,' she added fiercely.

'Oh, darling, you can't do that. Think how it would look. Imagine what Richard's mother would say. No, I'm afraid you're going to have to do as Emma says and wear the dress. I'm sure it will look stunning on you.'

'Yes, it will,' Emma agreed eagerly. 'And we've just got time to do your hair.'

'Thank you, Emma, I'm quite capable of doing my own hair,' Natasha told her grimly.

She was trapped and she knew it, but she could cheerfully have murdered her cousin when Emma paused by her bedroom door to remind her dulcetly, 'Remember your promise... If Luke...'

Just for a moment, Natasha was tempted to tell her she had changed her mind, but she didn't. She knew quite well that if Luke Freres did try to make trouble between Emma and her fiancé, she would have to stop him. Emma, for all her flightiness, her giddiness, genuinely did love Richard, and really had toned down her wild behaviour as she tried to conform to the standards expected by Richard's family.

Privately Natasha thought that, the sooner Richard and Emma were free of the constraint of Richard's family, the more chance of success their marriage would have. It was fortunate indeed that Richard's first parish was so very far away in Northumberland, where there would be no risk of criticism and interference from his mother. Given the chance, Natasha suspected, Emma would make a very good, if somewhat unorthodox vicar's wife. She genuinely cared about people and understood them, which was more than anyone could ever say for Mrs Templecombe, who expected everyone to live up to the same impossibly high standards as herself.

Twenty minutes later, as the first guests arrived, Natasha stood despairingly in front of her bedroom mirror wondering if she was out of her mind.

She had washed her hair, and blown it into the same stylish bob in which Emma wore hers, although minus the raffish spiky fringe which Emma adopted. With her hair worn in this style she acknowledged that there *was* a fleeting resemblance between Emma and herself, if one discounted the disparity in their heights.

Yes, the hair was all right, but as for the dress...

On, it looked even worse than she had expected. The hem finished at least a couple of inches above her knees, the deep *décolleté* Vs at the front and back of her bodice somewhere that fell just short of her waist. Cleverly sewn into the front of the dress were two pieces of soft shaping which allowed the observer to entertain himself while imagining that the slightest movement of her torso was likely to expose far more of her obviously naked breasts than merely the cleavage between them, yet ensuring that such a sartorial disaster was simply not possible, so that she could not claim as she had intended that she could not wear the thing for fear of disgracing them all by baring her chest to the entire assembled Templecombe clan—something her mother, whose taste was very sharp-edged, would never have allowed.

'Oh, you're ready, then.'

Natasha swung round, her appearance forgotten as she stared at her cousin. Emma was wearing something that looked as though it had been designed for a prim little puritan; grey silk with a huge white collar and cuffs and a delicate bell-shaped skirt that made her look fragile and delicate.

'I've brought you these,' Emma told her. 'Black, silk stockings and satin shoes. I know you don't have any.'

Gritting her teeth, Natasha threatened, 'I don't know why I'm letting you get away with this, Emma. You had it all planned, didn't you? I look like the original scarlet woman, a fitting contrast to my demure little cousin.'

'No, you don't. You look stunning,' Emma told her flatly, and a little wistfully. Her cousin would much rather be wearing the black dress than the grey, Natasha recognised, humour coming to her rescue, while she would have felt much more at home in Emma's puritan outfit.

'Your mother chose this for me. She said it was bound to create a good impression.'

'Oh, it will,' Natasha agreed humorously. 'Pity she got her faiths mixed up, though. As I recall there never was much love lost between the *aficionados* of the high church and the Plymouth brethren.'

She saw that she had lost her cousin and sighed a little. 'All right, I'll wear your dress, Emma, but only...only because you haven't given me any option, and only because I realise how important it is to you that Richard's family accept you, although you know I suspect that Mrs T would respect you far more readily if you stood out against her and were your own person. Richard loves you for yourself, you know. If he'd wanted a carbon copy of his mother he'd have chosen——'

'Louise Grey. Yes, I know that, but his mother doesn't. She's still convinced that a miracle is going to happen between now and the wedding day, and that Richard is going to open his eyes and realise that it's Louise he loves and not me. And with that beast Luke to help her... If you'd been at the engagement party and seen the way he looked at me...'

'In this? Come on, Emma, be your age. Any man——'

'No, not that kind of way,' Emma interrupted her irritably. 'He looked at me...as though...as though I were a bad smell under his nose. Horrid man. You weren't there...you don't know.'

Natasha had missed the engagement party because she had been away on business, persuading a very difficult and jealous Italian manufacturer to allow her father to reproduce some of his designs for the English market.

'Look, I'll have to go down in a minute. I am grateful to you, Tasha. I don't know what I'd have done if you hadn't offered to help.'

'Offered?' Natasha protested indignantly, but Emma was already closing the door behind her.

CHAPTER TWO

SHE had never liked wearing stockings, Natasha reflected crossly—a fact which Emma had obviously remembered, since she had supplied her with a suspender belt as well as the impossibly fine black silk hosiery she was now wearing. And as for the height of these heels... She felt as though she were perched on stilts, towering above all the other women present.

Was it just her own self-conscious awareness of how very much more provocative the dress was than anything she would personally have chosen to wear that made her feel as though she were the cynosure of all eyes, or was it just because she was taller than Emma that she felt that the dress, startling enough when Emma had worn it, on her was not so much teasingly sensual as a direct and flamboyant statement of availability?

She had never in the space of one short half-hour collected so many admiring male glances nor so many disapproving female ones, nor was it an experience she would want to repeat, she decided irritably after she had fended off the fourth attempt of one of Richard's ancient uncles to detach her from the rest of the guests.

'I see Uncle Rufus has been making a play for you,' Emma commented teasingly as she came up to her.

'At his age, he ought to know better,' Natasha retaliated acidly, and then added, 'And don't think I haven't realised exactly why you blackmailed me into wearing this...this garment, Emma. With you dressed as though butter wouldn't melt in your mouth and me looking like the original scarlet harlot——'

'In black,' Emma interposed dulcetly and then giggled. 'I can't wait to see Richard's face when he arrives and sees us. He's been delayed and he won't be here until after dinner. He'll be bringing Luke with him.' She twisted her engagement ring nervously with her fingers. 'You won't let me down, will you, Tasha? I couldn't bear to lose Ricky—not now. I never thought I'd ever feel like this. I never imagined I could ever become so emotionally dependent on anyone. It frightens me a little bit.'

Natasha's stern expression softened. 'I'm sure Luke Freres doesn't have any intention of trying to come between you, but I won't go back on my word, Emma. Even though I positively hate you for making me wear this appalling outfit. Stockings as well, and you know how much I loathe them.'

'Really?' Emma giggled again, giving her a coy look. 'Men adore them. Richard said——' She broke off and groaned. 'Oh, no, here's Mrs T bearing down on us, I'm off.'

'Coward,' Natasha whispered after her, as Emma adroitly whisked herself out of the way, leaving Natasha to face Richard's mother alone.

'Well, Natasha, this is a surprise,' Mrs Templecombe said critically as she frowned at her.

'We don't expect to see *you* wearing that kind of outfit.'

Natasha had never particularly cared for the dean's wife, although she had never attracted her criticism in the same way as Emma. That was the trouble about living in a small place where you had spent all your life. You knew everyone, and everyone knew you and felt free to air their opinions and views of your behaviour—even when you were long past the age when such views were welcome or necessary.

'Anyway, isn't that the dress Emma wore when she and Richard became engaged? I told her then it was most unsuitable.'

'Which is why she passed it on to me,' Natasha told her evenly. Much as she herself might sometimes disapprove of Emma's behaviour, she was not going to aid and abet Mrs Templecombe in criticising her cousin.

'Well, I must say I'm surprised to see you wearing it.'

'I'm a career woman, Mrs Templecombe, and setting up my own business doesn't allow me either the time or the money to waste on clothes shopping. To tell the truth I was grateful to Emma for offering to lend it to me.'

A lie if ever there was one, but Richard's mother seemed to accept it at face-value.

'Yes. I must say it was rather adventurous of you to open your own shop, and selling ecclesiastical fabrics to the general public.'

Her face suggested that what Natasha was doing was somehow or other in rather poor taste, making

Natasha itch to say rebelliously that the cloth wasn't sanctified, but instead she contented herself with murmuring, 'Well, they're very much in vogue at the moment, and are being snapped up by people with a taste for traditional fabrics who can't afford to buy the original antiques.'

'Ah, there you are, Lucille. Such a pity there isn't time to show you round the gardens before dinner. I particularly wanted to show off the new section of the double border. We've planted up part of it with a mixture of old-fashioned shrub roses, underplanted with campanula and a very pretty mallow.'

Smiling gratefully at her aunt, Natasha adroitly excused herself, marvelling on the unsuitability of some people's names as she walked away. Surely only the most doting of parents could have chosen to name Richard's mother Lucille. Her second name was Elsie, which she much preferred and which everyone apart from Emma's mother was wise enough to use.

If her aunt and mother were nothing else, they were certainly marvellous and inspired cooks, Natasha admitted when the main courses had been removed from the table and the sweet course brought in.

Another bone of contention between the ecclesiastical fraternity and her own family was the large pool of temporary domestic assistance her mother and aunt could call upon from the wives and daughters of some of the factory's employees, who would cheerfully and happily help out on the domestic scene when necessary. This willingness to do such work stemmed as much from her aunt's and mother's treatment of those who supplied such help as from the generous wages paid by her father, both women being keen believers in the motto 'Do unto others . . .'

It was a constant source of friction at the deanery and elsewhere in the cathedral close that they, who were frequently called upon to involve themselves in all manner of entertaining, were hard put to it to get so much as a regular cleaner, but then, with Mrs Templecombe to set the tone for the whole of the cathedral close, it was not perhaps surprising that they would find it difficult to hold on to their domestic help.

His mother, as Richard cheerfully admitted, had been born into the wrong century and adhered to an out-of-date and sometimes offensive policy of 'us and them'.

As it was a warm evening, once the meal was over the guests were free to wander through the drawing-room's french windows, on to the terrace overlooking the gardens. Natasha escaped there, avoiding the fulsome compliments of her coterie of elderly admirers, and the fierce glares of their wives.

Really, she reflected, as she stood breathing in the scented night air, she had had no idea that being a siren involved such hard work. It was just as well she had no ambitions in that direction.

In the distance, the cathedral bells tolled the hour. The bells were one of the first things she missed when she was away from home. Her little house inside the city was almost in the shadow of the bell tower, and she had grown used to timing her telephone calls to avoid clashing with their sonorous reminder of the passing hour.

However, much as she loved the cathedral, much as she enjoyed the pomp and ceremony of its religious feast days, much as she adored the richness of its fabrics and embroideries, if she ever got married she would want a simple ceremony: a simple, plain church, flowers from her aunt's garden, a few special friends and only her very closest family.

She didn't envy Emma her big wedding in the least, and she certainly did not envy her all the palaver that went with it. What she did envy her in a small corner of her mind was having found someone she loved and who loved her in return. Sighing to herself, Natasha wondered if she was ever going to totally grow out of what she now considered to be a silly, immature yearning for that kind of oneness with another human being.

She had lived long enough now to recognise that marriage was a far from idyllic state, one that should only be entered into after a long, cool period of appraisal and consideration, and preferably only if one had developed nerves of steel and was devoid of all imagination; and yet, even though she knew all this, there were still nights like tonight when the soft, perfumed air of the garden led her into all manner of impossible yearnings...

She slipped off her shoes and walked to the edge of the terrace away from the haunting scent of the roses climbing on the wall, and it was while she was standing there, looking out across the shadowed garden, that she heard a familiar voice exclaiming,

'Emma, darling, there you are!' and felt a pair of male hands on her shoulders.

Immediately she turned round, saying wryly, 'Sorry, Richard, I'm afraid it's not Emma, but Natasha.'

'Tasha? Good heavens!'

At another time, the disbelief in his voice would have amused her, but now for some reason it merely served to underline her own aloneness.

'For a moment I thought... You and Emma normally look so different. I'd never have mistaken the two of you. I... You look so different...'

Richard faltered into the kind of silent eloquence of a man who had confidently flung himself off the top of the highest diving-board, only to discover that the pool below him was empty of water, but Natasha took pity on him and said drily, 'Luckily for you, I'm prepared to take that as a compliment, even if it was a rather back-handed one. I think you'll find Emma's in the drawing-room talking to your mother.'

'Tasha, I'm sorry. I didn't mean...'

'I know you didn't,' she agreed wryly, and then added severely, 'Just don't do it again.'

'I suppose I'm so much in love with Emma that I can't think of anyone else. I saw you out here wearing her dress—— Why *are* you wearing it, by the way?' he asked awkwardly. 'I mean, it isn't your sort of thing at all, is it?'

'Oh, isn't it?' she asked quizzically, watching him flush uncomfortably, irritated without knowing why that he should automatically assume that she didn't have either the ability or the desire to be seen as a sensual woman.

In fact, she was so engrossed in the shock of discovering that she could feel such illogical irritation that she didn't realise they weren't alone until he looked abruptly away from her and said eagerly, 'Luke, come and meet Emma's cousin, Natasha. Natasha, I'd like to introduce you to my, or rather my father's cousin, Luke.'

Without knowing why, as she turned round Natasha felt both vulnerable and nervous.

The man walking along the terrace towards her had the familiar Templecombe features of a tall, athletic frame, good bone-structure and a shock of dark hair, but in him some rogue genes had added features which neither Richard nor his father possessed, she recognised uneasily.

Whereas the most common expression on the faces of Richard and his father was one of benign, almost unworldly kindness, on this man's face was an expression of hard cynicism; his eyes, unlike Richard's, weren't brown, but a light, pale colour which seemed to reflect the light, masking his expression. He was taller than Richard, and broader, somehow suggesting that beneath his suit his body was packed with powerful muscles and that it had been used in far more vigorous and dangerous ways than playing a round of golf. Natasha, who had never in her life experienced the slightest curiosity or arousal at the thought of the nude male body, suddenly found herself wondering helplessly if the dark hair she could glimpse so disturbingly beneath the crisp whiteness of his shirt cuff grew as vigorously and as masculinely on other parts of his body, and if so what it would be like to feel its crispness beneath her fingertips.

She stiffened as though her body had received a jolt of electricity, and heard him saying evenly and without any inflexion in his voice at all, which somehow made it worse, 'Emma's cousin. Ah, yes, I thought I recognised the dress.'

'Yes, so did I. In fact I thought for a moment that Tasha was Emma.'

'Really?'

Natasha watched, fascinated, as the dark eyebrows rose indicating polite disinterest, and then said hurriedly, 'I think we'd better go in. Emma will be wondering——'

'If you've borrowed her fiancé as well as her dress,' the cynical voice suggested, causing Natasha to grit her teeth and force back the sharp retort springing to her lips. He might move in the kind of circles where people swapped lovers as easily as they changed clothes, but if he thought that he could come here and insult her by suggesting... But what was the point in quarrelling with him? As a painter he might be worthy of her admiration, she thought angrily as she stalked past both men, realising too late that she had not retrieved her shoes, but as a man...

'Won't you need these?'

Seething, she turned round to discover that he was holding her shoes. Damn the man; he must have eyes like a hawk. Of course, as a painter he would be used to monitoring every tiny detail. Her heart started to jump erratically as he came towards her. His wrist and hand were tanned a rich brown, and as she put out her own hand to retrieve her shoes she noticed how pale and somehow delicate her own skin looked against his, how fragile her wrist-bones—so fragile that, if he were to curl his fingers around her wrist, he could break it as easily as he might snap a twig.

She gulped and swallowed, furious with herself for her idiotic flight of fantasy, almost snatching the shoes from him with an ungracious mutter of thanks.

Richard, keen to find Emma, had already gone inside, and she wished that his cousin would follow suit, she decided resentfully as she put the shoes on the terrace and then started to step into them.

As she slipped on the first one, the heel wobbled alarmingly and she kicked the other shoe over. Cursing the uneven paving of the terrace, she started to bend down to pick it up and then tensed as Luke Templecombe said coolly, 'Allow me.' He was already holding the shoe and there was nothing she could do other than grit her teeth and stoically concede defeat as he suggested mockingly, 'I think it would be much simpler if you put your hand on my shoulder to steady yourself. The ground here is very uneven—hardly suitable for this kind of footgear, but then when ever did a woman consider suitability of prime importance when choosing what to wear?'

Natasha opened her mouth to deny his unfair comment, and then closed it again, her whole body going into shock as she felt his fingers close round her ankle.

'Silk stockings,' she heard him murmur, and then, unbelievably, his hand travelled up her leg, resting briefly on her knee before travelling expertly along her thigh, stopping on a level with the hem of her skirt.

For almost thirty seconds Natasha was too mortified to speak, to do anything other than tremble in furious indignation. When her paralysed vocal cords were working again, to her intense chagrin all she could manage was a very mundane and choked, 'How dare you? What do you think you're doing?'

'I thought I was accepting the none too subtle invitation I was being given,' he told her laconically. 'No woman who wears black silk stockings and that kind of dress is doing so because she *doesn't* want to be looked at and touched.'

Natasha was furious.

'How dare you?' she repeated, almost stammering in her rage. 'I suppose you're the kind of man who believes that women are never raped—that when they say no, they always mean yes. For your information, I am wearing this dress and these stockings, not for the disgusting reasons you have just suggested, but because——'

She stopped then, realising that she could not tell him exactly why she was dressed as she was. She looked wildly at him and saw that he was still watching her with cynical amusement, waiting for her to go on, and instead of completing her sentence she said thickly, 'Oh, go to hell!' and stormed rudely past him, ignoring the mocking laughter that followed her, so upset that she was physically trembling, that she wanted nothing more than to rip the dress from her skin and to consign it and the stockings to the fire, and then to bury her head under her bedclothes and give way to the relief of a prolonged bout of tears.

No one...no one had ever infuriated her like that, nor insulted her like that...no one had ever made her feel so many confusing or violent emotions within such a short space of time.

Emma had been right; the man was loathsome, abhorrent, dangerous...

Very dangerous, she acknowledged, giving a tiny shiver. Very, very dangerous indeed.

CHAPTER THREE

IT WAS the dress, Natasha told herself shakily half an hour later on her way back downstairs from her bedroom, to which retreat she had escaped to recover her poise and pull herself together.

It *had* to be the dress. It couldn't be anything else. Surely nothing in her manner could possibly have given him the impression that she actually wanted... She swallowed hard, furious with herself for the shaky, nervous feeling invading the pit of her stomach—the feeling that said that underneath her anger, underneath her shock and fury had lain a very discernible and disturbing quicksilver flash of pleasure in the way his fingers had brushed her skin.

As she paused just inside the open drawing-room door, taking in the normality of the scene in front of her, it seemed impossible to believe it had actually happened.

The trouble with you, my girl, she told herself shakily, is that you're too used to men regarding you as being as sexless as an elderly maiden aunt. Where's your sense of humour? No doubt scores of women would have been highly flattered by his approach.

As she skirted the room, keeping a wary eye out for Luke Templecombe and wondering what on earth Richard's mother was likely to say if she told her what had happened, she saw her cousin and

Richard standing hand in hand gazing foolishly into one another's eyes, the epitome of a young couple in love.

'Stopped sulking, have you?'

She froze as the softly spoken words just brushed the tip of her ear. Intense waves of sensation washed right down over her body from that spot to the tips of her toes, making her want to curl them in protest. She just—*just*—managed to stop herself from turning round, and instead gritted with acid sweetness, 'I wasn't aware that I was. If you'll excuse me, I must go and help my mother.'

'Not just yet.'

This time she couldn't prevent herself from swinging round as she felt the now familiar sensation of those lean fingers clamping her wrist and holding her captive.

She panicked immediately, hissing furiously at him, 'Will you let me go? What is it with you? Does it turn you on to...to force yourself on women?'

The smile he gave her was feral, making her shiver inwardly.

'Does it give *you* a thrill to force yourself on men—visually, at least?'

Natasha discovered that she had clenched her fingers into a fist; she also discovered that nothing would have given her greater pleasure than to hit the hard male face staring into her own with the open palm of her hand—a discovery which shocked her into stunned silence. No man had ever made her feel like this...infuriated her like this...insulted her like this.

'For your information, I am wearing this dress because *I* happen to like it,' she lied flagrantly.

'Do you, or is it the sensation of male eyes following your every movement that you like? Come on, be honest—no woman wears a dress like that unless she wants a man to look at her and be sexually aware of her.'

There was nothing she could say. In her heart of hearts, she knew what he was saying was perfectly true.

'Admittedly I suppose it's possible that a naïve woman might perhaps foolishly wear such a dress for one particular man, forgetting in the heat of her—er—desire that something intended to arouse only one particular male was likely to have the same effect on every male who sees her in it.'

Natasha stared at him and then said huskily, 'If that's meant to be an apology——'

'It isn't,' came back the crisp response. 'I don't consider I have anything to apologise for.'

He had released her wrist and as she stepped back from him, rubbing her wrist as she glared at him, even though the pressure he had exerted had not hurt her at all, he bent his head and murmured softly against her ear, 'Think yourself fortunate it was only your leg I touched. The combination of that black silk jersey and the knowledge that you aren't wearing a damn thing underneath it tempts far more than a man's gaze to linger on your breasts. Personally, I've always considered that a woman with anything over a thirty-two B chest should never be seen in public without her bra, but I must admit that you've gone a long way to change my mind, sexually if not aesthetically, although I would suggest that such a cleavage *is* rather gilding the lily; a simple high neckline would have been just as alluring and far more subtle.'

Natasha gaped at him in disbelief.

'You look like a little girl who's suddenly seen her grandmother turn into the wicked wolf,' he taunted her. 'Surely you knew the effect your outfit was going to have?'

Out of the corner of her eye, Natasha saw Mrs Templecombe watching them frowningly. The last thing she wanted was for Richard's mother to realise how upset she was, and so, ignoring his remark, she said brittly, 'Richard and Emma make a good couple, don't they? I think they'll be very happy together.'

'Do you?' He gave her a sardonic look. 'Personally I'd have thought them exceptionally ill suited.' He saw the outrage darken her eyes and added cruelly, 'Your cousin has to be one of the most light-minded females I have ever come across, while Richard is destined to be a Templecombe in the same mould as his father and his before that. He's a dedicated, very serious young man, who at the moment is infatuated by a pretty face and a willing body. Do you honestly want me to believe that they have the remotest chance of happiness together? I give them six months or less before she's as bored as hell with playing at being the vicar's wife and is looking around for the kind of diversion I caught her enjoying last year—on the very night she and Richard announced their engagement.'

Natasha discovered that her heart was thumping frantically, as though she had suddenly and frighteningly come face to face with something she found dangerous. And this man *was* dangerous, she recognised inwardly, both to Emma's happiness and to her.

'What exactly are you trying to say?' she asked him unevenly.

He gave her a long look.

'Oh, come on, don't tell me you don't know about your cousin's premarital fling with Jake Pendraggon. I myself saw her leaving his house the very morning after she and Richard announced their engagement.'

As she looked into his face, any thoughts of trying to explain, to make him understand vanished, and she heard herself saying coldly, 'I think there must be some misunderstanding...'

'*I* don't think so—the facts spoke for themselves. Facts which I suspect Richard remains ignorant of, poor fool. And if she was unfaithful to him on the very night they got engaged... She was wearing that dress you've got on tonight.'

Without stopping to think, Natasha drew herself up to her full height and lied determinedly.

'You mean you *think* you saw Emma. In actual fact *I* was the one you saw. I arrived home too late to attend the party. I rang Jake and he invited me to go round. Emma had come home by then. She knew I didn't want to drive back to my own place and get changed, so she offered to lend me her dress. Jake likes his women to look...'

'Available?' he supplied silkily for her.

* * *

'Hello, Luke. You two certainly seem deep in conversation.'

Both of them swung round at the sound of Emma's voice. Richard was standing beside her and, as though she had been fabricating lies all her life, Natasha said smoothly, forcing a light laugh, 'Emma, you'll never guess what—Luke saw me leaving Jake's house last year, after your engagement party, and he actually thought I was you.'

Somehow or other Emma managed to look not just shocked but affronted as well. 'I did help Jake out with some research on his book,' she said stiffly, 'and there was some silly gossip at the time. I think you found it quite amusing, didn't you, Tasha? Are you still in touch with Jake?'

'No,' Natasha told her curtly, suddenly very annoyed with her cousin. It was one thing to help Emma out of a difficult situation; it was quite another for her cousin to openly brand her as Jake Pendraggon's lover.

'Richard tells me you won't be able to make it for the wedding, Luke,' Emma was saying.

'No, I'm afraid not. I'm tied to a commission I accepted some time ago.'

It was said so urbanely and with so little regret that Natasha couldn't help reflecting that he was not really sorry to be missing the ceremony at all.

Suddenly she felt so exhausted, so drained that she could barely stand up. The pit of her stomach felt as though it were lined with lead; her head ached and all she really wanted to do was to go somewhere where she could be alone. Excusing herself, she hurried towards the door. Some fresh air might help to clear her head. Not on the terrace this time—that was too public, too visible. No, she could creep out of the back door and wander round her aunt's closed kitchen garden.

In the porch off the kitchen, she hesitated long enough to put on an old pair of trainers and the Barbour jacket her aunt used when she was gardening. She felt cold inside. Cold and empty in some way that made her want to hug her arms round her body.

As she let herself into the kitchen garden through the wooden door, she paused to breathe in the cleansing smell of her aunt's herbs. She wished it might be as easy to cleanse her mind, her soul of the besmirchment it had suffered tonight. It was no use telling herself that Luke Templecombe didn't know the first thing about her, that the woman he had insulted and scorned was not really her at all. She still felt sore, humiliated, defiled...

There was enough light from the moon for her to see the brick paths quite clearly. There was a seat under the wall, framed by an arbour of grapes which her aunt kept out of sentiment, claiming that the fruit they produced was worse than useless. She went and sat down on it, leaning back and closing her eyes, breathing deeply as she tried to unwind. It took her several concentrated minutes of forcing herself to breathe evenly and deeply before she felt she was properly back in control of herself.

That infuriating man. She prided herself on her calm, unflappable nature, but he had well and truly pierced the barrier of her self-control and revealed a woman of emotions and feelings even she had not known existed. Don't think about him, she warned herself as she felt her tension returning, but it was a very difficult mental command to obey when his cynical, vaguely piratical features insisted on forming themselves against the darkness of her closed eyes.

'Ah . . . Titania by moonlight.'

The too familiar, drawling voice shocked her into opening her eyes and staring in disbelief as she saw the object of her thoughts standing in front of her.

Too disturbed by his presence to guard her words, she said acidly, 'Well, you're certainly no Oberon, but we're definitely ill met.'

She stood up abruptly, intent on escaping from him just as quickly as she could. He was standing several feet away from her and it should have been easy, but for some reason her feet seemed to be stubbornly glued to the path, while he moved easily and lithely towards her, blocking her exit.

'What *is* it you want?' Natasha heard herself asking breathlessly, helplessly almost, and inwardly she railed against the weakness in her voice, and her folly in asking the question.

He seemed to think so too, because he laughed, a soft, dangerous sound that raised the flesh on her arms, his teeth a brief flash of white in the dimness of the garden.

'Such sweet innocence. You sound about sixteen years old, but it won't wash, my dear. You know exactly what I want.'

He took a step towards her and then another, while she stood there like a transfixed rabbit, unable to move.

When he took hold of her, his hands sliding beneath the heavy fabric of her borrowed Barbour, she shuddered deeply, and, as though he found the sensitive reaction of her flesh intensely satisfying, he murmured against her ear, 'I've been wanting to do this all evening.'

Distantly Natasha was aware of his sliding the heavy jacket off her shoulders, and binding her to him with arms hard with muscles she could feel even through the fabric of their clothes. His head angled towards her, blotting out the moon. Panic attacked her as she suddenly recognised her own foolishness in not escaping earlier. Her mouth had gone dry; her lips felt stiff and cold. She badly wanted to touch them with her tongue, a nervous reaction, and one which she was well aware he would read as intensely provocative. She could see the clear white of his eyes and the light reflective gleam of his iris. She could even see the hard angle of his jaw and the firm curve of his mouth. Soon that mouth would be touching hers... Soon... Was she mad? she wondered in a frantic surge of reality. Had he cast some sort of spell over her, to render her so quiescent and submissive?

His mouth only a breath away from her own, he told her softly, 'I've been wanting to do this all evening, wondering how you would feel and taste.'

'Well, I haven't,' she countered jerkily, trying to pull back from him and escape, but it was too late.

As she turned her head to avoid his kiss, he caught hold of it, sliding his palm along her jaw, imprisoning her so that she couldn't move her head without hurting herself, his voice edged with mockery and cynicism as he told her, 'You're a liar.'

And then he was kissing her—not roughly or cruelly as she had always naïvely imagined men *did* kiss women for whom all they felt was an emotionless physical ache, but with such great subtlety, such instinctive awareness of her own needs and responses that it was as though the whole world had caved in around her, leaving her floating helplessly in a dimension she had never even imagined existed.

The pressure of his mouth moving against her own was at once so caressive, so knowing, so persuasive, that she simply didn't have any defences against it. Despairingly she recognised that, while her mind might not have wanted this intimacy, her body certainly had, and, humiliatingly, he must have been aware of that wanting even though she herself had not.

Helplessly unable to stop herself giving him the response he demanded, she heard him make a small sound deep in his throat, and felt her own flesh thrill in recognition of what it meant. His hand was no longer cupping her face; instead it was caressing her throat, pushing aside the shoulder of her dress so that his fingers could caress the smooth, pale flesh he had revealed.

Even though she could feel the fabric sliding away from her skin, even though she *knew* from the slightly rough contact of his dinner-jacket against her skin that the bodice must have slipped away to reveal her breast, she made no attempt to stop him, no attempt to do anything other than clutch at his shoulders and gasp a tiny sound of shocked arousal as his lips caressed the smooth line of her throat, and his hand slid into the gaping bodice of her dress to completely free both breasts, first to his touch, then to his gaze, and finally to the caress of his mouth.

And now he wasn't either gentle or restrained and, shockingly, in response to the demand of his mouth she felt fierce surges of pleasure and desire wash through her body, so powerful, so compulsive that she cried out in protest when his mouth released one breast before turning to the other, her hands clenching on his shoulders as her newly aroused senses silently urged him to repeat the agonisingly arousing caress.

When he did so, she trembled violently in open response, causing him to linger over the sensitive nub of flesh he was enjoying, before lifting his head to mutter against her mouth, 'You've been driving me crazy with the need to taste you like that all evening, *and* you know it, you little witch. Richard says you have a place of your own near the cathedral. Let me...'

It was like being immersed in a bath of icy water. Where she had been swept away by sensations, emotions so totally foreign to her that in his arms nothing had been more important than the pleasure he was giving her, now abruptly she came back to reality and suffered a corresponding surge of self-revulsion.

How many times in the past had she quickly and coldly turned down those men foolish enough to imagine that she could possibly want a sexual relationship with them on the strength of an acquaintance that could be counted only in hours? It was a hazard of that part of her work which involved travelling and buying abroad. Never once had she been even remotely tempted to indulge in that kind of brief sexual thing. It was something she utterly and completely abhorred.

She had always believed that, for her, sexual desire was something she would only experience for someone with whom she was deeply and passionately in love, which was why, as Emma had taunted her earlier, she was still a virgin. And yet now here she was in the garden of her parents' home allowing a man—and not just any man either, but one she had already decided she disliked and distrusted intensely—to caress her so intimately that she had given him the impression that she was ready to go to bed with him.

Perhaps something of her feelings showed in her face, because suddenly he had released her and he now stood watching her . . . waiting.

Quite what would have happened if she hadn't heard her mother calling her name, Natasha wasn't sure. As it was she could only feel immense relief and gratitude that she was saved from making any explanation, from saying anything other than a husky, 'I must go,' before practically running away from him.

It was only later when she was helping her mother to serve coffee and a light supper to their guests that she remembered she had left her aunt's jacket in the garden. She shivered, her face suddenly pale, causing her mother to say anxiously, 'Tasha, are you all right? The last thing we need now is you going down with a summer cold. What on earth were you doing in the garden anyway?'

'I had a headache and wanted some fresh air,' she responded tensely, while she surreptitiously searched the room, unsuccessfully looking for Luke Templecombe.

It wasn't until she saw Emma half an hour later that she discovered he had gone.

'You can relax now,' her cousin told her cheerfully. 'Luke's gone, thank goodness. Oh, and thanks for letting him and Richard think that it *was* you leaving Jake's house.'

'I still think it would have been better for you to tell Richard the truth,' Natasha told her. 'He loves you and I'm sure he'd understand.'

'Not yet,' Emma told her positively. 'He does love me, but I don't think he's sure enough of me yet to believe that I could spend the night with Jake simply working with him. I was right about Luke, wasn't I? He really is horrible. He's fantastic-looking, of course, and a wow with the women according to Richard, but I bet inside he's as cold and hard as ice. I can't see him ever allowing himself to fall in love, can you? Richard says Luke's very anti-marriage—considers it a trap and all that kind of thing. Apparently his parents were very unhappy together, but because his father was a Templecombe there was no question of divorce. They married at the end of the war, and Luke's mother had been in love with someone else. He was killed and so she married Luke's father, but it didn't work out.

'His father died when Luke was fourteen years old. An overdose of sleeping tablets. Accidental death, according to the authorities, but Richard says Luke always believed that he killed himself when he found out that Luke's mother was having an affair with someone else and that she was leaving her husband. He never forgave his mother. He ran away from home when he was sixteen and virtually worked his way around the world. Richard says he feels rather sorry for him—personally I think he's the pits, don't you?'

'He certainly isn't someone I'd like to see a lot of,' Natasha agreed hollowly.

Impossible not to feel some sympathy for the unhappy child he must have been, but he wasn't a child any longer; he was a man—a cruelly cynical and dangerous man. A man who would have taken her to bed simply to ease a physical ache without feeling the slightest degree of liking or respect for her as a human being. She shivered convulsively, and decided grimly that as soon as tonight was over she was going to take Emma's dress, and her stockings and her silly high-heeled shoes and throw the lot of them on the fire, and if Emma ever, ever asked her to do anything to help her again she would most definitely refuse.

'What's wrong?' Emma asked her curiously. 'You look as though you're thinking of murdering someone.'

'Mm... would it surprise you to know that that someone is you? Don't ask me for any more favours, Emma. I don't think I could survive it.'

'What? Not even being godmother to our first child?' Emma teased, laughing when Natasha said fervently,

'No... not if he or she is going to inherit your aptitude for getting into trouble.'

CHAPTER FOUR

'How do I look? Is my veil straight?' Emma asked Natasha anxiously for about the tenth time.

'Yes. It's straight. And you look wonderful,' Natasha assured her firmly and truthfully.

Emma, in her cream silk wedding dress and wearing the veil that had been their grandmother's, was a breathtakingly beautiful bride. Now, as she prepared to leave for the church with Sara, the other bridesmaid, Natasha bent to kiss her cousin's cheek and then picked up the full skirts of her own dress, hurrying Sara out of the room and downstairs.

The soft cream of their dresses with their apricot sashes were almost as lovely in their way as Emma's stunningly beautiful gown, Natasha admitted, pausing briefly to check the neckline of her own in the mirror and adjust its off-the-shoulder puff sleeves.

Thank goodness Luke Templecombe wasn't coming to the wedding. She was still smarting and sore from her run-in with him at the pre-wedding dinner, still too sharply aware of how intensely she had reacted to him.

There had been sighs of relief all round this morning when they had woken to find the sun shining on a perfect summer's day, although as yet none of them had had time to appreciate it as the whole house had been busy with comings and goings from first thing onwards.

The reception was being held here at the house in a marquee which a skilled team of workmen had erected two days ago. Now, firmly ushering Richard's sister ahead of her, Natasha opened the front door and smiled at the driver of their waiting car. Sara was still scowling. Sulking still over Emma's refusal to allow her to wear pink, no doubt, Natasha reflected as she firmly ignored the younger girl's sullenness and remarked on their good luck with the weather.

The ceremony was taking place at the cathedral, of course. Her own father was giving Emma away. As their car drew up and they got out she heard the appreciative murmurs of the onlookers.

'Everyone's arrived,' her mother told her, hurrying up to her. 'Richard doesn't look in the least nervous.'

'Pa is,' Natasha told her with a grin.

Earlier, suddenly and unexpectedly emotional, Emma had hugged her tightly, tears in her eyes as she whispered, 'Thanks for everything, Tasha...and especially for letting that pig Luke think it was you he saw leaving Jake's. Thank goodness he can't come to the wedding. I'd have been like a cat on hot bricks wondering if he was going to stand up and denounce me when they got to that bit, you know, "If any man..."'

'Yes, I know,' Natasha agreed. 'Although I'm sure he'd never have done anything so dramatic. It's not his style. He prefers a more subtle form of cruelty.'

Emma had given her an odd look, started to say something and then stopped, and no wonder. But fortunately she had been too caught up in her own thoughts to ponder too much on the bitterness in Natasha's voice.

Natasha would never, never forget the way he had treated her in the garden. She went hot with fury and chagrin just to think about it . . . just to remember. And underneath that emotion ran another darker, shameful awareness of how frighteningly he had aroused her.

She saw the car arriving with her father and Emma. As Emma climbed out on to the pavement Natasha knew that she was not the only person discovering that her breath had lodged in her throat and that her eyes were unexpectedly misty.

She was just about to hurry forward to help her cousin with her dress when Sara suddenly said excitedly, 'Oh, good, there's Luke! He's made it after all. Wonderful!'

Luke . . . Luke here . . . ? Sara had to be wrong. He had said quite firmly that he would not be able to attend. He couldn't just change his mind like that—not without letting anyone know.

For some odd reason Natasha's heart was beating furiously fast. She knew she ought to move, to hurry forward to Emma's side taking Sara with her, and yet her whole body seemed to be held in a state of suspended shock. Sara was calling out Luke's name and waving frantically. All she needed to do was to turn her head . . . just a few inches . . . No one would ever notice . . . and he would be directly in her line of vision.

The mere fact that she wanted to turn her head jolted her back to reality. The man was a barbarian, cruel and feral, for all his cloaking sophistication. She knew...she had felt the sharp claws of his contempt, the savage teeth of his cold desire. She shivered suddenly, reminding herself that this was Emma's day, and that if her cousin knew that Luke was here it might spoil things for her.

Resolutely ignoring the temptation to turn her head, she took hold of Sara's arm and hissed in her ear, 'Not now, Sara. You can talk to Luke later,' and quickly tugged her in Emma's direction.

Fortunately her cousin was so busy worrying about the delicate lace of her veil that she had not had time to look around her. Hopefully, by the time she did, Luke would have disappeared inside the cathedral with the rest of the guests.

For Natasha, the moving simplicity of the wedding service was overshadowed by her knowledge of Luke's presence. Contrary to the fears Emma had expressed earlier, he did not stand up and denounce her, but then Natasha had never thought that he would. No, his denunciations now were all for her, she thought bitterly as the triumphal surge of the wedding march filled the cathedral and the doors were drawn back to admit the hot brilliance of the afternoon sun.

It was over. Emma and Richard were safely married and there was nothing that Luke Templecombe could do about it, no matter how unsuited he might think them.

What she couldn't understand, she decided uneasily, following Emma back down the aisle, was what he was doing here. It had seemed so certain that he could not attend the wedding, and yet here he was.

She had no idea where he was sitting, nor did she intend to look, but Sara's excited 'Luke!' sent prickles of unwanted sensation burning under her skin, drawing her attention instinctively to his tall, dark-suited frame.

For a moment their eyes met and locked. Something dark and challenging flickered in his, setting up a warning pulse at the base of her throat. When she touched her skin there the betraying gesture drew his attention. The sensation of him looking at her was so strong that she could almost feel the heat of his gaze burning her skin, could almost feel the savage possession of his mouth as it fastened over that frightened pulse.

She felt sick, faint, shocked into a maelstrom of panic and fear. And yet why? What was there to fear? What could he possibly do to her here among her friends and family? What could he possibly *want* to do to her? He had come here to see Richard married, that was all. It was insane of her to think she had read in that feral glance he had given her, that challenging clash of their eyes, another darker purpose.

Why on earth would he want to seek her out? He had made his contempt of her all too plain already, and yet she discovered even once she was outside in the warmth of the sun that her skin felt oddly chilled, that her throat was aching with tension and that she was almost visibly trembling.

All around her was the wash of people's voices, congratulations and laughter, people giving instructions as they were shepherded towards the waiting cars.

No photographs were being taken outside the cathedral. It was deemed unseemly and so everyone was waiting for Emma and Richard to leave so that they could make their way back to Lacey Court.

Only when she was safely inside their own car did Natasha feel able to relax. She ached to turn her head and search feverishly to see where Luke was, what he was doing, but she refused to give in to her weakness. It was fear that was making her feel like this, fear and anger, and of course shock...and yet beneath them lay something else—a dangerous, elemental sexual excitement whose existence tore at her pride, at her self-respect.

'Are you OK?'

Sara's unexpected question made Natasha open her eyes and look at her.

'Yes, yes. I'm fine. Why?'

'You look awful,' she was told untactfully. 'Really white and sick. You didn't want to marry Richard yourself, did you?'

'No, of course I didn't,' Natasha told her shortly. 'I've just got a bit of a headache, that's all...'

Her response seemed to satisfy Sara, who immediately changed the subject and said blissfully, 'I'm so glad that Luke's here. He's wonderful. Much nicer than Richard.'

Natasha's mouth twisted cynically.

At her side Sara was still chattering. 'I'm going to make sure he sits next to me. I'll change the place cards——'

'You can't,' Natasha told her sharply, 'You're on the top table, remember.'

Sara was pouting sulkily. 'Well, I don't see that that matters. I suppose Emma has put me next to some ghastly boy.'

'I've no idea,' Natasha told her shortly. Her heart was still pounding at the thought of finding herself on the same table as Luke, and yet why? Why should she feel this...this fear? Antagonism, dislike, resentment...yes, she could understand herself feeling all these emotions, but fear? And fear of what? Surely not of his repeating that savage caress he had bestowed on her before?

The car had stopped. They were home. She could hear Emma's excited voice. As she climbed out of the car, other cars were arriving... Her parents...Richard's family... And there, in the expensive Jaguar saloon, Luke, dark and predatory, and looking just a little alien in some way among the laughing crowd of guests.

Emma had seen him now, her face expressing her indignation as she hissed to her new husband, 'What's he doing here?'

Richard looked puzzled.

'I don't know. He said he wouldn't be able to make it.'

'Well, it's going to put out all the numbers,' Emma told him indignantly.

When Richard looked helplessly at her Natasha stepped in, saying soothingly, 'I'm sure we'll be able to squeeze him in somewhere.' Somewhere as far away from her as possible. 'I'll go and have a word with the caterers.'

She was only too glad of the excuse to get away, to hurry through the house to the kitchen to find the man in charge of the catering team.

'Yes, a place could easily be made at one of the tables,' he assured her, having listened to her question. She lingered for a few more seconds and then reminded herself that she had other duties, that she was Emma's bridesmaid.

When she returned to the garden the photographer was busy with Emma and Richard. She watched them absently, her senses straining to find Luke so that she could keep well away from him, but she wouldn't allow herself to turn her head.

'Ah, Natasha. My dear...'

She smiled automatically at Richard's mother, and then went cold as she saw Luke standing with her.

'I know you've already met Luke. Such a wonderful surprise that he managed to make it for the wedding after all.'

Woodenly, Natasha said nothing, staring fixedly ahead and then gritting her teeth as he seemed deliberately to step into her line of vision.

Her eyes were on a level with his jaw. She could see the rough growth of beard shadowing the clean-shaven flesh.

'Luke, you remember Natasha, Emma's cousin, don't you?'

'But of course... Quite a metamorphosis,' he added softly under his breath, so softly that

Natasha knew only she was meant to hear it. She felt her skin heat with indignation and resentment, and then saw the way he was looking at her. Like a cat at a mousehole.

'Please excuse me,' she said frigidly. 'They'll be waiting to finish the photographs.' Her face still hot, she walked away. How dared he look at her like that—with that cynical half-smile that said that he knew all her secrets, all her vulnerabilities? He knew nothing about her. Nothing at all.

'Not dancing?'

Natasha stiffened as she heard Luke's voice in her ear. She had left the marquee and come outside for a few minutes' respite from the tension of continuously smiling and talking, trying to appear natural while at the same time trying to avoid Luke. And now here he was behind her, making her spine tingle with tension and her body suddenly go hot and weak.

'I wanted a few minutes alone,' she told him pointedly, refusing to turn around. Not because she was afraid to confront him. After all, what had she done? Nothing...

Nothing other than to present him with a totally false impression of herself. An impression that said she was both sexually experienced and sexually available. But dozens of other women must give him that same message; there was nothing particularly remarkable about her... No reason for him to project towards her this aura of male arousal and awareness. He couldn't want her. And she certainly did not want him. And yet...

She shuddered at the shocking, contrary feeling deep inside her, and then flinched as he reached out and touched her bare shoulder.

'Are you cold?'

He must know that she was not, because his fingers were now tracing the line of her collarbone, stroking it almost, lazily and carelessly, ignoring her attempt to move away from him.

'You're quite an actress,' he murmured. 'Today, the cool demure cousin of the bride, the epitome of what women of Richard's mother's generation believe a young lady should be.' His voice mocked her and then dropped to a harder, dangerous tone as he added, 'And yet the last time we met you were the epitome of an eager wanton, a woman of passion and desire.'

'I must go.'

How weak her voice sounded. How uncertain and hesitant, faintly breathless and nervous—not as she would have wanted it to sound at all.

'Not yet... No one will miss us if we stay out here a little longer.'

Her heart was thumping frantically fast. She didn't want to stay outside alone with him. She wanted to be with everyone else. Where she would be safe... But safe from what? He wasn't threatening her in any way. He wasn't even touching her any more, and dangerously, in view of all she knew about him, her skin actually seemed to miss that cool contact with his fingers.

'You rather intrigue me, you know,' he told her, moving round so that he was facing her.

'Oh. Am I supposed to find that flattering?'

'Don't you?'

Reaction kicked at her stomach. He knew too much... Saw too much.

'No,' she told him shortly. 'And now, if you'll excuse me, I must go back.'

She side-stepped him, expelling a shaky breath of relief when he let her, and then just as she thought herself safe he reached out and circled her wrist, shackling her to him.

'Not yet,' he told her softly. 'You realise, don't you, that you're the reason I'm here today?'

'No.' She made the denial instinctively, choking over the word as he coolly drew her to him and into his arms.

Why was he doing this...and why was she letting him? She was a fool, an idiot, bent on self-destruction. She tried to escape but it was too late. His mouth was already hard and warm on hers. His hands were smoothing down over her back. In another moment her body would be pressed the whole length of his and he would be doing to her what he had done before.

Panic engulfed her. She didn't want this... She hadn't invited it. But she hadn't rejected it either, an inner voice taunted her. She struggled to pull herself away from him, to evade the drugging pressure of his mouth.

'Luke... Luke, where are you?'

Natasha gasped in relief as she heard Sara calling Luke's name.

'Luke, you promised me this dance.'

She thought she heard him curse under his breath as he released her, but her heart was pounding so heavily that she was surprised she could hear anything above its roar.

As she stepped away from him she saw that in the moonlight the flesh around his mouth was tight with anger. He hadn't wanted to let her go, she recognised, as Sara spotted them and came rushing over.

'Oh, there you are. This is our dance. Emma wants you,' she told Natasha dismissively. 'She says she's ready to get changed.'

Natasha was only too happy to escape.

'You look pale. Are you OK?' Emma asked her when they went upstairs to her room.

'Yes. I'm fine.'

'Fancy Luke turning up like that...and he's given us a very generous cheque.'

'And that makes everything all right?' Natasha asked her bitterly. 'Emma, less than a month ago you were convinced the man was going to destroy your whole life.'

'Well, that's what I thought... I still think he *might* have done if you hadn't pretended to be me. Has he said anything more about that to you?' she questioned anxiously.

'No,' Natasha told her abruptly.

Somewhere in the marquee Luke would be dancing with Sara. She told herself that she was glad that Richard's young sister had interrupted them, that the last thing she would have wanted was to be forced to endure the intimacy he had been pressing on her, and yet some tiny part of her body remained unconvinced, and the flesh of her mouth felt tender and sensitive so that when she touched it with her fingertips she could still almost feel the sensation of Luke's mouth there.

Three hours later, when the last of the wedding guests had gone, including Luke, Natasha felt more exhausted than she had ever done in her life. It wasn't just the wedding itself, it was the strain of avoiding Luke—of avoiding confronting the duality of her responses to him.

On the surface were her natural resentment, her ire, her fury, and yet beneath them ran a dangerous flow of counter emotions. Arousal, desire, sexual excitement. Emotions as unfamiliar to her as they were unwanted.

Emotions she must get firmly under control because they had no place in her life. No place at all. Neither had Luke Templecombe.

CHAPTER FIVE

WHY was it, Natasha wondered grimly three weeks after the wedding, that the phone always chose to ring with the particularly irritatingly imperious summons when she was either halfway up or halfway down her small four-storey home's flights of stairs, and therefore forced to race either up or down them to silence its aggravating demands.

Another person—an Emma no doubt—would probably have cheerfully allowed it to ring. Or have an additional phone socket installed on the first-storey landing, she decided breathlessly as she reached the door of her workroom and flung it open, dashing across the room to snatch up the receiver, saying quickly, 'Natasha Lacey.'

There was a small silence of a kind that made a tiny thrill of premonition race down her spine, and then a faintly mocking male voice drawled, 'And a rather out of breath Natasha Lacey at that. Very flattering, I must say.'

The voice, the lazy amusement, the sexual self-confidence were all of them instantly recognisable, as was the sharp thrill of betraying sensation that burned through her. But after them came panic and then fear. Why was Luke Templecombe telephoning her? Just for a moment she was tempted to pretend that she hadn't recognised his voice, or, even better, that she didn't remember him at all, but caution warned her that to do so would be to enter into a very dangerous game indeed. One at which she suspected he was adept and skilled, and one for which she already knew she had no talents at all, so instead she said as coolly as she could, 'Luke—what an unexpected surprise. If you've been trying to get in touch with Richard's parents, I believe they've gone away for a few days.'

He didn't take up the polite fiction she was offering, saying after a small pause, 'No, it was you I wanted to talk to. I have some business in the city next week. I'll be staying over for a couple of days. Richard's parents are very kindly allowing me to use the deanery as a *pied-à-terre*. I'll be there for three days. I'd like to take you out to dinner.'

To say she was stunned was a massive understatement, Natasha thought muzzily as she stared silently out the window. She had never expected Luke to get in touch with her again, and never, ever, in her wildest imaginings visualised him calmly inviting her out. Her workroom had been warmed by the sun all day, and initially when she had rushed in she had found it almost overpoweringly hot. Now suddenly she shivered, rashes of goose-flesh breaking out over her skin.

She had tried so hard to dismiss that sharp, fierce sexual arousal she had experienced in Luke's arms, to pretend that helpless spiralling sensation of her body bursting to life beneath his hands and mouth had never happened, to obliterate from her memory the dangerous knowledge that Luke had been physically aroused by her, had wanted her, telling herself that she was a fool if she imagined that he was doing anything other than deliberately and consciously using his maleness in that way to punish her, knowing almost just by looking at him that his experience of life, of human emotions and vulnerabilities was light years away from her own, reminding herself that his particular brand of maleness was both potent and dangerous, particularly to someone like her, who did not have the experience to combat it.

Had they met in different circumstances, had she not unwisely allowed Emma to persuade her to adopt a persona that was not really hers, had he been introduced to her as she really was, Natasha suspected that Luke would have treated her with the same good-mannered but distancing politeness she had witnessed him exhibiting to such good effect on Richard's mother. It was partly her own fault that he had reacted to her in the sexually predatory manner he had, and it had stunned her to discover how naïve, how defenceless, how very unaware of her own vulnerability she had been.

She had never believed it was possible to react so immediately and so intensely to a man one didn't very much like. It had shocked her to discover within herself a hitherto hidden streak of recklessness so contradictory to her normal carefully controlled behaviour. A recklessness which whispered provocatively that perhaps it was time she had the experience of a Luke Templecombe in her life. So had spoken the serpent to Eve!

Now Luke was ringing her up, asking her out, and she was not so naïve that she didn't realise that it wasn't her conversation he wanted. This kind of experience, this casual, emotionless assumption that she would welcome what she knew would only be a brief sexual fling with him chilled her, bringing home to her her own danger.

She took a deep breath and, before she could give in to the temptation churning recklessly inside her, said shakily, 'I'm sorry... That won't be possible.'

The silence from the other end of the line was almost menacing. He obviously wasn't used to being turned down, she told herself, trying to whip up enough anger to subdue the dangerous *frisson* of yearning twisting inside her. If she accepted and went out with him, it would lead to all manner of complications. He thought she was one of his own kind, and when he discovered she wasn't it would lead to embarrassment and maybe even pain. The mere fact that she was tempted to accept warned her how dangerously vulnerable she was. It was pointless allowing herself to ignore the facts, to indulge in silly, impossible daydreams.

For her own sake, she had to make sure that he did not get in touch with her again.

'So you're not free next week,' the silky voice enquired.

She took a deep breath, knowing what she had to say.

'I'm sorry, but I'm not free at all.'

'I see.'

How odd that two words said in such an expressionless manner could convey such a wealth of ironic innuendo.

Later she acknowledged painfully that she ought to have left it there, simply said goodbye and replaced the receiver, but the same impulse that had made her feel guilty and responsible enough to help Emma out of so many ridiculous situations now pushed her to add, 'In fact, I can't imagine why you should think that I might want to see you again.'

There was a small silence and she thought for a moment that she had gained ascendancy over him, and then as smooth as cream and far, far less palatable came the words, 'Really? I have memories of a certain handful of minutes which tell a very different story. However, I can quite well understand why in these health conscious times you might not want to be seen as a woman who shares her bed with two lovers concurrently. You must forgive me. I must be becoming rather less astute than I have always believed myself to be. I didn't realise that you were already involved elsewhere...'

It was just as well she was alone, Natasha reflected as she felt the indignant anger scald a hot, burning tide across her body. How dared he insinuate... Her fingers tightened around the receiver. She ached to let him know just how wrong he was, to give voice to her fury and resentment that he should dare to criticise *her* behaviour, to imply that it was her fault that he had assumed that she was both available and willing to play sophisticated sexual games with him. But she couldn't do so without betraying Emma.

Even so, she was angry enough to say icily, 'Even if I weren't, I assure you that I would have no interest whatsoever in pursuing our acquaintance.'

With that she slammed down the receiver, but not before she had heard him saying cynically, 'Odd...that wasn't the message I received at all.'

Hateful, hateful man! How dared he assume...? how dared he suggest...?

She was still pacing her workroom half an hour later when the phone rang a second time. She looked at it doubtfully, half inclined to let it ring, and then, telling herself that she was being stupid, she made herself pick up the receiver.

The sensation she experienced when she discovered that her caller wasn't Luke Templecombe wasn't entirely one of relief. Which told its own betraying and dangerous story, she reflected grimly as she tried to concentrate on her telephone call.

It was rather a long one, and when it was over she found herself torn between relief and a rather disturbing sense of disappointment. What she ought to be feeling was elation, she chastised herself. It wasn't every day that she received such a prestigious commission.

An invitation to select and quote for fabrics to complement the renovation of a Carolean manor house which was presently being converted into an exclusive private hotel wasn't the kind of commission that someone in her position could afford to be blasé about. What was even more heart-warming was that the owner of the hotel had seen some fabrics she had supplied for someone else and had liked them so much that he had immediately found out her name and got in touch with her. He was anxious to keep the flavour and period of the house as authentic as possible, he had told her, bearing in mind the fact that, being in a hotel, the fabrics would be subject to the kind of wear and tear not recommended for rare antiques.

He had suggested that she spend a week at the house as his guest so that she would have plenty of time to absorb its atmosphere and consider what fabrics would best complement it. Although she had pointed out to him that she was no interior designer, he did not seem to think this a problem, telling her briskly that he would much prefer to have the opinion and suggestions of someone with a genuine feel and flare for the period rather than a designer intent on meeting some fashionable criteria without proper thought for the ambiance he wanted to give the place.

It was the kind of challenge she had often day-dreamed about, but never imagined actually being given, Natasha acknowledged. If she had received this kind of offer before meeting Luke Templecombe it would have filled her every waking thought, but now her gratification was tinged with an odd reluctance to accept a commission which she knew would take her out of the city when Luke was due to visit it. Why, when she already knew that the worst thing she could do was to fall into the trap of letting herself believe that by some miracle Luke was going to take one look at her, realise how badly he had misjudged her and immediately announce how much he preferred the real Natasha?

Not only was she a fool for imagining anything so impossible could actually happen, she was also dangerously close to the border of some kind of emotional suicide if she actually *wanted* Luke to... To what? To desire her? To pursue her? To what end? The kind of involvement she had determinedly avoided all her adult life—the kind of involvement that was based on emotionless sexual need on the man's part, and something frighteningly close to total emotional and permanent commitment on the woman's?

She had always known that within herself lay this deep pool of emotional vulnerability, this capacity to give herself completely and absolutely to one man and one alone. What she had never known was how easily the man in question could be someone like Luke Templecombe, the kind of man who was, of all his sex, least likely to either want or be able to share the intensity of her emotional commitment.

It was just as well that only she knew of that momentary surge of reluctance to accept the commission she had been offered. Telling herself that what she was experiencing was probably nothing more than a good old-fashioned and probably overdue dose of totally unsuitable sexual responsiveness, she resolved to put Luke Templecombe right out of her mind.

Three days later, irritated with herself for her inability to close off her mind against its insidious clinging to her memories of Luke, Natasha was walking in Lacey Court's gardens, trying to clear the persistent headache which she knew was born of a combination of lack of sleep and mental unrest.

What increased her self-anger was the knowledge that, instead of wasting time spending so much energy and emotion dwelling on a man who ought to have no place in any sane woman's thoughts, she should have been concentrating on preparing herself for what was the most important commission she had ever received.

A year ago, a month ago even, had someone told her that she would have actually been in this kind of emotional state, where she preferred day-dreaming impossible daydreams about a man whose every word and gesture was completely opposed to everything she believed went to make up the type of man who most appealed to her to concentrating her every thought and effort on the most exciting challenge of her new career, she would have dismissed them as insane.

Now *she* was the one who was dangerously close to insanity. She had to be, to be virtually yearning as helplessly as a teenager over a man whom every protective instinct she possessed told her it was imperative she kept out of her life.

The trouble was that she had other instincts—deeper, more dangerous, and innately stronger instincts, instincts she had never dreamed existed until Luke had so shockingly awakened them; instincts which recklessly told her that, no matter what the risks, the dangers, she *must* allow her body the self-indulgence of experiencing all the pleasures it knew Luke Templecombe could show it.

As a child, Natasha had often stood on a bridge, looking down at the water flowing below, and experienced the dangerous sensation of being pulled towards that flow. Now she was experiencing that sensation again, only this time it was Luke Templecombe who was the magnet which drew her so dangerously, or rather the sexual spark he seemed to have ignited inside her.

She stopped her pacing, grimacing in self-disgust that she, who had always been so fiercely fastidious, so intensely protective of her own physical privacy, should experience this overwhelming surge of sexual hunger—the kind of hunger she had never associated with women like herself, the kind of hunger that kept her awake at night and made her body ache in a thousand unfamiliar and tormenting ways, that caused her, when she did sleep, to wake up from dreams of such intensity and sensuality that merely to remember odd flashes of them was enough to make her skin burn and her mind flinch.

'Dear me, surely it isn't my poor delphiniums that are causing that glower. I know this pink variety is somewhat frowned on by the purists, but they do add a certain balance to this section of the border.'

Natasha forced a smile as she saw her aunt approaching her, but it didn't come easily—something which the other woman obviously recognised, because as she stood beside her she asked quietly, 'Is something wrong, Tasha? This commission perhaps . . . I know it's a wonderful opportunity, but——'

'It isn't the commission,' Natasha assured her, and then realised what her denial had admitted.

'There is something, then?' Helen queried, confirming her thoughts.

For a moment Natasha was tempted to fib. She was a woman, not a child. This was the kind of problem she ought to be able to solve by herself; talking about it would do nothing other than to confirm what she already knew—that she had made the right decision in making it plain to Luke Templecombe that she did not want to pursue any kind of relationship with him. However, she had admitted too much to lie now; she was not blessed with the kind of inventive tongue which allowed her to fabricate deceit, and so she said quietly, 'It's nothing really. It's just that I got myself into a rather silly situation with someone and——'

'By someone I imagine you must mean Luke Templecombe,' her aunt interrupted her, concealing her own compassion when she saw the way Natasha looked at her. This niece of hers was so vulnerable, so different from her own ebullient, lightweight daughter.

Shocked, Natasha rushed into unguarded speech. 'How did you know? I mean...'

'I saw him follow you out into the garden, the evening of Emma's pre-wedding dinner.'

Despairingly, Natasha closed her eyes and then opened them again, suddenly longing to unburden herself.

'Let's go and sit down,' her aunt suggested, leading the way to a sheltered stone bench situated to give the best view of the high summer border.

Humbly Natasha followed her. As soon as they were seated, she found herself pouring out everything in a disjointed, confused spate of words, so unlike her normal concise, often guarded conversation that Helen Lacey felt her concern increase.

Listening to Natasha's breathless speech, she found time to mentally chastise Emma's part in the confusion, thinking it typical of her flighty child that she should involve her more serious cousin in what by rights should have been her own problems, with scant regard for the possible consequences to Natasha.

'So perhaps because of the way you were dressed, and certainly because you had stepped so protectively into Emma's shoes, Luke mistook you for——'

'For Jake Pendraggon's lover,' Natasha agreed, adding quickly, 'Not of course that Emma and Jake were lovers. I suspect she simply wanted to make Richard jealous.'

'Well, she certainly succeeded, and to such effect that when it became necessary she could not rely on his believing the truth. She behaved very badly—very badly, involving you in what should have been her own problem. I suppose it wouldn't be possible to tell Luke the truth?' Helen hazarded, suspecting that there was more to the story than she was being told.

Her cautious, defensive niece would not normally be sent into such a state by the unwelcome advances of a sexually predatory male, so what was different about this one? She suspected she already knew, and her heart ached for Natasha.

'I *can't* tell him the truth...' And not just because of Emma. Her own pride would not allow her to do so. And not just her pride. For some reason she didn't want to see the bored uninterest she already knew would creep into his eyes once he learned the truth about her—that she was a dull, undesired twenty-seven-year-old virgin, who had been entrapped into playing a role for which she was completely unsuited, and who was now so scared by the results of that role-playing that she was forced to admit the truth.

'Oh, dear,' was her aunt's only very mild comment.

As she looked at the older woman, Natasha knew quite well that her aunt had correctly interpreted the complexities of her emotions.

'I take it, then, that this new commission has arrived at a most fortuitous time?'

'Yes,' Natasha agreed shakily, glad that she didn't have to put into words her fears that if she stayed in the area she would be all too vulnerable to any pressure Luke decided to put her under. She said as much to her aunt.

'Mm,' the latter agreed, 'a very dangerous young man. I thought so the moment I set eyes on him, and I can't help wondering if it was entirely wise of you to suggest to him that you're involved with somebody else.'

'It was the only thing I could think of to put him off,' Natasha told her. 'It certainly seemed to work.'

She winced a little, remembering his acerbic, almost cruel comment.

'Perhaps,' her aunt agreed, 'although he struck mc as a man who has no compunction whatsoever about meeting whatever challenges life chooses to throw his way. As you say, it's probably just as well that you're going to be out of his reach for the next few weeks. He is very compelling, Natasha, almost overpoweringly so, and very attractive.'

'So is fire,' Natasha retorted drily, 'providing you don't get too close to it.'

Her aunt gave her a shrewd, compassionate look. 'I see. Like that, was it?' She saw Natasha's expression and smiled reminiscently. 'I haven't entirely forgotten what it feels like, you know. Even when one gets to my age, one isn't automatically rendered unsusceptible to one's emotional and physical needs. Just look at that iris,' she directed, drawing Natasha's attention to the flower in question. 'Isn't it the most perfect colour?'

It was, and Natasha said as much, recognising that her aunt wished to turn their conversation away from any more personal confidences.

'This border always looks its best at this time of year,' her aunt continued, as they left their seat and started to walk towards the house, 'although this year I'm wondering about extending its life by underplanting the perennials with autumn flowering bulbs.'

They continued to discuss the garden until they had returned to the back door, where her aunt left Natasha, announcing that she had to go and check on the progress of her sweet peas.

For the rest of the time left before she was due to leave for Stonelovel Manor, Natasha stalwartly refused to allow her thoughts any leniency to wander in the direction of Luke Templecombe. It wasn't easy; temptation had a way of presenting itself to her in so many plausible guises that sometimes even she herself was deceived.

The fact that this, her most challenging and potentially most demanding commission to date, made it necessary for her to involve herself in a certain amount of preparatory research before leaving Sutton Minster helped.

Her knowledge garnered during her recent investigative trips to Florence in particular had already equipped her with an excellent store of knowledge to draw on, and even more a supply of contacts in that city whom she hoped would be able to supply the various decorative items she wanted to suggest to Leo Rosenberg as ideal to complement the rich damasks and tapestries she wanted to use.

In Florence there were frame-makers, adept at copying any frame a client chose to desire, small, old-fashioned workshops tucked away in narrow down-at-heel streets where every kind of panelling, moulding or other decorative item of work could be produced as skilfully today as it had been centuries before. These craftsmen were expensive, of course, but she had gained the impression from Leo Rosenberg that this venture represented something that was more than a mere commercial venture.

On her father's advice, she had made some discreet cautionary enquiries via her bank, for as her father had warned her, for someone like herself, newly established in her own business, the financial hardship of buying for a client who then turned out not to be in a position to pay for goods ordered on his behalf could destroy her business and leave her with a burden of debts she could never repay.

The bank reports were good, and some further enquiries made by her solicitors elicited the information that Leo Rosenberg was a man in his early fifties who by judicious buying and selling of property had built up a reputation as a shrewd entrepreneur.

His decision to buy Stonelovel Manor and convert it, not into expensive and sought after apartments, but instead into a luxury country house hotel had caused some surprise in financial circles, but the general force of opinion seemed to be that Leo Rosenberg had the Midas touch when it came to his business affairs.

Having reassured himself that his daughter was not going to be drawn into financial over-trading, Natasha's father offered to give her whatever help she might need in completing the commission.

'I've got to get it first,' Natasha reminded him, the night before she was due to leave for Stonelovel. She was poring over maps at the time, checking up on the best route from her home to the manor, having decided not to use the direct route of the M4, and then to cut across country, but instead to take her time and enjoy a quieter if more circuitous route that meandered through the countryside.

Only she knew that she had deliberately decided to leave a full day before she had originally planned, because suddenly in the middle of the night she had woken up from a dream in which Luke Templecombe had presented himself at her front door a day before he was due to arrive. Wishful thinking or presentiment? What did it matter? What did matter was the aching, yearning burden of temptation the dream brought her, the almost uncontrollable desire to simply give in and let fate carry her where it willed.

But allowing someone or something else to take over her life, to make her decision for her, and thus to abdicate from the responsibility of any decision about it, was not and never had been Natasha's way, so she sturdily fought down the wakening, desirous wash of dangerous allure trying to erode her self-will, and decided to leave a day early.

A quick check by telephone to the number Leo Rosenberg had given her confirmed that it would be in order for her to do this.

'Leo is at present abroad,' his secretary informed her, but a room had been organised for her at the house, and his staff had been primed to expect her. 'The place is full of workmen at the moment, but Leo should be back tomorrow. You'll want to have a good look round the house, of course, and that's why Leo thought it would be a good idea for you to stay there for a few days, to get the feel of the house; and I know he wants to talk to you about his own ideas and plans for the ambiance he wants to create.'

Now, knowing that she wanted to get an early start in the morning, Natasha checked through the samples of fabric she had put on one side to take with her, and then went meticulously through the portfolio of photographs she had culled from various magazines, the brochures she had obtained from various manufacturers of reproduction furniture, and all the other details she had meticulously gathered together, including her all-important notebooks from her trip to Florence.

This was the most important challenge of her career, and she was not going to allow anything or anyone to deflect her from giving it her full attention—especially not Luke Templecombe.

'I'll be leaving early in the morning,' she told her parents as she stood up, 'so I'll say goodbye now and I'll try not to disturb you in the morning.'

'You'll ring us when you arrive, won't you?' her mother queried anxiously. 'The roads these days——'

'I'll ring you just as soon as I can,' Natasha soothed.

She knew that she was taking the only sensible course open to her, that in this instance flight was definitely safer than fight, but her pride chafed at the necessity of it, wishing that she had the courage, the armour to confront Luke.

But it wasn't confronting him she feared; it wasn't that at all... What she feared was the enemy within herself, the alien, invidious physical desire he seemed to stir up inside her with so little effort. *That* was why she was running away. Had she not felt that desire, had he simply been another unwanted male importuning her, she would have had no compunction at all about staying and making it plain to him that he was wasting his time, but she doubted her own ability to tell him she didn't want him when her body had so plainly and shockingly already given her a very different message indeed.

And yet why was she allowing herself to get into such a state? Almost the first thing that had struck her about Luke was his male pride, so sharp-edged and honed that it almost bordered on arrogance. *Why* was she so afraid he would attempt to pursue her when she had told him she was involved with someone else?

Though he was no saint sexually himself, she had known instinctively that he was a man who would not share—a man who would never tolerate his current lover's being involved with another man. She had said enough to him surely to ensure that he must have lost whatever interest he had had in her, and yet beneath that logical certainty ran another kind of knowledge, a thread of instinct and deep feminine awareness that warned that, no matter what she might have told him vocally, her body had given him other, subtler, but no less emotive messages which he might just choose to believe in preference to her spoken words.

He was above everything else a man of intense pride, and who could tell? He might just choose to take it into his head to force her to acknowledge that, no matter how much she might say she did not want him, that she was involved with someone else, physically she desired *him*. And if once he did that...

She shivered suddenly, goose-bumps a rash of intense sensation along her skin as her body treacherously remembered how it had felt to be in his arms.

Stop it, she told herself. Stop it now before it's too late.

Thank goodness she had been offered this commission so opportunely. Without it, without the necessity of taking herself away from him, she doubted that she would have found the strength to do so voluntarily.

CHAPTER SIX

'DO COME in. Suzie, Leo's PA, rang and warned us to expect you. Aren't we being lucky with the weather at the moment?'

Acknowledging the older woman's pleasantries, Natasha followed Leo Rosenberg's housekeeper into the house.

She had arrived five minutes earlier, knocked on the door and introduced herself, and as the older woman invited her inside Natasha paused to study her surroundings.

'Leo intends to keep the reception-rooms as much as possible as they already are. Upstairs, of course, there's a great deal of work to be done; rooms have to be divided, bathrooms et cetera, but then of course you'll know all about that.'

Before Natasha could confirm or deny her comments, the housekeeper was leading her through the hall, opening a door set in the rear wall.

'We've tried to give you a room where you won't be disturbed too much by the workmen, but as you can see everything's rather chaotic at the moment,' she apologised, raising her voice so that Natasha could hear her above the sound of men whistling, electric drills whirring and the general hubbub of people working.

'We're all sleeping on the top floor at the moment, and I'm afraid we're having to use what used to be the servants' staircase, which is rather narrow; Leo intends to have lifts installed, discreetly of course.'

The stairs were narrow, and very twisty in places, but Natasha, used to the vagaries of her parents' home and her own steep four-storey little house, was far less breathless when they reached the top than her guide.

'Your room's down here,' the housekeeper told her. 'No private bathroom, I'm afraid, although you won't actually have to share with anyone else. Leo's organised a suite for himself at the other end of the house, in what will eventually be his private wing. My room is at the top of the staircase, and at the moment no one else is actually staying here.' She paused outside a white-painted door, and opened it.

Stepping inside, Natasha saw that she had been given a room with a big window which faced north, and which would be ideal for her to work in. It was a good-sized room, equipped with a double bed, a couple of comfortable looking armchairs, a desk, an easel and even an open fire.

'Leo said that you'd need somewhere where you'd be able to work in private as well as sleep. This was the room the architect used when he was drawing up the original plans for the alterations. I hope it will be all right.'

'It's ideal,' Natasha assured her, giving the woman the warm smile which always transformed her face, banishing the faintly aloof elegance which it had in repose, and drawing the immediate response of a relieved smile from the other woman.

'Well, that's all right, then. I'm afraid I've rather been dreading your arrival. I wasn't sure if Leo had warned you what to expect. He tends to talk about the house as though it's already been transformed, forgetting to warn people about the realities of the work in progress.'

'You've known him a long time?' Natasha hazarded.

'Yes. My husband used to work for him when he first set up in business, then, when George was killed in a road accident, Leo asked me if I'd like to come and work for him. It was a real lifeline. George and I had no children, no family at all to speak of... That was fifteen years ago and I've been with Leo ever since. He even offered to send me on a special course, so that I could run the hotel as its housekeeper once all the work is finished, but it would be too much responsibility for me and I told him so.'

So the ruthless, efficient entrepreneur of her father's business reports had a human side, Natasha reflected as she listened. Certainly his enthusiasm and love for the house had suggested that he was far from being the typical hard-headed type such men were generally assumed to be.

'I'll leave you to get settled in, then. Leo is coming down tomorrow to go round the place with you.'

Natasha had been hoping to explore the house on her own before meeting her client, but, having seen the extent of the work in progress on the fabric of the building, was forced to admit that it might be wiser to wait until Leo Rosenberg arrived in case she got in the way of the workmen.

'Would it be all right if I explored the gardens?' she asked the housekeeper now. 'I don't want to get in anyone's way.'

'They haven't started work on those as yet, so I should think that will be all right. Leo did say that if you were interested there were some books and papers in his study describing various changes which have been made to the place over the years.'

'I'd love to see them,' Natasha agreed.

An hour later, wandering around the neglected kitchen garden, reflecting on how much her aunt would enjoy the challenge of restoring it to what it must have once been, the guard she had placed on herself slipped, and without even knowing how it had happened she found herself thinking about another garden... another time... about a certain evening and a certain man. Before she knew what she was doing, in her mind's eye she saw Luke walking towards her front door, ringing the bell, waiting impatiently, and then, when there was no response, walking away. As she watched that departing back, she had an insane impulse to run to her car, to drive home just as fast as she could so that... So that what? So that she could open her heart and her mind to the inevitable pain which would follow any involvement with a man like Luke? What was the matter with her? She had never thought of herself as being a masochistic type before. Quite the contrary.

It had been a lovely day, and here in the enclosed kitchen garden it was almost hot, and yet still she shivered visibly, a violent tremor of sensation running through her body. Why was she reacting like this, feeling like this, aching, yearning, hungering like this, when she knew that the man responsible for these unwanted, dangerous feelings could offer her nothing other than an emotionally barren physical affair?

She stopped in front of what had once been a bed of herbs, and bent automatically to remove a large chickweed while her thoughts went round and round in the same tormenting circles.

'It's a disgrace, isn't it? I saw you walking from my study window and I thought I'd better come down and introduce myself.'

Natasha straightened up, flushing a little as she saw the amused and faintly speculative eyes of the man who had approached her.

Tall, somewhere in his early fifties, still dark-haired with a penetrating, thoughtful gaze, he made her all too conscious that the appearance she must be presenting was hardly the one she would have wished to present.

'Leo Rosenberg,' he introduced himself, shaking her hand firmly, ignoring the particles of soil clinging to her, and giving her a genuinely warm smile as he asked, 'Do you know much about gardening? I confess I'm at a loss to know where to begin with this one. What I'd like is to restore it as far as possible to something approaching a style in keeping with the house, although, bearing in mind that this is going to be a hotel, allowances will have to be made for the inclusion of tennis-courts et cetera.'

'I'm not an expert on gardens, I'm afraid,' Natasha confessed, 'but my aunt is, and I know she'd love to get her teeth into something like this, starting virtually from scratch——' She broke off, flushing again. 'I'm sorry. It's just that I was thinking about her... about how much she'd enjoy the challenge of this garden.'

'She needs a challenge, does she?' he asked astutely, causing Natasha to reflect that she was already beginning to see just what made this man so financially successful.

'I think so, although she'd probably disagree with me,' Natasha admitted as she fell into step beside him. She hadn't introduced herself, but it was obvious that he knew who she was.

'Knows a bit about this kind of thing, does she?' he enquired, making a sweeping gesture towards the area they were just leaving.

'An awful lot,' Natasha agreed. 'It's her hobby, and the gardens at home are her special province. I hadn't realised you were arriving this afternoon,' she continued a little more formally. She didn't want him to think she had been taking advantage of his absence to simply waste time. 'Your housekeeper told me you were arriving tomorrow to go over the house with me. I didn't want to disturb the workmen.'

'No, best not to,' he agreed, explaining, 'I managed to get away earlier than I expected. There's something wonderfully relaxing about coming back to this place.'

He stopped and breathed in deeply. Despite his age and occupation he looked remarkably fit, Natasha noticed, the involuntary movement of his chest as he breathed in betraying a solid muscle structure, devoid of excess flesh. Her thoughts were confirmed when he removed his jacket and slung it over his shoulder.

'Yes, I must admit I don't envy you working in London,' Natasha admitted.

The grin he gave her was endearingly boyish.

'Not London on this occasion. I've just flown in from New York and, as you say, here is infinitely preferable. That's why I intend to retire—to retain one wing of the house for my own private use, and live what's left of my life at a more relaxed pace.

'Unfortunately, in order to do that, initially I'm having to put in a lot of extra time getting everything sorted out. This aunt of yours—where can I find her?'

His question startled Natasha into an automatic reply, and she was even more startled when he frowned and then said thoughtfully, 'Laceys . . . of course . . . Ecclesiastical Textiles. I ought to have realised. You've virtually grown up in the business, then?'

'Yes, although I did brcak away from it for a while.'

Funny how easy it was to talk to this man, Natasha reflected. He had that same gift of genuine interest in others which she so admired in her aunt.

Thinking of Helen made her wonder a little guiltily how the latter would react if Leo Rosenberg did call on her. Perhaps she ought to warn her—

but then she had no idea if her new client was simply making conversation or whether he was seriously considering asking her aunt to help him with the restoration of his garden.

'I'm sorry if I'm pushing you a bit, but I've got an unexpected meeting in Amsterdam tomorrow, and if we could go round the house together now, and then go over the architect's plans...'

'I'd love to,' Natasha assured him. 'I've been doing as much reading up on the period as I can, and I've brought some samples with me, plus some sketches. As far as the bedrooms go, obviously you're going to want them to work from a practical point of view, as well as echo a feel for the period. Where the reception-rooms are concerned, I'm not sure just how much authenticity you had in mind. Obviously again the rooms are going to be used.'

'Used, yes, but we expect that the kind of guests we attract will have a genuine interest in and respect for antiques. Naturally, I'm not suggesting we re-create a Carolean interior exact in every detail—that would be impossible—but to some extent, encouraging the guests to believe that they have stepped back into the past, that they are staying somewhere which genuinely reflects a feeling for the period in which it was first built. I'm not suggesting using original antique fabrics, even if they could be found—such things more properly belong in museums and collections—but new fabrics, copied from original designs, made in the traditional way.'

Several hours later, when Leo Rosenberg had shown her the length and breadth of the house,

Natasha found herself liking him even more than she had done at first.

Wisely she had allowed him to lead the conversation. She always found it easier to help a client once she had discovered exactly how they felt about their home and its role in their lives, and, despite the fact that primarily Leo had called her in to provide interior design for the hotel, she had quickly discovered that the house meant far more to him than merely another business venture.

'There's nothing I'd like more than to simply keep the place as a private home,' he confided when they were back in the small cluttered room he was using as a temporary office. 'But, as the last owner discovered, it takes enormous revenues to maintain a place like this as a private house. I simply could not afford to do it. Sooner or later I'd have to sell and watch it being split up into separate units, its ambiance lost . . .

'I called in a team of consultants, got them to advise me on the best way to make a place like this pay its own way. They came up with the idea of converting it into a select country house hotel—the kind that caters for a maximum of ten couples and is more like joining a private house party than staying at a hotel. The American and Japanese in particular love that sort of thing. As you know, Charlie, the chef, is Roux-brothers trained. What I need to find now is a first-class hostess-cum-housekeeper——'

He broke off, grinning slightly shamefacedly. 'I'm sorry, but I'm afraid I do tend to get carried away once I start, and you're a very sympathetic listener.'

'Won't your wife——?' Natasha began, but he shook his head, cutting her off.

'I'm a widower. My wife died five years ago. She'd been ill for a long time. She developed a progressive wasting disease after the birth of our son.'

Natasha made a soft sound of sympathy, and then, sensing that it wasn't a subject he wanted to pursue, said quietly, 'I've got a rather interesting article upstairs which you might like to read. I came across it by chance, but it's very informative. It's about the resurgence of interest in traditionally patterned and made fabrics, and I think you'll find the section on damasks and brocades of particular interest. As you may know, my father's factory mainly produces ecclesiastical cloths, although he is extending his range to include several non-ecclesiastical traditional designs. However, there are factories in Italy mainly, in and around Florence, where they still have the original pattern books which they have used for centuries, where they can still produce what is virtually, in everything but age, an original seventeenth-century cloth.

'It's expensive, of course,' she warned, 'and I would suggest only for use in certain carefully selected places.'

By the end of the evening, Natasha had discovered that her latest client was not a man who believed in wasting time once he had made up his mind about something. Subject to his final approval, he had virtually given her *carte blanche* to go ahead with designing and furnishing, not only the bedrooms for the new hotel, but the reception-rooms as well, and with a budget which made her gape a little at him.

'The kind of guest I want to attract will expect it,' he told her, but it seemed to Natasha that he was being a little defensive and she warmed to him even more, sensing his desire to clothe the house in the very best raiment he could afford out of love for it, rather than out of a far more businesslike desire to win the approval of potential guests.

As she had discovered, when it came to the small wing of the house which he was retaining for his private use he had very definite ideas about what he wanted, but he had obviously done his homework, and where fabrics were concerned he had made it plain to Natasha that he was perfectly happy to be guided by her.

'I have a small collection of paintings which I intend to hang in the long gallery of my own wing. A friend of mine is going to advise me as to their placement. I've been scouring the auction houses and dealers for suitable pieces of furniture for my own wing. As far as the hotel is concerned, most of the furniture will have to be reproduction and purpose-built, in a style in keeping with the period, of course.'

It was after one in the morning before Natasha was finally able to go upstairs to bed. He would be leaving for Amsterdam first thing in the morning, Leo Rosenberg had told her, but she was to stay on as originally arranged until his return, when hopefully they would be able to finalise the initial colour schemes for the individual guest bedrooms.

As they said their goodnights, it occurred to Natasha that at heart Leo Rosenberg was a lonely man, even though on the surface he seemed to have everything in life that a human being could want, and her own heart felt chilled and heavy as she prepared for bed and contemplated her own future. A lonely future. A future without love, without passion...without Luke, who, she reminded herself hardily, was hardly likely to furnish her with either love or passion, but merely with the base coin of physical desire. Was she really stupid enough to believe that she could ever be happy with that kind of relationship? Of course not!

So why was she wasting so much time, so many thoughts, so much heartache in thinking about him, in wanting him? *Wanting* him? She sat up in bed and shuddered. *Why* did she want him? Why was she behaving in a way that for her was so out of character? She already knew that Luke had nothing genuine to offer her, nothing that for her could make the dangers of their relationship worthwhile.

With this new commission to fill her thoughts and her time, it ought to have been the easiest thing in the world to put him out of her thoughts. Instead...instead, here she was lying sleepless in a strange bed, knowing that if she closed her eyes, if she allowed herself to relax, she would end up as she had ended up on so many nights recently, reliving every touch, every word, every heartbeat of the time she had already spent with him, and that, worse, within seconds of admitting his memory into her thoughts she would be aching for more than mere memories, that she would be... She made a soft sound of distress in her throat and turned over, thumping her pillow, telling herself that she was her own worst enemy, that she had to forget him, to put him right out of her mind, and concentrate not on fictional fantasy but on reality.

CHAPTER SEVEN

IT WAS three days before Natasha saw Leo Rosenberg again, three days during which she worked extremely hard, both on preparing detailed drawings for each of the guest bedrooms and the reception-rooms, and on mentally closing the doors of her mind against the all too intrusive thoughts of Luke Templecombe which continued to plague her.

Of the two, preparing the drawings was by far the easier. She would go to bed at night, convinced that she was so exhausted both mentally and physically that she would be asleep the moment her head touched the pillow, only to find that she was wrong and that her aching, yearning body recalcitrantly refused to allow her the peace she needed.

On the third night before Leo's return, exhausted by a struggle which seemed to grow harder with time, rather than easier, she gave in and allowed her thoughts to conjure up impossible fantasies in which Luke suddenly appeared to sweep her off her feet, to hold her and kiss her as he had done on that never-to-be-forgotten night, but this time without anger, without cynicism, without the divisive resentment of her sex which had come across to her so clearly on that occasion.

All human beings had their own private defence systems, and, given the history of Luke's childhood, it wasn't impossible to understand that the fact that his mother had left both him and his father for another man, plus the tragedy of his father's eventual suicide, could have resulted in a resentment and mistrust of the female sex which had manifested itself in his relentless sexual pursuit of her.

She was no psychologist; she didn't need to be, she admitted, to recognise that she was looking for excuses, for explanations to offset the apparent deliberate emotionlessness of Luke's sexual overtures.

Moving restlessly in the comfortable bed, she lectured herself against the folly of believing that it was possible for Luke to change. Why should he? He obviously didn't want to. He was obviously quite happy with his way of life. She might not be sexually experienced, but it had been easy to see that Luke wanted only an emotionless sexual relationship with her.

Relationship. She smiled painfully to herself in the darkness. What made her think he wanted to take it that far? If she was brutally honest with herself, she had no reason to believe that Luke wanted anything more than simply to take her to bed, and then, once having done so, to forget her.

Why did that hurt so much? Her first instinct of dislike for him, her first rational awareness that he was cold and dangerous—they had been right. Just because later he had made her sexually aware of him, and just because her rebellious body for some unknown reasons of its own refused to forget or ignore that awareness, that did not mean she had to start looking for reasons, for excuses, for hope...

She shivered a little. It was her own upbringing, her own moral code that made her search for that leavening hint of emotion, of feeling, because she found it so difficult to accept that she could actually want a man who embodied everything she had always disliked in the male sex.

It had caught her off guard, shocked her, frightened her, that she could so easily be put into this state of emotional and physical turmoil, that she should have fled her home rather than confront him, that she should be lying here awake, thinking about him, wishing...

Wishing that what? That, like some romance-story hero, he would simply not take no for an answer, that he would overpower her veto with the strength of his determination and desire and thus remove from her the burden of decision, effectively consenting to a relationship which held nothing, none of those virtues she had always believed a man-to-woman relationship should hold?

The very thought revolted her. She had always prided herself on making her own decisions, on refusing to allow others to take any responsibility for them. If she ever allowed this physical attraction between them to develop, it would be because *she* had made a decision to do so, not because she had closed her eyes and simply allowed Luke to drag her into it so that she could then turn round and blame him.

If she ever allowed... her stomach turned over at the enormity of what she was thinking. What was happening to her? She had come here thinking that simply to remove herself from Luke's presence would be enough to cure her of this ridiculous desire she seemed to be suffering. She had genuinely believed that, kept mentally on her toes by her new commission, there would be no space in her mind for any thoughts of Luke...

How wrong she had been. Exhausted mentally and physically though she was, deep inside her body was a hunger, an ache which she knew would later cause her acute emotional and moral anguish, but which now was so sharp, so searing that she knew that if Luke were to open the door and walk into her room that ache would be a scream of physical need she might find it impossible to deny.

But why? Why now? Why this man? Why this intensity? It shocked her that her body could turn traitor on her like this, that she could want like this, ache like this, and above all it shocked her that she could experience this intensity without the saving grace of love.

She woke up tired, with dark circles round her eyes, knowing that today was the day she would have to present her suggestions and recommendations for Leo's approval.

Wearily she got up, and subjected herself to the hopefully energy-stimulating shock of a cold shower, shivering as the cold water burned goose-bumps into her shrinking flesh, forcing herself to endure the small punishment, knowing from experience she would feel the benefit of it later.

Her body wasn't something she was used to dwelling on overmuch. She was lucky in that she didn't tend to put on weight, and if privately she considered that she was a little on the slim side when compared to other women's rounded curves, her slenderness hadn't appeared to deter Luke. Far from it.

She stood quite still beneath the still-gushing shower, clutching her sponge to her breasts, oblivious to the water pelting her skin, oblivious to everything other than the heat stirring deep inside her body—a heat that made her face flush with shock and pain.

It was only the sudden damp warmth of her face that made her realise that she was crying.

And well she might, she acknowledged in anguish. She ought to cry for very shame that in her thoughts she had already committed self-betrayal, that in her thoughts she had shared with Luke those intimacies she was deceiving herself she had too much self-respect, too much pride, too high a moral code to share in actual practice.

Which was worse, she asked herself wearily later as she got dressed—to allow herself to imagine in the privacy of her most secret thoughts that she and Luke were lovers, and then to pretend to be angered and offended by the knowledge that he should want her merely as his sexual partner, or to admit honestly to herself that she wanted him, and to recklessly give herself to him, knowing that in doing so she was breaking every one of her self-made rules, and yet knowing at the same time that this was something she had to do, a need she had to appease, an experience she had to have? Was she really such a coward that she could allow herself the intimacy of Luke's body in the secret darkness of her thoughts, but could not permit that same intimacy in reality simply because it was not cloaked with words like 'love'?

In the end which of them was the more dishonest? Luke or herself? Shamingly, she already knew the answer.

Leo arrived rather later than expected. It was closer to lunchtime than just after breakfast when he drove up to the house in the Jaguar D-type vintage sports car that was his pride and joy, and he wasn't alone.

To her surprise, Natasha saw her aunt seated in the car next to him, her laughing face turned towards him, her hair windblown and tousled. For a moment Natasha was too surprised to speak, and watched in silence as Leo helped her aunt out of his car.

'Leo...Mr Rosenberg has brought me to see his gardens,' her aunt explained breathlessly as soon as she was within earshot. Her face was flushed with a pretty and unfamiliar colour which could have been caused by the breeziness of the open-topped car, but there was a sparkle in her eyes, a certain something in her manner as she turned to wait for Leo to lock the car and join them, that caused Natasha to wonder speculatively if there was rather more to her aunt's arrival than merely Leo's enthusiasm for renovating and restoring the house and its gardens.

'You see I took up your recommendation,' Leo announced as he joined them. 'And Helen has very kindly consented to come and give me the benefit of her advice——'

'I'm no expert,' Helen Lacey interrupted him. 'Merely an enthusiastic amateur.'

'A very gifted enthusiastic amateur,' Natasha put in.

'Extremely gifted,' Leo agreed. 'Having seen what you've achieved at Lacey Court, I must confess I'm rather reluctant to let you see how much the gardens here fall behind.'

'I'm sure you'd be far better advised by a qualified horticulturist or designer,' Natasha heard her aunt saying as the three of them fell into step. 'Although I must admit it is the kind of challenge I've always longed to take up.'

'Wait until you've seen the extent of the work that needs to be done,' Leo advised her. 'And our guests will expect to have such facilities as tennis-courts.'

'And croquet,' Helen advised him, 'especially if they're Americans. You've probably even got enough ground for a polo field as well. Now *that* would be a draw.'

'Polo,' Leo mused. 'It's very fashionable, of course.'

Listening to them, Natasha reflected rather wryly that they had almost forgotten she was with them, and she wondered if they were as aware as she was of how well they fell into step with one another, not just in practice as they walked towards the house together, but in theory as well, both of them equally enthusiastic about the house and its possibilities. Listening to them talk, she quickly realised that this could not possibly just be the first time they had met.

Her suspicions were confirmed over lunch, when Leo mentioned that he had called on her aunt immediately after his return from Amsterdam and they had had dinner together, followed by a lunch in town, when he had invited Helen up to London for the day to see his offices there.

Watching her aunt and Leo Rosenberg together, Natasha was suddenly aware of a devastatingly and totally unfamiliar sensation of aloneness, of longing... for what? she asked herself derisively. For Luke Templecombe?

While her aunt spent the afternoon exploring the garden and its possibilities, Natasha was closeted in the office with Leo as they went over her carefully prepared notes and schemes.

'These are ideal; just what I wanted,' Leo told her positively once they had finished.

'And the costings?' Natasha pressed anxiously, knowing that some of the fabrics she had chosen for the reception-rooms were expensive.

'Fine,' Leo assured her, adding, 'I might be a businessman, but I'm not a philistine, Natasha. I realise that the kind of quality we're discussing here doesn't come cheap, and nor should it. How soon could you start work here? The contractors are due to finish upstairs at the end of the month, and the sooner you can get started after that...'

Quickly Natasha assessed her present workload. She had several small commissions on hand which could either be completed or shelved to allow her to start work at the time Leo was requesting. Some time or other she would need to make a trip to Florence. Some of the fabrics she would like to use, not to mention the other decorative items she had included in her presentations, would mean a personal visit to the craftsmen concerned to check that what she wanted could be produced within her provisional budgets.

She explained all this to Leo, and waited hesitantly while he considered.

'I'd like to have the place ready for opening by Christmas, to catch the Christmas market which would be particularly lucrative.'

Christmas! Natasha took a deep breath. It would be pushing things a bit, and completion for that date would to a large extent be dependent on the ability and willingness of her Florentine contacts to provide her with what she wanted on time.

'I think I could manage it,' she told him cautiously. 'Depending on my suppliers. As far as the fabrics for the bedrooms are concerned, these will come from my father's factory, and I can virtually guarantee delivery on them, plus a good discount off normal prices, but for the fabrics for the reception areas, good though our stuff is, it cannot compare with the fabrics from Florence which I'd like to use, and I have no control over the supply date for those.'

'I understand,' Leo assured her, 'and I don't intend to have any penalty clauses added to our contract.'

He saw her surprise and smiled wryly, 'I trust my instincts in these things, Natasha, and any true entrepreneur who tells you he doesn't do the same thing is lying. My instincts tell me I can trust you—and not just because I'm already halfway towards falling in love with your aunt,' he added with a grin as he stood up.

Natasha gaped at him and he laughed again, a little ruefully this time.

'She said you'd be shocked. I suppose to someone of your age the very idea of a man in his fifties falling in love——'

'No...no, you're wrong,' Natasha told him quickly, and then admitted honestly, 'I was only thinking this afternoon what a good couple the two of you make. I just didn't expect you to——'

'To what? To admit that, having spent the years since my wife's death telling myself that I'd never want to marry again, I've suddenly discovered that I was wrong. Life's too short to let pride stand in the way of love and happiness; that's something I *do* know. The moment I met your aunt, I realised she was someone who was going to be important to me. It was like having a light suddenly switched on in a dark place in my life, illuminating its darkness, warming its coldness. And I believe she feels the same way about me.'

'Is that why you're giving me this contract?' Natasha asked him hesitantly. 'Because you've fallen in love with my aunt?'

He frowned at her. 'No. If I didn't think you were up to the job, your relationship to Helen wouldn't make the slightest difference.'

Listening to him, Natasha believed him and was relieved. Much as she wanted the contract, she wanted to earn it on her own merit and ability and not for any other reason.

'I notice you've suggested several fabrics for the long gallery. As I said, a friend of mine is going to come down and advise me on the best placement of my art collection in the gallery, and I think I'd like a final decision about the fabric for the windows and the window-seats to come from him.'

Natasha nodded her head. The fabrics she had tentatively selected for the gallery were traditional tapestries in muted designs and colours to blend in with the old panelling—fabrics which would not detract from the main purpose of the panelled gallery which was to be a display case for the paintings Leo had collected, the majority of which he had already told her had been painted at the height of the Victorian mania for Gothic revival, and would thus be in keeping with the ambiance of the house.

'At the moment the paintings are in storage. I'm having them delivered here when the men have finished working on the gallery, which should be about the same time as they finish work on the bedrooms. We can make a decision about a fabric for the gallery then.'

Agreeing with him, Natasha smiled a little sadly to herself as she saw the way his gaze kept straying to the windows overlooking the garden. He was anxious to rejoin her aunt, Natasha could see, and so she diplomatically asked if he would mind if she went up to her own room to make a few telephone calls.

From her bedroom she could see down into the neglected kitchen garden, and that same earlier stab of awareness of her own single state knifed through her again as a quick glance through her window showed her the sight of Leo and her aunt walking arm in arm along one of the overgrown paths, stopping to study something, so deeply engrossed in one another that she automatically stepped back from the window, feeling that her observation of them, no matter how accidental, was somehow an intrusion into their privacy.

Alone, though, it was impossible to stop the demons of anguish tormenting her as she contrasted the closeness, the warmth, the mutuality of emotion and feeling between Leo and her aunt with the total lack of any such feelings which had characterised the interlude she had shared with Luke in her parents' garden. How appropriate that Leo's and her aunt's relationship should be shared with the warmth and light of the sun which bathed the garden, while hers with Luke had been cloaked and hidden in moonlight.

She tried to tell herself that she was glad she had escaped from him, but somehow, despite the ferocity of her thoughts, they had a hollow, unconvincing ring to them.

She didn't have any time alone with her aunt until just before the latter was about to leave.

The three of them had had dinner together, and now Leo was upstairs collecting some papers he needed prior to driving Helen back to Lacey Court on his way back to London.

Her work here was nearly finished for the time being, Natasha confirmed to her aunt. There was little more she could do until the workmen had finished, and she had made arrangements with

Leo's housekeeper that she would return for a few days at the end of the month just to check that she was still as satisfied with her plans, once she was able to study them in the context of the completed bedrooms.

'You'd better have a key, then,' the housekeeper told her. 'You'll be coming down on the bank-holiday weekend, and I shan't be here. I'm having a couple of weeks with my cousin in Bournemouth.'

'While we're on our own, there's something I think I should tell you,' her aunt murmured, as the housekeeper went in search of a spare key. 'We had a visitor yesterday, or rather *you* had a visitor.'

The kick of sensation that was pure visceral pleasure made Natasha tense her stomach muscles as she waited for her aunt to continue. Her mouth had gone dry, she discovered, and the tension invading her body made her feel as though she were poised like a diver on a high board.

'Was it . . . was it . . .?'

'Luke Templecombe,' her aunt supplied drily for her. 'Yes, it was, and none too pleased to discover that the pigeon had fled the nest, so to speak. Unfortunately when he arrived I wasn't there, and when I came in your mother had already told him where you were.'

Her heart gave a tremendous bound, a sharp sensation of excitement quickly followed by an equally intense feeling of sickness that made it impossible for her to do anything other than stare at her aunt while the colour came and went in her face.

'I agree with you, he *is* a very dangerous young man, all the more so because he is also so very intensely male. He wants you, Natasha, and something tells me he isn't going to be put off by this tale you've told him about there being someone else. It might even add spice to the game.'

'Yes,' Natasha agreed tonelessly. Her betraying burst of euphoria had faded into a miasma of anguish and misery. 'But that's all it is to him . . . a game . . .'

'Meaning what?' her aunt asked gently. 'That to you it's something more?'

Natasha shook her head. 'Not yet, but it could be if I let him——' She bit her lip and corrected grimly, 'If I allowed myself to . . .'

'To take him as your lover?'

'I was going to say to become involved with him. Oh, it's hopeless . . . useless.' She swung round miserably. 'I can't understand why I should want him the way I do. He's everything I most dislike in the male sex: cold, cynical, unable to react to any woman other than as a sexual object.'

'It's called sexual attraction,' her aunt told her drily, 'and, make no mistake about it, it's a very potent force. If it's any consolation to you, I got the impression that he resents it just as much as you do. I could tell from his expression that he bitterly resented having to ask where you were. He's an intelligent man, Natasha; he'll have guessed exactly why you're running from him. He'll know quite well that if this supposed commitment of yours to someone else meant a damn there'd be no need for you to run.'

'He thinks I'm a sexually experienced woman with a list of lovers behind me as long as his own,' Natasha told her despairingly. 'Even if I were to...to allow things to develop...how could I tell him? How could I explain?'

'That you lied to him to save Emma's hide? You might be surprised. He might——'

'What? Be thrilled out of his mind to discover that I'm still a virgin?' She shook her head. 'This isn't fantasy, Helen, it's reality. He doesn't want me for my ignorance and lack of experience because they involve responsibilities he doesn't want to take on. He wants someone who can match him on his own ground...someone who knows the rules...someone whom he can discard as easily as he picked up once he's grown bored.'

'And what do you want, Tasha?' her aunt asked her softly. 'Do you know?'

Natasha grimaced.

'Not really. I want him, physically, very badly indeed, and believe me, just admitting *that* takes as much courage as I have. I can't begin to tell you what admitting it has done to my self-esteem. I thought I was above that kind of sexual need. I thought——'

'That you weren't *human*. My dear, all of us are that. If it's really that bad, if you really desire him so intensely, why not——'

'Have an affair with him? How can I without explaining...without betraying——?' She bit her lip. 'No, it's impossible.'

'Nothing's ever impossible,' her aunt reminded her warningly, 'but, if it's any consolation to you, he has left Sutton Minster and gone back to

London. I saw Lucille Templecombe yesterday and she told me that he'd gone—'

She broke off as the housekeeper came back triumphantly carrying a spare set of keys.

'I'll have to check with Leo, of course, but I'm sure he won't mind.'

'What won't I mind?' Leo asked, walking into the hall, and in the general stir of explanations and arrangements Natasha was able to push Luke Templecombe to the back of her mind.

But not for long. She was leaving Stonelovel Manor in the morning to return home, and once her aunt and Leo were gone and she was back upstairs, laboriously checking through her list of suppliers to ensure that she had all the details she was going to need when the time came to make firm orders, she found herself sitting staring into space instead of working, trying to damp down the fierce, searing heart-burning inside her at the thought of Luke coming in search of her... and finding her... Her defences were pitifully weak—so weak that he would have no trouble in breaching them if he chose to do so, and the worst of it was that more than half of her wished that he might do so, that he *might* take the burden of decision from her and commit her to the course that her rebellious flesh longed to take.

Wryly, she acknowledged that she was in for another sleepless night.

CHAPTER EIGHT

MORNING had arrived, but Luke had not, and today Natasha was due to leave the manor and return home. She told herself that she was glad that Luke had chosen not to put in an appearance, to test her will-power, to defy her denial of her need for him, but she knew that it wasn't entirely true.

It still shocked her that she should feel this intensity of desire, this awesome, enervating, sharp physical need, but slowly she was coming to accept it as fact, to even test out its alienness by surreptitiously studying the workmen who were still busy on the house, but despite the plethora of male muscles and sexuality, despite the keenly interested scrutiny she had received from more than one pair of male eyes while she had been checking out the layout of the new bedrooms, no sharp *frisson* of sensation had stirred her body, no erotic awareness of them as male and herself as female, no aching, painful need like the one that Luke had made her feel, and she wasn't sure whether to be relieved or disappointed by this discovery.

It was late afternoon when she finally got in her car and set out for home, unwillingly admitting to herself that she had perhaps deliberately delayed her departure, just in case Luke should put in an appearance.

Fool, she derided herself, as she drove home. Common sense told her that her aunt was wrong in believing that Luke intended to seek her out. Why should he? Even she with her lack of experience could see that he was the kind of man who would never go short of female companionship. Why should he bother to pursue her?

It was a surprise when she got home to discover that her aunt wasn't there.

'I can't understand her,' Natasha's own mother complained. 'Since she's met this... this man she seems to have changed completely. She never used to want to go anywhere, and now... well, we hardly ever see her. When I asked her how long she was going to be away, she said that she really didn't know, that Leo had business in New York, and that they would probably fly from there to Switzerland.'

'Stop fussing, my dear,' Natasha's father intervened. 'Helen is old enough to know her own mind. Personally I'm only too pleased to see her taking an interest in life again.'

'She *did* have an interest in life. She had the garden,' was Natasha's mother's slightly peevish comment.

Natasha repressed a sympathetic sigh, suspecting that her mother was missing the close companionship the two of them had shared.

'Leo really is very nice,' she comforted her mother, 'and he's as good as told me that he's in love with Helen.'

'Well, I suppose she does deserve some happiness. She's been alone long enough.' Natasha watched as her mother gave a small shiver, and looked across at her own husband. 'If the two of them develop a permanent relationship, though, I'm going to miss her.'

'Me, too,' Natasha agreed, and then lightened the slightly sombre tone of the conversation by adding, 'I know someone who won't, though—Richard's mother. She blames Helen for the supremacy of our garden.'

'Oh, yes, that reminds me, Natasha. Someone called here asking for you while you were away—Richard's cousin, a very handsome young man.'

'Yes, Helen told me,' Natasha said neutrally, trying to keep her voice as calm as possible, but sensing that her father wasn't altogether deceived, from the thoughtful look he gave her. Anxious to get off the dangerous subject of Luke Templecombe just as quickly as she could, she turned to her father and said quickly, 'If you've got some time to spare, I'd like to go over the schemes Leo's agreed for the bedrooms at the manor. We'll be using the company's fabrics for the bedrooms, although I'm going to need some special lots dyeing to accommodate the full colour ranges I want to use. Leo will get the full discount on the lines we already run, but he understands that the special orders will cost more.' She went on to explain to her father that, wherever possible, the original features of the house had been retained so that some of the guest bedrooms had their original panelling, while others had had items such as wardrobes and other necessities put in, including the new partition walls hidden behind new panelling, most of which had been left in its natural state and then limed to achieve a soft, weathered silvery finish.

It was for these rooms that Natasha needed the special dye runs of fabric, knowing that they would need slightly softer colours than the very rich shades the company normally produced.

'Does this man—Leo—does he intend to live in the house or——?'

'Oh, yes, he's retained the small, original wing for his own use. It's beautiful: five bedrooms, three each with their own bathrooms, plus the most marvellous original panelled gallery overlooking the enclosed kitchen garden, which he intends to keep for his own private use. That was why I put him in touch with Helen. He was complaining that he couldn't find anyone to advise him on replanning and replanting the gardens. That reminds me,' she added, turning to her father, 'I'm going to need to make another trip to Florence some time in the near future, so if there's anything you want while I'm over there . . . I know exactly the fabrics I want for the long gallery—something which isn't going to detract from the paintings Leo intends to have hung on the walls, and yet which is rich enough to set off the panelling and the stucco ceiling . . .'

Natasha had eight hectic days plus one full weekend in which to clear her desk and her outstanding commissions, before she had to return to the manor. This necessitated her working well into the evenings and her free weekend as well, but she didn't mind.

The hard work helped to stop her thinking about Luke—well, almost . . . She was past the stage now of expecting to hear his voice each time the phone rang, past the stage of experiencing that savage thrill of fear-cum-excitement at the thought of seeing or speaking to him.

She told herself that it was for the best that he hadn't got in touch with her, that her most sensible course of action by far was to put him completely out of her mind and out of her life. She told herself as well that one day there would come a time when she would look back on the whole incident and marvel at her own idiocy and the narrowness of her escape from a situation which could only damage both her self-esteem and her self-respect, but she still avoided walking in the gardens at night; she still found it hard to sleep. She still felt her body tense with something that wasn't entirely dread when the phone rang or someone knocked on her street door.

On the Thursday afternoon preceding the bank-holiday weekend, she packed for her return journey to the manor, intending to leave a little earlier than she had originally planned in order to avoid the early holiday traffic.

The weather forecast for the weekend was promising good weather, which meant that the roads were bound to be busy. Never an entirely happy driver in heavy traffic at the best of times, Natasha had no wish to be caught up in queues of impatient and thus perhaps over-reckless drivers.

She arrived at Stonelovel just as the housekeeper was on the point of leaving. The older woman looked flustered and hot, and obviously didn't want to be delayed.

As she stepped into the waiting taxi, she called out to Natasha, 'Oh, by the way, I've put you in the same room. I hope that's all right. There's plenty of food in the fridge.'

Thanking her, Natasha unlocked the door and went inside.

The house seemed oddly quiet after the busy hum of workmen. The air in the hall was still full of dust. It floated in the sunlight pouring in through the now renovated and uncovered leaded windows on the stairs.

What she really ought to do first was to unpack her car, but the impulse to walk through the now empty rooms and inspect them at her leisure was far too tempting, Natasha acknowledged.

Work was still in progress on some of the reception-rooms, but for the first time Natasha was now able to see some distinct resemblance between the detailed architect's drawing Leo had shown her and the rooms themselves.

Everything in the house that was original had been meticulously and carefully restored, huge fire-places uncovered, having been hidden behind centuries of 'improvements', panelling freed from its clogging coats of paint, plaster ceilings revealed by the removal of lowered false ceilings.

In the end she spent far longer than she had anticipated slowly going from room to room, picturing them as they had been in her mind's eye from the photographs Leo had taken of the house when he first took it over and marvelling at what had been achieved in such a relatively short space of time.

It helped having the money to be able to employ expert craftspeople, she acknowledged, but money on its own wasn't enough... without Leo's enthusiasm... his love for the house...

Her imagination took fire as she explored, mentally clothing the rooms in the fabrics she had already chosen.

The discovery that it was almost eight o'clock in the evening and that she had spent several hours lost in the magic of bringing to life these empty rooms forced her to abandon them and return to her car to collect her things.

As she carried them upstairs, she wondered wryly if it was the euphoria of realising almost for the first time how confident she actually felt about achieving the effects Leo wanted, of discovering, when she admired the handiwork of the craftsmen responsible for the restoration of the house, that she too was part of that same team, *her* skills equal in Leo's eyes at least to theirs... or if it was simply the fact that she hadn't eaten anything since her late breakfast and was therefore extremely hungry.

Hungry, but too euphoric, too restless to settle down to anything so mundane as preparing a meal. Fortunately the housekeeper had stocked the refrigerator thoughtfully and generously—there was a large cold cooked chicken, plus a wide variety of salads, fruits and vegetables—and, slightly guiltily telling herself that she would make up for her laziness in the morning, Natasha made herself a thick chicken sandwich using wholemeal bread and several slices off the chicken.

What she needed to do now, she told herself firmly as she ate it and drank a cup of coffee, sitting at the kitchen table, was to go out and have a pleasant relaxing walk through the grounds to bring herself down into a less elevated state.

Tomorrow she could throw herself thoroughly into her work; tonight she needed a good night's sleep. Tonight, if she dreamed of anything, she wanted those dreams to be of fabrics, not of Luke Templecombe. He had already disturbed far too many of her nights...and far too many of her days.

Having quickly washed up, she opened the back door and stepped outside. It had been a warm day, and the air was now pleasantly cool, refreshing enough to make her want to breathe in deep lungfuls of it, and yet not so chilly that she needed to go back inside to find something warm to put on over her jeans and Tshirt.

Knowing that she was going to be the only occupant of the house, she had only brought with her a handful of casual clothes, the kind she felt most comfortable in while working: old worn jeans, comfortable baggy sweaters. She nearly always bought men's jumpers, liking their length and generosity. In the winter it was cold upstairs at the top of her house in her workroom and she generally wore them over the top of thermal vests, plus warm shirts to retain her body heat. In summer they were equally effective over something thinner.

It would be relaxing now to walk round the kitchen garden and to exercise her overactive brain in imagining what it might be transformed into with her aunt's skill.

The house, built in the reign of Charles II, would just about have been settling into its surroundings when his niece Mary married her Dutchman. It was during that period that the vogue for gardens composed of vistas, contained in yew hedges, for topiary work, and for neatly designed beds, of the type which in France were known as parterres, had been at its height.

At Lacey Court they had a knot garden designed by her aunt which made use of two different shades of green hedging which was universally admired, but here in this walled kitchen garden her aunt would have so much more scope for her skills. How lucky she was loving not just the man, but his home, and on top of that to be granted the munificence of such a wonderful professional challenge as well.

Not that anyone deserved that happiness more than her aunt. It was completely wrong of her to feel so...so what? Envious...of another's happiness? She stopped walking abruptly, instinctively turning her face towards the shadows, even though there was no one else there to read her expression.

Since meeting Luke Templecombe, she felt as though her whole life had been turned upside-down, as though she had been forced to confront facets of herself she had never previously realised existed, facets she wasn't entirely at ease with.

Driven by the restlessness that possessed her, she walked out of the walled garden, following a path which she knew led through the gardens to the perimeter of the estate and from there to join a pathway, now overgrown in many places, which ran along the inside of the boundary fence.

It was later than she had expected when she eventually got back. Almost midnight, in fact, and, although she felt physically exhausted, mentally she was as alert and on edge as ever.

She went upstairs to have a bath and prepare for bed, and it was just as she was stepping out of the bath that she saw the sweeping illumination of a car's headlights coming down the drive.

Puzzled rather than alarmed, she dried herself quickly, and then pulled on her discarded outer clothes. It could only be Leo returning unexpectedly at this hour, and she had bolted and barred the doors, preventing him from getting in. She knew that, even if he noticed the omission of her underwear, he was hardly likely to comment on it. She had witnessed the way he looked at her aunt, heard him describe his feelings for her, and had known that they were genuine.

Running quickly downstairs, she headed for the main entrance hall just as he reached the door from the other side. She heard him inserting his key, and called out to him, 'I've bolted the door from the inside, Leo. I'll just open it for you... You're lucky I was in,' she added. 'I'd virtually only just got back from a long walk and I was in the bath when I saw your car headlights.'

She was smiling welcomingly as she slid back the final bolt and unsnapped the lock so that she could open the door. As she did so, the light from the hallway spilled outside illuminating the man standing there. Immediately her smile died, to be replaced by disbelief and a shocked wave of intense awareness that burned up in a tide of colour, crimsoning her skin.

'Luke,' she whispered, faltering, instinctively stepping back as he came forward, her eyes wide with apprehension and shock. 'You shouldn't have come here,' she told him huskily as he came into the hall and closed the door behind him. 'I told you I didn't want to see you again. You've made a mistake if you——'

'I'm afraid *you're* the one who's made a mistake,' came the laconic reply. 'I haven't come here looking for you, Natasha.'

The shock of his casual, uncaring disclaimer silenced her, freezing her ability to reason or think—to say anything beyond a stammered and defensive, 'Then why *are* you here? You——'

'Leo asked me to come down and check over this gallery of his, to advise him on the placing of his collection, and this is the first opportunity I've had to do so.'

Sickly Natasha stared at him, her skin burning with chagrin and embarrassment as she realised that he was telling the truth. Why oh, why had she assumed that he had come here in pursuit of her? Why on earth hadn't she kept her mouth shut, let him explain his appearance?

'Leo didn't say anything to me,' she said, turning her back on him and missing the narrow-eyed scrutiny he gave her.

'No. Well, maybe he didn't think it important. I take it that visitors are still sleeping upstairs on the third floor?'

Still keeping her back to him, Natasha nodded. 'There's no one here but me,' she told him awkwardly.

'Yes, Leo did mention that the place would be empty apart from the designer he'd hired. Stupid of me, perhaps, but I never made the connection between that comment and yourself.'

Natasha felt her face burn anew. A none too subtle reminder of her idiotically self-betraying assumption that he had come in search of her.

'It's late,' she said jerkily. 'I was just on my way to bed.'

'So I see,' he murmured as she turned round. His glance was resting on the soft, unrestrained thrust of her breasts beneath her bulky top and Natasha had a momentary and far too telling awareness of how it had felt to have his hands and then his mouth caressing their softness.

She drew in a sharp, unstable breath. Hadn't she made enough of a fool of herself already tonight, without compounding that stupidity? The last thing she wanted now was for Luke to become aware of her reaction to him.

'I thought you were Leo,' she snapped defensively, as though answering an unspoken question, and then watched uncertainly as something happened to the bones of his face, compressing them somehow so that the air of relaxed mockery died from his eyes and was replaced by a hard, penetrating sharpness that took her breath away and made her stomach clench in silent agony.

'Did you, now?' he said softly. 'I'm sorry I disappointed you.'

'So am I,' she retorted recklessly, and without giving him any opportunity to retaliate she fled, hoping that her exit in the direction of the stairs looked a lot more controlled and self-possessed than it felt.

Luke here... She couldn't believe it. It was like something out of the very worst of her nightmares—or the very best of her daydreams. She shuddered a little at the knowledge of her own contrary feelings. Luke here...Luke sleeping under the same roof. How long did he intend to stay? How long?

Much to her own surprise, having been convinced that the knowledge that Luke was sharing the same roof with her would mean yet another restless night, not only did she sleep exceptionally well, but she actually managed to oversleep as well, waking up to find the sun shining into her room.

The house felt quiet and empty, as though there was no one else in it apart from herself, as though at some time during the night Luke had left.

Angrily she quelled the sharp stab of pain caused by that thought. If he *had* left, she ought to be relieved, not disappointed. However, when she went downstairs, there was a note on the immaculately clean kitchen table, reading simply, 'Am working in the long gallery. Perhaps you could spare the time to show me the fabric samples Leo tells me you have selected for the windows.'

It was only natural of course that he should want to make sure that she wasn't thinking of using some totally unsuitable fabric which might completely ruin the atmosphere of the gallery and draw the eye away from the paintings, but her professional pride was scorched with resentment that he should make it so obvious that he might want to veto her suggestions.

She wondered what time he had started work. It must have been early. She herself was no stranger to working long hours and making early starts. She wondered if he perhaps thought that she made a habit of lying in bed until the morning was half over, and once again her professional pride revolted.

She made herself some filter coffee and found a grapefruit in the fridge, rejecting the temptation to skip breakfast, knowing that the amount of work which lay ahead of her might mean that she had to miss lunch. It was always the same—once she got involved in her work, she tended to resent any interruption which took her away from it.

The coffee was hot and reviving and, on an impulse she didn't want to examine too closely, she poured out two more mugs of it, carrying them with her on a tray as she made her way to the gallery, stopping off first in Leo's office to collect the samples she had left there the previous evening.

When she opened the door to the gallery, Luke was standing surrounded by half-open packing cases, hands on his hips, a frown darkening his eyes.

He looked up briefly as she walked in and, ignoring the sharp tightening sensation that coiled through her body, Natasha said as calmly as she could, 'I thought you might like a cup of coffee.

I've brought my samples with me, and once you're ready to look at them...'

Several of the paintings had already been removed from their crates and she looked curiously at them as she put the tray down on the floor.

Watching her, Luke said drily, 'If you're wondering how much they're worth, I can assure you that Leo has made a very good investment.'

Natasha was astounded, as much by the cynicism in his voice as by his comment, and she swung round, forgetting to be cautious and on her guard as she said in surprise, 'Why should I be in the least bit interested in their material value? I was simply curious about them, that's all. Naturally, from a professional point of view——'

She stopped as she saw the way his mouth twisted.

'Professional. Is that what you consider yourself to be?' Luke taunted her. 'You get your latest lover to let you play at decorating his new acquisition and on the strength of that you consider yourself professional.'

Natasha was astounded—so astounded that for a moment she couldn't do anything other than stare at him with her mouth open, and then, realising how idiotic she must look, she snapped it closed and said through gritted teeth, 'For your information, Leo is not my lover, and even if he were...even if he were...I do not need to...to have sex with my potential clients in order to get their business. And as for not being professional...'

She lifted her head and stared proudly and furiously at him.

'All right. So maybe I don't have any paper qualifications, and certainly normally I would not be taking on a commission as large as this one. I'm not a designer and have never pretended to be. But I *do* know about fabric, especially the kind of fabrics Leo wants for this house. That's why he contacted me in the first place. However, if you, with your wealth of experience and knowledge of these things, feel that he'd be better served employing some fashionable interior design house, then no doubt you'll tell him so. Right now it isn't your personal and prejudiced views of my qualifications for this job that I want, but simply your views on the fabrics I've selected for the furnishings here in the gallery.'

Without giving him any chance to intervene, she swept on, carried away by the hot swell of rage and, yes, pain as well, that moved so powerfully within her.

She had always known that he despised her, even more, she suspected, than he had desired her...but it had been as a woman that she had thought that he had held this contempt for her...not as a human being.

What did he know of her skill or lack of it?

She said as much, throwing the question at him like a challenge, and then confronting him, breathless, and more angry than she could virtually ever remember being.

'I saw Jake Pendraggon's Cornish house featured in a magazine article,' he told her drily. 'Whoever wrote the article was discreet, saying merely that the place had been decorated by a close friend of Mr Pendraggon's, but it isn't difficult to put two and two together.'

'To make five,' Natasha told him through gritted teeth. 'I did not decorate Jake's house, and neither am I having an affair with Leo. In fact——'

'Prove it,' he interrupted quietly, so quietly that for a moment she thought she must have misheard him, but then he repeated, 'Prove it by having dinner with me tonight.'

Have dinner with him? What on earth would that prove? Not that she felt the need to prove anything to him—anything at all. But that was a lie, she acknowledged, as she looked from his face, set into an expression of cynical awareness that she would refuse his invitation, to the samples she was still holding in her hand. She *did* need to prove something to him. She wanted him to acknowledge that her skill in her own field was worthy of recognition and praise; she wanted to see the cynicism die out of his eyes, to be replaced by... by what? Respect!

Prove it, he had challenged, and of course she was far too mature, far too sensible to give in to that kind of emotional pressure, and yet still she heard herself saying recklessly and shakily, 'All right, I will, but only if you'll stop treating me as though I'm going to drape this place with hundreds of yards of totally unsuitable chintz and fussy bows, and instead look at these samples I've chosen—if not with a totally unbiased eye, then at least with the closest you can manage to one. I realise that you don't like... that you want to...'

To think the worst of me, she had been about to say, but he substituted for her before she could do so.

'That I desire you physically. Yes. Inconvenient, isn't it? For both of us. And don't pretend you don't know what I mean, that you aren't equally turned on by me as I am by you. You daren't let yourself come within five yards of me, and I feel exactly the same way about you. The simplest solution would be for us to have sex with one another right here and now, and get the whole thing over and done with. Both of us know quite well that, once the itch has been scratched, once we've exorcised whatever need it is that has attacked us so inconveniently, it will die as quickly as it flared into life, but woman-like of course you can't be honest enough to face reality. You want me just as much as I want you but——'

Natasha stared at him in stupefaction, the colour slowly fading from her skin and then rushing back in a low wave of mortification.

'I do not want you,' she snapped frantically at him. 'And the reason I don't want to... to come too close to you is... is that I like my own personal space remaining uninvaded... by anyone.'

'You're lying,' Luke told her flatly. 'But have it your own way. I'll tell you this, though—if you think that by playing coy and hard to get you're going to get me chasing after you, you can think again. I never play those kinds of games.'

'No, I don't suppose you do,' Natasha agreed. Suddenly she was cold, a deep, biting, inward cold which had nothing to do with the temperature. 'You like to play your own game, by your own rules, don't you, Luke? But here's one woman who isn't going to join that game.' And then recklessly, because suddenly she was so tired, so sickened, so miserably aware of how foolish she had been in even allowing into her most private thoughts the kind of idiotic fantasy which had led her into believing that somewhere beneath the hardness, beneath the cynicism, beneath the tough outer shell lay a real human being, with real emotions, and real desires, she told him shakily, 'I can't change the way you think of me, Luke. I don't even *want* to, but I will tell you this. No matter what you do think, you don't know me. Yes, I desire you. Yes, I want to make love with you—and I choose those words deliberately, not out of some kind of stupid, self-deceiving emotionalism because I need them to cloak a physical need in some kind of disguise, but because for me that's what any physical act of intimacy between two people must have.'

'Are you trying to tell me that if I lied to you, if I told you I loved you, if I wrapped up my need in pretty, meaningless words, you'd go to bed with me?'

'No,' she told him firmly and truthfully. 'I know you don't love me, and I admit that doesn't stop me wanting you, but you're talking about that wanting, that desire as though it's something you resent—some weakness for which you can only feel contempt. Perhaps I *am* naïve, stupid, self-deceptive, but I believe that even when there is no "love" as described by the poets and writers between two people, there can still be tenderness, caring, mutual respect, laughter, pleasure and a true giving . . . of wanting to give and to please. But of course for that both people concerned would need to be well-adjusted, mature human beings, with the capacity to see the foibles and weaknesses of themselves and of others, and yet be able to live with them, to feel compassion and understanding for them . . . and we both know that you can never feel like that, Luke—not while you're still a little boy, hating your mother for leaving you, unable to understand what could have motivated her, wanting to punish her and to go on punishing her and totally unable to see beyond your own needs to hers. Here.' She walked up to him and shoved the samples towards him, not bothering to see if he picked them up or let them fall.

'These are the fabrics I thought most suitable for in here, depending on the colours of the paintings and their frames. I've deliberately tried to choose those which will fade graciously into the background, rather than clamour for attention. If you don't approve of them, I suggest you take it up with Leo. Now I'm afraid I have work to do.'

As she walked towards the door, she prayed she would get there without collapsing. She was in shock, she recognised, as she opened the door. It was shock that had made her react like that, berate him like that, and yet, she acknowledged as she opened the door and passed through it, she had spoken the truth as she saw it.

Even so, her tender heart ached for the look she had seen momentarily and so painfully in his eyes when she had accused him of still hating his mother, of resenting her for deserting him and, because of that, punishing her sex by holding it in contempt. He was an intelligent man, and one who must have already seen in himself this schism, this vulnerability. He hadn't needed her to point it out to him.

CHAPTER NINE

FOR the rest of the day, Natasha made sure that she kept out of Luke's way.

She was angry with him and angry with herself as well, and yet underneath that anger ran a deep vein of compassion for him . . . pity almost. A pity that she knew quite well he would not want.

She had seen so illuminatingly in those self-betraying words of his the reality of what his physical desire for her meant to him, the paucity and worthlessness of it, and had discovered that despite her own pain, her own anguish in wanting this man, in loving this man who, she now recognised shockingly and far, far too late, could not and would not want to share those feelings, she still felt that of the two of them he was the worse off. How truly appalling it must be never to be able to allow oneself to feel anything for another human being other than that cold, clinical desire only tempered to heat by dislike and contempt. No, despite her own anguish at recognising what she suspected she had always known—that her own physical desire for him was only one part of a complex range of emotions and needs, which for convenience's sake the human psyche lumped together under the word 'love'—she would not have wanted to change places with him, to experience the cold inner emptiness that he must suffer, that he *had* to suffer in the knowledge that, no matter what the emotions of his partner in any sexual intimacy, all he could feel in return was physical satisfaction and emotional sterility.

Half of her urged her to pack her things and leave the house, now before there were any more confrontations between them, but the other half said stubbornly that she had work to do and that to leave now would surely be to confirm to Luke that she was, as he had so sneeringly told her, lacking in professionalism. And so she stayed, working at an exhausting pace, trying to banish from her mind the knowledge that Luke was in the house with her, trying to force herself to believe that she was completely alone, but every now and again her defences broke down, and she would sit staring into space, confronting the unwanted knowledge that she loved him as well as desired him. She had known it irrevocably in that moment when she had flung her accusations at him, and had then looked into his eyes and seen the shocked confusion darkening them, like a child cruelly and wantonly hurt by the uncaring actions of an adult. In that moment she had ached to go to him, to hold him, to protect and cherish, not just the man, but the child within him as well, in the age-old way of women in love.

She loved Luke Templecombe; she shivered in the thrill of horror that iced her spine. There was only one way to deal with such an all-encompassing, idiotic folly, and that was to shut herself off from it, to starve it of her thoughts, her attention, her concern, to resolutely ignore what she felt in the hope that without the nourishment of wanton hope and desire it would slowly die. Slowly and painfully, she acknowledged, shivering again. Did she have the strength to endure that kind of pain? Did she have any alternative other than to do so?

Not really.

At six o'clock, she stopped work, recognising that if she did not eat soon she would probably not eat at all.

She opened the kitchen door cautiously, relieved to discover that the room was empty, and then left it open so that if Luke should decide to come down here he would realise she was there and go away again. He must, she recognised, have as little desire to see her as she had him.

She tried not to remember that he had asked her out to dinner, tried not to fantasise about where such an invitation might have led.

It would potentially of course have led to his bed, but once there, no matter how much physical pleasure he might have given her, emotionally he would have destroyed her. Not because he didn't love her—there could still have been tenderness between them, respect, pleasure and a thousand other positive emotions—but because he had shown her so clearly how he viewed, not just her, but the whole of her sex, and she had known then that for her no amount of sexual expertise could cancel out that deep inner contempt, that basic lack that would have meant he was rejecting her as a person, even at the very moment when he possessed her most intimately.

Without much enthusiasm, she made herself a cold meat salad, and sat down to eat it at the kitchen table.

She was halfway through it when Luke walked in. Immediately she stiffened, her throat closing up against the wave of emotion that struck her.

His jeans were coated with a film of dust; she could smell it on his skin, and see the way it was ingrained into the flesh of his throat and face as he came towards her.

She saw the way his mouth tightened as he looked down at her half-eaten meal. A man's mouth said so much about him. Luke's was sharply defined, mobile, the full curve of his bottom lip openly sensual. She focused on it for a handful of seconds too long, suddenly aware that she felt oddly dizzy.

'I take it, then, that you won't be having dinner with me tonight, after all.'

The mockery in his voice brought her back to reality. She dragged her attention away from his mouth and retaliated wryly, 'Something tells me that everything you do or say has its price, Luke, and I'm afraid that no meal, however excellent, would be worth the payment I suspect you'd ask.

She watched as mockery gave way to disbelief and then anger.

'If you're seriously suggesting that I'd expect you to go to bed with me simply because I'd bought you a meal...'

She could see that he was furious with her, but recklessly she didn't care. Let him see what it felt like to be insulted and treated with contempt.

'I'll have you know that I am not the kind of man who expects a woman to pay for a meal with her body.'

'And neither am I the kind of woman who has sex with a man for no other reason than that she feels fleeting physical desire for him,' Natasha retaliated. She pushed aside her half-eaten meal and stood up. 'It's been a long day, and I'm tired, Luke.'

As she started to walk past him, he said curtly, 'Wait.'

Involuntarily she stopped.

'You left these in the gallery,' he told her, handing her her samples of fabric.

She took them from him automatically, flinching as her fingers brushed his skin, dazed by the knowledge that even such a brief physical contact could stir her emotions so deeply. It was hard not to imagine what she would feel like given the freedom to touch him more intimately, to explore the male shaping of him, to feel the aroused movement of flesh and muscle...

He was already turning away from her, making her shakily relieved that he couldn't read her mind.

As she turned towards the door, she heard him saying almost gruffly, 'I owe you an apology, by the way. No one without an excellent knowledge of the period and its furnishings could have chosen those particular fabrics. There's one there—a tapestry in a similar shade to the panelling...'

For a moment Natasha was almost too stunned to speak. He was apologising, actually apologising, and more—admitting that she had knowledge, that she had skill. She knew very well that she ought not to let his words go to her head like wine, that she ought to suppress the delighted euphoria bubbling inside her, that it was ridiculous that she should feel pleasure, gratitude almost, in his reluctant words of praise. It was all she could do to say sedately, 'Yes, I know the one you mean. I liked that too, but of course the final choice depends on Leo's views. I had hoped to narrow it down to say three or four fabrics, but first I'd need to see the paintings and their frames.'

'I've virtually unpacked them all now. I've got a layout planned as to how and where they should be hung, but until they are I doubt that you'll be able to make any firm decision. It's going to be a couple of days at least before I get to that stage.'

'That's all right,' Natasha told him. 'I've plenty of work to be going on with in the meantime.'

Was he hinting that she ought to leave? Or was she becoming oversensitive? She decided that she was. After all, it couldn't matter to him whether she stayed or not. Now that she had made it plain that she wanted far more from a relationship than he was ever likely to offer, she doubted that he would continue to want her.

She was just turning away from him when he said abruptly, 'Natasha, I owe you another apology. I should never have implied that you got this contract because you were sleeping with Leo.'

'No, you shouldn't,' she agreed shakily.

'Not prepared to accept my apology?' he queried, watching her. 'Well, I suppose I can't blame you for that. Physical desire can lead a man into all manner of folly, and I suspect that today I've just about run the whole range of them. I'd like us to make a fresh start—forget everything that's happened. Will you do that, Tasha? Will you have dinner with me tonight, just as though we are two people who have just met, and having just met both want to discover a little more about one another? There won't be any strings, I promise you that. I haven't yet reached the stage of having to trick women into going to bed with me.'

She could well believe it. Logic, common sense, self-protection urged her to refuse, urged her to remember that, although he had apologised, nothing had really changed. He was still the same man he had been this morning...still the same man who had made it so painfully plain to her just what he thought of her and of the rest of her sex, and yet disturbingly she heard herself saying, 'Just as long as you realise that it will only be as two colleagues that we're dining together, Luke, and not as two potential lovers.'

What on earth had she done? she asked herself shakily when she got to her room. Why on earth had she agreed, exposed herself to further danger, further pain? She had no answers, only an intense aching desire to be with him . . . to share something with him, even if it could only be her enthusiasm for her work. And if he should break his word, if he should try to persuade her... Well, then she would just have to tell him the truth, she decided recklessly—or at least enough of it to make sure that he would not make love to her.

* * *

She suspected she knew exactly how to do that. She would simply tell him that she was a virgin, that she was not, as he had obviously assumed, a woman of experience and sexual knowledge. Once he knew that, once he realised how little physical pleasure and how much emotional danger there could be for him in his possession of her, he would cease pursuing her. Sadly she recognised the truth that her innocence, her total commitment both emotional and physical, which another man might have cherished and revered, were both unnecessary and unwanted as far as Luke's desire for her was concerned. To him they would be burdens he would not want to assume, and the mere knowledge that they existed would be sufficient to kill any lingering desire he might have for her.

She had only brought casual clothes with her, but there was after all no need for her to dress up...to impress or please, to tantalise or arouse. In the end she opted for a plain cotton skirt in soft cotton stretch jersey teamed with a white sleeveless polo-necked top. The outfit looked and felt cool, and, she felt, covered enough of her body to make it plain to Luke that she was not covertly trying to attract him.

He was waiting for her when she went downstairs. Like her he had showered and changed. They looked at one another almost equally warily, she recognised, as he opened the front door for her and waited until she had locked it behind her.

'I've booked a table at a small place only a few miles away. It's on the river, and they specialise in fresh-water fish dishes. I should have checked first that you do like fish.'

'I do,' Natasha assured him, waiting while he unlocked his car and then opened the passenger door for her. He was careful not to touch her any more than was strictly necessary, and she sensed that he was deliberately distancing himself from her sexually. Let's start again, he had said... But start again to what purpose? As he set the powerful car in motion, she reminded herself that he had not forced her to accept his invitation and that she was here with him by her own decision.

He made some comment about the countryside around the house, and she responded in kind.

'Leo is thrilled with the house,' she offered tentatively, trying to follow his example and make innocuous small talk. 'He told me he fell in love with it the moment he saw it.'

'Yes. For all his astuteness where business matters are concerned, Leo is a romantic at heart, and I'm afraid people are somewhat inclined to take advantage of that fact once they recognise it.'

A hint that he believed that *she* might try to do so? Natasha shot him a wary look. He was concentrating on his driving, his profile hard, sombre almost. She realised with a small shock that she had never seen him smile—not properly, not with real warmth—and that knowledge saddened her.

The restaurant was, as Luke had told her, only a short distance away, its car park already almost full. As she got out of the car, Natasha could hear the murmur of the river, blending with people's voices.

'It is possible to dine outside,' Luke told her, guiding her across the car park, 'but I thought it would be more comfortable, if less romantic, inside.'

Natasha shot him another wary look, but there was nothing to be read in his controlled expression.

'Mm,' she offered brightly. 'We'd have both been bitten to death by midges outside anyway.'

The restaurant was small and low-ceilinged, its furnishings softened with the patina of gentle aging. She could well understand why it was popular, she reflected, looking appreciatively around her.

The restaurant had a small private bar, but when she refused Luke's offer of a pre-dinner drink they were quickly ushered to their table. A good one, Natasha noticed, with a view of the river and yet out of sight of the people eating outside.

She studied her menu in silence, sharply aware of the speculative glances Luke was attracting from most of the female diners. She couldn't blame them. He was well worth looking at, and she after all shared their vulnerability to his good looks.

Their waiter was hovering expectantly; she returned her attention to the menu, choosing a trout mousse, followed by salmon as her main course.

'I think I'll have the same,' Luke agreed, asking her if she had any preference as to wine.

She shook her head. She had no real taste for alcohol, and said as much.

'Mineral water, then, I think, for my guest,' he told the wine waiter, selecting a bottle of wine for himself.

Now that she was with him, she felt ridiculously self-conscious... almost as awkward as a teenager, and yet during her months in Florence she had dined with some of Florence's most notorious flirts without so much as a qualm.

But then she had never been vulnerable to them in the way that she was to Luke.

'Tell me something about your work... how you first became interested in it,' he invited her over their first course.

Obediently she did so, admitting to herself how flattering it was to have his attention focused on her, to be discussing with him a world in which they both shared an interest, albeit on different levels.

'What about you?' she asked him. 'I know that you travelled a great deal before you started painting.'

Tactfully she didn't say just how she had gained that knowledge, nor that Emma had been scathingly acidic about his morals and lifestyle.

'I didn't travel, I worked my way around the world,' he contradicted her flatly, ignoring her tact. 'And if you know that, then I'm sure you know why. In fact, I comprehend from your remarks earlier on today that someone has furnished you already with a potted history of my life... or at least of the less appealing aspects of it.'

Caught in the act of breaking a piece of bread, Natasha discovered that her hands were trembling and that the soft roll was being crumbled to nothing while she fought to conceal her distress and her compassion.

'I'm sorry,' she apologised softly. 'I shouldn't have said what I did earlier.'

'Don't apologise. You had every right to voice your feelings and thoughts, unappetising though I found them. No one likes being brought face to face with aspects of their personality they'd rather not recognise. I might not agree with all of your accusations, but certainly there was enough truth in them to make me——'

He broke off abruptly, all the colour suddenly leaving his face as he stared at someone out of Natasha's view. Unable to stop herself, she turned round to see what had caused the shock etched into his features.

An older couple were dining at a table several feet away from them, the man silver-haired, expensively dressed, slightly portly in a way that suggested both wealth and self-importance, his female companion younger, but not young. In her fifties perhaps... unless that too smooth complexion, and too taut skin was the result of the surgeon's knife rather than nature. Suspecting that it probably was, Natasha studied them discreetly, unable to see what it was about them that had had such a profound effect on Luke. The woman's clothes were a trifle youthful and close-fitting for someone of her age perhaps, her laughter too high and girlish, her flattering concentration on her companion hinting perhaps at desperation rather than delight, but why that should cause Luke to look as though he had virtually seen a ghost she had no idea.

As she looked back at him, anxiously she saw him lift his wine glass to his mouth and virtually drain the contents. His hand was shaking slightly, and Natasha only just managed to hold back the exclamation of concern springing to her lips.

He had barely touched his trout, she recognised, and he barely touched the main course that followed it either, although he emptied the bottle of wine.

Throughout the meal, while he contrived to talk to her, she was conscious that his real attention was on the couple seated behind her. Much as she longed to ask him what was wrong, she felt unable to do so, and when at last they got up and left the restaurant she was conscious of a sense of relief, almost as though she had been holding her breath, waiting for something unpleasant to happen. She had refused a sweet, suddenly anxious to be back at the house and away from the restaurant, but Luke had ordered himself a brandy and to keep him company she'd accepted a cup of coffee.

Half an hour later, when they left, she was relieved to see that what he had had to drink appeared to have had no physical effect on Luke at all. Perhaps because she herself was so abstemious, she was over-reacting a little, she accepted. Certainly she had seen men drink far more than Luke had consumed tonight and still claim that they were completely sober.

His introspective, almost distant mood which had begun in the restaurant seemed to have deepened. It was almost as though she wasn't there, she acknowledged sadly as she walked with him out to the car.

And yet why should she feel rebuffed, rejected almost? They had come out to dinner as temporary colleagues, thrown together by circumstances. She had made it plain to him that her acceptance of his invitation was not a prelude to having sex with him, and throughout the meal he had treated her with courtesy and respect. Now if he was a little withdrawn, a little preoccupied by his own thoughts, wasn't she being rather foolish in wishing for something more personal . . . more intense?

Luke stopped beside the driver's door of the car, and then frowned.

'I think it might be as well if you drive,' he told her. 'That is, if you don't mind . . .'

'Not at all,' she reassured him, adding that the car was a similar model to her father's which she had on occasion driven.

Luke handed her the keys and walked round to the passenger door, leaving her feeling slightly hesitant and a little surprised by the knowledge that she had perhaps misjudged him a little. She would have thought he was a man who always insisted on being in control both of himself and of others, and yet tonight in asking her to drive he was virtually admitting that he was not.

Her frown deepened a little as she climbed into the driver's seat, adjusting it to suit her smaller frame, while Luke virtually slumped into the seat beside her before reaching for his seatbelt.

Natasha realised as she set the car in motion that her earlier surmise that the alcohol had not affected him had been wrong.

'I'm sorry about this,' she heard him saying indistinctly. 'Either that damn wine was a lot stronger than it ought to have been, or the more moderate way in which we all live these days has lowered my capacity for alcoholic consumption far more than I realised.'

He was massaging his forehead as though it ached, Natasha noticed, and she was sure that the grim set of his mouth was caused by more than the fact that he had had too much to drink. In fact she was pretty sure that it had something to do with the couple who had absorbed so much of his attention, but a reluctance to pry and be rebuffed for doing so kept her from saying anything.

The big car was a delight to drive after her own more workaday model, but she was glad that she had had the experience of her father's Daimler to familiarise her with the lightness of the power steering as she tackled the winding road that led back to Leo's house.

Throughout the drive, Luke sat silently staring out of the window, patently lost in his own thoughts. And those thoughts couldn't be happy ones, she was sure, Natasha recognised as she brought the powerful car to a halt in front of the house.

As she climbed out, she wasn't entirely surprised to discover that her body was stiff with tension, as though she had been locking her muscles against some kind of external pressure.

They went inside together, the coolness of the hall striking chill against her warm skin, making her shiver slightly and suggest, 'I'm going to make myself a cup of coffee. Would you like one?'

'To sober me up?' Luke derided, suddenly seeming to snap out of his private absorption to focus on her. And then, frowning suddenly, he apologised, 'I'm sorry. Yes, coffee would be a good idea.'

He followed her into the kitchen, making her aware of his height and physical strength in a way that was becoming achingly familiar.

As she switched on the bright fluorescent lights of the kitchen, Natasha reflected with relief that here in these mundane and unromantic surroundings she ought to be able to banish the rebellious thoughts and impulses that tormented her. Here, away from the soft, cloaking darkness outside, she should surely be able to close her mind to those unwanted memories of Luke's body against her own . . . of Luke's mouth . . . of his hands . . .

Her own started to shake as she prepared the coffee. Desperate to force herself to treat him just as though he were a casual acquaintance, she said quickly, 'I haven't thanked you for dinner. It really was kind of you.'

The explosive sound he made stilled her, her body suddenly gripped with sharp tension.

'Was it? Are you really trying to tell me you enjoyed it? Don't bother to lie, Natasha. It was a disaster,' he said harshly, 'and all because of that damned woman!'

Natasha couldn't move, dared not turn round, as she waited, wondering if he would tell her just what it had been about the other couple that had affected him so deeply.

'She looked so much like *her*—could have been *her*, in fact...if I didn't know that she's living in South America with her latest lover...'

'Her?' Natasha felt compelled to ask, but in her heart she already knew whom he meant.

'Yes, her—my mother,' Luke grated harshly, confirming her thoughts. 'Remember, Natasha? The woman who made me hate your sex...who deserted me and made my father kill himself.'

Whether it was the wine that had unlocked the iron control he placed upon himself, or whether it was the sight of the woman he claimed looked so much like his mother, Natasha had no idea. She only knew that the sight and sound of him in so much mental and emotional anguish acted on her own emotions like a powerful magnet, drawing her across to him, making her reach out automatically to encircle his rigid body with her arms, and to hold him tightly and securely as though he were a hurt child, rocking him instinctively against the comforting softness of her own flesh, while she reached up to smooth the dark hair off his forehead and murmur the age-old litany of comforting words that women had used as a placebo against pain since the dawn of time.

She had no thought for herself, for her own feelings or needs, no fears that her comfort would be rejected or mocked, only a deep, instinctive need to succour and heal. It was the embrace of woman for all that was vulnerable and mortal in man, completely non-sexual, completely selfless...a true giving of support from one human being to another.

'You were right in what you said this morning. I *have* been punishing your sex for her desertion...her broken promises.'

Natasha felt him shudder against her, and she knew sadly and instinctively that once this moment of intimacy was over he would resent her for witnessing what he would consider to be the weakness of self-betrayal. Whether it was alcohol- or emotion-induced or a combination of both, she had no idea; she only knew that he was suffering and that she must offer him comfort.

'It's over, Luke,' she told him softly. 'You must let the past and its pain go. Stop torturing yourself. It wasn't your fault.'

She knew, the moment he tensed against her, that she had found the centre of the emotional abscess that poisoned his life. Inside she wept silent tears for him, and for all the children who, hurt and confused by the complexities of adult emotions, believed that they were to blame for the breakdown in adult relationships, who took upon themselves the heavy burden of guilt and despair...who believed that it was something in them that caused their parents to leave them.

She had been lucky. Her parents had had a good marriage. She had had the benefit of the secure home which Luke had not.

'It wasn't your fault,' she insisted, ignoring the resistance she could almost feel emanating from his flesh, ignoring his unspoken desire that she stop. 'Whatever caused your mother to leave was caused by her own needs and feelings, Luke. There are women to whom the sexual side of their nature will always be paramount... more important than their marriage vows—more important even than their children. You can't blame yourself for the fact that your mother was... is one of those women.'

She felt him shudder, and then he said thickly, bitterly, 'So what ought I do? Accept the fact that she didn't love me?'

'If you can,' Natasha agreed steadily. 'For your own sake.'

She felt him move against her in rejection of her words, his voice stronger, harsher as he derided, 'What are you trying to do, Natasha? Play the amateur psychologist? Well, it won't work. You haven't told me anything I don't already know.'

He started to pull away from her and, as he did so, she lost her balance a little, falling against him so that he reacted instinctively and immediately, catching hold of her around her waist to steady her.

He was looking directly at her, and there was no way she could tear her own gaze away. Her heart started thumping erratically.

By some complex alchemy that she was way beyond understanding, she knew that he was going to kiss her... knew it and did nothing to stop him.

'Natasha.' He said her name softly, slowly, almost as though he were tasting it, and a *frisson* of sensation tingled down her spine, an awareness of how much she wanted, needed to be held close to him.

Surprisingly, when his mouth touched hers its touch was gentle, caressive, without the sexual domination he had shown her before.

It was a kiss more of need than desire, she recognised in surprise; it was tender rather than passionate, and, sensing his need, his pain, she responded to it generously, lovingly, wanting to ease his anguish, to somehow make him whole again, to restore to him what his mother had taken away.

CHAPTER TEN

QUITE when desire overtook compassion, Natasha had no idea. One moment, or so it seemed, they were embracing without the urgency of desire, the next...

The next, Luke's arms had tightened around her, his body hardening against her, his hands moving urgently over her as though he wanted to make her aware of every pulse-point of his body. And all the time his mouth was moving on hers, caressing, arousing, feeding the hot, aching sensation that had erupted deep inside her body in response to the feel of his flesh against her own.

The sudden realisation of what she was doing, of what she was inviting, hit her, and she tried to drag her mouth from his, to lift her body away from its dangerous intimacy with his, but Luke stopped her, one hand tangling in her hair as he held her mouth beneath his own, the other spanning the small of her back, so that every movement she made to try and wriggle away from him only served to enforce on her the knowledge of his arousal. That knowledge proved too much for her own weak flesh. It had ached and yearned for this intimacy for too long, had fed itself on memories and dreams that faded into nothing beside the sharp reality of his proximity.

Luke's hand was still tangled in her hair, cradling the back of her head, but there was no need now for him to hold her prisoner beneath the passionate heat of his mouth, no need for him to bite in sensual demand at the soft curve of her bottom lip, tugging erotically on its full tenderness, until she whimpered softly beneath the burden of her own desire and clung recklessly to him, opening her mouth to his possession in the same way that she knew she had already opened her heart . . . and would surely soon open her body. That knowledge made her tremble, not in fear, but in a frightening awareness of how committed to him she actually was . . . How hopeless her belief that, somehow or other, by refusing to admit the truth, she could make it easier for herself to shut him out of her life and her heart. As though somehow she could actually prepare herself for the time when he wouldn't want her, when she would simply be another body he had desired and then forgotten.

She loved him . . . she always would love him. He merely desired her. That should have stopped her. But even as the thoughts passed through her passion-dazed brain she let them slide away, wanting, needing, aching for the narcotic he was offering her, even while she knew that its pleasure would be an arid one, that she would eventually have to confront the truth and with it her own pain.

Hazily she wondered how it was that she could so easily cast off her self-respect and pride, her moral beliefs and ethics, and then, as Luke's hand tugged her top out of the waistband of her skirt and slid under it, finding and moulding the soft curve of her breast, her ability to think, to reason, to do anything other than feel disintegrated completely.

She could hear someone breathing shallowly, quickly, each breath interspersed with soft sounds of need, but only realised distantly that it was the sound of her own arousal she could hear. All her attention, her concentration was focused on the pleasure Luke's touch was giving her, on responding to the hard demand of his mouth with passionate, almost fevered kisses.

Distantly she was aware of Luke removing her top and then her bra, unaware that she herself had begged him to do so, until she heard him whisper thickly against her skin, 'There . . . is that better? Is that what you wanted, Tasha?'

His voice was more slurred now than it had been when they left the restaurant, the words thick and unsteady, making her tremble with eager expectancy.

He was kissing her throat, while his hands cupped and caressed her naked breasts. She arched up towards him, moaning softly, and then gasping with pleasure as she felt the sharp pressure of his teeth raking the soft curve of her shoulder, making her twist and turn frantically against him, silently inviting him to repeat the caress over and over again until her body was alive with sensations . . . vibrating with need and desire.

She had no will, no needs, no desires, other than those he conjured up inside her, and when he lifted her against his body, arching her back in his arms so that he could repeat against her breasts the caresses which had already made her shiver with arousal and need, she didn't even hear herself cry out the sharp, anguished sound of intense desire.

But Luke did, and the pressure of his mouth increased until it seemed to Natasha that her whole world was concentrated on the tender area of flesh that Luke was drawing into his mouth, bathing with liquid heat and then tormenting with such rhythm and overwhelming intensity that the pleasure he was giving her was almost unendurable.

Only when he released her swollen, aching nipple did she come back to reality to discover, as he slid her slowly down his body until her feet touched the floor, that she could barely stand, so weak did she feel.

She was trembling from head to foot, aching with a teeth-clenching need that shocked her.

'Outwardly so very cool and controlled, and inwardly, so deliciously passionate,' Luke was saying softly in her ear. 'If I didn't know better I could almost believe that no one has ever touched you like that before.'

His hand reached out towards her breast, the pad of his thumb brushing her engorged nipple as though unable to resist its aroused allure.

'You're so soft,' he told her. 'So tender. I can't wait to feel how you respond when I taste you here.'

His hand left her breast to brush lightly against the front of her skirt, the merest pressure of light fingers barely touching the mound of her sex, but it triggered off such a reaction inside her that Natasha could hardly believe what was happening to her. His words...his actions...his intentions...all of them hit her at once, her body reacting to them so overwhelmingly that she had no defence against them.

The thought of his mouth touching her so intimately, which ought to have been so shocking, so unthinkable, had suddenly become a refined form of deliberate torment, a promise of pleasure, so desirable that she felt faint from the need it induced.

'I want you, Tasha.'

The words echoed through her body, increasing her aching tension.

'Let me take you to bed. You know how good it's going to be for us, don't you? We're both adults. Experienced. We both know.'

Instantly Natasha tensed, the husky, compelling words breaking through the bubble of desire blinding her to the truth. He thought that for her, as for him, this would be nothing more than simply another sexual encounter, and it was *her* fault that he thought that. She ought to tell him. She *had* to tell him. Panic clawed inside her as she realised that she had left it too late for any explanations . . . that he would not be pleased to discover now that she was still a virgin . . . that he was in no mood to listen to any immature outpourings of insecurity and need. And yet if she didn't stop him . . . if she let him continue . . .

She shuddered sickly, knowing what she must do, dragging herself away from him to say huskily, 'Luke, I can't. I'm sorry.'

For a moment he simply stared at her, and then as she watched she saw first disbelief and then anger darkening his eyes, and automatically she stepped back from him, crossing her arms defensively over her exposed breasts, suddenly aware that once again they were antagonists and not lovers.

'I think you mean you *won't*,' he countered acidly. 'Not that you *can't*. Punishing me, Natasha? Stupid of me, but I thought you were above those kind of games. Still, I suppose I should have guessed, realised that after all, underneath all that soft compassion, you aren't any different from the rest of your sex. Oh, you're perfectly safe,' he told her, watching with cynical eyes the way she flinched back from him. 'I'm not going to force myself on you, if that's what you think . . . or want,' he added with unforgivable cruelty. 'I couldn't even if I wanted to,' he added brutally. 'Odd how even the sharpest desire can so easily die...or be destroyed.'

He left her standing in silent agony and disbelief as he walked away from her and closed the door behind him. She stared numbly round the kitchen, blinking in the strong light, her attention focusing briefly on the crumpled piece of fabric that was her top, her hand reaching for it automatically while her brain tried to come to terms with what had happened.

She tried to tell herself that it was for the best . . . that this way there would be less pain, less trauma, but her tormented, aching body refused to believe the panacea she was trying to offer it.

At some point she woke from an uneasy sleep disturbed by the sound of a car engine, but it wasn't until she woke up in the morning and went downstairs to discover that Luke's car had gone that she realised what that sound had meant.

Luke had gone.

She tried to tell herself that it was for the best, that in the circumstances she could hardly have faced him with equanimity. Even without his presence, her skin burned hotly when she remembered how he had made her feel . . . how she had openly and self-destructively responded to the way he made her feel. He had every right to feel angry with her, she acknowledged miserably. She ought never to have allowed things to get so far. She ought to have told him, stopped him . . .

But her weakness did not justify his total denunciation of her sex. She could understand that the rejection of his mother, followed by the suicide of his father, had been painful experiences for a young boy on the threshold of entering manhood, but surely with maturity must have come the realisation that not all women were the same, just as not all men were the same, that people were individuals . . . Unless . . . unless he had simply found it easier to blot out that knowledge, to tell himself that all women *were* like his mother and thus, in doing so, protect himself from further hurt, from the vulnerability that came through loving someone. And she sensed that, although he had not said so, Luke *had* loved his mother, which was why he had taken her desertion so badly. It was easy to understand how a young and impressionable boy might have reacted, might have told himself that all women were the same, and how the man that child had grown into would go on telling himself the same thing because believing it made him feel safe, inviolate.

It was not his fault that he should feel the way he did any more than it was hers that she should be unfortunate enough to love him.

What was his fault and hers was that both of them, knowing how diametrically opposed their beliefs and needs were, had allowed themselves to be carried away by that destructive surge of sexual desire, which both of them knew could only lead one way.

Yes, it was best that he had gone, but that did not stop her from wandering helplessly around the gallery, compulsively touching the things she knew he must have touched...the crates...the paintings...letting her fingers move blindly over them as though in doing so they could give back to her their memories of his hands moving on them, in the same faultless, dangerous way her body had recorded the sensations he had conjured up within it, playing and replaying them until she was so sensitised by her memories, so aware of the shocking intensity of her own need that she ached to be able to close her mind and body against him. To forget that she had ever known he existed.

Her aunt and Leo returned while she was still working at the house, both of them so obviously bursting with happiness that Natasha was not surprised when Leo announced proudly that Helen had agreed to marry him.

'Of course, he's only marrying me so that he'll get a cheap gardener-cum-housekeeper,' Helen teased, but the look in her eyes when she looked at him totally belied any real belief in her words. That they were deeply and sincerely in love was obvious and, while she was thrilled for them, at the same time Natasha was appalled to discover that she had to look away from them because of the weak, selfish tears clouding her eyes.

Leo insisted on opening a bottle of champagne so that their engagement could be toasted, and, although she tried to respond cheerfully to their excitement, at the first moment she got Natasha escaped to her own room.

How selfish of her, to allow her own feelings to shadow someone else's joy. She only hoped that neither of them had noticed how difficult it had been for her to smile and join in their pleasure, even while she was truly pleased for them.

When her aunt knocked briefly on her bedroom door and called out her name, Natasha got up to let her in.

'What's wrong?' Helen asked quietly without preamble. 'Or can I guess? Leo has just told me that Luke Templecombe was here over the weekend. My dear, I had no idea. If I had... Leo seems to think that Luke must have left in something of a hurry. Apparently he was to havc hung Leo's paintings in the gallery, but all he seems to have done is uncrate them. Leo seems to think he must have been called back to London on urgent business. He said something about Luke being commissioned to do a portrait of one of the Royals.'

'He left last night,' Natasha told her, and then, unable to hold back her grief, she poured it all out:

her love for Luke, her discovery of the contempt and dislike he harboured for her sex, his belief that she, like him, was sexually experienced and that because of that she would be willing to enter into an arid, meaningless sexual relationship with him.

'Even if I were what he thought of me, it wouldn't make any difference. I still wouldn't want him on those terms. I couldn't...' She shuddered, knowing how easily she could, knowing how frighteningly easy it would have been for her to let go of her cherished beliefs, how frighteningly easy to give in, not to Luke, but to her own need, her own love. 'A self-destructive love,' she told Helen, painfully, intent on revealing every nuance of her own despair, admitting that she was as much to blame for Luke's departure as he was himself, not seeking to hide from her aunt her own role in what had happened.

'It was my fault. I allowed him to think...to believe...'

'Natasha, he's an experienced man,' her aunt pointed out gently. 'He must have seen...have realised.'

'No,' Natasha denied, gulping emotionally, unable to lay bare that final self-betrayal, to disclose that her reactions to him, her response to him had not been that of a woman who was sexually unawakened or hesitant.

'My dear, I'm so sorry. If there's anything I can do...'

'There isn't,' Natasha told her, biting hard on her bottom lip. 'I've just got to learn to live with it. No one asked me to fall in love with him, Helen,' she said painfully, 'least of all Luke himself. I knew right from the start just what he wanted from me. I told myself I could deal with it. I even told myself that I was being honest with myself, but it wasn't true. I realise now that part of me kept on hoping for some kind of adolescent miracle. You know the sort of thing—that he would look at me, and that everything would change...that he wouldn't just want me but that he would love me as well.'

She heard her aunt sigh and said thickly, 'Yes. Ridiculous, I know...stupid as well. Especially when I've always prided myself on my common sense, on my ability to control my emotions.'

'All of us are vulnerable when we love,' her aunt pointed out gently. 'Men as well as women. It sounds to me as though your Luke is frightened to death of allowing himself to love anyone.'

Her Luke. Natasha felt the aching tug of pain arch through her. If only he were her Luke.

'It's too easy to make excuses for him, to say that his mother's rejection allows him to behave the way he does, as though he's still a child and not a man.'

'I agree, and to be quite frank with you, darling...even if he could bring himself to say he cared about you, I shouldn't like to see you get involved with him.'

'There's no chance of that,' Natasha told her grimly. 'He's probably even managed by now to forget that I ever existed. After all, why should he remember?'

Her aunt sighed, getting up and patting her hand commiseratingly.

'If there's anything Leo and I can do...'

'Nothing,' Natasha assured her, 'other than forgive me for being such a selfish misery. I am thrilled about your engagement. When's the wedding to be?'

'December. There's no real need for us to wait that long, but the house should be finished by then. Leo wants us to have a proper wedding, as he calls it, and I must admit I'd like to be married in the same church where I made my first vows to your uncle. It sort of completes the circle, if you know what I mean, and besides, your mother would never forgive me if we opted for a quiet little ceremony. She and Leo are rather alike in both enjoying a little pomp and circumstance.'

Natasha laughed. 'Does Emma know yet?'

'No... I'm going to ring her tonight to break the news. I'm just hoping that Richard's work in his new parish will allow them to attend the ceremony, which is why we've opted for the first week in December.'

'Mmm. Well, if Leo's expecting to open the hotel for Christmas, as he told me he wanted to do, I'd better get myself off to Florence and order the fabrics we're going to need.' She gave her aunt a too brilliant smile and said shakily, 'If you want to look over the schemes I've chosen...'

'Good heavens, no,' her aunt assured her. 'That's your field, not mine, Tasha, and I know whatever you've chosen will be exactly right. Leo has been raving about you, you know. He's most impressed.'

'I've been lucky to get such a wonderful commission,' Natasha told her, her face clouding as she remembered the accusations Luke had thrown at her. Odd that they could hurt so deeply, cut so sharply, when surely by now she ought to be inured to pain, but every time she remembered was, like the first time, acute, heart-wrenching anguish.

Two weeks later she left for Florence, without having heard a word from Luke. Not that she had expected to. Nor hoped? Not even in the privacy of her own thoughts was she prepared to admit just how much she had hoped, or how unwisely.

She left for Florence, armed not just with detailed notes on the fabrics she needed for Leo's house, but also with various commissions and messages from her father, knowing that the time she spent there would be frantically busy, and hoping that somehow or other business would prove to be the magic panacea she so desperately needed to stop her thinking about Luke, yearning for him, aching for him.

Her mother had commented disapprovingly before she left, 'Darling, you're getting too thin. You look positively haggard. Doesn't she, Helen?'

Above her mother's head, Natasha and her aunt had exchanged a wordless look.

'I expect it's because she's working so hard,' Helen Lacey had dismissed, adroitly rescuing her, and then directing Natasha's mother's thoughts to another channel by commenting, 'I hope I'm wrong, but I rather think that Emma is going to make me a grandmama. There was a hint to that effect in her last letter.'

'Surely not so soon,' Natasha had heard her mother expostulate. 'I thought they intended to wait. At least, that's what Richard implied.'

'Richard may have implied it, but Emma obviously had other thoughts. And when did she want to wait... for anything?' the latter's mother had asked drily.

Emma having a child—not just any child, but the child of the man she loved. Something sharp had twisted painfully inside Natasha... something that was not envy, but rather a hopeless, helpless longing for something she knew could never be. And yet if she had not stopped Luke... if she had not insisted... she could now be carrying his child. She could now be looking forward to the compensation of having the child to love where she could not have the man. And she *would* have loved it, and in doing so would have shown Luke what? That he was wrong about her? To what purpose? Was she really so stupid, so criminally selfish that she would have allowed herself to conceive a child, knowing that that child would never know the love and care of its father. Had she really travelled so dangerously far down such a self-delusory road?

She was thinking of Luke when her plane landed in Florence, but then when did she not think of him? He had become almost a compulsive obsession with her, something she was unable to let go of, something she doubted she actually wanted to let go of.

In Florence she was welcomed warmly by those she had come to do business with, her expertise and knowledge recognised and admired.

She was, after all, her father's daughter, and in Florence, where generation upon generation had developed their skills in working and using the rich textiles she had come to buy, they well understood the passing down of knowledge and flair from one generation to the next.

Every night, every lunchtime found her eating with the family of one or other of her contacts, made welcome among them, and treated by most of them in much the same way they might treat a favourite niece.

She was beautiful, young and just a little triste—something that all Italians, but especially the Florentines responded to with all the passion and compassion of their Mediterranean heritage.

It was in the salon of one of her father's oldest contacts that she saw the magazine. It was lying half open on a sofa, so that when she moved to pick it up the first thing she saw was Luke's face staring back at her.

She dropped the magazine as though it burned, her face turning white and then red, her eyes blurring with emotion.

Her hostess, the mother of four teenage daughters and an adored and spoiled only son, saw what had happened, and discreetly led her young guest away from the others on the pretext of showing her some new curtains she had made.

Gratefully Natasha tried to pull herself together, to appear calm and normal, but when she left the house she heard herself asking awkwardly if she might borrow the magazine, her eyes avoiding the compassion in those of her hostess as her request was granted.

Once back in her hotel room, she devoured the article, drinking it in as though it were a life-giving elixir.

The writer was praising Luke's talents as a portraitist, hinting that he was now receiving Royal patronage, and asking him what had made him make the switch from landscapes to portraits.

It was all a question of growth, was Luke's response. A question of answering a need within oneself for development.

From the arch tone of the writer's article, Natasha guessed that she must have been attracted to Luke. What woman would not? She spent a miserable evening imagining the two of them making love—or having sex, as Luke would no doubt have described it.

She stayed in Florence for almost a month, working so hard that she completed all her commissions ahead of schedule and discovered some new sources of supply which ought to have thrilled her, but which only caused her to reflect that if she was not successful in her emotional life, then at least where her business was concerned she was not the same kind of failure.

She arrived home on a cold, windy day to find a message waiting for her from Leo asking her if she could possibly drive down to the manor because the first of the curtains for the bedrooms, made up from the fabrics supplied by her father, were now ready for hanging and he wanted her to be there to supervise this task.

Once such news would have thrilled her, but now she felt little more than a brief flare of surprise that so much time had passed. Was it really almost six weeks since she had last seen Luke? It was so fresh in her memory that it might almost have only been yesterday.

Luke...Luke...Luke...why oh, why could she not stop thinking about him, aching for him, loving him?

Why could she not do what she knew to be the sensible thing, the only profitable thing, and cut him out of her memory, forget that she had ever known him?

Because she was a fool, that was why, she told herself as she drove down to Stonelovel. She had learned from her mother that her aunt and Leo were both at the house, Leo supervising the work on his own private wing, and her aunt involved in the replanning and replanting of the gardens.

It was a relief to know that she wouldn't be in the house on her own. She had no wish to fall into the trap of daydreaming about Luke—something she was sure she would be tempted to do if she was alone.

Her aunt had never looked better, Natasha reflected, sitting sipping a welcome cup of tea while she listened to her enthusing over what she had managed to achieve.

Natasha had arrived half an hour earlier. She had been given her old room, as the guest rooms in the private wing were not yet ready for occupation, and she tried not to contrast her aunt's air of glowing happiness as she described how much progress they had made on the gardens with her own awareness that time, her life itself, both seemed to have become dragging burdens that were sometimes almost too heavy to carry.

It had been a cold, wet drive, and she had half expected to arrive to find her aunt's work impeded by the weather, but it seemed that nothing could dash her spirits.

'Once it's stopped raining—*if* it stops raining—I'll show you round.'

'And in the meantime, *I'll* show you round the house,' Leo announced, walking into the room to join them.

Later on, as she followed Leo and Helen from room to room in the hotel part of the house, Natasha could well understand Leo's pleasure in what had been achieved. All that was needed now were the finishing touches which would be provided by her fabrics.

Natasha found she was holding her breath, not wanting to go inside when Leo insisted on showing her the gallery, but once she had stepped inside it looked so different from the last time she had seen it that she managed to force herself to ignore the fact that it was here that she had been with Luke, talked with him, argued with him . . .

'Luke came back, then,' she commented huskily, unable to stop herself from admiring what had been achieved. It would be the easiest thing in the world to close one's eyes and be transported back to the seventeenth century. Even knowing that the paintings and portraits were in the main Victorian reproductions of paintings of the Elizabethan and

Stuart periods, it was easy to believe that they were genuinely of that period.

They had been hung in such a way as to mirror photographs Natasha remembered seeing of traditional panelled galleries of the Stuart period. Places where the ladies of the household would walk on rainy days, pausing to gaze down out of the windows, when the view inside palled, to admire the complexities of the herb and knot gardens set out below.

'Yes. He was here last week,' Leo responded. 'In fact, he——' He broke off suddenly, probably warned by a discreet look from her aunt, Natasha suspected, as she transferred her attention from the paintings to the other couple.

'It's wonderful,' she told them honestly. 'And when the fabric for the curtains and window-seats arrives... Well, all I can say, Helen, is that you'd better order your Tudor court costume right now.'

She asked several questions about the paintings which genuinely did interest her, and learned that Leo had been collecting them over a long period of time, even before he had acquired the house.

By some heroic effort she managed not to mention Luke's name, nor to invite any kind of comment or information about him.

They spent the evening discussing the wedding. Natasha excused herself fairly early on, saying genuinely that she was very tired.

As she went up to her room, she told herself that she was glad that Luke had finished working in the gallery and that there would now be no fear of his returning...of their meeting, but the knowledge did not make her heart feel any lighter, nor did it ease the burden of misery she was carrying.

CHAPTER ELEVEN

NATASHA had spent a busy morning organising the hanging of the curtains which had been delivered while she was in Italy. The firm who had made up the fabrics sent out a team of four from Bath to work under Natasha's supervision. She had dealt with them before, and the girl in charge of them was around the same age as Natasha herself, a pretty, plump brunette who, as Natasha already knew, was a bit of a daydreamer, inclined to see everything through rose-tinted glasses.

When she had finished enthusing about the house, she said enthusiastically to Natasha, 'You must be so excited about the wedding. It's a real romance, isn't it?'

They were alone in the gallery where Natasha had taken her to explain just how she wanted the Florentine fabric to be cut and draped once it eventually arrived. They had left the door at the end of the gallery open, and neither of them saw the man approach the open door, and then hesitate there.

'Yes, it is,' Natasha agreed.

'The wedding is being held in your home town, Mr Rosenberg says. Your mother must be so excited.'

'She is,' Natasha agreed. 'This will be her second wedding this year. My cousin was married earlier in the year.'

'I think it's wonderfully romantic. To have met almost by accident. If you hadn't been working here——' She broke off, flushing a little, and suddenly looking both flustered and excited as she stared at the door.

Natasha, who had her back to it, immediately turned round. The room seemed to spin dizzily around her as she saw Luke standing looking back at her.

'Luke...'

She wasn't even aware of saying his name, never mind the curious and half-envious look the other girl gave her, as the latter said quickly, 'Oh, heavens, I've just remembered I promised Jenneth I'd make some notes on what you want in here, and I've left my notebook downstairs. Shan't be a moment.'

Too bemused to stop her, Natasha couldn't drag her gaze from Luke as he stood to one side to allow the other girl to pass, and then walked into the room, closing the door behind him.

He looked different somehow. He was thinner, that was it, she recognised, greedily drinking in the sight of him, aching to be able to run up to him, to hold him and touch him.

His eyes, she saw, were glittering with a hectic, almost too brilliant fierceness, his mouth curling in a familiar line of anger and contempt, and her heart, which seemed to have stopped beating, suddenly started to flutter with frantic little beats that made her breathless and dizzy.

'So. You're going to marry Leo. I suppose I shouldn't be surprised. I ought to have guessed. But you see, Natasha, you really did deceive me. I really had begun to believe that you were different, that you were honest, that you would never lie or deceive.'

'I...haven't lied to you,' Natasha managed to tell him, her throat choked with shock and bewilderment. Why on earth did Luke think she was marrying Leo?

She opened her mouth to correct him and explain, but already he was sweeping on, refusing to allow her to say anything, his anger growing with every word he uttered, feeding on itself, until she too felt the white-hot heat of it infecting her own calmer emptiness.

It was like standing on the edge of a gathering storm, she thought distantly as his words, his scorn and his rage thundered around her until she had to shut herself off from what he was saying. Her face burned at the injustice of his anger, at his stupidity in assuming that she could ever commit herself to anyone other than him.

'What...nothing to say for yourself?' he snarled at her when he had reached the end of his contemptuous denunciation. 'Well, perhaps this will give you something to think about. Do you know why I came here today, Natasha? I camc hcrc to apologise to you. To tell you that you were right and that I was wrong...to tell you that I'd done some thinking and some heart-searching since I last saw you and that you were right...I was punishing all your sex for my mother's desertion...and more...I came to recognise that the reason I wouldn't let myself make any emotional contact with a woman was because I was frightened, terrified of being hurt again the way my mother hurt me.

'I came here to tell you all of that, Natasha, and to ask you if you and I could begin again. Make a fresh start. If you could perhaps teach me a little of your compassion, your generosity...if somehow or other we could find a way of making something out of whatever it is between us. And what do I find? I find that the woman who had lectured me so earnestly, so emotionally, the woman I had at last managed to let myself believe in, is nothing but a sham. God, at least my mother was honest in her rejection. At least she didn't pretend.'

He had been standing half a dozen yards or so away from her, but now, as she turned towards him with dazed, shocked eyes that focused helplessly on his face, he closed that gap between them, taking hold of her so ruthlessly that there wasn't time for her to escape him.

'You wanted me,' he whispered rawly. 'You still want me.'

'No.'

Her denial was meant more as a plea that he listen, that he allow her to explain than a contradiction of his accusation, but either he did not understand that, or he chose to misinterpret it, because as she pleaded breathlessly to be released his hands gripped her wrists and he hauled her against his body. She could feel the heat coming off it, the anger... the arousal.

He kissed her once, a fierce, contemptuous pressure of his mouth on hers that bruised and punished, and then again, equally fiercely, but this time with a compulsive raw desire that made her tremble weakly against him, her body sagging against the heat of his, her mouth instinctively softening, giving.

She heard him groan, a savage, angry sound that echoed her own frustration and need. His hands moulded her body, shaping it against his own, running over it with angry, restless movements that conveyed his need and his resentment of it.

One hand gripped the back of her neck, burrowing into her hair, the pressure of his kiss forcing her head back so that her body grew taut like a bow. His other hand spanned the base of her spine, pushing her against him, moving her in a shockingly open simulation of the physical act of sexual possession.

Somewhere deep inside her she felt shock, anger, and self-contempt, but overruling any kind of logical and civilised emotion was her own fiercely compulsive need to respond to him as aggressively and wantonly as he was doing to her. One part of her shockingly almost gloried in the knowledge that, even while he claimed he hated and despised her, he still wanted her. She discovered that she liked that, with a stab of shock bordering on that with which a lifelong vegetarian might suddenly and totally inexplicably discover a taste for blood-red meat.

It should have sickened her. Instead she found it euphorically exciting, as though in some way by arousing this anger, this need, this compulsive desire within him, she was punishing him, hurting him . . .

Hurting him . . . She grew still abruptly. Hurting him. How could she want to do that? Because he had hurt her? Was that any real excuse?

He had lifted his mouth from hers. She focused on it and saw that it was slightly swollen and bruised, that there was a small bite on his bottom lip. She reached out and touched it automatically, frowning when her fingertip came away marked with a spot of blood.

'Yes, you little hell cat, you did that,' Luke told her thickly. 'And we both know that right now I could lay you down here on the floor and take you and make you scream with the pleasure of our lovemaking.'

Natasha had gone white, but she refused to allow herself to be beaten down by his words—not when she knew that he was equally vulnerable, more so perhaps, since she suspected that he had never before had to confront the kind of need he was now feeling for her.

Hardly knowing where the words were coming from, she heard herself challenging softly and recklessly, 'Do it, then, but I promise you this, Luke—it won't just be me who cries out in pleasure.'

She saw him go white as he released her and stepped back from her. On another occasion the shocked look in his eyes might almost have made her smile, but, now that reaction was beginning to set in, she was beginning to feel sick and shaky.

'My God, what kind of woman *are* you?' he breathed thickly. 'Does Leo know about this . . . about us? And don't tell me that he makes you feel the same way that I do, because I won't believe it.'

'I should certainly hope not, since Leo is about to become *my* husband, Mr Templecombe.'

Neither of them had heard Helen come into the gallery. Natasha focused on her briefly, frowning a little as though she barely recognised her. She could hear the exclamation of disbelief uttered by Luke. She could see the cool control of her aunt's face. Her own body felt as though it were about to disintegrate . . . to fall apart.

'Ah, there you are, Luke. Did you find Tasha?'

As Leo himself walked into the gallery, Natasha knew she had had enough. She made a strangled sound of pain, and rushed out of the open door, heading not for her room, nor even for her car which would take her safely away from Luke and his cruel accusations. She was hardly in a fit state to drive, and the kind of solitude she craved the most she knew she could most easily find in the neglected walled garden on which her aunt had not yet started work.

The paths were damp underfoot from all the recent rain; the air smelled green and fresh, the clean scent mingling with the richer, more fragrant one of the old-fashioned bourbon roses which straggled untidily against the walls.

She sat down on an old bench tucked away behind an overgrown corner.

She had been there an hour, maybe more, when the creaking of the gate opening warned her that her solitude was about to be destroyed.

She wasn't perturbed; she knew that Luke must have left long ago, driven back to wherever he had come from by the same intense anger which had brought him into the gallery in the first place.

She tried not to let herself dwell on what he had said to her, on how different things might have been if he had only realised how impossible it was for her to commit herself to Leo, to anyone else other than him.

She wasn't, she decided drearily, prepared to make explanations or apologies. Why should she? He was the one who couldn't recognise reality, who could not or would not see the truth. Whatever kind of relationship he had wanted to have with her, for it to succeed it would have had to be based on mutual trust, and that Luke did not and probably never could trust her had been made bitterly clear.

That kind of outburst, that kind of anger, that kind of sheer blindness could only be overlooked or forgiven in a man so deeply in love that the mere thought of losing the woman he loved caused him such intense pain that he reacted to it illogically.

And Luke did not feel like that about her. Luke did not love her. She made herself say it out loud.

'Luke does not love me.'

'Wrong, Tasha. Luke does love you, God help him,' Luke himself groaned.

She turned her head in disbelief and saw that he was standing less than three feet away from her, looking both unbearably haggard and ridiculously boyish at the same time.

'No, please, let me stay... apologise... explain. God knows, if you listened to me from now until the end of time I doubt I could apologise in full. Helen has told me everything.'

'Everything?' She frowned at him, rather like a child trying to understand an adult. 'You mean she's told you that she's marrying Leo?'

'She has told me that, and much, much more. Do you mind if I sit down?'

He sat down on the bench next to her, and Natasha instinctively edged away from him. She was too vulnerable to him even now.

'Tasha, why didn't you tell me how wrong I was about you? Why did you let me think that——?'

'I was available and sexually experienced,' she flashed at him. 'You know why, Luke. It was to protect Emma. She was afraid you would prevent Richard from marrying her.'

'What? How on earth could I have done that? Even if I had wanted to, it's plain that he's besotted with her.'

'You told me yourself you didn't think they were well matched, and Emma heard you telling Richard's mother that the wedding could be called off.'

'By Emma, not Richard. Look, your aunt's told me everything. And I can't say that any of it has exactly endeared Emma to me. Forcing you into that kind of situation. Has she no sense... have neither of you? You do realise how close I came that very first night to...'

'To what? Seducing me, in my parents' garden?' She allowed her disbelief to colour her voice, shading it with scorn and bitterness. 'Oh, surely not?'

'You don't believe me. You've affected me like no other woman I've ever met, Tasha, and I've met plenty. Do you honestly believe I react like this to every woman, that I feel like this about every woman, that I've ever experienced this kind of wanting, this kind of intensity before? It's a whole new territory for me, and, like any other animal, I find unfamiliar territory makes me aggressive and wary.'

'I don't know what you're trying to say to me, Luke, but really it doesn't matter. I think it's best that you and I forget we've ever met.'

'Better...for whom? Certainly not for me. I want you in my life, Tasha.'

'Do you? Well, I've got news for you, Luke—I don't want *you* in *mine*... Not as my enemy, not as my friend, and certainly not as my lover.'

She started to stand up, but when he said quietly, almost pleadingly, she recognised, 'Not even as your husband?' she sat down again, her body suddenly boneless.

'My husband?'

'That's what I came down here today to say to you. That I loved you and that I wanted to marry you.'

'To marry me? But——'

'I love you, Tasha. I realise now that I fell in love with you the moment I saw you, but I fought against it as all men do. Only with me the fight lasted longer and was far harder. Everything you said to me about my past and the fears I had brought out of it with me was quite correct. I was afraid to trust...to love. I was still blaming my mother, when, as an adult, I ought to have recognised . . . to have accepted . . . that she was probably as powerless to control her emotions and behaviour as I was mine. You were right when you said to me that for some women their lovers will always matter more than their children. It was my misfortune that my mother was one of those women.'

'And hers as well,' Natasha told him gently, putting her hand on his arm. 'I'm sure there must have been many times since she left you when she must have wondered about you and wished she had acted differently. It must be terrible for any woman to be torn between her lover and her child. She probably thought you'd be better off with your father. She couldn't have known what would happen.'

'It doesn't matter any more. I've come to terms with it. A little late in the day perhaps. And as for my crass stupidity in believing you were marrying Leo . . . Will you believe me when I say that it was jealousy, nothing more, nothing less, that drove me to say the things I did? I'd found out from Leo that you were coming down here. I'd been waiting, planning, desperately hoping that you would listen to me, that it wasn't too late . . . that you hadn't found someone else, and then to walk into the gallery and hear you apparently discussing your wedding . . .

'Put yourself in my place, Tasha. If our positions had been reversed, couldn't you visualise yourself behaving, if not as badly, then at least similarly?'

She could...so easily...so very, very easily. The mere thought of learning that Luke was marrying someone else, the mere thought of contemplating it was like a vice tightening around her heart, a physical ache of shock, rage and pain.

'We're both alike in so many ways—both intensely passionate, both intensely private people. We both cloak what we feel in an exterior disguise of self-control and coolness. I love you, Tasha. I can't make you accept that love, and I certainly can't make you accept me. I know that sexually I turn you on, but I'm not going to use that knowledge to pressure you. I'm talking about a lifetime's commitment, a relationship based on not just desire but on love, on trust, on half a hundred other things that I know damn well I've only just started learning about. I need you for that as well, Tasha. I need you to teach me how to love...not love...I've already learned that lesson—too well perhaps—but how to love others, how to show compassion, forgiveness. Will you do that, my darling? Will you help me, forgive me, trust me, love me?'

Even if she hadn't loved him so utterly and completely, Natasha knew that her heart must have been touched, not just by his words, but by the very real emotion he wasn't trying to hide. He would never change completely; he would always have that touch of arrogance perhaps, and certainly he would never find it easy to trust where others were concerned, nor to admit them closely into their lives.

Their lives. She smiled inwardly to herself, knowing that there had really been no decision to make. She loved him, and, while that could never have been enough with the Luke she had first met, *this* Luke, who was prepared to listen, to humble himself, to admit his misjudgments and errors . . . *this* Luke who could tell her that he loved her and lay bare his deepest most personal feelings to her . . . this Luke was a man she could trust as well as love. This Luke was someone with whom she could share her life.

'You know I can,' she told him quietly, and then added, 'It won't be easy, I know that, but I do love you, Luke, and if you love me . . .'

'I do. I might have been slow to recognise it, but once I did . . .'

'When did you?' Natasha asked him.

'That night we went out to dinner together. I think deep down inside I knew it before then, but that was the first time I admitted it to myself.

'Kiss me, Tasha,' he begged her. 'Show me that I'm not dreaming any of this.'

'Mm. I hope this isn't just a dream.'

'That's what you said to me the day you told me you loved me,' Natasha told her husband, laughing up at him. They were lying on their bed in the luxurious Caribbean villa they had been loaned for their honeymoon by one of Luke's clients.

'You're sure you don't mind, Luke . . . about being my first lover?'

'Don't be silly.' He picked up her hand and kissed her fingers slowly and lingeringly, watching with appreciative awareness the pleasure darken her eyes.

'I was surprised, I must admit, when Helen first gave me that pithy lecture on just how wrong I was about you, but I'd loved you before I knew there hadn't been anyone else and——'

'You...you weren't disappointed, then...the first time?'

They had been lovers before they were married. Luke had taken her away for a long weekend and had made love to her so tenderly, and then so passionately that he had banished all her fears that he might somehow find her inadequate, but now, womanlike, she felt a need to probe...to exact verbal confirmation of what she already knew.

'In what? Finding that I'd fallen in love with a passionately intense woman who'd had the good sense to realise that I was the perfect lover for her?' he teased.

Natasha balled her fist and pretended to hit him, protesting when he grabbed hold of her and rolled her underneath him. The tussle which ensued left her breathless with laughter, until she felt the familiar hardening of Luke's body against her own and the laughter disappeared.

'We're going to be late for dinner again,' she warned him as he kissed her.

'Who cares about food? I have an appetite of a very different and far more essential kind, don't you?'

She did, Natasha acknowledged. It amazed her that she could feel like this, respond like this, that there should have been this intensely passionate side of herself which she had never known existed until she met Luke.

'Hold me, Luke,' she demanded fiercely, whispering the words against his skin. 'Hold me and don't ever let me go.'

'Never,' he told her. 'You're mine now, Tasha, and you'll stay mine throughout eternity and beyond.'

TIME FOR TRUST

CHAPTER ONE

JESSICA heard the grandfather clock striking eleven. She lifted her head from her work, her concentration broken. The grandfather clock had been acquired through the ancient custom of exchange and barter still very definitely alive in this quiet part of the Avon countryside.

At first she had been very pleased with her 'payment' for one of her larger tapestries; she had even continued to be pleased when the thing had virtually had to be dismantled in order to be installed in the small hallway of her stone cottage, and had then required the services of an extremely expensive and highly individualistic clock mender.

In fact, it was only when she realised what the clock was going to mean in terms of interruptions to her concentration on her work that she began to doubt the wisdom of owning it.

Mind you, she allowed fair-mindedly, it did have its advantages. For instance today, if it had not interrupted her, she would doubtless have worked on until it was far too late to go to the post office. Today, Wednesday, was half-day closing, and she had a tapestry finished and ready to post to the exclusive shop in Bath which sold her work for her.

She had always loved embroidery from being quite small. She remembered how amused and then irritated her parents had been with her interest in it.

Her interest in tapestry had come later, when she knew more about her subject. She had spent a wonderful summer training at the Royal School of Needlework which had confirmed her conviction that her love of the craft meant that she wanted it to be far more than merely a hobby.

Now, five years after that fateful summer, she spent her time either working for the National Trust on the conservation and repair of their tapestries or designing and making tapestries of her own—some for sale through the shop in Bath, and others on direct commissions from people who had seen her work and fallen in love with it.

The tapestry she was working on today was one such commission. Her workroom at the top of her small cottage had a large window to let in the light she needed for her work. It overlooked the countryside to the rear of the small row of cottages of which hers was one. This view had inspired many of her designs; every day it changed, sometimes subtly, sometimes dramatically, and she knew she would never tire of looking at it.

She loved this part of the country with its quiet peace—just as she loved the solitude of her work and life-style. Both made her feel secure . . . safe . . . And those were feelings she needed desperately.

She shivered a little. How long was it going to be before she succeeded in wiping her memory free of the past? How long was it going to be before she woke up in the morning without that clutching, panicky feeling of sick fear tensing her body?

She still had nightmares about it . . . Still remembered every vivid detail of that appalling day.

It had started so normally—getting up, leaving her parents' fashionable London house for work. Her father was the chairman of the élite merchant bank which had been founded one hundred and fifty years previously by his ancestor.

All her life, Jessica had been conscious of her parents' disappointment that their only child should be a daughter. Nothing was ever said, but all the time she was at school, being encouraged to work hard, to get good results, she had known of her parents' real feelings. She ought to have been a boy; a boy to follow in her father's footsteps, to head the bank and follow tradition. But she wasn't—she was a girl . . .

Every time she heard her father say that it made no difference, that these days women were equally as capable as men, that there was no reason at all why she should not eventually take his place, she had sensed his real feelings—had known that she must work doubly hard at school, that she must do everything she could to make up to her parents for the disappointment of her sex.

She had known from being quite young what fate held in store for her. She would go to university, get a degree and then join her father in the bank, where she would be trained for the important role that would one day be hers.

'And, of course, it isn't the end of the world,' she had once heard her father saying to her mother. 'One day she'll marry, and then there'll be grandsons . . .'

But by the time she left university with her degree, she had known that she didn't want to make a career in banking.

Every time she'd walked into the imposing Victorian edifice that housed the bank she had felt as though a heavy weight descended on her shoulders, as though something inside her was slowly dying.

Her father's plan was that she would follow in his footsteps, learning their business from the bottom rung, slowly making her way up the ladder, moving from department to department.

Everyone had been kind to her, but she had felt suffocated by the weight of her responsibility, by the bank itself and its solidity. Whenever she could she escaped to Avon to stay with her godmother, an old schoolfriend of her mother's.

She knew that she was disappointing her parents—that they could not understand the *malaise* that affected her.

And then came the event that was to have such a cataclysmic effect on her life...

Warningly, the clock chimed the quarter hour. She mustn't miss the post.

Sighing softly, she got up, a tall, almost too slender young woman, with a soft, full mouth and vulnerable grey eyes. Her hair was that shade somewhere between blonde and brown. The summer sun had lightened it in places, giving its smooth, straight length a fashionably highlighted effect.

As it swung forwards to obscure her profile she pushed it back off her face with a surprisingly strong and supple hand. Her wrists looked too fragile to support such strength, but her long hours spent working on her tapestries had strengthened the muscles.

This particular commission on which she was working was for a young couple who had recently moved into a large house just outside Bath. He was predictably something in the City. She was pleasant enough, but slightly pretentious. They had two children, both as yet under five, but both boys were down to attend prestigious boarding-schools.

The tapestry, a modern one, was to be the focal point of a large, rectangular, galleried hallway and was to be hung so that it was the first thing that caught the visitor's eye upon entering the house. Jessica had given a good deal of thought to its subject matter.

Arabella Moore had said vaguely that she was quite happy to leave everything to her; she had apparently seen some of her work in the shop in Bath, and had additionally read the very good report that had appeared in a prestigious glossy magazine, praising Jessica's innovative skills.

'Something amusing and witty,' was the only specification Arabella had made, and Jessica only hoped that her client would be happy with her design. As yet she had not started work on the tapestry itself. The design was still very much at the drawing-board stage, awaiting completion then approval from Arabella.

As always when she was engrossed in a project, Jessica resented anything that took her away from it.

As she went to open her workroom door she heard an indignant yowl from outside and grimaced to herself, wondering what trophy Cluny her cat had brought back for her to admire. Cluny had been a stray, rescued one stormy November night, when she had found him crouched, wet and shivering, in her back garden. Now fully grown, he was sleek and black, and full of his own importance.

She opened the door and looked outside, giving a faint sigh of relief at the lack of any small, furry corpse. Cluny was a hunter, and nothing she could say to him seemed to make any difference, so she had had to learn to live with his uncivilised habit of bringing her back gifts of small, pathetic, lifeless bodies.

Everyone had a right to life, she believed that most passionately and intensely, and always had, but her belief had grown stronger and fiercer ever since she herself had come face to face with the realisation that her own life could end between the taking of one breath and the next, and despite the security of her cottage and the sheltered life-style she now lived, seeing only a few close friends, admitting no one new to her circle until she felt completely secure with them, there was still that haunting fear which had never really left her.

It had been a good summer, but now they were into October, and the blue sky beyond her window held the clear pureness that warned of dropping temperatures. She was wearing jeans and a thick woollen sweater, because, despite the fact that the rest of the cottage was centrally heated, she preferred to keep her workroom free of anything that might damage the valuable antique tapestries she sometimes worked on at home.

The cottage had a sharp, narrow flight of stairs which she preferred to keep polished in the old-fashioned way, a central runner kept in place with stair-rods—both the rods and the runner had been lucky finds at an antique fair. The runner, once cleaned, had proved to have a strength of colour which went well with the cottage's oak stairs and floors.

Only one or two of her prospective clients had ever remarked that surely modern fitted carpets would be both warmer and cleaner, and these clients had always proved to be the difficult ones—the ones to whom her work was something that had newly become fashionable and who really had no true appreciation of its history and art.

Downstairs she had a small, comfortable sitting-room with windows overlooking her tiny front garden and beyond it the main road that ran through the village, and a good-sized kitchen-cum-dining-room-cum-sitting-room which she had furnished mainly with antiques picked up here and there from various sales.

Only the kitchen cupboards were modern, and that was because the lack of space forced her to make the maximum use of every corner. Solid oak and limed, they had been built by a local craftsman and added a pleasing lightness to the low-beamed ceilinged room.

A scrubbed farmhouse table divided the kitchen area of the room from the sitting area. She had retained the open fireplace, and alongside it against the wall was a comfortable sofa draped with a soft woollen blanket and covered with tapestry cushions.

The stone floor was warmed by a collection of rugs, but the thing that struck strangers most forcibly about Jessica's home was the startling amount of vibrant colour. Those who had only met her outside her home assumed that, because she chose to wear camouflage colours of beige, olive and taupe, her home would echo these subtle but sometimes dull shades. Instead, it was full of vibrant rich reds, blues, greens and golds put so harmoniously together that the surprised visitor came away with the sensation of having been exposed to something exceptionally alive and warming.

No one was more aware of dichotomy between her habitat and her personal mode of dress than Jessica herself. Once, as a child, she had pleaded with her mother to be allowed to have a rich ruby velvet dress. She could see it in her mind's eye now, feel the delicious warmth of the supple fabric, smell its rich scent. Her mother had been aghast, controlling her own distaste for the dress by gently pointing her in the direction of another one in muted olive Viyella. And she had learned then that little girls who were going to grow up to run a merchant bank did not dress in rich ruby velvet.

Now out of habit rather than anything else she still wore those same colours gently dictated by her mother. Not that clothes interested her anyway— not in the way that fabrics, colours and textures did. Clothes were simply the means one used to protect one's body from heat and cold . . . and, in her case, to provide her with the protection of anonymity.

No one would look twice at a slender young woman, unremarkable of face and figure, dressed in dull, practical clothes. No one would pick her out as a target . . . a victim . . .

Her parents had never understood her decision to come and live and work in Avon. They had pleaded with her to change her mind, but she had remained steadfast, and she had had the report of her doctor to back her up. Peace and tranquillity, relief from pressure, a need to recuperate and gather up her mental strength—that was what he had advised.

That had been five years ago. Now her parents accepted, albeit reluctantly, that she lived a different life from theirs.

Her mother had never given up trying to coax her back to London. Every few months she had a fresh attempt—still hoping, perhaps, for that all-important grandson—but Jessica shied away from the commitment that marriage involved. She was free for the first time in her life, and that was the way she intended to stay. Marriage meant responsibilities, duties, putting others' feelings first... She didn't want that.

In her hall she picked up her parcel and let herself out into the small front garden. The sun was warm, but the air cool once she stepped into the shadows. She paused to admire the dwarf Michaelmas daisies she had planted much earlier in the year. Their rich massing of purple, mauve and lilac pleased her and she bent to touch their petals gently. Gardening was her second love, and she planted her garden in much the same way as she worked on her tapestries, but with the artist's fine eye for colour and form.

The post office was the only shop in the village; the nearest garage was ten miles away in the small market town, and the post office was very much the focus of village life. Mrs Gillingham, who ran it, knew all the local gossip and passed it on to her customers with genial impartiality. Jessica interested her. It was unusual for so young and pretty a woman to live so very much alone. Martha Gillingham put her single state down to a broken romance in her past, romantically assuming that it was this relationship which had led to her arrival in the village and to her single state.

She was quite wrong.

Jessica had never been in love. Initially because there had never been time. At university she had worked desperately hard for her degree, terrified of disappointing her parents' hopes for her, and then when she joined the bank everyone had known exactly who she was—the daughter of the bank's chairman—and that knowledge had isolated her from the other young people working there.

And then, after what had happened, the last thing on her mind had been falling in love. She liked her single state and was content with it, but something in the speculative way Mrs Gillingham always questioned her about her private life made her feel raw and hurt inside, as though the postmistress had uncovered a wound she hadn't known was there.

Not that there was anything malicious in her questions. She was just inquisitive, and over the years Jessica had learned to parry them with tact and diplomacy.

Today she had the attention of the postmistress to herself. She was just waiting for her parcel to be weighed when she felt the cold rush of air behind her as the door opened.

The postmistress stopped what she was doing to smile warmly at the newcomer, exclaiming, 'Good morning, Mr Hayward! Are you all settled in yet?'

'Not yet, I'm afraid.'

The man had a deep, pleasant voice, and even without looking at him Jessica knew that he was smiling. She had heard from the milkman about this newcomer who had moved into the once lovely, but now derelict Carolean house on the outskirts of the village, but so far she hadn't actually met him.

'In fact, I was wondering if you could help me,' he was saying, and then added, 'but please finish serving this young lady first.'

The faint touch of reproof in his voice startled Jessica, giving the words far more than the form of mere good manners.

She turned round instinctively and was confronted by a tall, almost overpoweringly male man, dressed in jeans similar to her own and a thick sweater over a woollen shirt, his dark hair flecked with what looked like spots of white paint, and a rather grim expression in his eyes.

There was something about him that suggested that he wasn't the kind to suffer fools gladly. All Jessica knew about him was that he had bought the house at auction, and that he was planning to virtually camp out in it while the builders worked to make it habitable.

He had arrived in the village only that weekend, and had apparently been having most of his meals at the Bell, the local pub, because the kitchen up at the house was unusable.

She had heard that he worked in London, and that being the case Jessica would have thought it would be more sensible of him to stay there at least until such time as his house was habitable.

Mrs Gillingham had finished weighing the parcel, and, summing up the situation with a skilled and speedy eye, quickly performed introductions, giving Jessica no option but to take the hard brown hand extended to her and to respond to his quick 'Please call me Daniel,' with a similarly friendly gesture.

'Jessica Collingwood...' His eyebrows drew together briefly, as though somehow he was disconcerted, the pressure of his grip hardening slightly, and then he was relaxing, releasing her and saying evenly, 'Jessica—it suits you.'

And yet Jessica had the impression that the flattery was an absent-minded means of deflecting her attention away from that momentary tense surprise that had leapt to his eyes as he'd repeated her name.

Mrs Gillingham, eyeing them with satisfaction, went on enlighteningly. 'Jessica makes tapestries, Mr Hayward. You'll have to go and look at her work,' she added archly. 'It's just the sort of thing you're going to need for that house of yours.'

Jessica gritted her teeth at this piece of arch manipulation and hoped that Daniel Hayward would realise that this arrant piece of salesmanship was not at *her* instigation.

It seemed he did, because he gave her a warm, reassuring smile and then said ruefully, 'Unfortunately, before I can hang any tapestries on them I'm going to have to have some walls. This...' he touched his hair gingerly '...is the result of an unsafe ceiling collapsing on me this morning.' His face suddenly went grim and Jessica shivered, recognising that here was the real man, the pure male essence of him in the hard, flat determination she could read in his eyes.

'I've sacked the builder I was using for negligence, and I was hoping you might be able to give me the names of some others from whom I might get estimates...'

Mrs Gillingham pursed her mouth, trying not to look flattered by this appeal. 'Well, there's Ron Todd. He does a lot of work hereabouts...and then there's that man you had to do your kitchen, Jessica. What's his name?'

'Alan Pierce,' Jessica informed her, helplessly being drawn into the conversation, wanting to stay and bask in the warm admiration she could read so clearly in Daniel Hayward's lion-gold eyes, and at the same time wanting desperately to escape before she became helplessly involved in something she sensed instinctively was dangerous.

'Oh, yes, that's it... Well, he's very good. Made a fine job of Jessica's kitchen. You ought to see it...'

Numbly Jessica recognised that she was being given a very firm push in the direction Mrs Gillingham had decided she was going to take.

No need to enquire if Daniel Hayward was married or otherwise attached. Mrs Gillingham was a strict moralist, and if she was playing match-maker then it could only be in the knowledge that he was single.

Helplessly, torn between anger and a strange, sweet stirring of excited pleasure, she found herself stumblingly inviting Daniel to call round and see how Alan Pierce had transformed her two small, dark rooms into her large, comfortable living kitchen.

'But, of course... you must be busy... and...'

He started to say that he wasn't, when suddenly the post office door banged open.

A man came in, masked and holding a gun. He motioned to them all with it and said gutturally, 'Over there, all of you!'

Mrs Gillingham was protesting shrilly. At her side, Jessica was dimly conscious of Daniel Hayward's protective bulk coming between her and the man, but he couldn't protect her! Nothing could. It was her worst nightmare come back to haunt her. She started to tremble, dragged back into that time in the past—that awful, unforgettable day that had changed the whole course of her life...

CHAPTER TWO

JESSICA had left for work at eight o'clock as she always did. She liked to arrive at the bank at the same time as the other staff. Her father arrived later, his chauffeur dropping him off outside the bank's premises at about nine-thirty.

There was nothing remarkable about the day. It was late March, cold and blustery still, with no real hint of spring. She was wrapped up against the cold wind in the navy wool coat which seemed to be the uniform of ambitious, career-minded young women, her hair styled sleekly in the expensive bob that her parents liked so much, its colour subtly enlivened by monthly visits to an expensive Knightsbridge hairdresser.

Beneath her coat she was wearing a navy businesslike suit and a striped cotton blouse which more resembled a man's shirt than a woman's.

On her feet she had good quality, low-heeled leather pumps, and when she got on the tube she mingled anonymously into the crowd of similarly dressed young women.

The bank, like others of its kind, was situated inside that part of London known as the 'City', several streets off Threadneedle Street, taking up a prominent corner position in a small square.

The commissionaire greeted Jessica with a smile that held just that hint of knowing deference. She was acutely conscious of the fact that, while she was *supposed* to be treated just as any other junior member of the staff, she was in fact being handled cautiously with kid gloves not just by her fellow workers, but also by her superiors, all of whom were very conscious of the fact that she was the chairman's daughter.

It wasn't an enviable position, despite what some of her contemporaries thought—she had overheard one of the other girls making catty remarks about her in the cloakroom. She felt set apart from the other girls, alien to them, all too aware of their muted hostility.

Not that being her father's daughter actually afforded her the type of privileges they seemed to think. In the evening, when they were out discoing and enjoying themselves, *she* was at home being catechised by her father as to what she had learned. Her degree did not exempt her from sitting all her Institute exams, and she was all too conscious that he was expecting her to do well.

The pressure on her, well-meant and proud though it was, kept her weight a little under what it ought to be for her height. Even now, early in her working day, she was conscious of an unhealthy tension across her shoulder-blades.

Tonight was the night she went to advanced evening classes for embroidery; the one bright shining pleasure in her otherwise tension-filled week.

She knew that, no matter how much she strove, working in the bank was never going to be anything other than a duty, and a reluctant one at that, but she just couldn't bring herself to disappoint her parents—especially her father—by telling them that she could not fulfil their ambitions for her.

This particular morning there was no commissionaire on duty, but when she turned the handle on the door of the back entrance to the bank, which the staff used on arriving and leaving, she found that the door was unlocked.

She walked into the familiar Stygian darkness of the narrow Victorian passage that led to the offices and cubby-holes at the back of the banking hall proper.

The first thing that struck her as she emerged into the general office was the silence . . . the second was the group of masked, armed men, one of whom was advancing grimly towards her, the rest holding the other members of the staff in a silent, threatened group.

'Get over there and keep your mouth closed.'

Her body trembling with shock, she did as she was instructed. It took several seconds for it to fully dawn on her that this was that most dreaded of all events within the banking community—an armed bank raid.

In such events, all bank staff were instructed not to try to do anything that might risk either their lives or those of others.

As she joined the silent group, Jessica saw that her father's second in command was among them, his normally highly coloured fleshy features a shade of old tallow. As her father's second in command he was in charge of one set of vault keys, while the bank accountant held the other. Together every morning they would unlock the vault so that the cashiers could collect cash for their tills.

Whenever necessary, and never normally on a regular basis, fresh supplies of cash were delivered from the nearby Bank of England. Only yesterday, late in the afternoon after close of banking hours, they had received an exceptionally large consignment of cash, and Jessica realised in sick fear that somehow the thieves must have known of this.

In retrospect, the ordeal of waiting while each member of staff arrived and was duly imprisoned with his or her colleagues seemed to be dragged out over a lifetime of unimaginable terror and shock.

None of them had any way of knowing what was to happen to them...whether they would all emerge unharmed from their ordeal.

On this particular day, Jessica knew that her father was not due into the bank until after lunch, having a morning appointment with an important customer. It seemed the thieves knew it as well, because just as soon as they were sure that all the staff had arrived they took them all at gunpoint to one of the large safes beneath the branch and shut them in it under armed guard.

Still forbidden to speak, and under the silent, masked threat of the gunmen facing them, they felt tension fill the room like a sour taste in the air.

All of them were close to breaking-point, but still it came as something of a shock when one of the other girls, the one who had been so catty about her working in the bank, suddenly called out frantically to their guard, '*She's* the one you ought to be concentrating on. She's the chairman's daughter. She's far more use to you than we are.'

Jessica held her breath, her chest painfully tight with anxiety and fear as the gunman turned slowly in her direction. Through the slits in his mask, she could see the icy glitter of his eyes. He motioned to her to step forward. When she hesitated, John Knowles, the accountant, bravely stepped in front of her, saying quickly, 'She's just a girl. Let her be.'

When the gunman hit him on the side of his head with the butt of his gun, a massed audible breath of shock rippled through them all.

Shaking with tension, Jessica obeyed the gunman's instruction to step forward. He walked slowly round her, the sensation of him standing behind her making the hairs rise in the nape of her neck.

So this was terror, this thick, cold sensation that bordered on paralysis, freezing the body and yet leaving the mind sharply clear to assimilate the vulnerabilities of her position.

The sound of the safe door opening took the gunman from behind her to join his fellow members of the gang. In the low-toned conversation they exchanged Jessica caught her own name, but not much else, and then to her horror she was being told to walk towards them. Flanked on either side by a gunman, she was escorted from the safe.

Hearing the safe door clang closed behind her was the very worst sound she had ever heard. Behind that closed door were her colleagues, safe now, surely, while she...

'Better take her upstairs to the boss,' the second gunman instructed the first.

The 'boss' was a powerfully built man with the coldest, shrewdest eyes she had ever seen.

'Chairman's daughter, is she?' he repeated when informed of her status.

'Yeah. I thought we could get a good ransom.'

A quick turn of the 'boss's' hand silenced her jailer.

'We'll take her with us,' the 'boss' announced chillingly after studying her for several seconds. 'She can be our insurance.'

What followed still haunted her in her nightmares. Blindfolded and gagged, she was bundled out of the bank and directly into the kind of armoured vehicle normally used by security companies. Once inside she could sense the presence of other people, even though they remained silent.

The van was driven away and she heard someone saying, 'How long do you reckon before anyone can raise the alarm?'

'Bank's supposed to be open in five minutes. That should give us half an hour or so before anyone realises what's happened... It will take them a fair time to break into the safe. The only other set of keys are held by the chairman, and he's out in Kent.'

'By the time they do get hold of them we'll——'

A sudden curse obviously reminded the speaker of her presence and he fell silent. She was sitting on the floor of the van, bound, blindfolded and gagged. Her body ached from the pressure of the hard floor and the fear-induced tension. She was sure she was going to die, to become another statistic of violence and greed, and when the van finally stopped and she was bundled out and half dragged, half carried up flight after flight of stairs and then pushed in a dank, foul-smelling room she was even more convinced that this was the end.

She heard the door close but dared not move, not knowing how many members of the gang were preserving a silent vigil around her. The silence went on and on, a relentless pressure against her stretched eardrums, like a soundless, high-pitched scream, battering at her senses.

Time lost all meaning. Her arms and hands were numb, but still she dared not move, picturing the armed man perhaps sitting in front of her, watching her. Her throat was dry and sore, but she couldn't ask for a drink. Her body ached, and cramp ran like a violent wrenching wire from her left calf to her ankle.

Outwardly motionless and controlled, inwardly she was falling apart, suffering the most appalling imagined fates, wondering if whoever had said those immortal words 'a brave man dies once, the coward a thousand times over' had really any awareness of the true terrors created by the imagination—terrors which had nothing whatsoever to do with one's ability to endure actual physical pain.

At some point she slipped into a semi-comatose state that gave her some relief, a sort of self-induced, drugged miasma of mental agony which separated her from her physical body and its discomforts. She couldn't move at all... couldn't do anything other than sit there where she had been left, straining her ears for some other movement in the room.

Quite when she began to realise she might be on her own she had no idea; perhaps it was when the quality of the silence struck her as being empty. She held her breath, listening anxiously for the sound of other breath, trying not to imagine the grinning faces of the gang while they witnessed her pathetic attempts to use what senses were left to her to work out if they were there.

If they were there... She was almost sure they weren't. Which meant... which meant that she was alone.

She ought to have felt relief, but instead she felt all the blind, frantic panic of a helpless child deserted by its parents. She couldn't move—her wrists were bound and so were her ankles, and her wrists were tied to some kind of pipe.

She heard a noise—not a human sound... The hairs on her arms stood up in terror as she felt something run across her bare leg. She wanted desperately to scream, but couldn't remove the gag nor scream through it.

Panic engulfed her; she tried desperately to pull herself free, and succeeded only in rubbing her wrists raw on their bonds so that the broken skin bled.

After panic and terror came dull, destructive acceptance. She was going to die here in this unknown place, and she might as well resign herself to it.

How long had she been here already? Hours... but how many?

She tried to think constructively, but it was impossible. All she wanted now was oblivion, escape...

When the door finally opened, her rescuers were all moved to different degrees of shock and pity by what they saw.

A telephone call to the bank had announced that any attempt to find her or them during the next five hours would result in her death, but that if no attempt was made to track them down for that period then her father would be informed of where she could be found.

Since the police had no idea of where to start looking for the thieves, they had had no option other than to comply with their demands, and against all their expectations they had actually received the promised call later in the day giving the address of a slum-clearance flat in a high-rise block where she could be found.

To Jessica, the debriefing that followed her imprisonment was almost as gruelling as the imprisonment itself, although in a different way.

The whole nightmare affair had left her perilously close to the edge of a complete mental and physical breakdown, with the result that she had finally told her parents that she could not return to the bank, and that instead she was going to use the small inheritance left to her by her maternal grandparents to train for a career much more suited to her now fierce determination to live as quiet and safe a life as possible.

Of course her parents had protested, especially when they had learned she intended moving to Avon.

There was no reason why she couldn't continue to live at home in London and practise her career from there, they told her, but she refused to be swayed. London was now a place that terrified her. She couldn't walk down a busy street without being overcome by the feeling that someone was walking behind her, stalking her—without the fear she had known in that small, frightening prison coming back to drag her back down into the pit of self-destructive fear she was only just beginning to leave behind.

In the end her parents had reluctantly given way on the advice of her doctor, who had told them that she needed to find a way of healing herself and coming to terms with what had happened.

That healing process was still going on, and now, suddenly and shockingly, she had been dragged back into that remembered horror.

She saw the gunman coming towards her and started to scream. He lashed out at her with the butt of his gun. She felt a stunning pain like fire in her shoulder, followed by a cold wash of paralysing weakness, and knew that she was going to faint.

When she came round, the small post office was full of people. She was lying on the floor with something under her head and someone kneeling beside her holding her wrist while he measured her pulse.

She looked up cold with fear, trembling with the remembered shock of the past, and encountered the warm gold eyes of Daniel Hayward. His look of warmth and compassion was reassuring and comforting. She tried to sit up, conscious of her undignified prone position and the curious glances of the people standing around her.

As she looked round the shop, Daniel Hayward seemed to know what she was looking for and said quietly, 'It's all right. He's gone.'

'Gone?'

She looked bewildered, and it was left to Mrs Gillingham to explain excitedly, 'Mr Hayward was ever so brave. He reached right out and took the gun off him, and told me to open the door and shout for help.'

While Jessica looked uncomprehendingly at him, he said humorously, 'Not brave, really. I simply made use of the excellent distraction you provided by drawing our friend's fire, although such a course of action is not really to be recommended. You'll be lucky if your arm isn't out of action for a good few days, I'm afraid.'

Her arm . . . Jessica tried to lift it and gasped as the pain coursed like fire though the bruised muscles.

'It's all right...nothing's actually broken,' Daniel Hayward was telling her reassuringly. 'But that was a nasty blow you took, and there's bound to be some very considerable bruising. Look,' he offered quietly, 'why don't you let me take you home? I've got my car outside. Mrs Gillingham has sent someone to fetch the doctor, but I think you'll feel much more comfortable lying on your own bed than lying here...'

He was so understanding, so concerned, so gentle in the way that he touched her, gently helping her to her feet. She couldn't ever remember a man treating her like this before, nor herself wanting one to. Almost instinctively she leaned against him, letting him take her slender weight as he guided her towards the door, politely refusing the offers of help showered on them both.

'I suspect the police will probably want to interview you later,' he told her gently as he settled her in the passenger seat of an immaculate and brand new Daimler saloon. Her father always drove a Daimler, and she was aware of a certain, unexpected nostalgic yearning for her parents' presence as he set the car in motion.

The last time she had seen them had been Christmas, when she had paid a reluctant duty visit to her old home. She had been on edge and nervous the whole time she was there—not so much because of her old fear of London's crowds and anonymity, she had recognised in some surprise, but because of her deep-rooted guilt, and fear that somehow or other her parents would succeed in gently pressuring her into returning to her old life... a life she knew she could no longer tolerate because of the restrictions it placed upon her.

Although the gulf between them saddened her, although she was still consumed with guilt in knowing that she had let them down, she still found her new life immensely fulfilling—immensely satisfying and pleasing in an entirely personal and difficult-to-explain way, other than to say it was as though she had now found a piece of herself which had previously been missing, and that in doing so she had completed her personality, making it whole.

'Which house is it?' Daniel Hayward asked her. 'Mrs G said it was along here somewhere...'

She gathered her thoughts and indicated which house was hers, conscious of the discreet twitching of curtains as he stopped the Daimler outside and then got out.

Her neighbours were elderly and very kind, and would doubtless be all agog with curiosity and shock once they heard what had happened.

It had been idiotic of her to react like that. The man had obviously not been much of a threat after all, but she had panicked remembering...

'I think I'd better carry you inside,' Daniel told her easily. 'You still look pretty groggy.'

She wanted to protest, but she felt too weak, her body fluid and amorphous as he swung her up into his arms. It was only a short distance to her front door, but long enough for her to feel the measured beat of his heart and to register the strength in the arms which held her.

Such intimacy with another human being was alien and unfamiliar to her, and yet beneath the rapid thudding of her pulse, beneath the dregs of fear induced by the attempted robbery, and beneath even the instinctive, defensive coiling of her muscles as they locked in protest against the sensation of being so completely within the physical power of someone else, ran another feeling, slow, golden, like a full and lazy river warmed by a summer's heat, its flow so deceptively slow that one wasn't aware of the relentlessness of its strength until it was too late to swim against it.

Her heart seemed to miss a beat and then another; her fingers curled into the roughness of his sweater, and, as though he sensed what was running through her mind and the enormity of her struggle to comprehend the bewildering range of the conflicting emotions she was suffering, he looked at her, the golden eyes calm and gentle, almost as though he knew her fear and was reassuring her.

As he unlocked the door to her house and carried her inside she had the crazy feeling that an intimacy had been born between them that cut through the normal barriers of convention and defensiveness which held the sexes apart. It was as though at some very deep level they had reached out and communicated wordlessly with one another, and that that communication held a silent promise for both their futures. What futures? She was alone, independent, by preference, by choice.

It was odd to hear him ask her quite mundanely, 'Shall I help you upstairs, or...?'

She shook her head.

'No... The sofa in the kitchen will be just as comfortable as my bed,' she told him quickly. 'It's through that door.'

He put her down and then announced that he intended to stay with her until the doctor arrived to check her over, softening his statement with a warm smile. In repose his face possessed a hard purposefulness which in other circumstances would have repelled her. It made him look too much like the fiercely competitive and power-hungry men who moved in her parents' social circle.

The thought disconcerted her, and as he released her he frowned and asked curtly, 'What's wrong? Did I hurt you?'

The words seemed to echo warningly inside her, making her shiver with the knowledge of how easily this man *could* hurt her, and then she looked up at him and saw only the concern softening the harshness of his face, and the anxiety shadowing the clear golden warmth of his eyes.

She shook her head, half marvelling at how at ease she felt with him, almost as though he were an old and valued friend.

But he was a stranger—outwardly at least—and she was perhaps reading more into his kindness than she ought, taking up more of his time than she ought, allowing him far more into her life than she ought.

As she struggled to thank him and offer him an opportunity to leave, he stunned her by taking hold of her hands and holding them firmly within the grip of his own.

'I'm staying,' he told her evenly.

His palms were slightly calloused, the strength in his grip reminding her of his maleness. Comforting her. In reality the last thing she wanted was to be left alone to relive the horror of that other time...to remember the choking, destructive horror of the fear she had experienced then. That must be why she felt almost like clinging to him, why she wanted to be with him.

While they were waiting for the doctor he made them both a cup of tea, nodding approvingly when he saw the squat canisters with their differing blends of leaves so much more flavorsome than the dull uniformity of mass-produced tea-bags.

The one he chose, Russian Caravan, was one of her own favourites, drunk piping hot, its taste sharpened with a slice of lemon.

He let her sip hers in silence and then said, complimenting her, 'I like this room. It's comfortable... lived in. It has the kind of ambiance I want for my own place.'

Jessica laughed, amused that this obviously wealthy man whose house, even in its present state of dereliction, was far grander than her own small cottage should admire her simple décor.

'I should have thought for a house like yours you'd have wanted to get in interior designers,' she commented.

To her surprise he shook his head.

'No. The house is going to be my home, not a set piece that looks like a photograph out of a glossy magazine. Mind you, I'm a long way from the decorating and furnishing stage as yet. As I discovered this morning, there's some pretty bad damp damage, and an awful lot of restoration work to be done, simply to bring the fabric of the building up to scratch. At the moment I'm virtually camped out in a couple of rooms.' He grimaced wryly. 'I was hoping to get the worst of the repairs over before Christmas, that's why I'm so damned annoyed with this builder.'

'Wouldn't it have been more sensible to stay in London at least until the house is habitable?' Jessica asked him, curiosity about him overcoming the dull ache in her arm.

'Sensible, perhaps,' he agreed. 'But there comes a time when living and working at the hectic pace demanded by city life begins to pall. My business necessitates my working in the City, but I don't have to live there. Once I'd made the choice to move out...' He shrugged meaningfully, and Jessica guessed that he was a man who, once he had made a decision, seldom changed his mind.

'Your business...?' she asked and then hesitated, wondering if her questions were too intrusive. She had never felt anything to match the fierce need she was now experiencing to know everything there was to know about this man. He filled her senses, absorbing her attention to the exclusion of everything else, and these sensations were a phenomenon to her. She found it hard to understand how she, normally so cautious in her dealings with others, could feel so at ease with this stranger, and yet at the same time so keyed up, so buoyed up by his presence that everything in her life now seemed to be coloured by her reactions to him.

She sensed his hesitation in answering her question and flushed uncomfortably. Was she being too pushy, too inquisitive? After all, she had no previous experience to go on—no past relationships in her life to show her how to deal with the sensations he was arousing inside her.

But at last he answered her, his voice oddly sombre as he told her almost reluctantly, 'I'm an economist. I work in the City.'

An economist. She guessed vaguely that he was probably involved in some way with the stock market, and, knowing how secretive people involved in the sales of stocks and shares sometimes had to be, she felt she could understand his reticence and quickly changed the subject.

'Quite a few City people have moved out this way recently, although we are a bit off the beaten track. It isn't unknown for the village to be snowed in in a bad winter,' she warned him, but he laughed and seemed unconcerned by the threat of not being able to reach the City.

'What about you?' he challenged her. 'I've already heard all about your tapestries. In fact, I suspect that the marvellous creation I recently admired hanging on a friend's wall was designed and made by you, but surely from a selling point of view you'd do better living somewhere, if not central to London, then, say, like Bath, where there's a thriving interior decoration industry.'

'I don't like cities... or crowds,' she told him shortly. The ache in her shoulder was nagging painfully. 'I prefer to live somewhere quiet.'

'And isolated?' he probed skilfully, the golden eyes watching her as she looked at him in startled defensiveness. 'It wasn't so difficult to deduce,' he told her gently, as though answering her unspoken question. 'A very attractive and clever young woman living alone in a tiny rural village; a young woman whom it is obvious was not born and bred here, and whose skills have a much wider field of demand than her environs suggest. What happened?' he asked gently.

Tears clogged her throat. This was the first time anyone had asked her about the past; the first time anyone had seen past her defences and guessed that there was more to her desire to live so quietly than merely a love of the Avon countryside. She wanted to tell him, and yet conversely was afraid to do so. Why? In case he dismissed her fears as trivial and foolish as her parents had done? In case he was embarrassed by them as her London friends had been? Or just in case he simply did not understand the trauma of what she had endured and how it had affected her?

Panic suddenly overwhelmed her, followed by the old dread of talking to anyone about what she had endured—a fear which her doctor told her probably sprang from an atavistic belief that, in somehow refusing to talk about her ordeal, she was succeeding in shutting herself off from it, and that her reluctance to talk about it sprang from a deep-rooted dread that, once she did, her old terror would mushroom and overwhelm her, growing beyond her control to the point where it dragged her down and consumed her.

Her throat muscles locked, her body suddenly tense as she sat crouched on the sofa, defensive and inarticulate, the half of her brain that could still reason knowing that he must be wondering what on earth he had said to spark off such a reaction, and dreading him withdrawing from her.

A sound beyond the room distracted him. He lifted his head, frowning, and then said quietly, 'I think the doctor has probably arrived. I'll go and let him in.'

Tactfully he offered to leave her alone with the doctor, but she shook her head, wanting his presence, feeling protected and comforted by it, and yet at the same time feeling guilty, because she was imposing on him.

When she tried to say as much he shook his head and then took hold of both her hands, saying quietly, 'No, never... I want to stay.'

And then he smiled at her, and in the warmth of his eyes she saw a promise that dazzled and awed her. He shared her awareness of that instant and shocking recognition, that sensation of feeling inexplicably attuned to one another. She had heard of people falling in love at first sight. Was this what had happened to them?

But falling in love was an ephemeral, laughable thing that only happened to the reckless and impulsive, and she was neither of those. There was nothing shallow about the way she felt about him. No. This was more than a sense of recognition, of knowing that here was a man who seemed to understand, as though by instinct, everything there was to know about her—about her fears and apprehensions, about her weaknesses and strengths. Indeed, it was almost as though he possessed some deep inner knowledge of her that enabled him to recognise her every emotion and feeling.

He deliberately busied himself clearing away their china mugs and emptying the teapot while the doctor asked her to remove her sweater and examined her injured shoulder and arm.

Already both were painfully swollen, showing evidence of the bruising that was yet to come.

'Mm... Nothing's broken, but you're going to find that arm painful and stiff for a few days, I'm afraid. I think it might be as well to rest it in a sling at least for the next forty-eight hours.'

It would have to be her right arm, Jessica reflected wryly as the doctor rummaged in his bag for an antiseptic pack containing the requisite sling.

'I can leave you some pain-killers,' he suggested, eyeing her thoughtfully. 'Generally speaking, when a patient suffers extreme shock as you have done I can prescribe a mild sleeping tablet...'

Jessica shuddered and shook her head. She remembered the drugs she had been prescribed before, supposedly to help her sleep, but which in reality had doped and numbed her to such an extent that they had actually intensified her struggle to come to terms with her residual fear once she was without the crutch they offered.

'Sensible girl,' the doctor approved. 'A mild sedative isn't necessarily addictive, but I don't like prescribing them unless it's absolutely essential. If you want my advice, perhaps a good tot of brandy in your bedtime cocoa is just as effective.'

And equally addictive, Jessica thought to herself, but he was an old-fashioned doctor, with his patients' welfare very much at heart.

He closed his bag and turned to leave, pausing by the door to frown and ask, 'You live here alone, don't you?'

Jessica nodded, a cold finger of ice touching her spine, and she asked quickly, 'What's wrong? The man didn't escape, did he? I thought...'

'No, nothing like that,' he was quick to reassure her. 'It's just that with that arm you might be better having someone staying here overnight with you. Just in case you're tempted to dispense with the sling and overstrain the muscle. I could have a word with Mrs G——'

'There's no need,' Daniel intervened unexpectedly. 'I shall be staying here tonight.'

Jessica gasped, but the small sound was lost as the doctor nodded his approval and opened the door saying, 'No... No, there's no need to see me out. Nasty business altogether. Who'd have thought, in a small village like this...? Lucky thing you acted so promptly, young man...'

His voice faded away as Daniel ignored his protests and escorted him to the door. Jessica waited tensely as the door closed and she heard Daniel walking back to the kitchen.

'Yes. I know,' he said calmly as he came in. 'I jumped in there without consulting you, but I thought you'd prefer my presence to that of Mrs G, good neighbour though she is. If I was wrong...'

Jessica shook her head. He wasn't wrong at all, but they hardly knew one another. Until a few short hours ago they had been strangers, and, despite the fact that she felt drawn to him in a way she had never before experienced, the habits of a lifetime could not be so easily overthrown. She plucked nervously at her sweater with fingers that trembled a little, unable to bring herself to look at him in case she saw mockery in those too perceptive gold eyes.

'You're worried about what people might say about my staying here, is that it?' he asked her quietly.

Instantly her head shot up, her eyes blazing with pride and anger.

'Certainly not,' she told him curtly. 'I'm not so narrow-minded nor insular. I prefer to set my own standards for the way I live my life, not pay lip-service to other people's.'

'Then what *are* you afraid of?' he asked her gently, dropping down on to the sofa beside her, sitting so close to her that she could feel the heat passing from his body to her own, an unnerving, vibrant male heat that made her body quicken and her muscles tense—in expectation, not fear. 'Not me, surely?'

How could she tell him it was herself she feared, and her out-of-character reactions to him?

'I'm just not used to sharing my home with anyone,' she told him evasively.

'I'm invading your privacy, and you're not sure how you feel about it, is that it? Well, I can understand that. Like you I, too, prize my solitude. Like you I've always preferred to live alone. However, there comes a time...'

His voice had slowed and deepened. Without looking at him she sensed that he had moved closer to her, felt it in the warm vibration of his breath against her temple, and quivered in silent reaction to it.

When he reached for her hand she let him take it, even though she knew what her trembling would reveal to him.

With his other hand he cupped her face and turned it so that he could look at her. The warm grasp of his hand was somehow reassuring, as though he knew what she was feeling.

'If I'm presuming too much... if I'm letting my own feelings and reactions blind me into believing that what's happening between us is mutual, then tell me so, Jessica.'

An idiotic shyness swamped her, and it was as much as she could do to shake her head, her throat clogged with emotional tension.

'There are so many things we still have to learn about one another... so many things we still don't know or share, but there will be time for us to discover and learn all those things. For now shall we simply let it be enough that we're here together at the beginning of a journey we both want to share?'

Gratefully Jessica nodded her head.

He was telling her that he wasn't going to rush or pressure her. He seemed to know how unused she was to everything that was happening to her, how alarmed she was by it, at the same time as she thrilled to the knowledge that he shared her feeling; she who had never wanted this kind of involvement suddenly wanted it desperately.

As she looked at him, she wondered blindingly what it would be like when he kissed her, and as though he had read the question in her eyes his own suddenly darkened awesomely.

'Don't,' he warned her huskily, and then added, 'Once I start touching you I shan't be able to stop.'

Shockingly, her body responded to his warning so intensely that for a moment she was almost tempted into reckless incitement of the desire she saw burning in his eyes. She looked at his mouth and felt her body tremble. She reached out to touch her fingers to the male texture of his lips, to explore their shape and form, and then sanity prevailed and she drew back, her face betraying her own bewilderment.

Fighting to master the temptation flooding her, she said unsteadily, 'Tell me about your house. How did you find it? What do you plan to do with it? You're our first really local migrant from London, you realise. There are others, but they live on the other side of Blanchester. What brought you out as far as this?'

She was desperately trying to distract herself, to bring herself back on an even keel, and so missed the sudden tension of his body, the brief hesitation as he replied, 'Chance, really. I'd been looking for a house outside London for some time, and then someone mentioned this village.'

'Someone mentioned it?' Jessica looked at him, frowning, and then her frown cleared. 'Oh, you mean your estate agents. Well, they must have been relieved to have sold the Court. It's been empty for almost two years, and it's been badly vandalised.'

'You don't have to tell me that,' Daniel told her wryly. 'When you feel up to it, I'd like to have your views on how best to redesign the kitchen. My existing builder is a bit short on imagination, and

I want to avoid the stereotyped blandness so prevalent among kitchen designers. It will be a good-sized room: two rooms, really, since I'm having the wall between it and what was at one time the housekeeper's room knocked down.'

Gradually the sexual tension was easing from her body, to be replaced by a genuine interest in his plans for the house. When he glanced at his watch and informed her that it was almost seven o'clock she could hardly believe it.

'Will you be OK if I leave you for long enough to go and collect a few things?' he asked her. 'I could ask Mrs G to sit with you...'

Jessica shook her head. 'I'll be fine. Really, you don't need to stay overnight. I——'

'I'm staying,' he told her gently. 'And don't you dare move from that sofa until I get back. Remember what the doctor said about not straining the muscles.'

It wasn't very difficult to obey him; in fact, it wasn't any hardship at all to simply sit there and give in to the luxury of day-dreaming about the promises that had been implicit in almost everything he had said to her.

She had never believed this would happen to her—that she would meet someone and fall in love so quickly and intensely that within a few short hours it would be impossible to imagine her life without him—but it *had* happened, and not just to her, but to him as well.

She closed her eyes and gave in to the temptation of imagining what it would feel like to have his mouth moving on hers, his hands touching her skin, exploring her body with all the delicate skill his touch had already promised.

A rash of goose-bumps broke out under her skin, a tense, coiling sensation invading her lower stomach.

Physical desire... Up until now she had been a stranger to such feelings, so what was it about this particular man encountered in such harrowing circumstances that had led to its birth now?

Were the feelings, both emotional and physical, which she was experiencing genuine, or were they some kind of by-product of her fear?

Deep within her a part of herself recognised that alongside her burgeoning happiness ran a fine thread of cautious reluctance, as though that part of her was unwilling to allow itself to be committed to what she was feeling for Daniel.

She was too exhausted to dwell on the matter. Upstairs in her workroom, the phone rang. That was her business line, and by rights she ought to go up there and answer it. She was doing quite well now, but not so well that she could afford to turn down business.

Daniel had been so kind to her. So caring. Surely far more so than she, as a stranger to him, merited, and it struck her that he himself must be a very well-adjusted human being to be able to reach out so readily and warmly to a stranger, disregarding the possibility of their rejection. She realised that in similar circumstances she would most probably not have offered the same Good-Samaritan-inspired kindness, not because she would not have wanted to, but because she would have been afraid, as she suspected many people were afraid, of having her offer misconstrued or, even worse, resented. If she had spurned Daniel's kindness and retreated into the prickly sharp shell she normally used to conceal her true self from strangers, she suspected that he would have treated her reaction with equally considerate and thoughtful kindness.

He was plainly a man of intense generosity of spirit, and it humbled her that he should choose to treat her as his equal when she knew that inwardly she was nothing of the sort. She tended to hold even people who knew her at a distance, deliberately refusing to let them trespass too far.

Daniel was the first person in a long time whom she had actually wanted to draw into her life.

After her ordeal her doctor had explained these negative feelings as resulting from the long years of self-induced pressure when she had forced herself to conform and to be the daughter her parents wanted her to be. That they were her own form of rebellion against that stifling pressure.

Now, in retrospect, she felt ashamed of the way she had panicked this morning. No one else had. Mrs G, older than her and a lot frailer, had managed to cope with the situation. Exhaustion was numbing her brain. She was too tired to think any longer. She looked at her watch. Daniel had been gone just over an hour. Where was he? Had he changed his mind, had second thoughts?

About what? she scoffed to herself. All he had offered to do was to stay the night with her on a purely altruistic and non-sexual basis. It was not as though, after all, he was about to move in with her as her lover.

But if he was—— Abruptly she stifled the thought. It was too soon, much too soon for those kinds of thoughts.

CHAPTER THREE

WHEN Daniel returned Jessica was asleep. He woke her gently, smiling down into her unmasked eyes as they opened and widened in pleased recognition.

'Sorry it took so long, but I had to go to the pub to explain why I wouldn't be in for my usual evening meal. Of course, they'd heard all about the raid and wanted to know if you were all right. Mrs Markham insisted on giving me a couple of cold chicken salads for tonight, and she said to tell you if there's anything at all she can do, any shopping you want done...'

Stupidly, the thought of such kindness made her eyes fill with tears. She only knew the landlady of the local pub very casually, although she had heard that she was a highly organised and very capable woman under whose management the Bell had risen from a rather lacklustre village pub to a favourite eating place for locals in the know.

'Hey, come on... What did I say?' Daniel teased her gently, producing a clean handkerchief and mopping up her tears as easily and casually as though he had been doing it for years; as though he had known for years of this idiotic weakness of hers for bursting into tears every time she saw a sad film or heard or read something that choked her with emotion.

'I forgot to ask earlier,' he added, 'but is there anyone you want to get in touch with?'

'Get in touch with?' She stared at him.

'Yes, you know... your family.'

'My family?' Her frown deepened, and then she said shortly, 'No... No...' Habit prevented her from lying, and forced her to say unevenly, 'My parents...' the words 'wouldn't be interested' stuck in her throat because she knew they weren't true. Her mother would be down here just as fast as her father's chauffeur could bring her, but her mother fussing around her, rallying her, coaxing and persuading her to return to London was the last thing she wanted right now, and besides... besides...

Selfishly, all she wanted was to be with Daniel.

To ease her conscience she told him quickly, 'My parents lead very busy lives. There's no point in worrying them about this. After all, it's only a bit of bruising.'

The look Daniel was giving her made her flush and feel oddly defensive. She had seen his hawk's eyes warm with compassion and concern; she had seen them dark with the beginnings of passion, but now for the first time she was seeing them harden fractionally, as though accusing her. But of what...?

'As you're being kind enough to go to the trouble of staying here tonight to keep an eye on me, the least thing I can do is to provide you with a meal,' she announced brightly, deliberately changing the subject and trying to get up.

'Not tonight, I think,' Daniel admonished her. 'The doctor said you were to rest... remember?'

'He said I was to rest my arm,' Jessica protested, smiling. 'The rest of me is fully functional.'

He had been watching her as she spoke, and suddenly something vibrant and masculine flared in his eyes and his glance dropped quite deliberately to her body, making a caressing and lingering study of its curves and angles before he said softly, 'It's far more than merely functional.' And then, while she was still flushing, he got up and asked, 'Which room am I to sleep in? I'll take this stuff up there out of the way, and then I suggest that for tonight at least we make do with Mrs Markham's excellent chicken and even better apple pie.'

The heat was still coursing through her body in the aftermath of his deliberate erotic scrutiny of her, and it took her several seconds to pull herself together enough to say distractedly, 'Which room? Oh, there are only two. The spare room faces the street.'

Her eyes focused betrayingly on him as he bent to remove his leather holdall from the floor.

The leather was soft and worn, the holdall unadorned with gimmicky logos, unostentatious and battered, but Jessica recognised its quality none the less. She suspected that had she looked inside it she would have seen tucked discreetly almost out of sight a name familiar to her from her father's luggage. It was his proud boast that he had been given his cases second-hand by an uncle, when he first went up to Oxford, and that he still found them far superior to anything that modern science could produce.

Seeing the familiar brown leather reminded her sharply of her parents and of the gulf that lay between them; a gulf she felt it necessary to maintain to preserve her own independence.

Oh, there was no open rift. Whenever her mother could coax her home they welcomed her with open arms, and she knew quite well that nothing would delight her parents more than to have her living with them once more. Nothing . . . unless it was the news that she was married and pregnant with a grandson. A grandson who would take the place in the bank which she had rejected.

The last time she had been home her cousin had been visiting with her parents. Jessica wasn't particularly fond of Emma. Her cousin was the only child of her mother's sister and her husband.

Emma's father was a country solicitor, and comfortably rather than well off. Jessica suspected that Emma had always resented the fact that her aunt and uncle were far more wealthy than her parents.

They had both attended the same private school. There were only a few months' difference in their ages, and while they were at school Emma had often behaved towards her in a way that was spiteful and jealous.

Now they rarely saw one another. Emma worked in a very expensive and up-market Kensington boutique, and she had long ago announced that it was her sole ambition to find a man rich enough to support her in the same style that Jessica's father supported his family.

'But so many marriages end in divorce, and if you don't love him in the first place...' Jessica had objected sharply, shocked by Emma's revelations.

'Judgemental Jessica, all pi and prudery,' Emma had taunted her. 'So what if it does? You can be sure that I'll make sure I don't come out of any divorce without a substantial sum of money. It's all right for you to look down and sneer. You don't know what real life's all about. Your father's a millionaire.'

'Money isn't everything,' Jessica had told her.

Emma had laughed shrilly. 'Only *you* could come out with a statement like that. Of course it isn't to you...'

That had been when they were both eighteen.

Later, after Jessica's ordeal, Emma had come to see her at home. On the verge of getting engaged to an extremely wealthy minor baronet, she had been seething with resentment and anger because her quarry had been snatched out of her grasp at the last moment by his domineering and extremely protective mother. When she heard that Jessica didn't intend returning to the bank, she had been derisive.

'My God...if only I had your opportunities. You're a fool, Jess. Turning your back on the bank and setting yourself up as some dreary little sewing woman. You're a fool. Do you know that?'

Jessica had ignored her jibes about her embroidery skills and refused to rise to her bait, but since then the disaffection between them had grown.

Emma had married, divorced, and was now looking for husband number two, or so Jessica suspected.

'Come back.'

The soft words made her realise that she had drifted off into her own thoughts.

Daniel smiled at her as he picked up his bag. Even beneath his thick sweater, she could discern the powerful play of his muscles.

A weakening sensation invaded her body as she stared at his supple back, imagining how it would look, how it would feel, to have that powerful, lean body close to her own. His skin would feel smooth and warm, like silk—no, not like silk, like the most expensive kind of satin. And beneath it she would be able to feel the hard, padded muscles and the long, male bones.

Her imagination conjured up pictures that made her face go hot. Guiltily she averted her eyes from his body, sternly lecturing herself on her wanton thoughts.

More for distraction than anything else, while he was upstairs she got up and walked over to the sink. She wasn't an invalid, after all. She had simply bruised the muscles in her arm.

She could fill the kettle left-handedly, and set about the preparations for their evening meal.

Cluny came in through the cat flap, miaowing demandingly. Obligingly she went to get a tin of cat food, automatically reaching for it with her right hand, and then stifling a sharp gasp as her bruised muscles locked and went into a stabbing flash of pain. She dropped the tin of cat food, instinctively nursing her bruised shoulder.

When Daniel came quickly into the kitchen, alerted by her cry of distress, he found her kneeling on the floor trying to recover the tin, which had rolled under the table.

'Leave it!' he told her, his voice so sharp and steely that she obeyed it instinctively, her face flushing with mortification as she realised that his tone was more suitable for addressing a recalcitrant insubordinate than a woman who considered herself both mature and under no one's authority other than her own, but before she could voice any protest he was at her side, tugging her to her feet with such concern that she forgot her anger.

'Why on earth didn't you wait?' he chided her when she explained what had happened.

'It's my arm that's bruised, not my legs. And, besides, Cluny was hungry.'

'Cluny?' He looked down and saw the cat, who was fixing him with a basilisk-like stare.

A smile tugged at the corners of his mouth.

'Ah, yes. I see . . . Cluny . . . For the tapestries, of course.'

'Yes,' Jessica agreed, pleased that he had recognised the connection. Not many people who were not knowledgeable in her field realised that she had named her cat after the famous Cluny tapestries. She liked the idea that, economist though he was, Daniel had an obviously wide-ranging grasp of things outside his own field. It pointed to a mind quick and generous enough to acknowledge that monetary matters were not necessarily the focus of everyone's life.

'Well, I think that for tonight at least Cluny will have to rely on me for his food.'

'But it seems all wrong, you waiting on me,' she protested as he firmly led her back to the sofa.

'Chauvinist,' he teased, and then added, 'I promise you I'm quite at home in the kitchen. My mother brought us all up to be self-sufficient.'

'All?' Jessica queried curiously.

'Yes. I have two brothers and a sister.'

Her envy showed in her face. 'How lucky you were. I'm an only child.'

'Only child, lonely child?' he hazarded as he opened the can and spooned out the contents into Cluny's bowl.

'Yes, I was. Oh, my mother did her best. She was forever dragging me off to parties, introducing me to the children of friends, but . . .'

'But?' Daniel queried, looking thoughtfully at her. 'But what? You didn't like them, you preferred your own company, or you wanted to punish your parents for not providing you with brothers and sisters?'

Jessica raised startled eyes to meet his. How had he known that? She had only recently discovered herself what had lain behind her stubborn refusal to break out of her loneliness, and then only by accident.

A chance remark by a client, wryly commenting that her six-year-old was very definitely punishing her for subjecting him to being an only child, had given her a startling and painful insight into her own childhood behaviour.

'It's all right,' Daniel told her kindly, studying her expression. 'I was the eldest in our family and there were times, believe you me, when I came close to hating my parents for providing me with three siblings, especially the twins.'

'Twins?'

'Mmm. David and Jonathon. You can see that my parents have a penchant for biblical names. The twins arrived when I was seven, and Rachel a year later.'

'Do you still resent them?' Jessica asked him curiously. It seemed impossible to imagine the man she had known today resenting anything or anyone.

He laughed. 'Sometimes. When the twins decide to come and dump themselves and their friends on me for unheralded visits as they tended to do when they were at university, but they're both working in the States now. David's a biochemist and Jonathon's in advertising.'

'And your sister... Rachel?'

'Ah, Rachel... Well, she looks set to surpass the lot of us. She's training to be a surgeon. Following in our father's footsteps, so to speak. He's a GP,' he added by way of explanation.

Jessica frowned. 'Was he disappointed that none of his sons followed him into medicine?'

'Not really. Why should he be?'

It was a question that she wasn't really ready to answer, leading as it must to disclosures about her life which she was not sure she wanted to make.

Daniel was so well adjusted in comparison to herself. How would he view her actions? She trusted his judgement, and yet something held her back from confiding in him, almost as though she were afraid to have her actions weighed and found lacking.

She was deeply conscious of the fact that her ordeal had given her a get-out from the bank which she had been seeking for a long time.

Because of what she had endured, her parents, in their concern for her health, had made it easy for her to follow her own inclinations, and there were occasions like now when she wondered if part of her had not seized on the opportunity which her mental and physical vulnerability had given her, and if she would have had the courage and determination to follow her own path in life without it.

'Something's bothering you,' Daniel said quietly. 'What is it?'

Jessica shook her head and managed a strained smile.

'I always look like this when I'm hungry,' she told him lightly. 'And I've heard that Mrs Markham's apple pie is something very special.'

She could see that he wasn't deceived, and tensed, waiting for him to press her, wondering how she would react, what she would say, but he didn't, and she wasn't sure if it was relief or disappointment she felt when he simply said easily, 'It is. I can vouch for that.'

Half-way through the evening they received a visit from the local police who wanted to take statements from both of them. While Jessica stumbled and hesitated over hers, conscious that she out of the three of them in the post office had been the only one who had panicked, Daniel, in contrast, delivered his calmly and efficiently, politely answering all the officer's questions.

When Jessica apologised for being so vague about her own recollections the officer comforted her. 'That's all right, miss. It's only natural, after the shock you've had. We've got the lad, of course, thanks to Mr Hayward here. Time was when that kind of thing was only a city problem.'

It was almost ten o'clock when he left. Jessica felt exhausted. The kind of deadening exhaustion that made the senses blur and the mind and body scream silently for sleep.

After he had escorted the police officer to the door, Daniel came back, took one look at her and pronounced curtly, 'You've had enough. I should have realised and——'

'And what? Thrown him out?' Jessica asked wryly. 'Would you mind if I went to bed?' she asked him. 'If I stay down here much longer, I'll be asleep on the sofa.'

'Can I make you a bedtime drink?' Daniel offered. 'Something hot and milky and spiced with something alcoholic, as the doctor suggested?'

Jessica shook her head.

She half expected Daniel to offer to carry her upstairs. Not that she needed carrying. It was her arm that was injured, after all. But he was cosseting her as though she were something vulnerable and precious. He didn't offer, though, merely standing at the bottom of the stairs watching her until she reached the top safely.

Another man in similar circumstances might have tried to make capital out of their intimacy, and the fact that he did not confirmed all the conclusions she had already drawn about him.

The house only had one small bathroom, and it had no lock, but she felt completely at ease with the fact that, for the first time in her life, she was sharing her home with someone else. Daniel wouldn't crowd her or push...

She winced as she tried to lift her arm to remove her sweater, and found she couldn't. It would be simple enough to call downstairs to Daniel for help, but although half of her ached for the intimacy of his hands on her body, even in performing such a mundane chore as helping her overcome the problems of her sore arm, the other half wanted to draw out the sweetness of this first stage of their relationship.

By the time she got into her nightshirt and to bed she was already half-asleep, her eyes closing and her breathing deepening.

She slept soundlessly for several hours, not stirring even when the stairs creaked under Daniel's tread and he hesitated outside her door for a few seconds before going on to his own room.

The nightmare started abruptly, quickly gathering terrifying momentum, a sickening kaleidoscope of too vividly remembered terrors and fears. The darkness choked and blinded her. She moved despairingly in her sleep, feeling the sharp remembered pain of bonds breaking her skin, of fear, acrid and sour in her mouth, and a dangerous fever in her head.

She tore at the gag against her mouth and screamed out in her panic, a primitive, splintering sound that tore at her throat muscles and woke Daniel instantly.

CHAPTER FOUR

WHEN he came rushing into her room, Jessica was awake as well, sitting up in bed, hugging her arms around her shaking body, staring blindly at the wall.

'Jessica. It's all right. Everything's all right. It was just a bad dream,' he told her soothingly, summing up the situation immediately and sitting down next to her on the bed, drawing her gently against his body so that her back was resting against the warmth of his bare chest, his arms wrapping over her own.

'It's all right, now. It's all right.'

He might have been soothing a frightened child, Jessica recognised numbly as his voice penetrated the miasma of terror that waking from her nightmare had done little to disperse.

'It's OK,' he told her softly. 'You're safe. What happened this morning...'

Immediately Jessica stiffened.

'Not this morning,' she managed to whisper. Her throat ached, probably as a result of her screams, she recognised as she swallowed against the pain. She would have to tell him the truth now, otherwise he would be entitled to think her neurotic at the very least.

'Not this morning,' she repeated hoarsely. 'Something that happened... before.'

Now it was his turn to tense, and oddly she was reassured by this evidence that he was not, after all, omniscient.

'Do you want to talk about it?'

The words came slowly, almost reluctantly, and the thought crossed her mind that she might have read too much into what he had said and done, into how he had looked at her, and that he might not want to be burdened by her confidences.

Immediately she started to withdraw into her protective shell and, as though he knew exactly what she was feeling, his hold on her tightened and he said raggedly, 'I don't want to push you into giving me confidences you might later regret, confidences that might make you resent me.'

He turned her towards him, so that the top half of her body was pressed flat and hard against his bared chest. With a finger that shook slightly, he traced the shape of her half-parted mouth.

'This is crazy,' he whispered to her. 'I've never experienced anything like this before . . . never felt such an instant rapport with another human being. I'm afraid of demanding too much from you, of frightening you off me.'

Jessica gave a shaky laugh, wanting to tell him that that was impossible, but suddenly too shy. The sensation of his callused fingertip moving so delicately against the sensitive flesh of her lips was playing havoc with her senses. She could feel the shallow thud of his heartbeat, and knew its excitement matched the rapid beat of her own.

'You don't have to tell me anything you don't want to,' he was whispering against her ear, and the temptation to turn towards him and incite him to slide his mouth over her own and kiss her as her senses told her he could kiss her almost overwhelmed her.

But now was not the time for making love. If they did, she would never have been entirely sure that she hadn't used the potent drug of his lovemaking to alleviate the fear that still lingered in her mind.

'I want to tell you,' she whispered back, and then added truthfully, 'I *need* to tell you.'

He listened in a silence she found hard to fathom as she told him the story of the bank raid and her kidnap. Only once did she surprise emotion in his expression, and that was when she mentioned being taken to the flat and left there.

'I didn't know they'd left me on my own,' she told him, shuddering still at the memory. 'I thought they were there, watching me.'

For a moment she forgot that she was here in the present, safe in his arms, in her own bedroom, and her body went rigid with the old, remembered fear.

Daniel neither spoke nor moved, simply holding her lightly as though her body had the fragility of an eggshell, but when she eventually recovered enough to turn and look at him his eyes were burning gold with murderous rage.

'It was all a long time ago,' she told him huskily.

'But you still remember it.'

'Yes...Yes... After I was rescued...well, I was ill for quite a long time. Nervous exhaustion. Shock. And then when I did recover, I didn't feel I could ever face going back into the bank. I'd realised, you see, that all my life I'd been trying desperately to be the person my parents wanted me to be, and that that person was not necessarily the real me. I know they were disappointed. I'd grown up knowing that it was my duty to follow my father into the bank, to take the place of the brother I'd never had. So, after I'd told them of my decision, I decided it was best to . . . to distance myself from them a little.'

'So you don't see much of your parents, then?' Daniel asked her carefully.

Unaware that she was almost wringing her hands with anguish, she told him, 'I daren't. I feel I can't trust them not to put pressure on me to go back.'

'To go back? To the bank, do you mean?'

'Yes. It means so much to my father. They don't really understand.'

'And because of *that* you don't trust them?'

Why was he making it sound like an accusation? She looked at him, but could discern nothing hostile in the clear, calm gaze of his eyes. Even so, she shivered a little, as though she had just been exposed to a cold draught.

'Not them, nor anyone involved with them,' she admitted tightly. 'You see, my father has considerable influence. In the early days, he used some of my friends to try and manipulate me into staying in London.'

'You're making your parents sound extremely selfish and hard-hearted,' he commented quietly.

Immediately guilt filled her. 'No. They aren't . . . not really. They just think that they know what's best for me.'

'A fault common to most parents,' Daniel told her, and then said lightly, 'So I take it that if I said that *I* knew your parents, you would banish me from your life forthwith. Is that right?'

She looked at him uncertainly, unable to tell from his expression whether or not he was teasing her. Her breath locked in her throat and for a moment she couldn't speak. When she did, her voice was raw with pain.

'I'd have to, you must see that . . .' She hesitated and then asked tensely, 'You aren't trying to tell me that you *do* know my father, are you?'

She had gone cold at the thought, everything that she was feeling revealed in her eyes.

Daniel was looking at her, his eyes sombre.

She felt the breath leak from her chest.

'I don't want to talk about it any more,' she told him shakily, knowing her question was idiotic. Of course he didn't know them; she was becoming paranoid.

'I think I've spent enough time now feeling sorry for myself. I know my parents love me,' she added painfully. 'Neither of them would force me to go back, but I'm terrified that living with them, seeing my father's disappointment, would force me to give in. You see, the bank's been headed by a member of our family ever since its inception. If I don't marry and produce a son—— '

'Is that what you intend to do?' he asked her thoughtfully.

'No!' Her response was sharp and immediate. 'At least, not to provide the bank with a chairman!'

'Well, in these volatile days of mergers and take-overs, I don't suppose it will be long before your father finds himself a partner to help him to shoulder the burden of command.'

He sounded so uninterested that Jessica immediately thought she was boring him.

'I'm all right now,' she told him quickly, trying to pull away from him. 'You must be exhausted. You've been so kind, and now I've ruined your sleep.'

'It was already ruined,' he told her briefly, his eyes resting betrayingly on the swell of her breasts.

Immediately she was intensely conscious of the thinness of her satin nightshirt, so demure with its long sleeves and prim neck, but the fabric itself was anything but prim, and neither was the way it moulded itself to the soft curves of her body.

Heat began to prickle under her skin. Her body, unused to the intensity of physical desire, reacted instinctively to Daniel's maleness, and her face flushed with mortification as she realised that the wanton hardening of her nipples was clearly visible to him.

'Jessica.' He breathed her name thickly, roughly almost, as though it were a protest. Her body shook with the force of her own emotions, incited by the message she could read in his eyes.

'I want you,' he whispered achingly. 'But now isn't the right time—for either of us.'

She knew it was true, but it shocked her that he should have needed to say the words. In her second-hand experience of male to female relationships and desires, it was always the woman who called a halt, not the man—the woman who thought beyond the immediacy of the moment.

'I'm sorry,' she responded tautly, and watched mesmerised as the golden eyes turned fiercely molten and beneath his skin the bones of Daniel's face tightened.

'For what?' he demanded roughly. 'For responding to me like this?' His hand touched the curve of her breast—instant heat, instant pleasure, instant awareness of how she would feel if he were to strip her nightshirt from her and stroke first his hands and then his mouth over her rebellious skin, stormed through her. Her body didn't want to listen to warnings or common sense. Her body wanted to submerge itself eagerly in all the pleasures it sensed he could give.

'Dan . . . iel . . .'

He felt the spasm of longing convulse her body, and his hand dropped from her breast to lie flat and hard, low down on her belly, so that the heel of his palm pressed against the swell of her pubic bone and his fingers curved round her, not so much in a caress, but in a gesture that acknowledged the extent of her need and sought to comfort her for it.

That he should know so easily everything she was feeling and experiencing should have embarrassed her. After all, she was *not* familiar with the rebellious arousal of her own flesh, nor with the emotions that churned inside her, but instead of embarrassment she felt a tender, aching swell of gratitude that he should be so aware of her vulnerability and seek to comfort her in it.

'I want you,' he told her raggedly. 'I want to stay here with you now, to take you in my arms and explore every satin inch of you. I want to kiss the hollow here at the base of your throat and feel the pulse of your life's blood go crazy for me. I want to hold your breasts in the palms of my hands, to feel you arching your back in supplication of my mouth against you here.' His free hand touched the hard crown of one breast and she shuddered delicately, breathing shallowly. 'I want to hear you cry out to me in need, your body moist and fragrant with the heat of arousal.' His fingers left her breast and stroked lightly against the valley between them, while the other hand—the hand that held her so intimately, and so, she had thought, detachedly—moved briefly against her, causing her body to yield and open.

The small, frantic sound she made in her throat was as much one of panic as of desire and, as though he knew exactly what she was feeling, his hand dropped to her thigh and stayed there.

'And that's only how I want to touch and see *you*. I could spend the rest of the night telling you how you're going to make me feel when *you* touch *me*.'

He got up off the bed and stood with his back to her, but not before she had seen the tell-tale signs of his physical arousal.

Her pulse-rate doubled. She wanted to tell him to stay, but she knew he was right, that it was too soon... far too soon for them to become lovers.

'Will you be all right if I leave you?' he asked thickly.

Jessica nodded and managed an unsteady, 'Yes,' watching him walk to the door.

'How are you feeling this morning?'

'My arm's very bruised and stiff.' They were both standing in Jessica's kitchen. She had woken up early and had dressed and come downstairs, only to find Daniel there before her.

For the first time she felt ill at ease and nervous in his presence. In the cold, clear light of the sharply clear October morning he looked so much more formidable than she remembered, so much more male... She winced inwardly, wondering how much of a fool she must have made of herself last night. Had he really withdrawn from making love to her because he genuinely felt it was too soon, or had that simply been a polite way of saying that he didn't really want her?

As she tried to follow her normal morning routine, she deliberately avoided looking at him, jumping when he reached out and removed the teapot from her grasp as he said firmly, '*I* meant every word I said last night, but if you're having any regrets... if you're beginning to wonder if this... this thing that's happening between us isn't something you want to pursue, you don't have to be afraid of saying so.'

He watched her gravely as her face betrayed her emotions.

'You must think I'm behaving like an idiot,' she told him helplessly. 'Heavens, I'm an adult, not a child!'

'Even adults have been known to regret in the cold light of morning things that happen in the blurring, protective darkness of night,' Daniel told her. For the first time there was a trace of cynicism in his voice.

'I don't regret telling you about...about the past,' Jessica told him firmly, and then added bravely, 'and I'm not having second thoughts about...about us.' She looked at him and said with helpless honesty, 'I'm just not used to this kind of intimacy. I've never felt like this before.'

'Neither have I,' Daniel told her almost fiercely. 'There's nothing in my past... *No one*,' he emphasised, 'with whom I've experienced a tenth of what I'm feeling now.' He stopped and pushed his fingers into his hair in a gesture of baffled self-irritation. 'I don't know how to handle this, either,' he told her in a softer, muffled voice. 'One half of me says, "Don't push her...Don't rush." The other—the old male hunting instinct, I suppose—says, "Make sure of her now, before someone else snatches her away from you.'

His admission startled her, softening her defences. She hadn't given any thought to his vulnerabilities and fears; she had automatically assumed that a man so obviously very much in charge of his life and himself would never experience the kind of doubts to which she was prey.

'Look,' he said gently, coming towards her and taking hold of her hands, 'I know you're trying to tell me that you don't want to be rushed into an intimate relationship because you haven't had that kind of relationship before, and, like anything unknown, at times it appears dangerous and a little frightening. I can't claim that you'll be the first woman I've made love with, but I *can* tell you you'll be the first woman I've loved, and so intensely that I feel I hardly dare let you out of my sight in case you disappear.'

Jessica sat down and stared at him. His open declaration of love stunned her.

'But it's too soon,' she whispered protestingly. 'We haven't even known one another twenty-four hours yet.'

'I knew the moment I saw you,' Daniel told her harshly. 'You looked at me and it was as though suddenly the world had shifted into brilliant focus... as though a missing piece of my life had suddenly slotted into place... I can't explain it or rationalise it, Jessica,' he told her grimly. 'And I know quite well if someone was standing here telling me what I'm saying to you, I'd probably not believe him. There is no rational explanation for what I'm feeling. And you feel it, too. You might not want to admit it, but we both know it's true.'

'It might just be because of the raid,' Jessica argued tensely. 'Things like that unleash all kinds of strong emotions——'

'I saw you before the raid,' Daniel reminded her, his voice low and rough so that, somehow, the sound of it almost seemed to touch her skin.

She hesitated for a moment, like a diver confronted with a particularly high board, and then, taking hold of her courage, she said huskily, 'I'm frightened, Daniel... Frightened of trusting myself to what I'm feeling...frightened of giving myself to——'

'To me?' he asked her savagely, shocking her with the violence of his voice and expression. 'Don't you think I feel the same way? Don't you think anyone committing themselves to another human being knows that same fear? I can't tell you what to do, Jessica. I'm already in too deep to draw back, or to give you any detached advice. What I think you must ask yourself is what you fear the most... Is it the fact that sharing your life with me will breach your protective solitude, or is it because you fear that the relationship won't last?'

'Both,' Jessica admitted painfully. 'Especially our relationship not lasting.'

'So you're not really sure about your own feelings...about their ability to endure?'

His question trapped her. Of course she was sure about what she felt, and had been from the moment she had realised that the rapport she felt for him wasn't based on gratitude for his help and kindness, but came from what she felt for Daniel himself.

'Or is it the strength of *my* feelings you doubt?' he asked her softly, watching her as betraying colour stained her pale face. 'There's nothing I can do or say that will convince you,' he told her quietly. 'Only time can do that. I want it all, Jess. You, marriage...a family...'

He saw her tension and his mouth twisted in an ironic smile.

'All right, I know you're not ready for that kind of commitment yet.'

'I need time,' she told him helplessly. 'You're so sure... so... I want to trust how we feel, but it's all so new to me. We need time to get to know one another properly.'

'Yes,' he agreed, 'starting with today. How about coming with me when I go to see the builders you and Mrs G recommended? I need to have someone who's going to treat the restoration of the house with a bit more care and consideration than the cowboy who brought down one of the bedroom ceilings.'

'Is the house listed?' Jessica asked him.

'No, but I want to make sure the work is done sympathetically and in keeping with the period of the house. I had planned to go over to Bath this afternoon. I've got an appointment at an architectural salvage place there. They're going to look out for some of the stuff I need. Come with me, Jess. Spend the day with me. I promise I shan't pressure you. You can't work, and we both know damned well that if I leave you here, before I'm clear of the village you'll be trying to work.'

Already he seemed to know her so well, while she... Sometimes she thought she knew him, and then suddenly she would be confronted by another, unfamiliar aspect to his personality that would check her.

Spend the day with him... Why not? After all, as he had said, she couldn't work. If she stayed in the cottage on her own she would only brood, and while they were in Bath she could possibly call at the shop and discuss any new commissions they might have for her.

'I'll come with you,' she told him quickly before she could change her mind. 'I could show you where the builder has his office—it's not far from Bath.'

Instantly his whole face softened.

'Good girl,' he told her softly, and then leaned towards her as though he was going to kiss her.

A fierce thrill of anticipation ran through her body, tensing her muscles.

But then he hesitated and drew back, saying ruefully, 'No, perhaps not... I promised I wouldn't rush you, didn't I?'

Cross with herself for her own sharp feeling of disappointment, she announced that there were things she had to do before she could go out—such as feeding Cluny and getting changed into something warm enough for the gusty autumn day with its sudden sharp spirals of wind and its cold, almost frosty air—and then waited tensely for Daniel to object, as she had so often heard the husbands and lovers of friends object when they were kept waiting. Instead he said agreeably that that presented no problems since he had a couple of phone calls to make, if she would allow him the use of her phone, and additionally that it would be his chore to clear away their breakfast things since her now painfully stiff arm would necessarily mean that it would take her longer to get changed.

Surreptitiously watching him as he deftly cleared the table and started to wash up, Jessica reflected that she had seldom seen a man so at home and at ease with domestic chores. Turning round and seeing her watching him, Daniel grinned, and explained, 'Early training. Since I wasn't the girl she so desperately wanted, Ma had to make do with my help when the twins came along. I drew the line at pushing the pram,' he added, still smiling.

'You mother wanted a *girl*?' Jessica asked him curiously, puzzled. 'But, surely...?'

'What—all parents want sons? Not so,' Daniel told her, shaking his head.

'You must have found that very hard,' Jessica said slowly, remembering her own pain on discovering how much her parents had wanted a son.

Daniel frowned.

'I said that my mother wanted a girl, not that she didn't love me, Jess. There is a difference, you know.'

She opened her mouth to deny his statement, and then closed it again, knowing that it was true that, although she hadn't been the son her parents had hoped for, they did undoubtedly love her.

Once upstairs, like any woman in love, the moment she opened her wardrobe doors she discovered she didn't have a thing to wear, or, more truthfully, she didn't have anything to wear that she considered worthy of inciting Daniel's admiration.

Why was it that women were so vulnerable where their physical appearance was concerned? she wondered idly, frowning over the perfectly adequate contents of her wardrobe. Why was it that their deepest and most instinctive feelings of self-worth sprang from their public image and the way that people reacted to it?

For Daniel, she wanted to turn heads as they walked down the street... For Daniel, she wanted others to admire and maybe even envy his choice of woman a little, and yet the contents of her wardrobe were geared for her working life, and living here in the country. Warm, practical clothes designed to withstand the elements, good-quality clothes, but clothes that were scarcely worthy of the description "glamorous".

Just for one fleeting and revealing moment she thought regretfully of the shopping trip her mother had insisted on taking her on the last time they had met. She had refused the enticement of the expensive designer-label clothes her mother had drawn to her attention, pointing out firmly that on her income she could scarcely afford such luxuries, and that, anyway, she had no need of them.

Useless now to regret the soft pastel cashmeres, the fine, delicate silks, the thin, narrow skirts...

Instead she removed from its hanger a pleated woollen skirt in dark blue and green tartan enlivened by bright red and yellow lines.

The skirt had been an impulse buy the previous winter, from an exclusive shop in Bath. With it went a soft yellow sweater, and the sleeveless gilet which was the same dark blue as the skirt, lined with the yellow of her sweater.

The outfit was completed by a scarf, gloves and toning tights.

As she looked critically at her reflection, she wondered if she had the right personality to wear such striking colours. There was no doubt that the outfit was vibrantly colourful, and she hesitated for a moment, torn between leaving it on or changing into something plainer.

The painful ache in her arm decided her. The outfit must stay.

Almost shyly, she went back downstairs. The kitchen was immaculate, and Daniel was waiting for her, reading one of her books on tapestries.

'I hope you don't mind,' he apologised, smiling at her, 'but this caught my eye. There's a panelled room at the Court, or at least there will be if I can find enough panelling to repair the damaged sections. I had thought of using it as my study—a tapestry would look very effective against the panelling.'

'Very,' Jessica agreed and then warned, 'Providing that the panelling is of the earlier type.'

'It's early eighteenth century, or so I'm told. I'm afraid I'm not an expert on such things, which is another reason why I want to get hold of a reliable builder.' He grimaced in self-disgust. 'I thought I was too old to be taken in by a cowboy.'

'It happens all the time,' Jessica sympathised. 'When I first bought this place, I was lucky. The estate agent was a local man and he recommended this firm to me. I think you'll like him. He's got his own idiosyncrasies,' she warned, 'and works to his own time scale. He can seem a bit taciturn at first, but he does do a good job.'

Daniel hadn't said a word about her outfit, but the way he looked at her kindled that same feeling in the pit of her stomach which she had experienced the night before.

'I think we'd better make a move,' he said huskily, verbally confirming his reaction to her. 'Otherwise I might just be tempted to forget that we've agreed to take things slowly.'

Once inside the Daimler, she realised that she wasn't going to need the gilet while they were travelling. Daniel had already set the car in motion, and she struggled to remove it, hampered by the constriction of her seat-belt and the painful stiffness of her arm.

'Hang on. I'll pull up and help you,' Daniel told her, bringing the car to a halt and releasing his own seat-belt to reach across and snap hers free. 'Turn sideways, and then you should be able to slide it off,' he instructed.

Sitting with her back to him while he reached forward to gently manoeuvre the top free of her arms, she could feel the warm heat of his breath stirring her hair, raising goose-bumps on the nape of her neck.

'There... that should do it.'

Had she imagined that light, delicate kiss brushing her throat as he lifted her hair free of her collar? She shivered a little, wishing she had the experience and nature to turn round and say, 'I've changed my mind. Take me home and make love to me.'

But even if she had, it was hardly the sensible thing to do—to commit herself so rashly and so completely.

But wasn't she already committed? Wasn't she already involved? Wasn't she even now going to suffer as she had never suffered before in her life, if he left her? And that was what frightened her—that he might grow bored, or change his mind, or simply discover that he had after all mistaken his feelings, and that, while he walked away from her with no regrets, she would spend the rest of her life mourning his loss.

CHAPTER FIVE

THEY were going first to see Daniel's house, and, although she had often driven past it on her way to the main road which led to Bath and the motorway, Jessica felt a tiny thrill of excitement at the thought of going inside.

Her love affair with old buildings had first begun long before she had reached her teens, when an aunt of her mother's had invited her to spend a week's holiday with her in Cheshire and had taken her round some of the country's wonderful mediaeval and Elizabethan houses.

It wasn't the grand palaces which appealed to her so much as the smaller, more homely buildings, lived in by what in those days had been minor branches of the nobility, and the new, wealthy merchant classes who so vigorously intermarried with them.

After all, it was those merchants who had been responsible for so many of the beautiful things which had enhanced those homes: carpets, rugs, silks and velvets brought out of the East.

Daniel's house had been built when the Carolean period was at its apogee.

Inigo Jones and Christopher Wren might have been heralding in the dawn of the fashion for Palladian architecture in fashionable London, but judging from its exterior Jessica suspected, and hoped, that Daniel's house might have retained at least some of its original panelling.

In an effort to divert her senses from their intense responsiveness to him, she asked him about this as they headed for the house.

'The panelling in one of the bedrooms is virtually intact, although the original plasterwork ceiling is badly damaged, and then downstairs there's the hallway, a passage, and what at one time was the library, although most of the library shelves have been ripped out by a previous owner.

'At some stage the sitting-room and drawing-room were 'modernised', unfortunately. My apologies for the state of the drive,' he added, frowning as he turned off the main road and in through two stone gateposts, now without gates, and drove along an unkempt, rutted drive.

The trees which must once have lined the driveway no longer existed, and where once presumably there had been a smooth sweep of lawn perhaps studded by fine specimen trees, there was now an area of rough, untidy grass, so that the house was visible not just from the drive, but from the road as well.

'How much land does the house have?' Jessica asked Daniel.

'About two acres, and this piece you can see at the front is probably the only bit that resembles anything approaching a garden,' he told her ruefully.

'The whole thing has to be cleared and redesigned, but at this stage I'm trying to concentrate on getting the house properly habitable.'

'If it's in such poor condition, wouldn't it have been wiser for you to have stayed in London until the work's done?' Jessica asked him, repeating less aggressively a question she had already asked.

'Wiser in some ways, perhaps, but I want to be on hand to make sure work is progressing as it should. I've got quite a lot of leave due to me which I intend to use to put all the work in hand, and I think I can oversee things much more easily from here than from the city.'

He saw the sadness shadowing Jessica's eyes as she studied the frontage of the house and asked with a frown, 'What's wrong?'

His sensitivity to her moods disconcerted her; she had deliberately kept her fellow human beings at bay for so long that she wasn't used to people picking up on her feelings.

'It's the house,' she told him. 'Poor thing . . . It looks so neglected and unhappy.' She flushed defensively when she saw that he was smiling a little. 'Houses do have feelings,' she told him crossly, guessing that he must think her a sentimental idiot.

'Well, then, let's go inside this one and you can reassure it and yourself as to my intentions,' Daniel suggested, stopping the car and switching off the engine.

Although she loved her small cottage, Jessica couldn't help feeling slightly envious as she studied the impressive bulk of the building. The cream stone had weathered over the years and in places the window mullions were either worn or missing.

'It doesn't look so bad from the front,' Daniel told her wryly. 'Wait until you see what some idiot did to the windows, presumably in an attempt to let in more daylight.'

As he spoke he guided her up the steps to the front door, and unlocked it. The hallway was windowless and dark until Daniel switched on the light. The solitary bulb dangling from a ceiling cord at the top of the building illuminated a good-sized rectangular room, its walls covered with linen-fold panelling which at some stage in its life had been painted black. Damp from an upstairs room was causing the varnish to peel back in one place to reveal the natural colour of the wood. The room smelled musty and uncared for. The plasterwork ceiling was cracked, with large pieces missing. Jessica gave a soft cry of protest when she looked down at the floor and saw the desecration of the once elegant parquet. A staircase led up to a galleried landing, part of which looked dangerously unsafe.

'I'm afraid most of the other rooms are much worse than this,' Daniel told her grimly, watching the expressions chase one another across her expressive face. 'Want to have a look at them?'

Jessica nodded.

It took them just over an hour to go over the house, and once they were back downstairs in the hall she could see exactly why Daniel had fallen in love with the place. She had also seen just how much work needed to be done, and as she listened to Daniel commenting determinedly and energetically about what needed to be done her admiration of him increased.

He had not taken on an easy task and, although he teased her about her indignant claim that houses had feelings, he had admitted to her that something in the house in its appalling dereliction had called out to him, and that, although half of him had said that it would be far more sensible to find a house that needed much less expensive restoration, he had not been able to resist the silent pull of the house on his senses.

'Now you see why I need a good builder,' was his final comment as they both gave one final look at the hallway.

Nodding, Jessica turned to head for the front door, and almost missed her footing on the uneven floor.

Instantly Daniel was at her side, his arm coming out to steady her, and then sliding so naturally and easily round her shoulders, drawing her into the warmth of his body, that she could find no worthwhile reason to make any move away from him as he asked her if she would like to see round the garden.

'I'd love to—if we've got time.'

'Plenty,' he assured her. 'I thought, if you were agreeable, that we'd stop for lunch on the way to Bath. I've heard there's a very nice place a couple of miles outside the city. An old manor house that's been converted into a hotel-cum-restaurant.'

Jessica thought she knew the place he meant. Somewhere she had only heard of by repute, from her more wealthy clients. She had been expecting they would have a quick snack lunch somewhere, and she couldn't help but feel flattered that Daniel should choose to take her somewhere so exclusive. Even so, she felt bound to demur, pointing out hesitantly, 'It's rather up-market, and I'm not really dressed for that kind of place.'

Instantly Daniel frowned, the look in his eyes making her flinch a little. 'It isn't your clothes I'm taking out to lunch, it's you, Jessica,' he told her roughly. 'You're the first *real* woman I've met in one hell of a long time. Clothes don't matter. People do... but if you'd rather lunch somewhere else...'

His unexpected compliment followed by his thoughtfulness touched her unbearably. She shook her head, unable to trust her voice, unprepared for the suddenness of it when Daniel abruptly stopped walking and swung her round so that they were standing breast to breast, thigh to thigh.

The warmth of his mouth moving against the coldness of her skin, touching the outer corners of her eyes with their betraying moisture before moving to her lips with a sudden, almost fierce urgency, obliterated every single atom of common sense she had ever had.

While his hands cupped her cold face and his mouth moved on hers with such piercing intensity, nothing else mattered other than that she respond to him—give herself up to him with equal intensity. When his hands moved beneath her jacket, seeking and then finding the fullness of her breasts, she gave a voluptuous sigh of pleasure against his mouth.

Hazily she was aware that if he chose now to lie her down against the crisp dying leaves and the long, untidy grass, and make love to her, she wouldn't want to do a thing to stop him.

When he didn't after all do any such thing, but instead broke the kiss, murmuring soft, regretful words against her mouth, withdrawing his hands from her body, she told herself stoically that it was just as well, that the grass would have been wet, that the wind was cold, that they could easily have been seen, while all the time her body cried fiercely in protest that none of that mattered, that it wanted him, and that it wanted him here, now, this minute.

Of course, it was impossible for her to completely conceal what she was feeling. Her face had gone pale and strained with the effort of fighting her desire.

'Are you all right?' Daniel asked her in concern, watching her, and then before she was forced to think up a fib to explain her pallor he swore softly under his breath, and apologised.

'Your arm—I forgot... Did I hurt you?'

Quickly she shook her head.

The gardens were, as Daniel had told her, overgrown and neglected to such an extent that it was impossible to imagine what they had once been.

'One of the local libraries might have some kind of archive material that might give you some clues,' Jessica suggested thoughtfully, listening to Daniel disclosing his concern about how to best deal with the problem of redesigning the garden. 'And, of course, there are books which give quite detailed illustrations and descriptions of period gardens from which perhaps you could establish a new design.'

Dreamily she studied the untidy, dying meadow grass and stubby saplings, seeing in their place hedges of dark green yew leading the eye down tantalising vistas into walks that hinted at secret, hidden arbours. She shivered, recognising how dangerously involved with Daniel she had already allowed herself to become—to such an extent that she could easily slip into thinking of this house as her own . . . this garden . . .

Daniel saw her shiver and, mistaking its cause, said firmly, 'Come on. You're getting cold—my fault for keeping you out here so long. Let's go and have some lunch.'

Half an hour later, still protesting that a sandwich and a cup of coffee would suit her admirably, Jessica found her arm being taken in a firm grasp as Daniel led her across the immaculate gravel forecourt of the small country hotel.

This was a house of much later period than his—early Victorian, Jessica guessed from its solid appearance. It had grounds of several acres, and a classic drive set between mature trees. Even from outside it was obvious that every conceivable care and thought had been lavished on its refurbishment and maintenance, and yet she found herself thinking loyally that she preferred Daniel's house in all its decay and decrepitude.

The restaurant was pleasantly busy, but they were lucky enough to get a table.

Daniel suggested that Jessica might like a pre-lunch drink, but she saw that he himself ordered only spa water, explaining that since he was driving he preferred to keep a clear head.

Mentally Jessica applauded him. She had known too many high-flying businessmen who seemed to believe that the country's drink-drive laws did not apply to them.

The hotel specialised in fresh food of the highest quality, served with light, delicate sauces that did not overwhelm or destroy its flavour. Jessica, who ordered salmon, discovered that the sauce served with it was one of the most piquant and delicate she had ever enjoyed.

Like Daniel she refused a pudding, enjoying instead the richly flavoured coffee and a piece of fruit.

Although Jessica had expostulated that she could find her own way from the architectural salvage firm's headquarters, where Daniel had his appointment, to the shop where they sold her tapestries, Daniel insisted on accompanying her there, and Jessica noticed the way her friend's eyes quickened with interest when they both walked into her small, pretty shop.

Very few women would be indifferent to Daniel's physical appearance, she suspected as she performed the necessary introductions.

Laura Grey had started her small interior design business four years ago, slowly building on her excellent reputation, careful not to allow the business to grow so quickly that she lost control of it, and thus of the quality of the work they did.

Now the cognoscenti considered her to be one of Bath's best interior designers, possessing as she did that happy blend of innovation plus sympathetic understanding of her clients' desire to have their own input into the finished appearance of their homes.

Discreetly she waited until Daniel had left before pouncing on Jessica and demanding to know, 'Where did you find him, you lucky thing?'

Tersely Jessica explained what had happened. It shocked her that she should feel this reluctance to discuss it with her friend.

She had met Laura shortly after she moved to the village, and liked her very much indeed. If pressed, she would have admitted that she was as close to Laura as she was ever likely to allow herself to get to anyone. She admired the other girl's business flair and respected and valued her judgement, and yet now, with Laura discussing Daniel's good looks with such obvious relish and sexual curiosity, she was conscious of a sharp pang of resentment coloured with a strong desire to let Laura know in no uncertain terms that Daniel was out of bounds, both as a subject of conversation and as a man.

Uncomfortable with her own feelings, she cut across Laura's flow of enthusiasm and said almost sharply, 'I only came in to see if you'd received the Thomson order safely.'

Laura paused, eyed her thoughtfully, and then said calmly, 'Yes. It came this morning. It's lovely, and I know the Thomsons will be thrilled with it. I'm taking it out to them tomorrow.' She paused, and then said frankly, 'You can tell me to mind my own business if you wish, Jess, but am I to take it that Daniel Hayward is someone special?'

Someone special... Jessica felt her heart race with a mixture of panic and happiness.

Half of her, the old cautious, protective half, was strongly inclined to deny the suggestion, but the other half, the new, feminine, joyful side of her personality that had suddenly flowered inside her, said recklessly, 'Yes... Yes, he is.'

Laura chuckled and then teased, 'There now, that wasn't so difficult to say, was it? I must say I'm impressed. All this time we've known one another there's never been a man in your life, and you've made it plain that that's the way you wanted things, and now you turn up with Daniel in tow, with such an obvious metamorphosis having taken place.' She laughed, her eyes twinkling. 'Mind you, I can't say I'm surprised. He is rather gorgeous. What was he doing in Little Parvham, anyway? Just passing through?'

'No. He's bought a house there.' Briefly Jessica explained the situation, and added generously, 'I don't know what he intends to do with the interior of the house once all the renovations have been completed, but if he does want an interior designer I'll recommend you to him.'

'He won't need me,' Laura told her, equally generously. 'You know far more about houses of that period than I do, Jess. You're an expert in the fabrics of that era—crewelwork, tapestries...'

'Not all of the rooms are true to the original period of the house,' Jessica told her. 'And I've no idea whether Daniel intends to restore the whole of the house to its original state. The drawing-room, sitting-room and dining-room have all been remodelled several times; the last remodelling evidently took place during the fifties,' she added ruefully, 'and involved the most deplorable modernisation of the windows, and a hideously unsuitable lowering of the ceiling height which has totally ruined the proportions of the rooms. All the original fireplaces have gone. There's some serious damp damage upstairs.' She gave a brief shrug. 'Daniel has an appointment with the builder who worked on the cottage for me. He's hoping he'll agree to undertake the restoration work.'

'Mmm . . . speaking of which, I was visiting a potential client today and she showed me the most marvellous old tapestry which has been in her family for umpteen generations. It's very badly worn in places, and I told her I'd have a word with you, and perhaps make an appointment for you to see it, to see whether you can repair it. I've sold nearly all the cushions you did, by the way, and if you could see your way to letting me have a fresh supply for Christmas . . .

'I also think it's time you were thinking about putting up your prices. Your stuff is ridiculously cheap, you know. I was in London last week, looking at things nowhere near the quality of your work, and the price——'

'Bath isn't London,' Jessica pointed out.

'Maybe not, but with the influx of people from the city . . .'

'I'll think about it,' Jessica promised her, and they were arguing amiably over the matter when the shop bell rang and Daniel walked in.

Her heart lifted at the sight of him as Jessica turned round and saw him. He was smiling at her, looking at her, as though he wanted to draw into himself the sight of her, his glance lingering for a moment on her mouth before he turned to make polite conversation with Laura, who was asking what progress he had made with the salvage company.

'Excellent. They think they may be able to match the panelling in the library, and provide fireplaces for most of the rooms. I fell in love with a staircase they've got there. It's after the school of Grinling Gibbons,' he told Jessica, 'but I'd like you to see it before I commit myself.'

The staircase in the house was badly damaged and abominable anyway, but it wasn't the thought of replacing it with something far more suitable that was making her pulse race so ecstatically, it was the look Daniel was giving her, the way he was consulting her, including her, making an open statement about her place in his life, and so naturally, so easily that she might always have been there. As easily and naturally as he slipped his arm around her as they left the shop, drawing her against his side, solicitous about her bruised arm, eager to hear how she had got on with Laura, and genuinely pleased for her when she passed on Laura's flattering comments about the standard and appeal of her work.

'Perhaps I ought to commission you now for a tapestry for the library,' he teased her. I might not be able to afford you once you put up your prices and your work becomes the "in" thing.'

Jessica shook her head. 'I won't allow that to happen,' she told him firmly. 'I love my work, and it's always a pleasure to work for people who share my love of it. The last thing I want is for my tapestries to become a fashion fad. Shown off today, like a new designer frock, and then thrown to the bottom of a cupboard tomorrow, because it's no longer the "in" thing. Just as long as I can earn a reasonable living, I'm content.'

He had stopped walking and she, perforce, had to stop as well. He turned to look at her, a grave, searching look that made her quiver inwardly.

'I love you, Jessica,' he told her quietly.

The middle of a windy, busy Bath thoroughfare was the very last place she had ever imagined receiving a declaration of love, but as she stood gazing back at him Jessica discovered that it wasn't the place that mattered, but the words and the man who said them.

A fervent response trembled on her lips, but she was too shy to make it, too unsure still—not of her feelings, or even really of his, but of trusting that this happiness could last, as though in some way she doubted her worthiness to be the recipient of such pleasure, like a child receiving the munificence of a longed-for and wholly unexpected Christmas gift of such magnitude that it feared the gift had really been intended for someone else.

'The builder,' she said shakily. 'We're going to be late.'

Was it disappointment that darkened his eyes, or irritation? His arm was still around her, but she couldn't be sure.

She heard him sigh, and then he said quietly, 'You're right. Come on, then. Can you direct me there?' he asked her as he opened the car door for her.

'Yes,' Jessica assured him. 'It isn't very far. Just a couple of miles outside the city centre.'

The builder ran his business from a small yard with an office attached to it. The building had originally been part of the stable block attached to a large Georgian house, and the sympathetic way the restoration work had been carried out was an excellent advertisement for his skills.

Jessica waited patiently as Daniel paused to inspect the stonework. The yard was a fascinating place. The builder was also involved in a small way in architectural salvage, though nowhere near as large or as well known as the company Daniel had visited earlier, and her eye was caught by some iron railings which she paused to admire as she waited for Daniel.

'These windows are very much the sort of thing I want for the house,' Daniel told her, pointing out the stone-mullioned windows to the building.

'They're new ones,' Jessica informed him. 'Alan Pierce employs a stonemason.'

She had offered to wait in the car while Daniel saw the builder, but to her pleasure he had insisted on her joining them.

He had talked of loving her, and, for her, love—real love—went hand in hand with permanency, marriage, children...but did loving someone mean the same thing to him? He had indicated that it did, but caution warned her not to take too much for granted. Life had made her wary, reluctant to trust her own emotions and judgements.

Daniel said he loved her; she certainly knew that she loved him, but somewhere deep down inside there were shadows...doubts. Was it because she had never considered herself to be the kind of person to look at a stranger and know instantly and irrevocably that she loved him? Was it because she had always had the vague idea at the back of her mind that love, when and if it ever came into her life, would grow from a relationship which was already well established, and not be this sudden, lightning thing, striking into her between one heartbeat and the next? Or was it because the feelings Daniel caused within her were so alien to her normal wary, controlled approach to life that she was half resentful of them—resentful and just a little afraid?

CHAPTER SIX

DANIEL'S meeting with the builder went well enough for the two of them to be able to agree that, once he had looked at the house and confirmed that the plans drawn up by Daniel's architect were compatible with the capabilities of his workforce, he would be able to start work almost immediately.

When Daniel looked surprised and pleased he went on to explain that under normal circumstances it would have been weeks, if not months, before he would have been able to do the work, but a barn conversion on which he had been due to start work had hit some last-minute snags, which meant a long delay while work went back to the planning stage.

Having made an appointment to meet the builder at the house in the morning, they set off back for the village.

Although she didn't say anything, Jessica's arm and shoulder were beginning to ache quite painfully. She thought she had done a very good job of hiding this fact from Daniel, until he pulled up in front of her cottage and said abruptly, 'I'm sorry. I've exhausted you. Thoughtless of me.'

He sounded so terse that Jessica felt for a moment that her weakness irritated him. Her father had always been rather intolerant of anyone less than physically one hundred per cent. It was his boast that he never caught so much as a cold, and that he had never in all his working life had to have time off through ill health, and so she said quickly, 'I'm not normally like this. I'm pretty tough really.'

As though he sensed the vulnerability and defensiveness hidden by her quick smile and light voice, Daniel caught hold of her good arm, sliding his hand down it. His fingers brushed the turbulent pulse, the delicate inner skin of her wrist, sending her pulse-rate into turbulent disorder. He turned her hand over, studying her palm so intently that she started to tremble, and then he lifted her hand to his mouth, dropping a light kiss into her palm.

'I wasn't criticising you, Jess,' he told her softly. 'I was condemning myself for being thoughtless.'

She looked at him, her breath catching on a ragged sigh as he read the emotions chasing one another across her face.

'Jess... Jess...' he said rawly, lifting her palm to his lips a second time, but this time their pressure was hard and forceful, and when she quivered under the assault of sensations rioting through her his tongue caressed the soft pads of flesh at the base of her fingers. When they curled in immediate reaction to the rush of pleasure swamping her, he bit gently into the soft mound at the base of her thumb, and then less gently, so that she shuddered violently, her eyes huge and dark with bewilderment.

'Don't look at me like that,' he muttered roughly, his thumb registering the too rapid thud of her pulse, his eyes monitoring the hectic flush staining her cheekbones, his body responding violently to her arousal.

'Why?'

Her lips parted softly on the question, a tiny frown etched between her eyebrows.

'Because it makes me want to do this.'

His hand cupped her head, sliding into her hair, his fingers hard and warm against her scalp. During the day his jaw had darkened with the new growth of beard, and when he kissed her the roughness of his skin against the softness of her own created a *frisson* of sharp pleasure that made her shiver inside and break out in a rash of goose-flesh outside.

She had never done anything like this before—never been kissed so passionately and demandingly in full sight of anyone who chose to walk past the car, and been so oblivious to that fact that if Daniel had started to undress her all she would have known was that now, at last, she was going to feel the delirious joy of his touch against her skin.

It was a car backfiring in the distance that brought her to her senses, making her pull back from him, her eyes still cloudy and confused by the suddenness and intensity of her own desire.

Neither of them spoke as they went inside, but Jessica was acutely aware of Daniel's hand on her arm, of the tension gripping him—the same tension that was still invading her. She sensed his impatience, his male desire to carry them both to the culmination of the feelings they had just shared.

They looked at one another in silence, but the air between them quivered with expectancy and anticipation. If she went towards him now, if she touched him, spoke to him, Jessica knew that he would make love to her. She wanted him to so intensely, her need so sharp and spearing, that it seemed incredible to imagine that she had ever hesitated or doubted. The Jessica who she was now, this moment, looked back in incredulous amazement at the Jessica she had been, unable to comprehend why she had had such doubts, such fears.

And then the phone rang, the sound shrill and imperious, fragmenting the fragile bubble of desire that held them both captive. Jessica reached for it instinctively, her voice unsteady and slightly higher-pitched than usual as she said her name.

'Jessica, darling, are you all right? I've been trying to reach you all day.'

'Mother... Is something wrong?'

Discreetly Daniel moved out of earshot to give her privacy, but there was nothing private she wanted to say to her mother. Strange that, while she loved her and knew that she was loved in turn, there were still these immense barriers between them.

'No, nothing's wrong. It's just that it's rather a long time since I spoke to you.'

Instantly Jessica felt guilty, uncomfortably aware of the low tone of unhappiness in her mother's voice.

Jessica suppressed her guilt.

'Are you sure you're all right, darling?' her mother pressed. 'You don't sound your normal self. Your father and I worry about you, living alone.'

'Living in London is much more dangerous,' Jessica pointed out wryly, and then, aware of the quality of her mother's silence, mentally cursed herself. No doubt her mother thought she was making an unkind reference to her kidnapping.

'Why don't you come home for the weekend?'

Jessica felt her stomach knotting as it always did at the thought of spending time with her parents, of being vulnerable to their subtle persuasion and coercion, and yet she heard the yearning note beneath the lightness of her mother's words.

'I can't, Mother,' she fibbed, hating herself for her own weakness. 'I'm afraid I've already got something on.'

'A date?' her mother enquired, her voice brightening.

A date... What would her parents say if they knew about Daniel? If they knew she had fallen in love? Not that she was going to tell them. Not yet. Not until she herself was sure.

Sure of what? Of Daniel? Of herself? As she muttered something non-committal and replaced the receiver the euphoria of her earlier mood of reckless certainty and confidence had gone, replaced by one of uncertainty and tension.

Daniel obviously sensed it. He gave her a thoughtful look and offered quietly. 'If you'd like me to leave...'

She shook her head. Part of her did. Part of her wanted to crawl back into the security of the solitary life with which she was so familiar, but another part of her wanted to break free of the old Jessica and her fears.

'No,' she said huskily. 'Please stay.'

And as they looked at one another across the width of the room she wondered if he realised that those were probably the most portentous words she had ever said.

As though he knew what she was going through, over the meal, which he had insisted on preparing, Daniel deliberately kept the conversation light and general.

He was interesting to talk with—not like some men, whose entire lives and interests were themselves and their careers. Daniel was widely read, and knowledgeable, drawing her out to talk about herself so easily and gently that she scarcely realised what he was doing.

At nine o'clock exhaustion suddenly hit her.

'You're tired,' Daniel said quietly. 'I'd better go.'

Go? Jessica stared at him. She had taken it for granted that he would be staying the night again.

He touched her face with his hand, his touch both reassuring and tender.

'I promised I wouldn't rush you,' he reminded her. 'But if I stay here with you tonight, I may not be able to keep that promise. We both know that.' He frowned and hesitated. 'I want your love *and* your trust, Jessica.'

She desperately wanted to beg him to stay, to push caution aside and say that she had changed her mind, that she was ready now to make the fullest kind of commitment to him, but the words stuck in her throat, a paralysing shyness silencing her, and by the time she had found her voice he was already on his feet and walking towards the door.

'I'll get my bag,' he told her quietly, and then added, 'Tomorrow, would it be too much if I asked you to be with me when Alan Pierce comes to go round the house? I'd like your views on anything he has to say.'

'A woman's touch,' Jessica said lightly, trying to mask her pleasure that he should want her there.

'No,' he corrected, watching her. '*The* woman's touch.'

He wouldn't let her go with him to the car, saying that it was too cold outside. He brushed his lips fleetingly against her forehead before firmly stepping back from her.

'Nine o'clock tomorrow?' he suggested.

Jessica nodded, and then offered almost shyly, 'If you want to make it a bit earlier, we could have breakfast together.'

'I'd like that, Jess.' He seemed about to say something else, but then stopped and opened the door.

The house felt empty without him, and yet, after all, she had only known him a couple of days.

Tiredly she went upstairs, wishing she had had the courage to ask him to stay, and yet admitting ruefully later, when she studied herself in the full-length mirror in her bathroom, that her bruised arm and shoulder, all swollen and now vividly coloured, purple and blue, were hardly appealing.

Morning brought an end to the brief interlude of blue skies and bright autumn sunshine. The wind had picked up during the night, blowing in pewter rainclouds and turning the whole landscape a dull, leaden grey.

Lethargically Jessica surveyed the contents of her cupboard and wondered what on earth she was going to give Daniel for breakfast. A trip to the local market town to stock up at the supermarket there was plainly called for, but she couldn't summon any enthusiasm for such an undertaking. She hated supermarket shopping at the best of times, and could never visit one without wondering how on earth mothers with under-school-age children managed. The old-fashioned corner-type shops might not have sold the wide range of goods supplied by supermarkets, but they had a friendliness, a warmth that was lacking from these huge soulless buildings. The worst time for shopping in them, as far as she was concerned, was early in the evenings or at weekends, when all the other shoppers seemed to be in family groups and she felt as though she was the only person there who was on her own.

She wondered curiously how Daniel lived, where he did his shopping. As a successful businessman no doubt he ate out a lot. Daniel... Was every path her thoughts took these days destined to lead her back to him? Was she already so dangerously involved with him that she couldn't, didn't *want* to focus on anything or anyone else?

As she closed the fridge door she glanced upwards towards the window, sighing as she saw the rain spattering against the glass, and then she remembered that tucked away in one of her top cupboards was an unopened packet of porridge bought on impulse one bitterly cold spring day and left unopened all summer.

She wasn't tall enough to reach the top cupboards in the kitchen without standing on a stool, but she had forgotten the weakness in her arm, and as she stood on the stool and lifted her arm to open the cupboard her bruised muscles protested, and the pain in them made her cry out in surprise and almost lose her balance.

'Jessica! What the devil...?'

The sight of Daniel standing in her kitchen, glowering at her while he set down the paper bags he was carrying and came quickly towards her, made her tremble so much that the stool wobbled even more. The floor was uneven and the stool not the safest thing to stand on, she knew, but her situation was surely hardly perilous enough to warrant either the grim look Daniel was giving her or the stifled curse he muttered under his breath as he crossed the kitchen and unceremoniously lifted her off the stool.

Once her feet were touching the floor, though, he didn't let her go.

She could feel the heavy thud of his heart through her thin sweater.

The heat from his body lapped her in a warmth which was rapidly making her own flesh burn. It was hard to keep her voice calm and steady as she asked, 'What did you do that for? I was perfectly safe.'

'Safe? Your front door was unlocked and open when I heard you cry out.'

The grimness was beginning to leave his mouth, and guiltily Jessica remembered that she *hadn't* checked that the door was closed and locked after she took the milk in.

'I forgot about my arm,' she told him breathlessly. 'That was why I cried out.'

'Idiot!' Daniel told her roughly. 'Don't you *know* that the majority of patients in Britain's outpatients' hospital departments go there through accidents caused in the home? What was it you wanted, anyway? I'll get it for you.'

She told him, and then explained about her near-empty fridge and her concern over what she was going to give him to eat.

'I've brought our breakfast with me,' he told her wryly, watching her nose twitch appreciatively as she focused on the carrier bags he had put down on the table. The unmistakable smell of freshly baked bread reached her, making her mouth water.

'You've been into Long Eaton,' she accused him. 'You must have been. That's the only place around here where they have a bakery.'

'I was awake early,' he told her. 'Mrs G had mentioned the bakery, and so I thought I'd drive over and see what they had to offer.'

'They make the most wonderful croissants,' Jessica began with regret. 'They use French flour and a special recipe...' Her voice trailed away, her eyes rounding with pleasure as Daniel delved into one of the carrier bags and told her,

'I bought some, and some of Mrs Neville's cousin Ann's very special blackcurrant conserve,' he added virtuously.

Jessica started to laugh, happiness rising inside her like effervescent bubbles, intoxicating her. She wanted to fling her arms around him and tell him how wonderful he was, but because by nature she was cautious and unused to expressing her feelings, she said mock severely instead, 'That conserve is wickedly expensive, and loaded down with calories.'

'Mrs Neville told me it's your favourite.'

It was the way he was looking at her, and not the words, that silenced her—the knowledge that he cared.

She reached out to touch him, her hand trembling a little as her fingertips found the hard line of his jaw.

'It is,' she said huskily.

And then she was in his arms and he was holding her, touching her, kissing her as she had ached for him to do every time she woke up during the night and discovered that he wasn't there.

'Much more of this and I'm going to start forgetting that I promised not to rush you,' Daniel whispered thickly against her ear, stroking the soft skin of her throat with fingers that trembled betrayingly. 'And I still haven't...'

She ached to tell him that she had changed her mind, that there was nothing she wanted more than to commit herself to him completely, but instead said softly, 'Haven't what?'

'Jess, about your parents...'

'No, please, I don't want to talk about them. I know you mean well, Daniel, but it's just that I can't trust them. We'll be late for the builder,' she reminded him jerkily.

She saw him look at her, an odd expression in his eyes, composed of wryness and something that was almost pain.

'Posting No Trespassing signs, Jess?' he said drily.

The builder arrived at Daniel's house just as they were getting out of Daniel's car. He showed no surprise at seeing Jessica with Daniel, and together the three of them set off on a tour of inspection.

It took them almost three hours, with Alan Pierce making copious notes.

He listened while Daniel explained exactly what he wanted to achieve, firmly agreeing with him when Daniel said that he wanted to use salvaged materials of the right period as much as possible, resorting to new only when there was no alternative available.

The builder, as Jessica already knew, had been apprenticed as a teenager to a small family firm of craftsmen working in and around Bath, so that unlike many modern builders he was fully conversant with many of the traditional forms of building, but, listening to him discussing the work with Daniel, what surprised her was Daniel's own expertise.

When she commented on it later when the builder had gone, he told her ruefully, 'It's only information culled second-hand from books and magazine articles, I'm afraid. Unfortunately I have no practical expertise. I've always been interested in architecture and old buildings. In fact, as a teenager I had dreams of qualifying as an architect.'

Jessica looked at him in surprise.

'Did you? What made you turn to the City instead?'

He gave a brief shrug. It was cold outside in the overgrown gardens, but he was standing so that he sheltered her from the worst of the wind. There was something intensely pleasurable about standing here with him, Jessica thought as she looked up into his face, waiting for his reply.

This morning he was dressed casually in a pair of faded jeans, a woollen shirt and a rather battered and very soft leather blouson jacket, and, watching him as he had enthusiastically and knowledgeably inspected rotting pieces of wood, crumbling stonework and plaster, as comfortably at home among the dirt and mess of the old house as the builder, she hadn't been able to help contrasting him with the other men she had occasionally dated—men introduced to her via her parents, men who dressed in expensive suits and who would never in this world have dreamed of crouching down on rotting floorboards to admire the workmanship in a piece of wainscoting.

He seemed to hesitate before responding to her question, causing Jessica to frown as she saw the faint shadows darkening his eyes.

'Necessity,' he told her at last, and then leavened the starkness of the word with its undertones of past unhappiness with a wry smile. 'I don't regret it now. I find the world of finance intensely fascinating and seem to have discovered my *métier* there.'

Jessica wondered if he would go on to explain in more detail, but hesitated to press him, not wanting to intrude on memories he might prefer to keep private. His hand on her shoulder guided her along a disused and overgrown footpath, and he stopped to examine a broken stone urn which looked as though it should have been one of a pair. It guarded a set of stone steps which led down to what must once have been a south-facing lawn surrounded by herbaceous borders and enclosed by a traditional yew hedge. Now all that remained was a tangled mess. The yew hedge had reached proportions that threw ominous shadows more suitable for a graveyard than a garden. Idly, Jessica used her imagination to project a mental picture of what it might once have been, believing the subject of Daniel's past closed, and then to her surprise he said abruptly, 'Do you mind if we walk for a few minutes? I find it easier to talk that way.'

She wanted to tell him that she didn't mind what she did as long as she did it with him, but such extravagant teenage idolatry was something she felt it wiser to suppress, and so instead she shook her head, allowing him to draw her closer against his side and to keep her there as he matched his pace to hers.

'You already know something of my background,' he told her. 'What I didn't tell you was that when I was sixteen my mother's sister and her husband were killed in a car crash. They had three children, all of them under seven; the youngest, Gemma, was only eighteen months old. My aunt and uncle were only relatively young. They hadn't been able to make any financial provision for the children in the event of their deaths.

'My parents made the decision to take responsibility for them and to bring them up as they had done us. I was taking my O levels at the time. In my imagination, I'd already decided on my future: university, including training with a firm of high-ranking architects. I didn't just want to be any architect. I wanted to be articled to the best there was. I wanted to travel—Italy, Greece, the old world and then the new, to learn all that was best in my field. My father had to explain to me that, with the added responsibility of three more children, it just wasn't going to be possible for him to finance me in the way that we'd planned; architecture is a seven-year course, you see.

'Of course, I could have gone ahead with my plans, worked my own way through university, got my degree and then built up my skill and reputation. It would just have taken a bit longer, because I wouldn't have been able to devote all my time to studying. But in those days I believed less in the value of ability and the will to succeed, and far more than I should have done in my right to an unhindered education.'

'But it's not too late,' Jessica counselled quickly, remembering her own misery when compelled by duty and love to try and turn herself into the person she believed her parents wanted her to be. He could still qualify, set up in practice...

'I no longer want to,' Daniel told her, and added, 'You're missing the point, which is that I wanted my success to be handed to me, that I believed I had a *right* to expect my parents to make it possible for me to succeed. I wanted to be an architect because it seemed to me to be a glamorous, potentially high-profile life-style. My love of design and buildings came second to my love of self.'

'It must have been hard for you,' Jessica murmured. 'To have all your hopes and plans dashed like that...'

'Maybe, but it taught me a great deal, and I like to think that I'm a better person from what I learned. You see, initially I behaved extremely badly—in the ways that only a spoiled teenager can behave badly. I let my schoolwork slide. I sulked and complained and generally made life unpleasant all round, culminating with the failure of my A levels. I was at a private school, and fully expected my father to pay for an extra year's schooling so that I could resit them. I hoped through my bad behaviour to pressure him into financing my career as an architect—and I deliberately blinded myself to the fact that, in financing that, he would have to deprive my cousins of the same kind of education he had given us. It came as a grim shock when he told me that, far from paying for an extra year's schooling for me and wasting several more thousands of pounds, he was going to use the money instead for my cousins' education, considering that they deserved it far more than I did.

'At first I thought he was simply making an idle threat. As the eldest, despite the fact that both my parents ensured that I took my turn with chores at home, I had somehow or other during my growing-up process collected the chauvinistic belief that as a son, and the eldest child, my needs and desires somehow ranked higher than those of my siblings and cousins. My father very quickly dispatched this error.

'Instead of going on to university, I had to leave school and find myself a job.'

He saw her face and smiled.

'It wasn't as harsh as you seem to think, and taught me several salutory lessons, through which I discovered my flair for matters fiscal. I also discovered how much more self-appreciation one's achievements bring when one has earned them for oneself.

'I had to go to night-school to get the qualifications to enable me to go on to university, and by that time I had discovered my hitherto unsuspected skill with figures, so I opted to take a degree in economics.'

'And your parents?' Jessica questioned.

'Unfairly proud of my achievements, so the others tell me. The youngest of my cousins is now sitting her A levels. Like my father and sister, she wants to go into medicine. She's utterly dedicated to the ideal of doing all that she can to work for the improvement of world health, especially in the Third World countries. When I think that through my selfishness I might have deprived her of the opportunity to fulfil that ideal, I can only thank God that my parents were wise enough and loving enough to stand firm with me. That's why...'

He stopped walking and turned to face her.

'Jessica, I have to tell you,' he began earnestly, frowning as he looked down at her, his eyes shadowed and dark so that suddenly her heart missed a beat, her mind already braced as though for a blow, already anticipating that he was about to tell her something she wasn't going to like, and then before he could speak they both heard something travelling along the drive.

Daniel cursed and released her.

'That will be my ex-builder. I told him to meet me here so that I could pay him off and make it clear to him just what I think of his shoddy workmanship. I think it might be an idea if you wait for me here,' he added purposefully. 'I suspect this isn't going to be pleasant.'

He was gone for just over half an hour, and when he returned he looked so grim and remote that Jessica found it impossible to ask him what it was he had been about to say to her when they were interrupted.

CHAPTER SEVEN

Two days later, prowling edgily around her workroom, Jessica acknowledged how much she was missing Daniel.

He had had to go to London the previous morning, and wouldn't be back until this evening, and already his absence was eating into her like a canker.

Her phone rang and she raced to answer it, subduing her disappointment when it was not Daniel on the other end of the line.

In fact it was someone from the National Trust, with which she had had dealings before, wanting to make arrangements for her to travel up to Northumberland to look at and potentially do some repair work on a tapestry so fragile that it had to be worked on *in situ*.

Jessica knew the tapestry, having been asked to inspect it on a previous visit. Her discussion with Jane Robertson, who was in charge of that section of the National Trust's restoration department, was a long one. She agreed to travel up to Northumberland and to stay there overnight so that she could make a thorough study of and report on the tapestry.

'We can put you up in the house itself,' Jane told her. 'We've got a couple of rooms which we keep for visitors. One of them has the most marvellous parcel-gilt four-poster bed. It's been restored, of course, and we've had new silk hangings woven. It's terribly romantic.'

Listening to Jane enthusing about the bed and its restoration, Jessica wondered wistfully if it would be possible for Daniel to go north with her. She tried not to allow herself to be tempted by images of the two of them sharing the watery bluey-green intimacy of the silk-hung bed. When she eventually replaced the receiver her palms were damp and her heart was pounding. She was so shockingly aroused by the power of her own thoughts that she knew if he were to walk into the house now...

As though deliberately on cue, someone rang the front door bell. The shock of it pierced her, sending a tiny message of excitement-cum-panic thrilling through her.

She positively raced downstairs, flinging open the front door, her face flushed and her eyes fever-bright with anticipation.

Only it wasn't Daniel who was standing there. It was Emma. She stared at her cousin, her smile dying, to be replaced by bitter disappointment.

'Emma,' she said dully, standing to one side so that her cousin could come in. 'What brings you here?'

Her cousin, as always, was dressed in the very latest designer-label fashion, her face perfectly made-up and her hair immaculate.

She raised her eyebrows as she stalked in—no other word could adequately describe the hauteur with which she moved, the very definite 'look at me' aura she deliberately invoked.

'A duty visit to my godmama.' She pulled a face. 'I thought I might as well call in and see you on my way back,' Emma told her smoothly. 'You don't look very pleased to see me, though. Perhaps you were expecting someone else,' she added archly as she followed Jessica into the kitchen-cum-living-room, grimacing faintly as she did so, and saying, 'Honestly, Jess. I can't understand how you can live somewhere like this. It's so small and ordinary. When I think of Uncle James and Aunt Harriet's house in Kensington...'

She gave a delicate shudder and then turned to Jessica, giving her one of her brilliantly unkind smiles, so that Jessica felt her toes curling in anticipation of one of Emma's more cruelly acid jibes.

'Still, it won't be for very long, will it?' Emma said softly. 'Aunt H. is cock-a-hoop about the whole thing. A summer wedding next year—just nice time to get everything organised. I expect the engagement will be announced at the usual family Christmas shindig. Quite a feather in your parents' cap. And, of course, so clever of darling Uncle James to keep it all in the family, so to speak. I must say, though, that I *was* surprised.'

Eyebrows raised, mouth pursed, eyes cold as winter ice, she turned to Jessica and said sweetly, 'Do you know, darling, I always thought that *if* you did get married, it would be someone frightfully worthy and intellectual. I never imagined for one moment that you'd fall in so easily with your parents' plans. Not after all the fuss you made when you decided to leave the bank. Of course, your father had to put a brave face on it at the time, and I know the whole family were rather miffed when he didn't take Cousin John's Paul into the bank in your place, but then I suppose he's always had something like this in mind. Finding himself an ambitious man, clever enough to take into the bank as a partner, and ambitious enough to actually accept such an archaic condition. It's all so frightfully Victorian, isn't it? And I suppose I shouldn't be all that surprised about Daniel's decision to go along with your father's plans. After all, he is frightfully hard-edged and ambitious, and he's never made any secret of the fact that money is very important to him, but you . . . well, my dear, *you* have surprised me,' Emma told her, folding herself elegantly into a chair and crossing her legs so that she could admire the silken elegance of their slenderness.

A smile of pure catlike pleasure curled her mouth as she removed one of her leather gauntlet-style gloves and drew her slender, long-nailed fingers along one slim calf.

'There's always something about black silk stockings, don't you think?' she said to Jessica and then smiled again. 'Oh, but then I forgot, since you became so independent and bucolic I don't suppose your budget stretches to such luxuries. Personally I'd rather die than wear those appalling nylon things you see so many people wearing—even with quite good clothes. You can't imagine the number of people who simply have no idea of real style.' She raised her head and studied Jessica's paper-white face with apparent surprise.

'Jess...what on earth's wrong? Have I said something I shouldn't? I must say I was surprised when I heard the news, but I didn't think you'd react like this to my knowing. Heavens, Uncle and Aunt seemed delighted. Uncle James opened a bottle of champagne when Daniel told him, and not just any champagne either. Vintage and absolutely delicious.'

Her small pink tongue touched her heavily glossed mouth as though remembering the taste of that very expensive champagne.

Something moved sluggishly and sickly in the pit of Jessica's stomach. She wanted to scream at her cousin to go away and leave her—leave her to come to terms with what she had just learned, leave her to rationalise all the disjointed information Emma had just given her—but Emma wasn't waiting for her reply, she was pouting and saying with a frown, 'And to think *I* was the one who introduced Daniel to your father.'

'*You* know Daniel?'

Jessica wasn't aware of speaking the words until she heard them resounding hollowly and painfully into the room.

Emma's eyebrows rose.

'But of course...I met him at Meriel Faber's divorce party. Meriel was furious when he took me home. She'd got her own eye on him. You'll have to be very careful, darling,' Emma warned Jessica. 'He's frightfully attractive, and very, very sexy...but then, it isn't as though you've fallen madly in love with one another, is it? So clever of Uncle James to offer to make Daniel a partner in the bank. I mean, there's no other way he could ever have achieved that kind of status off his own bat, and with the added promise of his son inheriting the whole lot . . . I promise you that will really put Cousin John's nose out.'

Jessica knew that if she stood there listening to much more she was going to be sick, no longer caring about anything other than the appalling ache burning inside her, the sick shock which had turned her skin clammy and her brain to papier mâché.

'Darling, you look so pale.' As Emma glanced at her watch, Jessica had the feeling that her cousin was secretly laughing at her, as though she knew. But how could she?

'I'm so sorry I can't stay longer, Jess, but I've got a date this evening.' She made a brief kissing noise in Jessica's direction, and pulled on her glove, her smile faintly malicious and triumphant as she paused by the door to say, 'Oh, and one word of warning, darling—don't be silly enough to fall for Daniel, will you? He's a real heartbreaker, or at least he was. I suppose he'll have to reform now that he's about to be a married man. Well, at least you'll be sure of one thing—you're getting a husband who's an excellent lover.' She was almost purring, and Jessica felt her nausea increase.

She waited until she was quite sure that Emma had driven away before staggering upstairs to her bedroom. Once there she crawled into the middle of the bed and lay there, her eyes burning and dry, her stomach still churning nauseously, her mind wrestling with the enormity of her own stupidity.

Daniel had not approached her as a stranger, but as part of a deliberate plan—a plan no doubt set up with her parents' approval, a plan to deceive her in the most cruel and destructive way there was.

And for what? So that her father could have his grandson, and so that Daniel—Daniel whom she had admired, whom she had liked, whom she had loved—could have a partnership in her father's bank.

She closed her eyes, aching to have the power to send herself back to a time before she had known Daniel. How gullible she had been! How stupid! There was no chance that Emma could have made up what she had told her. It had all rung too true. And yet...

She opened her eyes and stared at the telephone beside her bed.

It would be so easy to pick up the receiver and telephone her mother, ask her—ask her what? If she and her father and Daniel had deliberately deceived her? She started to shake, and curled herself up into a small ball of agonised misery.

What a fool she had made of herself, listening to him, believing him, opening her most private self out to him, loving him, and all the time he had been lying to her, letting her believe that he loved her.

When had he intended to tell her? *After* he had made love to her? she wondered cynically. *After* he had made sure of her, after he was confident enough of her to believe that she would accept his deception? Maybe he wouldn't even have told her until after he had married her—but no, that would have been impossible. He would have had to tell her beforehand... How sure of her he must have been.

Too sure. Much too sure...

Thank heaven she had found out the truth before it was too late.

A small voice mocked her inside, taunting her with the knowledge that it was already too late, but stubbornly she refused to listen to it. She and Daniel had not yet been lovers. She had still not given him that final commitment, and now she never would. Never. Never...

They had arranged to have dinner together, and because her pride demanded it she was determined not to let him see how much learning the truth had hurt her.

So, instead of lying sick and hurting on her bed, she forced herself to go through the motions of preparing for his return as though nothing had happened.

In the small sitting-room, she lit the fire and closed the woven, heavy curtains against the frosty air, switching on the lamps so that the room had an intimate, welcoming warmth.

In the kitchen she set about the preparations for dinner. When she chose she could be an inspired cook, and she chose now, thanking Providence that she had been out this morning and restocked her freezer and cupboards.

Then, when planning the menu, she had thought only of being alone with Daniel, of letting him know subtly how much she had missed him and how much she wanted to be with him. And so she had planned a meal of intimate simplicity. A lovers' meal eaten at a table illuminated only with candles in a room darkened with soft shadows.

She still needed those shadows, but now for a different reason. She had no wish for Daniel to see what she knew lay in her eyes. No wish for him to see how easily he could overrule her pride and her will-power.

No matter what he and her father might have planned, she was not going to be used by them. And to think she had almost wept when he had told her of his teenage dreams—of his supposed realisation that money and power were not the most important things in life. If only she had used her brain then, she might have guessed how deliberately that story had been invented and used. Only someone with a sure knowledge of her personality and her attitudes could have known just how much effect it would have on her. She remembered the way he had listened so sympathetically while she had told him about her past. God, how amused he must have been. Her fingers curled into tight, angry fists. Of course, her father would have told him already about her past, would have cautioned and warned him about what to say and what not to say, and yet, oddly, it wasn't against her father that her hatred and bitterness burned so fiercely.

Her parents loved her. They probably believed they were doing the right thing. They wanted to see her married, drawn back into the ambit of their own lives. Yes, for her father she could find excuses, but for Daniel there were none.

She heard his car long before it stopped outside, marvelling at her senses' ability and unerring instinct to pick out its now familiar sound.

She had deliberately switched off the light in the hallway so that he wouldn't see her face. She was wearing a dress she had found at the back of her wardrobe. A dress her mother had insisted on giving her last Christmas, for the family get-together they always had on Boxing Day.

It was silk velvet, long-sleeved and very fitted, curving to the shape of her body, drawing attention to the narrowness of her hips with its soft silk peplum. The back was slashed open in a deep V to her waist, the peplum had a silk frill that ran down to the hem and a silk bow strategically placed so that it resembled a provocative mock bustle. It was a sensual rather than a sexual dress—a dress that invited a man's touch, that hinted at the secret pleasure of its wearer's body.

It seemed poetic justice that she should be wearing with it the silk stockings which Emma had given her for her birthday, and the high-heeled satin shoes that drew attention to her slender ankles—every bit as slender and delicate as Emma's.

She was even wearing a subtle hint of perfume. She knew that she looked good, but there was no pleasure in the knowledge. Her appearance was a decoy—a means of keeping Daniel's attention occupied, so that when she chose to reveal to Daniel that she knew the truth and that there was no place for him in her life he would find the discovery as painfully shocking as she had found hers this afternoon, albeit for a very different reason.

It wouldn't be Daniel's *feelings* that would be hurt. Men like him didn't *have* feelings. They just had greedy bank accounts.

She let him in and stepped swiftly back into the shadows, not giving him the opportunity to greet her.

Deep inside her a nerve vibrated. If she allowed him to touch her, she would never be able to go through with it. She was still too vulnerable to him to withstand the sheer intensity of her own need.

'Jessica, is everything all right?'

The sharp words were not the ones she had expected. She had thought he would be so triumphant, so cock-a-hoop with his own success that he would not be able to see beyond the façade she was presenting.

They were in the kitchen now, and mercifully she had her back to him.

'I've missed you,' she told him huskily, and, after all, it wasn't a lie.

It was the wrong thing to say. She felt him walk towards her, bringing the small eddies of cold air from outside. Her spine tensed, the tiny hairs on her skin rising protectively as she willed herself not to turn round, not to do anything other than walk quickly away.

He followed her, stopping her; one hand on her shoulder firmly turned her towards him.

'Something *is* wrong,' he said quietly. 'What is it?'

Could he really tell, or was he simply guessing?

'No,' she lied. 'I was just worried that you might be late . . . the dinner——'

'To hell with the dinner!' Daniel said thickly. 'I've missed you, too.'

The emotion he was projecting caught her off guard. In his absence she had allowed herself to forget what a superb actor he was. She stood still, mesmerised by the fine tremble of his hands as they cupped her face, trembling like a sacrifice on the altar and completely unable to pull herself free. The hard, demanding pressure of his kiss took her by surprise, as did the urgency with which his hands slid over her body.

For a moment she weakened and let herself respond to him, let herself pretend that this afternoon had never happened.

'Oh God, Jess, you don't *know* what you do to me.'

The words muttered against her mouth broke the spell, enabling her to pull herself free of his arms and turn her back on him.

'Dinner's almost ready,' she told him shakily.

He looked at the table and said quietly, 'It looks as though we're celebrating.'

It was her cue, heaven-sent, and it was surely time to bring down the curtain while she still had the strength. She would have liked to drag the finale out until after dinner, to have lulled him into a false sense of security before denouncing him, but she couldn't rely on her own strength of will to last that long.

'We are,' she told him, and then with a composure she was proud of she poured them both a glass of wine and handed him one, saying evenly, 'I'm afraid it's not vintage champagne. My cellar isn't as extensive as my father's,' and then she raised her glass to her mouth and with a brittle smile said shrilly, 'Congratulations on your partnership with my father, Daniel.'

She saw the shock darken his eyes and knew she ought to have been pleased, but instead all she felt was a rolling tide of pain.

She couldn't prolong the farce any longer. What was the point? The very idea of revenge, or hurting him as he had hurt her, was risible.

'It's no use, Daniel,' she told him bleakly, putting her glass down clumsily. 'I know everything. Emma came to see me this afternoon. She told me——'

'Emma?'

'Yes, I know it all now—how you deceived me, lied to me.'

'Jess, let me explain——'

'Explain?' She laughed bitterly. Why had she imagined that, once he realised she knew, he would simply walk away from her in shame? She ought to have realised that men like Daniel didn't know the meaning of the word. Of course he would fight to hold on to what he wanted; of *course* he would use any means at his disposal to persuade and convince her. But she wasn't going to listen.

'Explain what? That it *isn't* true that this morning you and my father were celebrating your joining the bank? Tell me that, Daniel, and then maybe I'll listen to your explanation.'

He looked at her for a long time and then said quietly, 'Yes . . . it's true your father and I are partners, but——'

'No!' Jessica cut him short. 'Whatever you have to say, Daniel, I don't want to hear it. You've already deceived me once. Lied to me——'

'Lied?'

The anger in his eyes startled her. It wasn't what she had expected. It frightened her and undermined her determination. It wasn't the reaction she had expected. Pleas, excuses, explanations—these she had been ready for, but anger . . .

'You're everything I most despise in the human race, Daniel,' she told him, rushing quickly into her rehearsed speech. 'Everything I most detest and dislike. There's no place for you in my life, whatever my father might have told you. I won't marry a man who wants me because he sees me as a passport to my father's money—the key to unlock the bank's vaults. The only reason my father is giving you a partnership is because he wants a grandson.' She gave a high-pitched, hysterical laugh. 'But he'd be wasting his money, because there's no way I'd ever let a man like you, a man as contemptible and loathsome as you, make love to me.'

She lifted her hand in a theatrical gesture towards the elegantly set table with its romantic, flickering candlelight and said harshly, 'Yes, we're celebrating. We're celebrating my good fortune in discovering the truth about you before it was too late. You must have been so sure of me, Daniel. So very sure. Telling me you weren't going to rush me. But, you see, you were *too* sure, and now that I know the truth about you——'

'The truth? You know *nothing*!' He slammed down his glass of wine and advanced on her so quickly that there wasn't time for her to move. 'You're so ready to condemn, to criticise...'

He was in a towering, furious rage, and Jessica, who had only seen the gentle, easygoing side of him was transfixed by it.

'...and as for not wanting me—well, let's just see how true that is, shall we?'

She should have guessed, should have known that he wouldn't let her reject him. She hit out at him as he picked her up, but he dodged her blows with ease, laughing savagely under his breath as he carried her towards the stairs.

'So you know everything there is to know, do you?' he taunted. 'Somehow I doubt that, but I promise you this much—by tomorrow morning you will do.'

Shock closed her throat and froze her vocal organs. He couldn't be doing this—couldn't mean what she thought he meant. She had expected that once she denounced him he would leave, but she had underestimated him, and badly, and now for the first time she was frightened.

Frightened not of the raw male anger she had so obviously generated, but of her own leaping response to it. Frightened of the sensations his touch invoked. Frightened of the emotions she had fought all afternoon to subdue.

It wasn't true that she didn't want him. She *ought* not to want him, that was true, but she did, and humiliatingly she suspected he knew it.

Tell him to stop, tell him you've changed your mind—anything . . . anything to call a halt to what was now happening between them! But, while her feverish brain demanded that she take action, her pride refused to listen. She wasn't going to be the one to back down. She would show him, prove to him that she was stronger than her emotions, stronger even than her love, that she could put both of them aside and lie cold and unresponsive in his arms—that she meant every word of rejection she had thrown at him. Every word.

CHAPTER EIGHT

HER bedroom was in darkness and cold. She had not anticipated being up here with him, and a thin, sharp light from the hunter's moon pierced the curtains in an ethereal shaft.

Unerringly Daniel found his way to her bed, dropping her down on to it and pinning her there.

Her brain shrieked at her to abandon her pride and plead with him to stop this madness and set her free, but the words were locked behind her rigid throat muscles.

Her eyes dared him to do his worst, narrowing like a cornered cat's spitting hatred and disdain.

'I can explain, Jess, if you let me.'

She trembled on the brink of capitulation. What harm would it do? She wouldn't believe what he told her, of course, but it would buy her time, and maybe even . . .

She caught herself up, knowing her own weakness. If once she let him try to coax her round, if once she allowed herself to believe there might be an explanation . . .

'Explain.' She gave him a mirthless smile. 'Tell me that Emma was wrong and that my father hasn't made you a partner in the bank. Then I'll let you explain,' she goaded him and saw his mouth grow hard and grim.

'I can't tell you that,' he said crisply.

'Then you can't tell me anything,' she goaded, adding, 'If you rape me, Daniel——'

'Rape?' He drew in a sharp breath, his eyes brilliant with rage. 'Rape you?' She saw the way he fought to control his anger and trembled inwardly. 'Oh, I'm not going to rape you, Jessica, but I promise you this—you'll remember this night for as long as you live, and I promise you the memory of it is going to make you weep endless tears of regret and pain. How dare you deny what you feel for me? How dare you accuse me of something so base——?' He broke off, and her heart leapt. Perhaps after all she had been wrong. Perhaps there was an explanation. But hard on the heels of her joy came reality to bring her crashing back down to earth. Would she never learn? Of course he wanted to make her think, to make her question, to make her doubt . . . and then, once he had done so, he would use that success to build on, to cajole and coax her.

She *must* be strong, resolute. She *mustn't* allow him to sway her judgement.

'Nothing you can say or do will make me change my mind,' she hissed at him. 'Nothing!'

And only realised when she saw the glitter in his eyes the danger of the challenge she had thrown down at him.

'I'm not going to rape you,' he had said, and in her anguish and outrage she had overestimated her own ability to separate herself from her love for him.

Because, despite everything she *had* learned, despite everything she knew, shamingly, there was still love.

She shuddered beneath the force of it as he cupped her face and said harshly against her mouth, so that she felt the vibration of the words against the too sensitive flesh of her lips as well as heard them, 'You won't let me speak to you and explain, but there are other ways of communication. You say you despise me, hate me. I say you're lying, and that you're running away, turning your back on all that we could have shared, just as you turned your back on your parents. You're very good at cutting yourself off from things and people who you no longer want intruding into your life, aren't you, Jess? I can't *stop* you cutting me out of your life, but I intend to make damn sure that you'll never forget me.'

She had never seen him like this before, never guessed he was capable of such emotion, of such terrible, crushing rage. And yet there was no violence in the way his hands shaped her face, no desire to inflict physical pain, and if she hadn't been looking into his eyes and seen for herself the terrible dark bitterness burning there she might almost have felt that he was still the Daniel of yesterday, and that the whole nightmarish interlude with Emma and her revelations were just exactly that—a nightmare.

Listening to him, looking at him, she might almost have supposed that *he* was the injured party, that *she* was the one with the burden of guilt, who had betrayed their love. *Their* love. He had never loved her, never seen her as a woman, merely as the key to power and wealth.

His mouth touched hers lightly, delicately, sensitising the soft flesh of her lips, the tormenting friction making them moisten and cling, her heart and her body sending conflicting messages to her brain.

Where she had expected a roughly brutal attack, a clinical and malely arrogant attempt to force himself on her, she found instead she was being subjected to the subtlest and most undermining form of seduction.

The harder she tried to escape and break free, the more Daniel bound her to him with whispered kisses that caressed her skin and bemused her brain—light, tormenting touches that inflicted pleasure and not pain, and made her long to be free of the restrictions of her clothes so that her flesh could fully experience the tormenting drift of his hands.

'You love me.'

The words seemed to float into her mind, a magic litany that seemed to strengthen the flow of emotion sensitising her flesh.

The words seemed to lure her on, bemusing her mind, promising undreamed-of pleasures, suborning her mind until, sharply and painfully, she remembered the truth and recoiled from him, shivering with self-revulsion.

In the moonlit room he had an advantage which she did not—he could see the expressions chasing one another across her face, the pain and disillusionment, the bewilderment and anguish.

'Jessica, let me explain.'

Lying here, encircled by his arms, his breath warm and moist against her skin, her body sharply hungry for the pleasure it already sensed he could give it, she was tempted to give in, to let him lie and convince her, to let him take them both into a world of fabrication and let's pretend, but stalwartly she knew deep down inside her that the few hours of pleasure which allowing herself to be further deceived would give her would be outweighed a hundredfold by the anguish the memory of that false pleasure would eventually bring.

Summoning up the last of her will-power, she pushed him away and said fiercely, 'No! I already know all I need to know. You lied to me. I asked you if you knew my father. You said no. That was a lie, wasn't it? Wasn't it?'

He was sitting up, looking down at her, one hard hand on her shoulder pinning her to the bed. Why had she ever considered his eyes warm and tender? Now they were as flat and hard as stone, warning her not to press him too hard, but she ignored the warning, driven by demons of her own, by the knowledge that physically he only had to touch her and her body melted, ached, longed...

'You lied to me,' she reiterated. 'Tell me truthfully that Emma is wrong. That you don't know my father. That you've *never* met him. That he hasn't offered you a partnership in the bank.'

He looked at her for a long time, and then said rawly, 'I can't, but...'

She didn't want to hear any more. Stupidly, one tiny part of her had still hoped, had still prayed desperately that by some miracle she might have been wrong. Hating herself for that weakness, she wrenched herself away from him, surprising them both by her sudden surge of physical strength.

She heard the sound of fabric tearing as she moved, and froze, her eyes widening in shock as the shoulder seam of her dress split beneath the pressure of Daniel's grip and the silky velvet fabric slid downwards over her body, revealing first the pale gleam of her collarbone and then, while she stared at Daniel in frozen shock, the soft curve of her breast, her skin robbed of its colour by the moonlight, her throat, shoulder and now fully exposed breast turned to alabaster in its pale gleam.

An odd tension filled the room, a heavy, preternatural silence that seemed to press down on her, making it hard for her to breathe. Her heart started beating erratically. A pulse jumped in her throat and, unable to drag her gaze from Daniel's, she reached up to cover it protectively, only then realising how much of her body was revealed to him.

A fine shudder that had nothing to do with the bedroom's cool air ran through her body; she gulped in air and fumbled for the torn bodice of her dress, but it was too late. Against the chill of her breast she felt the warmth of Daniel's palm. Her pulse-rate rocketed into sharp acceleration.

'Daniel...No...' she denied huskily, but he wasn't listening to her. The air seemed to pulse with the sheer intensity of the emotional vibrations they were each giving off. Desire, anger, pain, and love.

As his hand slid caressingly around her breast, Jessica tried to draw air into her constricted lungs and found that she couldn't. Even before his thumb touched her nipple it was already erect and pulsing with an ache she prayed he couldn't feel. A channel of hot, feverish sensation ran like a cord from her breast to the pit of her stomach, tightening in a sharp spasm of sensation when he touched her, galvanising her flesh like a small electric shock. Instinctively she tensed against it, thus intensifying its power, her eyes turning dark and wild as she forced back the betraying reactionary shudder.

Half-paralysed with tension, she heard Daniel say her name and looked at him, trembling as she recognised the desire glittering in his eyes.

She hadn't bargained for this, hadn't allowed herself to think that a man hard and cold enough to deliberately plan to deceive her in the way Daniel had deceived her might be vulnerable to the overwhelming physical hunger she could see so plainly etched into his face.

He wanted her, and that wanting was real.

She lifted her hand to push him away, but somehow what should have been a gesture of repudiation became a tremulous caress as her fingertips trembled against his jaw and then slid helplessly towards his mouth, touching it as though she were reading braille. Mindlessly she absorbed the messages of this contact between their flesh, her body as still as that of a statue while she traced the fullness of his bottom lip, the clear-cut indentations at the corners of his mouth, the roughness of the skin above his top lip.

She felt him shudder and focused on him, her eyes betraying her bewilderment at her own behaviour. What *was* she doing?

She moved to snatch away her hand, but Daniel moved faster, his fingers closing round her wrist. She curled her fingers into talons, anger striking through her at this imprisonment, but his tongue was tracing spiral patterns against the soft flesh of her palm, ignoring the threat of the nails poised to rake his skin, and she discovered that the silk cord of desire linking her breast to the deepest, most female part of her body extended into other areas of her flesh. Her resistance melted, her body suddenly boneless, formless, pliable and soft, silently inviting him to mould it as he wished.

Without knowing she was doing so, she leaned towards him. His mouth found the pulse beating frantically in her wrist, and her hand touched the deeper, more vulnerable one in her throat, wondering what it would be like to feel his mouth there, claiming the hot pulse of her life's blood as though he knew that he was the one who gave it force.

An odd light-headedness engulfed her. She shivered and pressed herself closer to him, tensing as she felt the abrasive brush of cloth against the tenderness of her exposed breast. The cloth was in her way, a barrier that tormented her tender skin. Impatiently she pulled her hand free and tugged at the buttons on Daniel's shirt.

His skin wasn't like hers, pale and washed to silver by the moonlight. It was warm and golden, his chest deep and broad, silky with the fine dark hair that felt so soft to her fingertips, and yet when he seized hold of her, dragging her almost roughly against him, holding her mouth under his own while he kissed her with a suppressed violence that made her head spin, that same soft hair against her naked breast created such a wanton, delirious sensation within her that she wanted to tear off the rest of her dress and experience that same delicious friction on every centimetre of her skin.

As though her thoughts communicated themselves to him, she felt him reach behind her for the zip on her dress, and quickly strip it from her.

She shivered once as night-cooled air replaced the feverish heat of his body, and then reached towards him, silently and imploringly, beyond reach now of the voices that might have warned her against what she was doing.

As she lifted her hands towards him, Daniel caught hold of both of them, placing a kiss in each palm, and then holding them against his waist where the remaining closed buttons and his belt pressed into her skin.

Kneeling over her in the darkness, he was at once familiar and unfamiliar, and the tension that made her shiver was woman's age-old thrill of excitement-cum-apprehension as she looked into the face of her lover and saw there the uncontrollable quality of his desire, thrilling to it, and yet at the same time apprehensive of it.

And then, as his gaze fastened on her and became absorbed by the beauty of her body, apprehension turned to joy, mingled with a sharp surge of power. He wanted her; this man who was physically so much the stronger and less vulnerable of them both trembled at the sight of her body, his skin flushed with desire, his voice raw with need as he groaned her name, a plea for permission to reach out and touch her.

Blind, deaf and dumb to her own vulnerability, Jessica watched him, glorying in her power, her eyes slanting and narrowed like a hunting cat's, her smile secret and gently taunting. Without knowing what she was doing, she arched her spine, stretching voluptuously, watching him through half-closed eyes, noting the savagely indrawn breath and the hard tension of his muscles. Her hands left his body and one touched her own, hovering over the small triangle of silk that covered the heart of her sexuality. She frowned, her smile vanishing, her eyes clouding as the ache inside her intensified. She looked at Daniel and saw that he was looking back at her. What she saw in his eyes made her pulse leap. He unfastened the remaining buttons on his shirt, pulling it off and unceremoniously dropping it on the floor. The rest of his clothes were equally summarily dispensed with, every action underlined with a fierce urgency that made her heart race. She sat up, watching him, fascinated by the play of light and shadow across his body. When he pulled her against him, moulding her softness into the harder contours of his own body, the shock of the sudden contact with his flesh destroyed the last of her defences. All that she wanted, all that she needed was this—this blissful contact of flesh upon flesh...this heat...this pleasure...this delirium of joy that promised even greater joy beyond its boundaries.

She heard Daniel whispering to her, asking her things that should have shocked her, promising her things that made desire flood through her.

His hands touched her, shaped her, held her, removed from her the barriers of her stockings and briefs, and then shockingly, blissfully, cupped her, stroked her, and finally slid tormentingly against her, where she had ached for them to do, so that all the silver cords of desire running through her body became as taut as an archer's bow, the sensation dragging primitive sounds of pleasure from her throat, while her spine and her body arched and writhed and his mouth moved slowly and mind-destroyingly down the bared arch of her throat, and then further downwards until it rested between her breasts, ignoring their flagrant, thrusting demand to be pleasured by the raw heat of his mouth until she reached out and slid her hands into his hair, cupping the back of his head, feverishly urging him to give her the pleasure the flushed points of her breasts craved.

When he did, it was like nothing she had ever experienced. Her body trembled and convulsed, the shock of the sensations flooding through her betrayed in her eyes. Her body pulsed, ached, yearned towards him so that there was only intense relief in having the hard maleness of him surging against her.

Her breasts, swollen and tender, pushed eagerly against his chest, delighting in the friction of his movements against her, but that sensation, just like that of his hands on her hips, holding her, lifting her, and the sound of his voice, reassuring her, guiding her, were all subordinate to the need growing inside her.

She arched impatiently beneath him, crying out eagerly as his body responded to the invitation of her own and he entered her, offering her a momentary balm to the sharp intensity of her need.

But with each thrust of his body within her own the ache seemed to recede tantalisingly and tormentingly, always just out of reach of the satisfaction his flesh within her own promised.

Her nails raked his flesh, her teeth sharp and demanding, her body wild with need and inciting a similar savagery within his so that suddenly his movements were no longer controlled and tender, but fierce and elemental, like the eternal, relentless pounding of the sea against the land, driving her closer and closer to that place where the ache could no longer be controlled.

The climax came so quickly and was so earth-shatteringly powerful that it awed and half terrified her. She had a momentary glimpse of Daniel's face, his control shattered; he cried out something to her, his voice harsh and unfamiliar. She had a swift and terrifying awareness of reality and all that went with it, and then her body slid over the edge into darkness, carrying her mind with it.

She slept heavily and dreamlessly, awoken by the sound of her alarm. Her body felt unfamiliar and alien, voluptuously lazy, and yet at the same time sharply alive. In the harsh morning sun her skin seemed to possess a new luminescence, as though it glowed still with remembered pleasure. She turned her head and realised that she was alone as the memories came flooding back. There was a folded note propped up against her radio alarm with her name written on it.

She reached for it, opening it, her hands trembling.

'We *have* to talk. Daniel.'

We have to talk—and she knew about what. How he must be gloating! How he would enjoy ruthlessly reminding her of all that her foolish body had betrayed. He had found the way to entrap her now, and he wouldn't hesitate to use it again. She had no faith in her mind's ability to withstand the desires of her body any longer. Panic engulfed her. She had to escape, to get away...

And then she remembered that in a few days' time she was due in Northumberland. Jane wouldn't mind if she arrived earlier than planned. Daniel wouldn't be able to find her there. Neither would her parents. From that sanctuary, she would write to her parents and tell them that nothing on this earth would induce her to marry Daniel. That she would rather cut herself off from them completely than allow him to so much as lay a finger on her ever again.

She shuddered, clutching the bedclothes to her nude body, remembering how eagerly, how wantonly she had sought far more than the brief touch of his hands on her body last night. Far more. Well, now she had to pay for that weakness, that madness.

All the time she was making the preparations for her flight, her mind was punishing her with vivid mental flashes of tormenting memories of the past twenty-four hours, providing them in taunting mixtures of contrast: her anger and determination to eject Daniel from her life after she had learned the truth, side by side with her wanton, eager pleading for his lovemaking—images that made her stomach churn nauseously and her skin burn with hot, bitter misery.

She had no excuse to offer herself, no explanation nor reason; she had wanted him to make love to her, had eagerly and willingly aided and abetted him in her own mental humiliation.

With good reason had he laughed at her when she'd accused him of threatening her with rape.

Her hands shook as she packed the few clothes she would need; her mind wandered as she tried to concentrate on the far more important tools she might need.

Half of her resented her own weakness, in stealing away in fear, in not confronting Daniel and her parents and making her parents see what they were doing to her.

Her father wanted her married to Daniel, and had bribed him into agreeing, but she doubted that her father had realised just what methods Daniel would use to get her to consent to that marriage. She doubted that either her mother or her father realised how Daniel had damaged her, destroyed her. How he had tricked her into trusting him—into *loving* him.

The nausea rose up inside her again and she fought it down, hurrying through her preparations with a hunted, frantic tension that drove her until she was at last in her car and on her way north.

She was leaving without any letters, any explanations. She would write to her parents from Northumberland. And as for Daniel . . . She smiled mirthlessly and bitterly.

She had no doubt that once he discovered her flight he would realise how pointless it would be for him to pursue this charade of having some believable explanation for his behaviour. How could there be any kind of explanation? He had already admitted he couldn't deny that her father had offered him a partnership, and that he had accepted it. He was condemned by his own mouth.

Driven by the relentless pain of her own self-betrayal, she made good time to Northumberland, not stopping to break her journey other than when she had to refill her car with petrol.

The thought of food nauseated her. Her body was drawn tight with tension and revulsion—revulsion against herself, against her weakness, against that small pocket of rebellion deep inside her which said that her traitorous flesh wanted Daniel as its lover.

Symond Court was several miles away from its nearest village; a gaunt stone edifice that stood with its back to the North Sea and guarded from its vantage-point the empty countryside that surrounded it.

It was a house that had known many changes of fortune. Built originally by one of the Percies, it had passed out of their hands during a game of dice in the eighteenth century.

The man who won it had married a girl twenty years his junior on the strength of its possession, and her family, having discovered that, while he might own the house, he owned no wealth to support and maintain it, punished him for his deception by encouraging his wife into an affair with a prominent Minister of State.

The child of that affair was the only child of the marriage, and in due course he inherited Symond, but preferred not to live there, associating its bleakness with his own childhood.

In Victorian times it had seen a revival of its fortunes and had been sold to one of the new breed of monied men thrown up by the development of the railways. He had shrewdly married his eldest son to a daughter of the Percies, thus establishing for him a social respectability he himself could never attain. The house remained in the hands of their descendants until after the end of the First World War when, crippled by death duties, and having seen the deaths of his father, uncles, brothers and cousins, the sixteen-year-old who inherited it informed his trustees that he wanted it sold. For him the place would always carry too many memories of weeping women, of death and pain; he wanted to escape to somewhere where there was warmth and laughter. The land was sold off to various tenant farmers, the house and a handful of acres gradually falling into disrepair as the trustees sought unsuccessfully for a buyer.

The National Trust had taken it over thirty years previously. It wasn't a great house, nor a particularly famous one, but it did faithfully mirror the changes undergone by many English country houses in the centuries since it was built in 1690 to the present day.

The tapestries had been found hidden away in one of the attics, and after a good deal of research it had been established that they had originally been designed for the state bedroom, and that their designs had originated from Daniel Marot, Huguenot architect, who had been such a great favourite with William of Orange and his Queen Mary.

Jessica had been both thrilled and saddened the first time she saw the tapestries: thrilled by their beauty and rarity, saddened by their neglect and the signs of wear and tear. She had discussed then with Jane the work that would be necessary to restore and repair them.

At any other time the challenge of being invited to undertake this work would have delighted her, but during her long drive north it had been her present-day Daniel who had filled her mind to the exclusion of everything else, and not the Daniel Marot whose skill had originally designed the tapestries.

When she'd stopped to fill her car with petrol, she had taken the precaution of telephoning Jane to alert her to her early arrival.

'No problem,' Jane had told her warmly. 'In fact, I'll be glad of your company. The caretaker and his wife are away on holiday at the moment and the house is closed to visitors, so it's rather lonely.'

It had started to rain as she left the motorway, and now low grey clouds hung over the house, adding to its outward grimness.

The drive, bare of its avenue of once elegant limes, looked stark and uninviting, and Jessica shivered a little as she looked at the grim façade, aching for the warmth and security of her own home, for Daniel's arms...

She shuddered tensely, slamming her hand hard against the steering-wheel, hating herself for her own weakness. She had to forget him, to put him out of her mind, to stop thinking about him.

Jane was waiting for her as she drove round to the rear of the house and parked her car.

'Are you all right?' she asked in some concern as she helped her remove her luggage from the car.

Jessica gave her a tight smile, wondering what it was that had given her away, until they were inside the house and a quick glance in a mirror showed her her white, strained face, and huge dark eyes. The skin beneath them was taut and discoloured as though bruised. She looked, she admitted to herself, haunted.

'It's a long drive,' she said obliquely in response to Jane's question.

'Well, you've certainly made good time. I wasn't expecting you for another couple of hours at least. Let's have a cup of tea, shall we, and then I'll take you up to the tapestries. We've moved them into the workroom in the stable block. The light's much better in there. I'm afraid you're going to be cold, though. We daren't risk turning on the central heating. They're so fragile and brittle in places.'

The tea she made was hot and strong, with an aromatic, almost bitter taste. It scalded Jessica's throat, bringing her back to life. Watching her tremble suddenly, her face flooding with colour, Jane said quietly, 'I don't want to pry, but if you do want to talk...' She pulled a wry face. 'If it's man trouble, I've been there myself...more than once.'

Jessica smiled bitterly. 'Is it really so obvious?'

Jane grimaced apologetically.

'Well, yes, I'm afraid it is.'

Much as she liked her, Jessica couldn't talk to her. The hurt was still too raw, too new. All she really wanted to do was to crawl away somewhere and die, but she couldn't do that. She had to get over it, to go on...

She looked out of the window at the darkening sky and said, 'I think it might be a good idea for me to leave the tapestries until tomorrow. The light just isn't good enough now.'

'OK. I'll take you up to your room.' Jane hesitated and looked at her. 'I'm afraid I've got a date tonight, but I could cancel it if——'

Jessica shook her head. 'No, please don't—not on my account. I'm not very good company at the moment and, to be honest, I'd rather be alone.'

Jane gave her an understanding smile. 'Well, there's food in the fridge, and plenty of canned stuff in the cupboards. Just help yourself, and then tomorrow after breakfast I'll take you across to the workrooms.'

In normal circumstances the room Jane showed her to would have enchanted and delighted her; as it was, she barely noticed the rich damask of the hangings enclosing the bed, only half listening to her as Jane described how the pattern had been copied from a faded, torn scrap of fabric found during the renovation work.

'We had it copied in Lyons, using the traditional methods of weaving the fabric, and using modern dyes. Because the traditional dyes were so unreliable and faded so easily, we tend to forget how very rich and striking their original colours must have been—not to say garish,' Jane added with a grin, reaching out and touching the bed hangings, admitting, 'I love this shade of red, though. It's so vibrant and warm.'

The room had a fireplace, but, as Jane explained to her, no fire could be lit in it. 'Fire hazard,' she added pulling a face. 'We simply daren't take the risk.' She hovered for a moment, and then said awkwardly, 'Look, if you want some company, I could always cancel my date.'

It was only pride that enabled Jessica to lift her head and force a smile to her own lips.

'No. It's all right. I might *look* suicidal,' she said, striving to make her voice light and succeeding only in giving it a metallic brittleness, 'but I promise you I'm not.'

Not suicidal maybe, she acknowledged after she had reassured Jane and closed the door after her, but desperately aware of an inner aloneness, a coldness of spirit that pierced her, reminding her too painfully of how only a short time ago she had known the deep inner warmth that comes from close intimacy with one special person.

She thought she had known all there was to know about pain and loneliness, but she was beginning to discover she had not. When she had turned her back on her parents and the life they had planned for her, she had suffered, missed them, but that pain was nothing like the pain that rent her now.

Her body ached for sleep, just as much as her mind ached for release into oblivion, but both were denied her as she moved restlessly in the huge tester bed, her mind racked by self-contempt and anguish, her body racked with its longing to have Daniel beside her. Holding her, touching her, loving her...

With a low moan she turned on to her stomach, burying her face in her pillow. This was sheer stupidity, idiocy. If she allowed her thoughts to continue unchecked they would surely drive her to madness.

Cravenly, she longed for some magic pill which would miraculously wipe her heart and body clear of any memory of Daniel, but no such cure existed.

CHAPTER NINE

WORKING on the tapestries might be keeping her hands busy, but it was doing nothing to control the waywardness of her thoughts, Jessica acknowledged, lifting her head from her work and gazing unseeingly through the large north-facing window of the workshop.

She had been in Northumberland for two days, trying to concentrate all her energies on the task confronting her, but it wasn't working. Physically she might be here in Northumberland, but mentally, emotionally, she was still trapped in her bedroom at home, aching for Daniel, wanting him, loving him.

Her work was almost completed. Soon it would be time for her to return home. Jane had a busy social life and had invited her to join her this evening, when she was going out to dinner with friends.

Jessica had refused. She preferred to be on her own. There was no point in inflicting her misery on others.

Already it was mid-afternoon. Soon it would be dusk, and too dark for her to work. The evening stretched out in front of her emptily.

The house had a library full of books, and the small sitting-room Jane had invited her to use had a television set, but nothing held a strong enough appeal to wrench her mind away from its obsessive dwelling on Daniel.

She considered going to bed early, but the thought of going there, going compulsively over and over every second she had spent with Daniel, everything they had said and done, and then contrasting the rosy dream she had allowed herself to be drawn into then with the harsh reality of the truth, held no appeal either.

There had not been a moment from the time when she had last seen him when she had not been thinking about him. She had come up here to escape, to give herself a breathing space, but what if once she returned Daniel was not prepared to accept that she no longer wanted to see him? He was a determined man.

She was just watching the late evening news when she heard a car outside. She got up and went to the window, but it was too dark for her to see anything. It was still too early for Jane to be returning, and a tiny tendril of apprehension feathered down her spine. What if someone was about to break into the house? It contained many valuable pieces of furniture and paintings. And then the enormous, old-fashioned and very loud doorbell rang demandingly, and she dismissed her fears as idiotic and hurried downstairs.

It took her several minutes to deal with the complicated locks and bolts on the door, but foolishly, as she opened the door itself, she forgot to secure the safety-chain. She wasn't used to living with such elaborate security precautions, and it was only when the door was pushed open abruptly from the other side and Daniel strode in that she realised her own folly.

Stunned by the unexpectedness of his arrival, here where she had believed he would never know where to find her, she could only stare at him in stupefaction.

'Surprise, surprise!' he mocked her as he pushed the door closed with a gentle, and yet somehow rather intimidating, movement of his hand. He smiled at her equally gently, and she shivered, hating herself for her weakness.

That feeling which had invaded the pit of her stomach when she opened the door and saw him had nothing to do with hatred or anger.

It had been instinctive, automatic, indelible. She still loved him.

Shaken by her own stupidity, she turned away from him, thinking in some way that she might be able to remain stronger if she wasn't looking at him, if she was not being subjected to his effect on three of her five senses all at the same time; and the other two, touch and taste... She shuddered visibly, recalling all too clearly just how his body had felt beneath her touch, just how his skin had tasted...

'What are you doing here?' she demanded abruptly. 'How did you find me?'

She wasn't going to look at him, but the hair on the nape of her neck lifted gently in warning as he moved towards her and she felt the air behind her stir.

She froze, willing her body to repudiate him if he touched her. But he didn't, and only she knew just how much her recalcitrant body ached to feel the warmth of his hands on it.

'If you want to vanish completely, you shouldn't leave names and addresses on your answering machine,' he told her calmly.

Of course—that message from Jane. How could she have been so idiotic? And then shamingly she picked up on the cynicism in his voice, and whirled round, denying hotly. 'If you think I did that deliberately, so that you would come running after me...' Pain and anger choked her. 'You had no right to go into my house, to pry into my private things.' He was looking at her grimly, like an adult waiting for a child to finish a temper tantrum; his very lack of response to her accusations lashed her into a greater fury. 'You really are desperate, aren't you? I suppose it was naïve of me to think that once you'd discovered that neither lying to me nor seducing me were going to work, you'd give up.'

He was still watching her silently, distantly. Out of the corner of her eye she caught sight of her handbag, and, picking it up with an impulsive, bitter movement, she fumbled inside it and extracted a handful of silver, throwing it at his feet and crying fiercely, 'Thirty pieces of silver. That's the usual payment for a Judas, isn't——'

And then stood frozen with shock and horror at her own uncontrolled behaviour while he slowly picked up the money, and then said softly—too softly, her mind warned her—'You miscalculated. There are only twenty-nine pieces here, which means that I still haven't had full payment.'

He took one step towards her, and then another, and too late she saw how deceptive his distant calm had been. In reality he was far from calm; the lack of light in the hallway had not allowed her to see the hard glitter of anger-spiked bitterness in his eyes, nor to guess at the tension of his body beneath his seemingly relaxed pose.

He was going to touch her, kiss her, and once he did—once he did, no matter that that kiss was given in punishment and rage, she would be lost, as lost as she had been when they'd made love, clinging to him, crying to him to do with her what he wished, to make of her what he willed.

'What is it?' she cried out frantically, betraying more of her terror than she knew. 'What do you want?'

But she already knew what he wanted. He wanted her father's wealth, and ultimately her father's power. He wanted the bank, and to get it he was prepared to fulfil the conditions her father had set upon its acquisition. Marriage to her.

'Don't touch me,' she begged wildly, her self-control shattering under the tension of his slow advance towards her. She had already backed as far away from him as she could, and her skin burned as she heard her own shaming plea and recognised the panic and fear in her voice.

'Touch you?' He stopped and frowned, his mouth curling as though in disgust at the very thought, his expression suddenly changing as the rage died out of his eyes, the hot red glitter replaced by cold hardness. 'I haven't come to play games, Jessica. I'm not here on my own behalf, but on your mother's. Your father's had a heart attack. He's in Intensive Care. You mother needs you with her.'

She didn't believe it. He was lying to her—using another ploy to weaken her.

'You're lying to me,' she whispered, her face suddenly ashen. 'I don't believe you.'

'No, you wouldn't, would you?' He reached for her too quickly for her to avoid him, grasping her arm and dragging her towards the telephone on the table by the stairs.

Holding her arm in a grip so tight that she could already feel her flesh going numb, his eyes never leaving her face, he punched out a number into the telephone.

Jessica heard it ringing, and then when the ringing stopped he said tersely into the receiver, 'Intensive Care, Sister Allen, please.'

Jessica's head started to thud uncomfortably. What if he *wasn't* lying? What if it *was* true? What if her father's heart attack had in part been brought on by the discovery that she was refusing to fall in with his plans?

Anger, fear, pain...a conflicting mix of emotions gripped her as she stood there, her throat dry with apprehension, her eyes locked on Daniel's.

Holding the receiver slightly away from his ear, so that she could hear the voice on the other end, he said tersely, 'Sister Allen, I'm sorry to bother you. It's Daniel Hayward. How is Mr Collingwood?'

There was a moment's pause, and then Jessica heard a woman's voice saying quietly, 'Rather poorly at the moment, I'm afraid, Mr Haywood. As you know, he's had a major heart attack, and I'm afraid it's still far too early to give you any more information than that.'

Jessica stared at the receiver. She tried to speak, and found that her tongue had become thick and clumsy and that her head was buzzing. She saw Daniel put down the receiver and then turn to look at her, a frown replacing the grim hauteur with which he had been regarding her.

'Oh, God, don't look at me like that, Jess,' she thought she heard him saying, but the words were indistinct and fuzzy, and the world was turning dark all around her. She was being sucked down into a dark, cold vacuum, which she fought desperately against letting claim her.

Sick and dizzy, she was conscious of Daniel picking her up and depositing her in one of the hard antique chairs that furnished the hallway.

She wanted to close her eyes to blot out his face, but she knew that if she did she would lose consciousness completely. She had to focus on something to will herself not to give way to the panic and fear inside her.

'I'm sorry, I shouldn't have broken it to you like that.'

Compassion. Concern. She stared blankly at Daniel, her body trembling as though she were frozen. He was holding her hands, she suddenly realised, crouching down on the floor beside her, his thumbs registering the too rapid race of the pulse in her wrists.

'Let go of me, I'm all right.'

Her father in Intensive Care . . . Strange how she had never thought of her parents as vulnerable before. Strange how she suddenly felt as frightened and abandoned as a small child. She hadn't lived with them for years—rarely saw them—and if asked would have said that she was an adult and no longer dependent on them in any kind of way, but now she realised that it wasn't true.

She struggled to stand up, swaying uncertainly on her feet, her eyes blank.

'I must go home. My mother. Why didn't *she* ring me?' she cried out in sharp anguish.

Daniel was still holding her hands, still refusing to let her go.

'Perhaps she was afraid you'd refuse to come,' he told her quietly.

'Refuse?' She looked at him, her eyes dark with shock. 'but he's my father.'

'Yes, but you've made it very plain that you want to keep your life separate from theirs, haven't you, Jessica?'

'Because I couldn't be what they wanted. But that doesn't mean that I don't *love* them, that I don't *care* . . .'

She started to cry, her body shaking with emotion as she fought to control her feelings.

'I must go home. My things . . . I need to pack.'

'I'll do that for you,' Daniel told her. 'You just tell me how to find your room, and then we'll be on our way—at this time of night we should make good time.'

'We?' Jessica stared at him, and then said shakily, 'I'm not going back with *you*.'

The look he gave her made her feel small and ashamed, as though somehow she was behaving more like a child than a woman.

'I have my own car here,' she pointed out in a calmer voice. Naturally I——'

'Naturally nothing,' Daniel overruled her. 'You're in no fit state to drive, and if you're honest you'll admit it.' He saw her face and smiled unkindly.

'Yes, I know how much against the grain it must go that I'm the one to have had to break the news and witness your... distress. You've had a severe shock, Jessica, and if you won't consider the risk to your own life of driving several hundred miles while suffering from that shock, then at least think of the lives of the other people you might be putting at risk.'

She looked away from him, unable to deny the truth of what he was saying.

'Besides,' he added calmly, 'my car will make much better time than yours.'

'But you must be tired yourself,' she pointed out. 'You've only just arrived.'

Suddenly she realised how much he had taken on his shoulders, how very different his behaviour was from what she would have expected, but then she reminded herself of all that he stood to lose if anything should happen to her father, and of what a golden opportunity this must be to him to try to bring her round, to persuade her...

She ought to make a stand, to tell him that there was no way she was going to allow him to drive her back to London, but the thought of the long, tiring drive south, the knowledge that she was in no fit state to make that drive, silenced her.

'Your room?' Daniel demanded curtly.

Numbly Jessica told him, too drained to continue arguing. She watched with listless eyes as he went upstairs, and then, remembering his long drive and the equally long one ahead of them, she roused herself and went into the small kitchen which formed part of the caretaker's suite of rooms.

Jane had told her to make herself completely at home in this part of the house, and she knew the other girl would not mind her raiding the fridge in order to make some sandwiches and a flask of coffee for the homeward journey once she knew what had happened.

Thinking of Jane reminded Jessica that she ought to leave the other girl a note. She was just writing it when Daniel walked into the kitchen with her case.

'I've made you some sandwiches,' she told him curtly. 'I thought you might be hungry.'

She saw the surprise lighten his eyes and felt a momentary pang of remorse, a longing for things to be different, and even a rebellious wish that she had never opened the door to her cousin—never learned the truth.

'Something wrong?' Daniel asked her, watching her closely.

Hot colour scorched her skin. How he would laugh if he could read her thoughts.

In addition to filling a flask with fresh coffee, she'd poured them both a mug. She knew *she* needed the reviving, caffeine-induced surge of energy the drink would give, and she suspected that, although he wasn't showing it, Daniel must be feeling the effect of his long drive.

Turning away from him so that he couldn't see her face, she picked up one of the mugs and handed it to him, saying shortly, 'No, of course not.' And then suddenly, as though in denial of her claim, her hand started shaking, slopping the coffee on to the table, and to her horror she felt her eyes filling up with tears as a mixture of fear and urgency swept over her. Hating herself for being so vulnerable, she added bitterly, 'After all, it's not as though I've any reason to feel shocked and upset, is it?'

He gave her a cynical look. 'If you're trying to tell me those tears are for your father...'

His jibe stung and she retaliated bitterly. 'Just because I won't allow my father to run my life for me, it doesn't mean I don't love him... that I don't care... He *is* my father.'

'Is he? I had the impression your relationship with your parents was something you preferred to pretend didn't exist.'

His accusation hurt her, leaving her bereft of any defences, and too vulnerable to the small inner voice that told her that there must have been many times in the past when she had unwittingly hurt her parents, more so than she herself had ever realised, if it were true that her mother had felt so unsure of her response that she hadn't wanted to telephone her with the news of her father's heart attack. She had to remind herself that even now he was not above using her vulnerability to reinforce his own position, to emotionally coerce her.

'I never said that,' she denied sharply.

'Not in so many words, but you certainly gave me that impression. You don't trust anyone who knows your parents—hardly the sentiments of a loving child,' he taunted her.

'Maybe not, but they were certainly justified, weren't they?' Jessica accused, anger overtaking vulnerability. 'I may not share my parents' views on the direction I want my life to take, but that doesn't mean I don't care.'

There was a small silence, and then Daniel said grimly, 'Tell that to your father if——' He broke off, but she knew what he had been about to say. 'If he's still alive.'

Something broke apart inside her, spilling pain throughout her body, unleashing a veritable Pandora's box of emotions so complex and agonising that she wanted to cry out in protest against them.

'I can't be the daughter my parents want,' she said huskily, speaking her pain out loud. 'I *can't* sacrifice my life and emotions to the bank.'

Daniel had finished his coffee.

'Time to go,' he told her curtly, cutting across her emotional outburst.

It was only later, sitting next to him in his car as he drove south, that she remembered that he had never given her back the money she had thrown at him in such anguish and disdain, and for some reason she couldn't quite analyse that struck a tiny note of alarm somewhere deep inside her.

They were on the motorway, which was mercifully free of heavy traffic at this time of night, and Daniel had been silent for so long that it was a shock to hear him saying smoothly, 'I take it the bedroom you were in wasn't very warm.'

Astonishment made her turn her head to look at him, her expression unguarded and puzzled as she looked at his unreadable profile. He was concentrating on the road, not looking at her, even though she knew he must be conscious of her scrutiny. A car came up behind them, being driven far too fast, and he changed gear, pulling to one side to allow it to pass. The movement caught her attention, causing her to focus automatically on his thigh.

A huge wave of sensation washed through her, her body quivering as her mind fought against the images flashing across her brain. It shocked her that such a small, mundane movement could have the power to arouse images of such sensuality and intimacy, and her mind recoiled, horrified by what the conscious part of it considered to be an unforgivable invasion into the privacy of another person.

She had never before in all her life looked at a man and immediately conjured up a mental vision of him naked, aroused by desire, offering the pleasures of his body to her for her enjoyment. And what was even more disturbing was her own reaction to the wantonness of that imagery.

Confused and ashamed, she forced herself to drag her gaze from his body and focus on his face, her mind swimming with shock and bewilderment.

'My bedroom, cold?' she managed to stammer. 'I... No... I don't... What makes you think that?'

'The nightdress you were wearing,' he told her casually, momentarily and totally unexpectedly diverting his attention from the road to her.

'My nightdress?' She frowned, remembering how quickly she had packed for her journey north, wrenching out of a drawer a hideous winceyette nightdress which she had been given as a Christmas present one year, and by Emma, of all people.

She felt herself go hot and then cold as she realised that if Daniel had found her nightdress, then he had doubtless found and packed her underwear as well, although why she should feel so embarrassed at the thought of him touching her things she really had no idea. If she was honest with herself, anyway, it wasn't the thought of him touching the clothes he had removed from her drawer that disturbed her so much, but the remembered sensation of his hands removing them from her body.

'Yes... yes, it was cold. The house doesn't have central heating...' She realised too late that she was babbling a panic-stricken explanation and fell silent, not sure which of them she hated the most, herself or him.

'You realise that we still have to talk, don't you?' he continued calmly.

'Talk?' She jerked herself back to reality and gave him a bitter look. 'What about? You can't have anything to say that I want to hear.'

'No,' he agreed acidly. '*You* wouldn't. All you want to do is run away, to punish me the way you punished your parents.'

Jessica sucked in her breath, outraged that he should dare to accuse her.

'I thought you were a woman,' he went on inexorably, 'but you're not. You're a spoiled, selfish child who isn't capable of thinking beyond her own immaturity——'

'You're just saying that because you still think you can persuade me, convince me,' she interrupted him hotly, only to fall silent as he said coldly,

'No, Jessica. I have no intention of persuading or convincing you of anything. I was foolish enough once to offer you an explanation—an explanation of something that ought to have been taken on trust,' he told her grimly. 'But you *have* no trust. You couldn't wait to believe the worst of me, could you? You couldn't wait to reject me. Oh, no. I'm not your doting daddy. I'm not going to pander to you, coaxing and persuading you. Trust, love—they're two-way things, and if you think I want to share my life with a woman who doesn't respect me enough as a human being to know that I wouldn't deceive her without some very good reason——' He broke off and looked directly at her, and Jessica felt her heart plummet, and a horrid feeling of shame and misery engulf her. There was no love in his eyes, no warmth, no teasing, male appreciation, only a flat, metallic hardness that repudiated her and denied her, and for some reason she felt as though *she* were the one in the wrong.

'I don't know why you're telling me this,' she said fiercely. 'There's no relationship between us any more.'

'At least that's something we can agree on,' he countered coldly. 'All I'm doing is making my position clear. I'm here on your parents' behalf, not my own, so please disabuse yourself of any idea you might have that I'm going to try to coax or persuade you in any shape or form.'

'I'm glad!' Jessica snapped. 'Because it wouldn't work. We've both already agreed, it's finished.'

'Not quite,' Daniel told her silkily.

A tiny *frisson* of fear feathered down her spine. There was something in the way he spoke, something in the cold, hard way he smiled at her...

'There's still the matter of your twenty-nine pieces of silver. Poor Jessica,' he mocked cruelly. 'You couldn't even get that right, could you? One day, not very far from now, you're going to wish more than you've wished anything else in your life that you hadn't made that gesture, Jess.'

'Never,' she told him quickly. 'Never!' And then wondered uncertainly why it was that she was having such a strong premonition of danger.

It must have something to do with the power of his voice, she comforted herself, because there was absolutely no way he could be doing anything other than making the most outrageously impossible threats... Was there?

CHAPTER TEN

DESPITE Jessica's insistence that he take her straight to the hospital, Daniel took her instead to a small and very obviously expensive private hotel, where he stunned her by announcing that he had booked her a room.

'What for?' she demanded.

'Your mother will be at the hospital with your father. I suggest that it would be wiser to telephone and discover how your father is before rushing round there.'

While she could see the wisdom of this, Jessica felt compelled to point out that she could quite easily have gone to her parents' home in Kensington rather than come here with him.

'Do you have a key to the Kensington house?' he asked her quietly.

Jessica's face flamed. She didn't, of course.

'Your mother has enough to cope with without worrying about you. I told her I'd bring you to London and that I'd make sure you had a bed for the night.'

'Very sure of yourself, weren't you?' Jessica stormed at him. 'I suppose what you had in mind was my sharing *your* bed.'

She was stunned by the look of acid disdain he gave her. It silenced her, leaving her throat dry and her muscles tense.

'Now who's guilty of coercion?' he asked her softly, watching the colour rise up under her skin and then saying cruelly, 'If you want to make love with me, why not be honest and just say so?'

'I don't,' Jessica told him wildly, her heart pounding with shame and rage. 'And anyway, it wouldn't be making love—it would be just sex.'

She felt her heart plummet as he looked at her, his mouth twisting.

'You almost tempt me, but I don't have the time or the inclination to play those kind of games. There's a telephone here in the foyer. I suggest we ring the hospital from there, just so that neither of us gets any confusing ideas about each other's motives. I *was* going to offer to take you up to your room, but under the circumstances...'

Jessica had never felt so humiliated in her life, and the worst thing of all was that his accusation held a grim kernel of truth, even if she had only realised that fact herself after he had pointed it out to her.

As he walked across to the public telephone Jessica wished she had the strength to dismiss him and tell him that she didn't need his help, that she would make the call, but she knew that some part of her was frightened—frightened of what she might hear, frightened of the pain of learning that her father was dead, frightened of the burden of guilt that news would bring—and so, torn between resentment and anguish, she watched while he dialled the number and spoke once more to the ward sister.

The conversation was brief, and she was unable to hear it without joining him in the cramped intimacy of the booth—something she had no desire to do. Another weakness, another failing, she taunted herself bitterly as she waited for him to rejoin her, her stomach in knots of tension, her mind clouded by fears.

'He's holding his own,' he told her tersely. 'He's only allowed one visitor at the moment, and it's your mother's wish to stay with him.'

'Does she know? Does she know I'm here?' she asked him unevenly.

'Yes. I told her you were here. The best thing you can do now is to try and get some sleep,' he told her, turning his back on her, dismissing her, she recognised.

She swallowed and said painfully, 'If anything should happen to my father...'

'I've asked the hospital to let us know.'

She felt perilously close to tears, and ached for the warmth of his arms round her, holding her, protecting her...

What was she thinking? There was no safety, no warmth, no protection for her in Daniel's arms.

She went up to her room alone. It was well appointed, and a good size. Someone had already taken up her case, and there was also a thermos of coffee and a plate of delicate sandwiches, the sight and smell of which made her stomach lurch protestingly with nausea.

She spent what was left of the night tormenting herself with regrets for all that she had left unsaid and undone to show her parents how much she did love them.

Daniel had made her see the different and hurtful construction someone else might have put on the way she had so determinedly detached herself from her parents' lives—not knowing that it was because of her great fear that out of love for them she might commit herself to a life which she had known would ultimately lead to intense unhappiness for her.

Had she been as selfish and thoughtless as Daniel had implied? Perhaps she *could* have explained in more depth to her parents just why she had felt too vulnerable, too fearful of succumbing to the need she had felt in both of them, but more especially in her father, that she should be a part of the chain that linked the past with the future.

Only now, alone with the bleakness of her thoughts, did she realise that part of her fear, her resentment, had sprung from jealousy of the tradition which had made the bank such an important part of her father's life; as though, in turning her back on it, she was making a childish attempt to demand from him a statement that *she* was more important than the bank, like a child jealous of its siblings.

A flush of shame for her own immaturity stung her skin. Nothing would make her change her mind about the necessity for her to live her own life. She could never have made a career in the bank and found the contentment and satisfaction she found in her present work, but she could have explained in more depth, discussed, talked to her parents about her feelings, instead of seizing the excuse of her kidnap and thus foisting on them both, but more especially on her father, a burden of guilt that it was their fault that she had left the bank, that it was the bank raid and her subsequent ordeal at the hands of her kidnappers which had led to her desire to change her whole way of life, when in truth that had simply been an excuse she had seized upon because she was too weak to admit the truth.

Dawn came and brought no surcease from her mental anguish. Her head ached; she felt sick, alternately hot and cold as she tried not to let her imagination portray her father's death.

As her feeling of nausea grew she put her hand on her stomach and prayed grimly that the only reason for her nausea was her fear for her father. To have conceived Daniel's child would be the ultimate irony—her father would have his grandson, after all, or maybe a granddaughter, and she... She gave a fierce shudder and banked down hard on her too fertile imagination. Didn't she already have enough to worry about?

The discreet tap on her door startled her. For a moment she thought it might be Daniel, and the fierce thrust of emotion that speared her at that thought was its own betrayal, and didn't need underlining by the swift downward plunge of disappointment when the door opened and a smiling girl came in carrying a tray of tea.

Thanking her, Jessica poured herself a cup, her hand shaking when she recognised the aromatic blend she herself favoured first thing in the morning. Only Daniel could have ordered that particular tea for her, and to her consternation her hand wavered and her eyes filled with tears. When he had already hurt her in so many harsher ways, why it should be this small, deliberate hurting that should cause her to waver on the edge of breaking down, she did not know.

She looked at the phone. How long before she could ring the hospital? On impulse she picked up her clothes and hurried into the bathroom, showering and dressing before she had time to change her mind, leaving the cold tea undrunk as she found her handbag and let herself out of the room.

The hotel foyer was deserted apart from the receptionist on duty, as well it might be at this early hour.

Outside, the sun was struggling to emerge from behind a barrier of clouds, the air sharp and bitter, flavoured with the scents of the winter to come.

The commissionaire found her a taxi, and as it traversed the still quiet city streets Jessica realised with a shock how close it was to Christmas.

The knowledge brought a sharp stab of urgency, a need to see her father. Memories of past Christmases when she was a child flashed through her mind. How loved she had been, indulged but never spoilt. She closed her eyes in mental agony, wondering why it had taken Daniel to show her all she had deliberately blinded herself to.

Outside the hospital she hesitated, half yearning to turn back, afraid to go forward, afraid of the pain that might be waiting for her, and then a smiling porter asked her helpfully if she was lost, and she told him she was looking for the intensive care unit.

After he had directed her to it, he added warningly, 'Not that they're likely to let you in—not unless . . .' but Jessica was already hurrying away, suddenly in a fever of urgency to see her mother.

The doors to the intensive care ward were firmly closed. A nurse was seated outside at a desk, working on what looked like a horrendous mass of paper. She looked up curiously as Jessica approached her.

Awkwardly, Jessica gave her name, her tongue suddenly clumsy, her heart beating too fast with nervous dread.

'My father——' she began, and then broke off as the ward doors opened and her mother approached.

She hadn't seen Jessica, and the shock of seeing her normally immaculately groomed and coiffeured mother without her make-up, her face drawn, her hair untidy, traces of tears clearly discernible on her face seemed to seize her body in a paralysis of dread, and then her mother saw her and opened her arms to her, saying tremulously, 'Darling, it's all right. Your father is doing very well. He's over the worst now, and there's every chance that he's going to make a full recovery.' She gave a rather watery chuckle. 'His doctor says that this attack was a warning shot across the bows, and that if he takes heed of it . . .' She hugged Jessica tightly. 'Come in and see him for yourself.'

Shakily Jessica followed her into the ward, tensing at the sight of her father wired up to what seemed to be a formidable array of machinery, but he had seen her, and he was smiling at her, and suddenly she was overwhelmed with such a flood of love and awareness that it was impossible for her to speak.

'So Daniel found you,' her father said gently. 'He said he would.'

Daniel . . . The sound of his name brought her crashing back to earth, but she couldn't, wouldn't, do anything to spoil this moment, so she smiled and held tight to her mother's hand while the three of them shared the intensely emotional communion with one another.

Later, euphoric with relief, she went back to the Kensington house with her mother, surprised to discover how hungry she was, how suddenly alive and aware.

'I thought Daniel was going to come to the hospital with you,' her mother remarked as she made some coffee.

'I didn't want to disturb him,' Jessica fibbed. In truth she hadn't wanted Daniel to accompany her, and the note she had left him had been brittly polite and cold.

'No, he must have been exhausted,' her mother commented. 'I can't tell you how marvellous he's been. It's such a relief to know that the bank's in such capable hands. I can't help thinking that it's the stress and strain of these last few months which have contributed to your father's heart attack. The fear of the bank being taken over by some huge conglomerate whose ideology is totally different from your father's...I know that when Daniel first approached him with his company's offer, your father adamantly refused to consider it.' She chuckled reminiscently. 'He was furious when he came home. Outraged at this up-and-coming entrepreneur who dared to believe he could take over. And then, when he'd calmed down, he admitted to me that there were problems with the bank, that some of the shareholders might be tempted into selling their shares to one of those corporations that specialise in dawn raids on people whom they see as their competitors, followed by a rapid take-over of the company and then its destruction. Daniel at least, he admitted, wanted to maintain the bank as a going concern, to improve and enlarge its business activities, but his pride was stung a little, I think, by the knowledge that such a young man had built up a company large enough to take over the bank.' She smiled warmly at Jessica. 'That's something you and your father have always shared. Your pride.'

Jessica stared numbly at her.

'Mother, are you trying to tell me that Daniel has *taken over* the bank?'

Her mother looked puzzled.

'Well, yes, dear. I thought you knew that. Of course, there hasn't been an official announcement as yet. After all, your father and Daniel only signed the formal agreement a few days ago. Actually your father was rather cross.' She pulled a face. 'Of all the things to happen, your cousin Emma arrived in his office just as the formal signing was taking place. She had apparently ignored his secretary's request that she wait until your father had time to see her. Your father wasn't very pleased, I'm afraid, especially when his secretary told him that she found Emma actually eavesdropping outside his office door.'

The kitchen had started to spin dizzily around her. Jessica clutched the edge of the table, feeling she had stepped into a horrific nightmare.

'But I thought... I thought that Daniel was joining the bank as a junior partner.'

She saw her mother frown.

'Oh, no. What on earth gave you that idea?'

Jessica couldn't speak, and her mother mused maternally, 'We were so pleased when we learned that Daniel had bought a house so close to your village. I'm afraid, between us, your father and I must have bored him to tears singing your praises, but we're both so proud of you and all that you've achieved.' She bit her lip and added a little uncomfortably, 'Don't be cross with me, darling, but I'm afraid I did rather overdo the maternal bit a little in suggesting he might care to get in touch with you, but your father and I both liked him so much. I think it must be the eternal curse on all mothers that, where their children are concerned, they just can't resist matchmaking. I think he was rather uncomfortable about my suggestion, but obviously he did take me up on it.'

Her head whirling slowly and cautiously, Jessica began to question her mother, and what she learned made her tremble inwardly with sickening recognition of her own folly.

It was Emma who had lied to her, not Daniel. There could be no doubt about that, but, just to make doubly sure, she said as casually as she could, 'Emma called to see me a few days ago. She seems to know Daniel quite well.'

Her mother pulled a face. 'Well, that's another small problem we've had. Daniel was here for dinner one night when Emma arrived unexpectedly. She said she knew Daniel, and I asked her to join us, and I'm afraid I put him in a very embarrassing position. It turns out, although I suspect he's given us a rather sanitised version of the story, that Emma was introduced to him at a party some time ago, and that since then she's been making rather a nuisance of herself. He was quite blunt about it, and told us that he doubted that her feelings were in any way involved, and that it had been obvious to him from the moment he was introduced to her that she was, as he put it, on the look-out for a wealthy husband.'

Her mother spread her hands. 'What could I say? We all know that it's true. Of course, I apologised for putting him in an embarrassing position, but since then I'm afraid your cousin has been virtually hounding him. Your poor father was furious that she took advantage of her relationship with him to turn up at his office like that, and it was obvious she knew Daniel was there. I'm afraid he had to speak rather severely to her, and I also think that it was his interview with her that was at least partly to blame for his heart attack.'

She gave a faint sigh. 'I'm afraid there are people in this world who, like your cousin, can never be content with their lives, and so must always be searching for something more. I feel very sorry for her. Now tell me, darling—what do you think of Daniel?' she invited eagerly.

Jessica gave her a wan smile, her face totally devoid of colour. 'I'm sorry, Mum, but I'm not feeling very well... I...' She stood up unsteadily and raced for the downstairs cloakroom.

'It's just the shock of everything,' she muttered feebly once she was back in the kitchen with her mother fussing anxiously over her. She wasn't lying, after all—just not explaining exactly what kind of shock it was she was enduring.

'You must be exhausted,' her mother sympathised. 'I ought to be myself, but I think the relief of knowing your father is going to be all right has put me on some kind of elevated plateau.'

'I think it's called euphoria,' Jessica teased her weakly. Oh, how she wanted to be alone—needed to be alone—but she owed it to her mother to stay here with her. For once in her life, it was time to put someone else's feelings before her own. She was here to *help* her mother, not to burden her.

Later she was thankful for the constantly ringing telephone, for the people who had to be advised of her father's progress, for the hundred and one small jobs her mother found her to do, because they kept her physically occupied, kept her from being left on her own to dwell on the enormity of her misjudgement of Daniel.

'I can explain,' he had said, but she wouldn't let him, and now it was too late. She remembered the money she had thrown at him, the words she had said . . .

For three days she managed to keep up a pretence of normality, but on the third morning she answered the telephone and, on hearing Daniel's voice on the other end of the line, started to tremble so violently that she dropped the receiver and then fled to her room.

She wasn't surprised when her mother followed her there and said quietly, 'Do you want to talk about it?'

Surprisingly, she discovered that she did, grateful for the fact that her mother listened in silence, not interrupting until she had finished.

'Oh, Jessica,' she said sadly.

'Yes, I know,' Jessica whispered hollowly. 'He'll never forgive me. How could he? I've destroyed...what...whatever there might have been. But why didn't he tell me?'

Her mother was watching her pityingly, and she hadn't even told her the very worst of it—that shameful, irrational gesture of high drama that was now rebounding on her so cruelly.

'Perhaps he tried,' her mother said tentatively. Jessica started to deny it, and then remembered that there had been an occasion on which Daniel had seemed on the verge of saying something to her. And then, of course, afterwards, he had tried to explain, but she had refused to let him. 'If he still loves you——' her mother continued, but Jessica made a gesture of dismissal and said bitterly,

'Why not say, if I had loved him? I did...I do...but love on its own isn't enough, is it? I mistrusted him. I believed Emma without stopping to question what she was telling me. I refused to give him the benefit of the doubt, to listen when he asked me to. How much contact is Daddy likely to have with him, once...once he's back on his feet?' she asked obliquely.

Her mother sighed. 'Well, the plan is that Daniel will take over as chairman, but he has asked your father to stay on in an advisory capacity, and, of course, your father will retain his seat on the board. I'm afraid there will be rather a lot of occasions when he's likely to be a part of our lives. Of course, you no longer live here——'

She broke off, remembering just how close to Daniel Jessica did live, and it was left to Jessica to say quietly, 'Yes, well, in the circumstances, I'm sure it would be the best thing all round if I found somewhere else to live.'

There was a sad silence, and then her mother offered, 'Perhaps if your father or I were to explain?' But Jessica shook her head firmly.

'No. No more running. No more evasion. No more not facing up to the truth. I've learned that much, at least. No, there's only one thing I can do—must do.' She bit her lip and asked quietly, 'Do you . . . do you have a telephone number where he can be reached?'

Her mother frowned. 'Yes, I think so. It should be in your father's diary.'

It was, but the efficient secretary Jessica spoke to could offer her no other information than to say that her boss was unobtainable and taking a few days' leave of absence.

That left her with only one option.

She wasn't going to deceive herself. There was no going back, no remote chance of undoing the wrong she had done him, but at least she could apologise, admit her error, make it easier for her parents in their business involved with Daniel and make it clear to him that, whatever her private feelings, she was not, like her cousin, going to make a nuisance of herself. In fact, she was going to make sure that after she had delivered her apology—paid her debt, so to speak—there would be no chance of their paths ever crossing again. If they didn't she might, somehow, find the strength to go on living without him, but if she was subjected to the torment of seeing him . . . Her body shuddered with pain, her face deathly white.

Her mother willingly agreed to lend her her car when Jessica explained what she had to do, although she expressed concern about her physical health.

Jessica gave her a wan smile. 'I have to do it, Ma,' she told her. 'Please don't try to dissuade me.' She pulled a wry face and admitted shakily, 'If you did, I'm afraid I'm all too likely to succumb, and if I did that...'

Her voice tailed away, and she saw from the sympathetic way her mother was looking at her that she understood how important it was to her pride and self-respect that she admitted her error to Daniel—not because she entertained any foolish idea that he would forgive her, not even because she wanted to be forgiven, but because her own self-respect demanded that she do so.

It was going to be hard enough to build a life for herself without Daniel in it. It would be even harder if she also had to live with the knowledge that she had once again run away, found excuses for herself, refused to face up to her own responsibility for her own life.

She knew that Daniel wasn't still staying at the hotel to which he had taken her when he had brought her back from Northumberland. She knew he wasn't in his office. But that did not necessarily mean that she would find him at Little Parvham.

Nevertheless, she drove there, parking her mother's car outside the Bell and forcing herself to walk into the bar and ask the landlady if she knew where Daniel was.

The landlady of the Bell was a voluble, cheerful woman who enjoyed talking. After she had questioned Jessica about her own recovery from the shock of being in the post office when the would-be robber walked in, she informed her that Daniel was, to the best of her knowledge, out at his house.

Thanking her, Jessica made her way back to her car, battling against a cowardly impulse to find some reason for delaying the moment when she would have to face him and admit how she had misjudged him . . . when she would have to apologise to him and beg his pardon for the inexcusable insults she had thrown at him.

It was probably just as well that the road was empty of any other traffic, because her concentration was certainly far from exclusively focused on her driving.

She was shaking inwardly with tension and nausea when she eventually turned into the drive. There was no sign of Daniel's car when she haphazardly parked her own, but, assuming he had parked it to the rear of the property, she walked in through the open front door, hesitantly calling his name.

The silence of the dilapidated building was vaguely unnerving, but Jessica forced herself to walk into the middle of the hall, knowing that in reality her tension was not caused by the house, but by her own reluctance to see Daniel.

When her tentative call brought no response, she walked slowly upstairs.

What must have once been a very attractive gallery ran around three sides of the hallway, so that from below it was possible to look up to the roof and admire the ornate plasterwork of the domed ceiling above her, but where there must once have been an ornamental balustrade surrounding the gallery there were now yawning gaps, and as she reached the landing and glanced back down into the hallway below Jessica had a sickening sensation of giddiness. She had never liked heights, but, oddly, when she had been round the house with Daniel she hadn't been aware of the potential danger of the unguarded landing, and, frowning a little, she felt sure that when they had come round there had been some sort of protective rail running round the gallery at waist height.

If there had, it was now gone, and, keeping well back from the edge, she called Daniel's name again.

Silence... Frowning, she pushed open one of the bedroom doors and went to look down out of the window at the rear of the house. There was no sign of Daniel's car. He wasn't here.

Not sure whether it was relief or disappointment that was her sharpest feeling, she turned on her heel and walked out of the bedroom, closing the door behind her.

The floorboards on the gallery were uneven and warped—rotten in places, she recognised, frowning as she noticed the betraying signs of damp and decay when she really studied the floor.

Still frowning, she suddenly remembered that Daniel had not shown her this side of the gallery, explaining that the floorboards were in a very dangerously advanced state of decay, and that one of his complaints against his original builder had been the fact that he had removed the supporting beams from the hallway below without taking the trouble to shore up the floor with the appropriate props.

As she remembered Daniel's warning, Jessica moved forward quickly—too quickly, she realised, gasping with shock as the floor beneath her suddenly gave way, causing her to lose her footing and fall heavily.

The sensation of the floor falling away beneath her was one of the most terrifying she had ever experienced. She clung desperately to it as it tilted and then dissolved around her, crying out sharply in shock.

'Jessica! Don't move. Lie still.'

Daniel was here. She drew a shaky sob of relief and opened her eyes, quickly closing them again when she saw how much of the floor had given way beneath her, and how very precarious the one remaining strut was that supported her.

'Jess... Are you all right? Have you broken anything?'

Daniel was standing at the top of the stairs, his face unexpectedly strained, only yards away from her, but between where she was clinging to her strut and where he stood in safety was a yawning, empty gap where the floor had once been.

'Jess!'

She tried to concentrate. Her fall had winded her, her arm ached, but she was sure nothing was broken.

She started to shake her head, stopping when Daniel called out quickly, 'No, don't move—not yet...' but it was already too late. Jessica heard the ominous creak, felt the deathly ripple of movement that warned her that the joist couldn't support her for much longer. She looked down at the floor so far below her, and wished sickly that she hadn't, all too easily picturing what would happen to her vulnerable body if it plummeted on to it. Below her, the wreckage of the first fall had thrown up sharp spears of broken wood, and she shuddered, imagining them piercing her flesh, her organs...

'Jessica, listen to me. You can't stay there, the joist isn't strong enough. I'm going to lie down here and reach out to you. I want you to wriggle as far forward as you can.'

Jessica measured the distance between them in disbelief—no matter how much both of them stretched out, they couldn't bridge it.

'No,' she whispered croakily. 'No, it's too much of a risk.'

'All of life is a risk. Trust me, Jess. Trust me. I promise I won't let you fall.'

Trust me... All of a sudden hot, salty tears began to flood her eyes. What had she got to lose? If she fell, if she died...what was her life anyway, without him?

'Watch me, Jess,' he told her quietly. 'Watch me, and I'll tell you when.'

Her throat had gone dry and sore. Painfully she watched as he lay down on the floor and stretched out towards her.

'What I want you to do is to wriggle as far forward as you can, and then when I say jump...'

He couldn't mean it! But he did... 'Trust me,' he had said, but why should he put his own life at risk to save hers? Why should he give her so much when she had given him so little?

'Now, Jess...Now!'

Fear thrilled through her, but his command couldn't be ignored. She edged as far forward as she could, fighting to ignore the dreadful slow swaying of her precarious perch.

'Now...jump! Jump!'

Closing her eyes, she levered herself off her small platform. The sensation of falling...was sickening... She opened her eyes just as Daniel grabbed hold of her, hauling her unceremoniously on to the landing beside him.

The relief of it affected them both.

'What the hell were you doing up there?' Daniel demanded roughly, almost shaking her, while the tears poured down her face and she stammered huskily,

'I came to apologise. You weren't here...and...I fell.' She gave a deep shudder, and suddenly realised that he had stopped shaking her, but that he was still holding her. She tried to move away from him and immediately his hold tightened.

'Oh, no, you don't. Why did you *want* to apologise?'

So he was determined to extract his pound of flesh. Well, she could scarcely blame him.

All her carefully prepared speeches had gone completely out of her mind. She looked at him, and whispered huskily, 'Ma told me...about you taking over the bank. I realised Emma had lied to me. I just don't know what to say.'

She bit her lip and turned her head.

There was silence, and then he said softly, 'You could always try telling me that you love me.'

Her head snapped round, her eyes widening with anguish. 'Please, don't,' she begged, thinking he was deliberately taunting her. 'I know it's what I deserve, but I don't think I can . . .' and then to her horror fresh tears started to fall.

'Say it!' he insisted.

Through her pain she stared at him, and knew there was no escape.

'I love you.'

Again there was silence, and then he told her quietly, 'And I love you, too.'

'Don't,' she whispered brokenly, unable to bear the pain of his mockery.

'Don't what?' he mocked her, but his voice was rough and slightly unsteady. The way he was looking at her transfixed her, flooding her with a shock of hope.

'What is it you don't want me to do, Jess? Don't love you? Don't ache for you? Don't need you? Tell me *how* I can stop. Oh God, Jessica!'

And then he was kissing her, urgently, desperately almost, and her senses, starved of the intimacy of him, flooded her with their tumultuous response to him. She clung to him, kissing him back, opening herself to him, murmuring soft words of longing deep in her throat.

When he eventually released her, half laughing and half crying, she said the only thing that seemed to matter.

'Daniel, I love you so much. Can you forgive me? I was so wrong, so stupid . . .'

'We both made mistakes,' he told her gently. 'When I walked into the hall and saw you clinging to that joist, realised your danger . . . If I'd thought your lack of trust in me had killed my love—if I'd thought that, well, I very quickly realised how wrong I was, and I knew then that I'd rather go through that rejection a hundred times than see you die. And besides, it wasn't entirely your fault... I *could* have made you listen, explained. I *should* have told you earlier that I knew your father, but after what you said about not trusting people who knew your parents...' He gave a brief shrug. 'I was already committed...knew I loved you. I told myself I'd tell you the truth once I'd won your trust——'

'Mother told me everything,' Jessica interpolated. 'I should never have listened to Emma.'

'And I should have realised what a vindictive little soul she is, and been a little more careful in telling her that there was no place for her in my life and that I loved you. I should have realised she'd try to make trouble between us, especially after she gatecrashed my meeting with your father and overheard me telling him I was worried about the fact that I hadn't been able to tell you about my takeover of the bank, and that I didn't want my takeover as chairman officially announced until I'd had a chance to tell you about it. I was going to tell you that evening...had been screwing up my courage to tell you——'

'That money I threw at you,' Jessica interrupted unhappily. 'That was awful of me. There isn't any excuse. I was so unhappy.'

'Mmm...and you still owe me one piece,' he teased her, adding thoughtfully, 'Maybe you should give me a kiss instead.'

'Suppose I were to buy back the other twenty-nine pieces from you?' Jessica suggested instead.

He pretended to consider it. 'At what rate?'

'Mmm... A thousand per cent—one kiss at a thousand per cent for each of the twenty-nine pieces.'

'Twenty-nine thousand kisses? I don't know...how about twenty-nine thousand nights spent in my arms instead?' he murmured. 'Twenty-nine thousand...of course, you'd have to marry me. Now that I'm the chairman of such a respectable institution as Collingwood's I have my reputation to consider, you realise.'

'Twenty-nine thousand nights?' Jessica pretended to consider.

'In my arms,' he reminded her. 'Of course, if you're not sure you could meet such a long commitment, I could always...'

He was kissing her throat as he spoke, the words muffled against her skin.

'You could always what?' Jessica prompted huskily, trying to ignore this blatant seduction.

'I could always find some way of making the terms more acceptable.'

'In what way?'

He was still kissing her, his teeth nibbling provocatively at her vulnerable flesh, making her quiver outwardly as well as inwardly. 'Perhaps a small demonstration.' His hands were shaping her body, and she made a soft yearning sound deep in her throat, her fingers curling round his wrist, holding his hand against her breast while she moved her lips eagerly along his jaw, seeking his mouth.

'Never again,' he told her rawly, meeting the eager pressure of her kiss, 'never again are we going to let anything come between us.'

'Never,' Jessica answered. 'Never!'

How to enter

Simply sort out the jumbled letters to make ten words all to do with being on holiday. Enter your answers in the grid, then unscramble the letters in the shaded squares to find out our mystery holiday destination.

After you have completed the word puzzle and found our mystery destination, don't forget to fill in your name and address in the space provided below and return this page in an envelope (you don't need a stamp). Competition ends 29th February 1996.

Mills & Boon Romance Holiday Competition
FREEPOST
P.O. Box 344
Croydon
Surrey
CR9 9EL

Are you a Reader Service Subscriber? Yes ❑ No ❑

Ms/Mrs/Miss/Mr ______________________________

Address ______________________________

____

______________ Postcode ______________

One application per household.

You may be mailed with other offers from other reputable companies as a result of this application. If you would prefer not to receive such offers, please tick box. ❑

COMP495
B